Dear Readers,

Many times I've heard from readers that they have spent months and even years scouring bookstores to find copies of my early books, or that their own copies are dog-eared and falling apart. I'm pleased to know these books are so beloved, so I'm very happy that Sourcebooks is re-issuing four of my best novels from the first years of my writing career. I love the beautiful, colorful covers, which make these editions special. I hope you'll enjoy these books, whether they are new to you or old friends.

Yours,

Laura Kinsale

Uncertain Magic

LAURA KINSALE

sourcebooks
casablanca

Published by Sourcebooks Casablanca, an imprint of Sourcebooks, Inc.
P.O. Box 4410, Naperville, Illinois 60567-4410
(630) 961-3900
FAX: (630) 961-2168
www.sourcebooks.com

Originally published in 1987 by Avon Books, an imprint of Harper-
Collins Publishers

Printed and bound in Canada.
WC 10 9 8 7 6 5 4 3 2 1

One

RODERICA DELAMORE CLUTCHED HARD AT THE BILLOWING SILK folds of her father's pavilion as the horses came pounding down the turf. The blood-bay stallion was in the lead, a flash of living fire, pulling away from the challenger with each ground-eating stride as the crowd's rumble gathered to a piercing howl. The noise and emotion rose up around Roddy like a breaking wave, beating at her, drowning her, crushing the barriers that she'd built in her mind. Her cursed gift laid her open to everything, the sound, the sight, the combined aggression and excitement of ten thousand screaming spectators. The intensity of emotion threatened to overwhelm her, and she tore the silk with her twisting fingers as she sought madly for some way to block it out.

Her parents had been right—she should never have come. She should have stayed home on the quiet Yorkshire estate where her father raised his blooded running stock, safe in the country solitude. She was not ready for this; she'd had no concept of what it would be like to suffer the full force of her talent in the grip of a hysterical crowd. In desperation she narrowed her concentration to the animals, pushing away the tide of human feeling with terrific effort.

The trick worked. The impact of the crowd faded and changed, becoming a background roar of sound as Roddy let herself be sucked into the mind of the stallion in the lead, the bright bay, whose will and power filled her like a flood of molten fire. Her world became the world of the racehorse: the taste of copper and foam, the smell of sweat and crushed grass and hot wind; stretching, seeking, ears flicked back to the thunder of the challenger, eyes focused on the terrain ahead, reaching and reaching and reaching forward—

The sudden pain struck her as if it were her own. It shot down the stallion's left foreleg, and he broke stride for one fraction of a second, sending the jockey's live weight forward onto the horse's shoulders. The whip flashed, not hitting, but the brandishment was enough. The stallion sprang ahead. The pain increased. It grew, spreading across the animal's chest and striking into his neck and right leg. Still he ran, defying it, his stallion's mind set in aggression and pride—stay ahead, stay ahead, damn the pain—while Roddy pressed her fists to her mouth and bit down until her knuckles bled with vicarious agony.

In a back corner of her mind she was aware of fear, a human dread of the moment when the great beast would collapse and take down his jockey and the challenger behind in a savage tangle of flesh and hooves. She'd felt this kind of pain before, at home, when an exhausted gelding had collapsed of heart failure after a twenty-mile race between parish steeples. It was death, close and dreadful, and yet the stallion drove on, opening the lead. His stride lengthened, his black-tipped legs devouring turf like the rhythmic spokes of a giant wheel. As he neared the finish, the crowd noise rose to a crescendo. The pair flashed by Roddy. She was screaming, too, hardly aware of the tears that streamed down her cheeks for the animal's pain and courage, for the will that carried him past the finish a full length ahead of his rival, for the spirit that made him toss his head and fight the restraining hand of his jockey when every single step was anguish. She broke from her hiding place in the pavilion, in the rough stableboy's clothes and the cap she'd worn to conceal her bright blond curls, and pushed with unfeminine force through the mob that closed in on the victor.

She reached the stallion just as the silk-clad jockey swung off. A groom ran forward to take the puffing animal's bridle; his hand clashed with Roddy's as they both lunged. Roddy's fingers closed first and she tore the reins away.

"*Yo!*" he shouted amid the din, and made a move to yank them back.

Roddy screamed, "Don't move him!" forgetting entirely she was supposed to be a boy. "He'll die if you move him now!"

"Are ye crazed?" the groom cried. Roddy stumbled under his shove, then gritted her teeth and held her ground.

The stallion stood still beside her, awash in pain. He lowered his head, giving in to weakness for the first time, and at that motion the protests of the groom faded momentarily. But the man's pride was aroused now, his authority questioned. Roddy felt the stallion begin to tremble in delayed reaction. The groom made another grab for the reins. He captured them, pushing Roddy aside as he led the horse forward.

The stallion faltered, and went to his knees. All around, a dismayed cry flew up, and then a cheer as the horse clambered back to all fours. Roddy gave the groom a savage look. She felt the man's antagonism, sharp and quick as a stabbing knife in the wash of emotion from the crowd. She knew before he did it that he was going to drag the horse forward again. "Damn you! Don't—" she shouted, and found herself cut short by another voice that sliced across the noise.

"Leave it, Patrick. Let him stand."

Roddy stiffened, unused to being taken by surprise. She did not turn toward the newcomer—that was habit—but opened her special gift to his mind, expecting to pluck out a name and identity before she even saw his face.

Instead, she found only blankness.

That jolted her. She focused her gift more sharply. But the other remained a silence, a void, as disconcerting as the space where a newly lost tooth should have been.

A bubble of panic rose to her throat. For the first time in her life, Roddy felt herself reaching out instead of turning away, probing for emotion or thought instead of rejecting it. When finally she turned, it was as if she could not quite see the man beside her; only a vague figure, tall and elegant in a black coat and doeskin breeches. She spared a single glance up into his face.

His features came into focus with a sudden, wrenching clarity. He stood quite still amid the clamor, watching her intently, his eyes a startling blue beneath thick black lashes— light against dark, like the bright evening sky behind stark silhouettes. The expression on his fiercely carved face was closed, set in lines impossible to read. She blinked stupidly and gaped, like a person set down in a foreign country, unable to cope with an unknown tongue.

The silence spread to the watching throng, the real silence, the one her ears heard instead of her mind. Shouts and talk faded into hush. And in the crowd-thoughts behind the silence she found a name.

Her eyes widened. She looked quickly toward the stranger from under her lashes.

Saints preserve us.

Iveragh. The Devil Earl of Ireland.

She found herself in deeper water than she'd wanted. A lot deeper. She should have guessed. Oh, God, how had she not guessed? He *owned* the beast, for the Lord's sake. Rumor had been rife that the horse would go for a fortune to Lord Derby or the Duke of Grafton if it won today.

Roddy stole another look. The man could have been Satan himself, with his hell-black hair and burning blue eyes. Every improbable tale of the Devil Earl took on believability: if anyone could be a blackmailer and a thief and a pitiless corrupter of innocent maids, this was surely the man.

People moved. The crowd shuffled and shifted, and opened way again with that instinct they had for a fine coat and a gentleman's air. She knew the newcomer this time—Lord Derby himself, eager to lay his claim to the horse.

He hailed Iveragh and pumped his hand, congratulations on the win. "We'll call this an agreement." Derby pumped harder, looking sillier than he knew against Iveragh's trenchant silence. The excited lord babbled something about the next heat, and Roddy swung round in dismay. "Don't race him again! You musn't—"

"Gor—" The groom shoved her roughly. "Mind yer business, ye little bastard. The horse 'twere never better. Get on wi' ye."

Roddy thrust his hands away with hot indignation, remembering too late that she could hardly be taken for a lady of quality just now. She turned again to Iveragh—a look up to those uninterpretable blue eyes as steady as she could make it, which wasn't very. From somewhere she still had enough sense left to use her best country accents. "He ain't fit, m'lor'. He's sick. 'Twill kill him to run again. I've felt—" She stopped herself, knowing that these strangers would never believe in the talent that was taken for granted in her father's stable. "I've seen this before. 'Tis his heart, m'lor'."

"Sick, is it?" The groom moved a step. "Sick be damned, ye bleedin'—" Roddy felt his intention a moment before the action and stiffened—fool, fool, when she should have ducked—and the cracking blow took her across the face and sent her reeling into the solid wall of the earl's chest.

He caught her arms in a painful grip, but Roddy was too stunned by the bruising ache in her jaw to take more than passing notice. She hung a hazy moment in Iveragh's arms, then struggled up and tore herself free, going at the groom with all the fury of a wildcat, using nails and teeth and all the curses she had ever learned from her four rough-and-tumble brothers. She didn't bother to throw punches with only her puny weight behind them, but used her talent shamelessly, outguessing, dodging and biting and striking openhanded with ruthless efficiency, drawing blood more than once before she swung her leg up hard and kicked, catching the man squarely in the groin. He yelped and staggered back, bent double, and Roddy drank in his pain with satisfaction as the hisses and cheers rose up around them.

The stallion stood with his eyes rolling wildly. She went to his head to murmur reassurance. The animal's attack had subsided, but beneath the surface there was still a fatal weakness. If retired to pasture, he might survive. Another race would destroy him.

With an effort, she blocked out the mixed antagonism and amazement that flowed from the crowd and turned a defiant look on the unreadable face of Iveragh, "He hit me first, m'lor'."

The earl looked at her with his strange blue eyes. Roddy held the gaze and then faltered, dropping her lashes as a faint smile curved his lips.

"Fight dirty, do you?"

The words were soft, barely audible above the buzz of the spectators.

"He hit me." Roddy was on the defensive. "And he don't care a whit 'bout ta beast."

"Heart trouble." Lord Derby gave her a hard look. "Are you certain?"

Roddy glanced at Iveragh, seeing nothing she could fathom in the earl's dark face. The magnificent racing stallion was worth a king's ransom as a performer and a stud, but as a retired and broken racehorse he was useless.

"Yes, m'lor'," she said hesitantly, addressing Derby, and half expecting the earl himself to punch her for ruining his sale.

Derby turned to the man beside him. "We'll talk again. Perhaps after the next heat." He touched his hat brim. "Your servant, sir." He strolled away into the crowd that parted to let him pass.

Roddy was left to face the wrath of the Devil Earl alone.

She took a deep breath and turned back to the stallion, offering her hand to his silky black muzzle. The crowd still pressed around them, fallen into a waiting silence that unnerved her even more, for she knew what they were expecting. What they thought she deserved.

Cold-blooded murder.

Which didn't seem to be an unlikely event, Roddy thought morbidly, considering the reputation of Iveragh.

"So." His voice made her flinch with its chilly flatness. "Since you seem to have permanently disabled my groom, boy, perhaps you'll take over for him."

She looked up in confusion, but the earl was already turning away. The crowd muttered. She glanced around at all those sullen male faces and found herself with no better choice than to take the stallion's head and follow at a measured pace.

Her cheek ached, a stinging numbness that she feared would go black and blue. To take her mind off it, she kept alert to the horse's condition. The spectators drifted along behind, still hopeful of a scene, but the earl only led Roddy and her charge up the treeless hill toward the long row of thatch-roofed sheds where the horses were temporarily stabled. She expected undergrooms to run out to their aid, but no one came. The earl gestured toward an empty loose box, and with a sweep of his glacial blue eyes warned off the crowd that had followed.

"Untack him. His blanket's there," he said tonelessly.

Roddy ducked her head. To take off the stallion's saddle and bridle meant only one thing. He was scratching the horse from the next heat.

A walkover. The stallion's courageous win in the first heat was worth nothing, and now there would be a forfeit fee to pay, too, instead of the rich purse the horse should have won. She reached to obey the earl's order, replacing the bridle with a halter and dragging off the heavily weighted saddle. It was all unthinking routine, years of training in her father's stable. Now that the stallion's heart was steadier, she had to walk him to cool him out, stopping first to wet a sponge and squeeze a dribble of water into his nose and mouth. He stretched his lathered neck and stuck out his tongue, slurping at the thin stream.

By the time she had walked him once up the length of the shed and back, the earl was gone. From here, the crowd at the track was only a rumble on the wind, the words of the crier indistinguishable as he called the next heat. Her gift brought her nothing but a confused wave of agitation.

The tones of the distant voice changed. A shout of dismay went up from the mob.

They had announced the stallion's scratch.

She pursed her lips and kept the horse walking. He had believed her, that saturnine stranger. He had taken her at her word. It was gratifying, and scary, and something else—something oddly warm.

Trust, she thought, with a trace of wonder. *Blind faith.*

The earl did not return to the stable. A trickle of on-lookers began to arrive, curious to see why the stallion had been pulled. Roddy ignored their questions. She led the horse into his box, drew water and tossed hay with mute precision. Then she posted herself at the door, assuming an expression of silent haughtiness, a stony glare that she was certain was worthy of the earl himself.

❧

It was Mark who came for her. Long after all the races were over and the spectators had dispersed, the familiar essence touched her mind: her second-oldest brother, red hair and redder temper, storming along the shedrow toward her with murder in his thoughts. She cringed a little under the string of curses which ran through his mind when he saw her. The link between thought and words was so instantaneous that her family always spoke to her aloud, and Mark demanded in a furious voice, "What the holy devil are you doing here? Papa's out of his wits." He grabbed her arm and began to tow her along without ceremony, ignoring Roddy's voluble protests.

No one paid them any mind: a young gentleman with a ragtag, squealing stableboy by the ear. She went with Mark, half walking, half dragged, down the grassy hill to the gay row of grandstands and pavilions that lined the now-deserted track. She managed to get away from him long enough to straighten herself a little before she was marched forcibly into the crimson-and-gold tent where her father waited. Roddy began a quick apology, but her father silenced her with one stern look, a look that made her insides squeeze all sick and remorseful and scared as he dismissed Mark and yanked a curtain of silk across the door.

"Young lady," he hissed, the carefully arranged rolls of white hair at his temples quivering, "what d'you think you're about, running all over the heath like some hoyden? I thought we had an agreement."

"Yes, Papa," she said faintly. "I'm sorry."

"Sorry," he snapped. "Sorry. If your mother knew—" He broke off, and frowned at her. "What happened to your face?"

Roddy drew in a quavery breath at his thunderous expression. She thought of several cushioning lies, but she knew her brothers would have told the truth, and so she could do nothing less. "Someone hit me."

"Hit you!" It was a blast of shock and fury. "Good God, who had the impudence—*Iveragh*, that son of Satan, was it he?" Her father made a precipitate move toward the door. "By the devil, I'll kill him!"

"Certainly it wasn't, Papa," Roddy cried, waving her hands in a feverish tamping flutter, because they wanted to grab hold of him and pull him back and she knew that wasn't politic just now. "It was his groom. And I didn't come off so badly after all… I won the scrap."

"'Won the scrap,'" her father echoed, letting the folds of silk that formed a door drop back into place. He covered his eyes. "Sweet Heaven have mercy, my daughter won a mill with Iveragh's groom. If your mother knew—"

"I'm sorry, Papa." Roddy hung her head in misery. "I truly am."

He squared his shoulders under the thick pads of his frock coat, fidgeting with one blunt finger at the high collar points. "It's my fault. I should never have allowed you to come, much less let you dress yourself in this—this stable garb. Where in God's name was your sense, to go off with a scoundrel like Iveragh? Surely you could recognize what kind of man—" He stopped, reddening.

Roddy bit her lip. "I know his reputation, Papa," she said, and then blushed herself at her father's disapproving frown. "You know I understand these things better than a—a *normal* girl would."

"Capital," he said gruffly. "At nineteen, you're an expert on rakes and roués. If your mother hears of this—"

"You know she won't," Roddy said, and then added darkly, "If someone tells her, 'twill be a great deal too bad after all I've kept under the lid for Mark and the rest."

Her father cleared his throat in discomfort at that shaft. "Roddy. You're a female. Your brothers' conduct can hardly be held up as an example for your own."

The accumulated stresses of the day caught up with her at that, swelled and rolled and exploded. "Well—" she shouted, "what example shall I go by? Aunt Nell's? Shall I lock myself away where I never meet a living soul and try to forget this accursed talent I was born with?" She sucked in a breath and clenched her hands together, paced to the silk partition and turned back savagely on her heel. "Or perhaps Great-aunt Jane would be a better pattern. She only killed herself. Who could blame her? She loved her husband, and he couldn't bear to have her near him. I don't blame *him*, either," Roddy added bitterly. "What man could abide to have his mind an open book for his wife to read? To have her know every weakness, every fear, every secret that's too dark even for confession? What marriage could stand the burden of this damned... gift?"

"Roddy," her father said in an aching voice.

It made her throat hurt. The tears threatened, blurred, spilled over.

"Oh, Papa," she cried, turning to throw herself into his familiar arms. "This awful talent—sometimes I don't think... I can't stand... Oh, God, I don't *want* it! I don't want to live alone forever."

He clasped her tightly, not speaking, his anger forgotten as he let her feel all the force of his affection and support through the gift she despised. She wanted to stay there in his embrace forever, shielded from the confusion of anger and pain that bore down on her from the world outside. She could see the lies, feel the cruelty and greed so clearly, but she could never understand them. She felt as helpless as the dumb animals who lived under the whim of human will, unable to comprehend the tides of passion that swept around her. The methods of blocking she had so painstakingly taught herself were imperfect, easily broken down by extremes of emotion, leaving her vulnerable at just those times when she needed protection the most.

"Little Roddy," her father murmured. "Don't cry, darling. You won't be all alone. Your mother and I—you know you'll have us always, as long as we live." He stroked her trembling shoulder and touched her cheek. "You won't be like Nell; already you've come so much farther. It would have killed her to be within a mile of this place today, and you've managed beautifully."

Roddy shook her head with a vehemence that bumped his chin. "I haven't! I haven't done well at all. That match race—the first heat was more than I could stand. Even up at the stables with Lord Iveragh's stallion, it almost overset me when they began to cheer the finish of a race." She buried her face against his wide lapels. "I can't endure it, Papa. All the people—you were right. I should never, ever have come. I'll have to spend all my life stuck away in the country—" She drew a shaky, half-sobbing breath. "I'll never go to London, or dance at an assembly, or even be able to drive in the park. I'll never have my own family, little children to look after or watch grow up. It's s-so unfair. Why did it have to be m-me?"

Her father had no answer, and his helplessness and guilt only sank her deeper in despair. The Delamore gift passed to females from the male side of the family, and Roddy's father, like his father and grandfather and great-grandfather before him, had trusted to the fortune of siring sons one too many times. Her four brothers would most probably do the same, each hoping that the family penchant for boys would hold true. It was one of the cruel ironies of the gift that those who knew what it was to suffer it were not the ones who could pass it on. Her doomed great-aunt Jane had borne three daughters, and none of them had possessed the talent that Roddy had inherited through her father.

But she did not blame him. How could she? The alternative was never to have been born at all, and life was not so bitter as that. Not yet, anyway. But the memory of Great-aunt Jane was always there as an omen of what might happen if Roddy were so foolish as to try to live a normal life.

Normal. Now there was a word to cherish. Like love. Like the things she would never have, not for herself alone. Her parents loved her, and her brothers. But that was family. That was a child, and she was almost a woman now.

That wasn't Geoffrey.

Oh, Geoffrey, she thought. The tears swelled back into her throat. *My friend. My friend. Who doesn't want me.*

After a minute, she stood back a little, wiping at her blurry eyes. "I'm sorry, Papa. I shan't cry anymore. It's just been such a trial today, and I'm so very tired."

He squeezed her hands. "Go and change, then, and I'll have Mark find some dinner for you. You'd rather stay here than come to the inn?"

"Yes," she said quickly. "I couldn't face an inn—not tonight. It must be a sad crush."

He nodded. "Mark will stay with you. I've an appointment to dine with Bunbury at the Jockey Club—he dearly wants that colt of ours by Waxy. Can I do anything else for you now?"

Roddy shook her head. As he brushed aside the silken door, her father paused. "I'm sorry to have given you such a scold, darling. But when Mark found that you'd somehow gone off with Iveragh—" He made a clucking sound of distress. "Do stay clear of his like, Roddy. If your mother knew—"

"Oh, Papa," Roddy said, driven to a watery giggle by his obsession with her mother's disapproval. "Go on. Mama won't know what you don't tell her."

He smiled sheepishly and gave her a quick kiss. Then he was gone.

Roddy sat down on a cushioned stool and contemplated the well-worn jackboots that were an integral part of her disguise as a stableboy. Her homebound mother thought she was staying safely confined in the pavilion's ladylike quarters, but her father, more practical, had been easily swayed by the usefulness of Roddy's talent with his string of racehorses, allowing her on pain of utmost secrecy to dress so that she could go easily among the horse sheds.

It was not completely practicality. It represented something else, too: one of his small gestures, his little favors. He felt guilty, and so he gave her these secret treats. Gave her everything she wanted when she asked.

She'd been five years old when she'd first understood her difference. Before that it had simply been the way the world was, the way her parents were taller than she and her brothers had louder voices. It was a talent, her father had told her, something special, and she'd nodded, not understanding. She

musn't talk about it, her father had said; she musn't be unfair.
Don't carry tales. No one likes a tattle.

But the truth had come from her mother. It had happened
one day in Mama's bedroom, while Mama sat alone at her
dresser and fussed at her hair with shaking fingers. Mama was
afraid, and excited, and Roddy had peeped in anxiously. She'd
stood just inside the door, watching her mother, who tried to
smile in false welcome, which was a scary thing that had never
happened to Roddy before. Some people thought one thing
and said another. Never Mama.

Never Mama.

Roddy had walked forward, into that aversion, because
she was frightened and wanted her mother to like her as her
mother always did. Roddy hadn't understood, she'd only
wanted this thing that made her mother excited and happy
and miserable all at once to go away. She'd laid one hand on
Mama's knee and said, "Please don't, Mama. Don't go to that
man in the spinney."

"*What?*" her mother had said, with a jerk around and a
scared, awful roll of the eyes.

And slapped her daughter.

Roddy could feel it still: an unhealed wound, the shape and
length of her mother's fingers. The symbol of what Roddy
was. A freak. An aberration. The thing they all feared in their
deepest nightmares.

The fear was gone in an instant, covered with love and
remorse, and Mama had gathered Roddy in her arms and
cried and cried and begged for forgiveness. "Don't tell your
father," Mama had moaned. "I won't go; I won't go; I
didn't mean to hurt you. I never would have gone, darling,
I promise. Don't tell your father, please—oh, God—please
don't tell your father."

Roddy had not told. And her mother had not gone. Never
again had there been another man in her mother's life but her
husband. Because of Roddy.

Angel of Reckoning.

Two

TWO HOURS LATER, EASILY SHED OF MARK'S HALFHEARTED chaperonage, Roddy found Lord Iveragh's stallion where she had left him, looking lonely with his head hung over the door of the box. He greeted her with a soft whuffling, and Roddy gave him the handful of grass she had picked on the way. She peered into the box on tiptoe. His bedding was newly clean. That, at least. Sometime in her absence his groom had been back to care for him. She had begun to wonder, waiting all those afternoon hours alone.

The stallion nudged her, hungry after his effort of the day. Roddy smiled, and gave him a pat and a promise. She thought she might catch Old Jack, the Delamores' head groom, and have him cook a hot bran mash before he went to bed.

It was late when she returned, Old Jack having been long asleep and hard to rouse. She'd prepared the heavy bucket of steaming mash herself. After that it had been a long walk in the moonlight with only the sound of her own light song to keep her company:

> *Here is a pledge unto all true lovers,*
> *A pledge to my love where 'er he may be.*
> *This very night I'll be with my darling*
> *For many the long mile he is from me.*

Along the bare, rolling ridges of the heath she sang, where dry grass and horse-scent lay heavy on the breeze.

Ah la, then he came to his true love's window,
He knelt low down upon a stone,
Then through the glass he whispered softly,
Are you asleep, love, are you alone?

It was an old song, sad and dreaming, one of the sweet Irish airs that Geoffrey had taught her. As she reentered the maze of sheds and shadow, she left off her singing and kept her attention centered, occupied mainly with placing her feet and catching her breath and transferring the bucket from one hand to the other as her fingers went numb from the handle's bite.

It was a man's low voice that alerted her first. She stopped in the shadows, suddenly aware that the horse had a visitor.

He stood outside the box, speaking softly to the stallion as he leaned against the shed. She knew instantly who it was.

Not through her gift. Through the failure of it.

She squinted in the moon-tricky darkness, panting softly, and set down the bucket—slowly, slowly, so it did not rustle in the drying grass. He had abandoned his coat and neckcloth, and his shirt shone pale as the starlight, with sleeves rolled up and collar open. From the interior of the box, the stallion radiated satisfaction, having been finally fed, although he was looking for more when he sniffed Roddy and the bran mash. His fine head came out of the box, craning in her direction.

The earl stood back. "Greedy bastard," he said, in a tone that didn't match the words. "Deserve an extra measure of corn, do you?" He reached up and did something, she couldn't see what—patted the horse or flipped a stray piece of black mane onto its proper side. "To hell with you, then. I've hardly the blunt to feed myself. Not now."

The stallion swung his head up and down and then whinnied, demanding that Roddy quit dawdling with that fine-smelling mash. It was a funny thing, a small strange pleasure, to stand and listen to the earl's rich voice speaking softly in the darkness. Even the stallion liked it, which was why he was not making more of a fuss in his impatience.

The earl turned a little, leaning his shoulders against the shed and staring out into the night. In the moonlight, Roddy could see his face clearly, white and stark black with the shadows. He ran long fingers through his hair and down his face with a low groan. "We've lost it, old friend," he said. "You let me down." He lifted his face to the dark sky. "Ah, God. I can't believe it. *Iveragh*."

The name seemed to hang in the air, vibrating with love and despair. He turned, in sudden violence, and slammed his fist into the wooden shed with a blow that made both Roddy and the stallion jerk back in startlement. "Damn." It was vicious. "God damn them all." He moved as if to hit the shed again, but midway in his motion he checked the blow and stood still, his face a shadowed mask.

Roddy stared at him. She had thought at first he meant to strike the horse, but instead he let out a long, harsh breath of air, and buried his face in the animal's neck with a wordless sound of desolation.

It was then that the idea came to her.

She tilted her head.

To do such a thing—to even think of it...

But why not?

Why turn away from a chance—one chance—at the life that her gift denied her? He had trusted her. That counted for something. That counted for a lot.

She stood still, her mind racing, and then bent very quietly to pick up the softly steaming bucket of mash. She retreated in silence back behind the shedrow before going forward again, whistling warning with a loud, cheerful stable tune that Old Jack had taught her long ago.

By the time she turned the corner, the earl had composed himself. He looked up at her approach with cool disinterest.

Roddy smiled inwardly. An actor. A fine one at that, and Roddy was an excellent judge. He seemed suddenly fascinating, all the more attractive for his unpredictability. She nodded when she met his eyes, and gave him a brisk country greeting.

"'Evenin' to 'ee, m'lor'. I thought 'ee wudn't a-comin' back." She hefted the pail of bran. "I brung ta beast a bit o' hot mash, wi' yer permission, sir."

He gave her a narrow look, and nodded briefly. Roddy set the pail of bran in the eager stallion's box. She came out and closed the door, then took up a negligent position nearby, as if waiting for the horse to finish.

She half expected Iveragh to turn curtly away and leave, but he only stood, a little in the shadows where she could no longer see his face. She sought for something to say, some way to broach the subject that she wanted to discuss, but now that the moment was here, it seemed so outrageous an idea that she could think of nothing. Finally, after tapping her fingers nervously against the hard wood at her back, she blurted, "It near floored me, m'lor', that 'ee took me at me word this day and scratched ta beast."

He shrugged. "It pleased me at the time."

Roddy couldn't help herself; her eyebrows went disobediently upward as she looked at him.

He stared back at her gloomily, and added after a moment, "I'd a mind to give my groom a setdown."

Oh, certainly, Roddy thought. *A setdown for a groom. And scratching your horse only cost you your estate.*

She hid a wry smile in steady concentration on the tip of one boot. His stiff pride, maintained even in front of a mere stableboy, was perversely endearing. The plan in her head took on more appeal.

"'Er's a lovely beast, anyway," she said nonchalantly. "Me young missus would pay a pretty penny for him, I vow, even if he can't race no more. Put him to her Eclipse mare, she would. That'd be the Delamore stud, m'lor', up to Thomton Dale."

"Your mistress," he repeated, and Roddy thought there was the faintest trace of interest in his voice. "Mrs. Delamore?"

She jumped at her chance. "Oh, no, sir. Her daughter. Miss Roderica Delamore. She breeds her own stock, y'see. Happen she can spot a winner, too, even if she's not yet twenty." Which was perfectly true. At age twelve, Roddy had picked a black filly from her father's yearling crop that had gone on to win the Oaks in her third year, under Lord Egremont's colors.

"How happy for her," the earl said dryly.

"Oh, that ain't the half of it." Roddy warmed to her topic. "She's rich as Croesus, too—she's got three hundred thousand in her own name, free and clear, and all a-goin' to the man she weds. Come full into it a year ago."

He shifted a little, but did not move out of the shadow. "How do you happen to know that?"

She hesitated, frustrated by her inability to discern his true reaction. It was that blindness again, the uneasy sense of treading unknown ground. But he seemed by his question to be curious, and she plunged ahead. "'Tisn't rumor, m'lor'. She speaks of it now and then."

"You work in the stable?"

"Aye, m'lor'."

"You seem to be on rather familiar terms with a daughter of the house."

Roddy bit her lip, aware that she'd made a misstep. "Well, she ain't uppity, if that's what you mean," she said quickly. "Not silly and missish at all. She don't mind carryin' feed an' water if we're pushed down at the stud. For meself, I can't see why some town dandy hain't plucked her right up. An heiress like that. She even hunts. Make a fine wife for any man, I'd reckon."

The earl seemed to be looking at her rather oddly, but his position in the half-shadow made it hard to tell. "Perhaps she's ugly," he murmured.

"Ugly!" Roddy straightened indignantly. "I hardly think so. 'Tis just that they keep her locked away in the country. I'm sure she's as pretty as any London miss, and maybe more than some. An' she kin sing. Like a lark; they all say that. And dance," she added, determined not to miss any of her strong points. "Why, I've known her to dance all night at a ball!"

A small exaggeration. Roddy had never been to a ball, but she'd often slipped out of the house to whirl and leap in time to imaginary music when the moon was high and full.

She took a breath and went on recklessly, "You should see her. Why, I warrant she'd be pleased at the attention of a fine gentleman like yourself. You're just what she's looking for in the way of a husband, m'lor'."

He moved then, out of the shadow. Before she could prevent it, he had reached up with one smooth motion and flipped the cap from her head.

Roddy froze, with the bright loose curls tumbling down across her shoulders. She stared up into his face, turning crimson, feeling mortification paralyze every muscle and bone. Her mouth opened and then shut, fishlike, and no words came out.

"See for myself," he echoed softly. He touched her bruised cheek with one finger, tracing down her jaw, and a slow smile curved his fine mouth. "Perhaps I shall."

She blinked, distracted by the unexpected gentleness of his hand on her skin. His eyes looked very blue in the moonlight. He did not move away, and for one wild moment he was so close that she thought—but no, surely not, it wasn't possible...

Would the Devil Earl want to kiss a stablehand?

Of course not. Even if the stablehand *was* a girl. Roddy strained to catch some hint of what he felt, and found only that disconcerting blankness. In its loss, her other senses seemed to stretch and heighten. She felt the warm, faint touch of his breath on her skin, and caught a pleasant waft of tangy scent— masculine scent, which seemed new and familiar at the same time. His face was outlined in the moonlight in perfect curves and planes, so close that she could see the beat of his pulse beneath his loosened collar. She licked her lips; tried to make her breathing settle to a rational pace. She'd never been kissed before. It had always been something her brothers tried to do with the buxom little kitchenmaid if they caught her in the pantry. And the kitchenmaid liked it, even if she pretended not. Roddy steeled herself, determined not to flinch if he should try.

But the clatter of the stallion's empty feed bucket broke the spell. The earl dropped his hand and held out the cap. "Put this back on," he commanded. "I'll see you home."

Roddy hesitated, stupid and confused in the way the thing had gotten out of her control, and he acted for her, sweeping up the tangle of gold and pulling the cap over it with brisk efficiency. An instant later, Roddy found herself on his arm, being led firmly down the hill. She mumbled something about the stallion, and he shook his head. "Where are you staying? At the Star?"

"In my father's pavilion—" She stopped in chagrin, realizing that she had just established her identity beyond doubt.

The earl glanced at her. "You needn't look so disgusted with yourself, Miss Delamore. I'd guessed." He frowned down at her upturned face. "Your father allows you a fine measure of freedom. I saw him dining in town. Did he leave you alone?"

The implied disapproval aroused a quick resentment. "Of course not! He left my brother to watch me."

"Ah." He scanned the horizon. "Your brother must have amazingly good eyesight."

Roddy tried to pull her arm away. "It's none of your affair."

He stopped suddenly and caught her back. "But it is my affair. No young lady I intend to court is going to be found wandering Newmarket at night in the clothes of a stable lad."

Roddy stared up at him. "Court?" she repeated shakily.

"Yes." His face was as beautiful and cold as his namesake's in the moonlight. "Isn't that at what you were hinting so broadly, Miss Delamore?"

"Well—" Roddy floundered. And then: "Well."

He laughed, a sound that was tart and rich, like her first taste of champagne. "I perceive that you've lost your nerve. But I'm persuaded that the young lady who sent Patrick to grass with one well-aimed kick will come round."

Roddy could think of no answer for that, though she tried very hard. They reached her father's tent in silence. The earl stood aside and held up the silk, bowing as formally as if he were handing her back from a dance. "Good evening, Miss Delamore. It has been a pleasure. I shall be standing watch at a discreet distance until I see your brother return." He waited as she stepped into the tent, and then added, "In view of this rare demonstration of responsibility on my part, I would advise the postponement of any further plans you might have for the evening." He gave her a dark and charming smile. "Go directly to bed, my love."

❦

"I won't have him here," Mrs. Delamore declared, in a voice which Roddy and her father well knew.

"Matty, my dear." Her father spoke soothingly, but his movements were agitated as he took a brisk turn before the carved mahogany mantel. "Will you throw our good Cashel's friends in his face?"

Roddy's heart gave an old and familiar twist at the mention of Geoffrey's name. For half her life, it seemed, Roddy had been waiting. To grow up, to become a woman instead of the child she knew he thought her. But to Geoffrey, Roddy had never been more than a lovable waif with disturbing gray eyes, just as the small property he owned in Yorkshire was only a pleasant place for a holiday. Lord Cashel's heart was in Ireland, always, with the great estate that his family had held for centuries.

He adored his new Irish bride, too. It was a storybook kind of love, because Geoffrey was a storybook prince, perfect and kind and brave. Roddy knew that. She knew him to his toes. A man of principle, a man of ideals. He had his weakness—he liked a prettily-turned ankle almost as much as he admired a well-turned phrase—but he never suffered from the graver faults that plagued Roddy and the rest of mankind. Like jealousy. Like selfish spite. Roddy ached with it. No one would ever love her as Geoffrey loved Mary... unconditionally, no matter what Roddy's strange talent might be. It was too much to ask; Great-aunt Jane's marriage had been proof enough of that. Jane's husband, too, had adored his wife, until he discovered the witch-gift of the Delamores.

"Friend," Mrs. Delamore snorted, lifting herself to her greatest height, which came well below her husband's broad shoulders. "The man's not fit to kiss a viper, far less call Lord Cashel his friend."

Roddy's father took a sturdy swig of his brandy. "Dearest, you must understand. Geoffrey's been close to Iveragh since they were boys. I simply don't see how we can exclude him from the dinner party without giving offense."

"Nonsense." Her mother tapped her palm with her fan and eyed her husband suspiciously. "There must be horses in it."

Roddy wanted to smile. Sometimes it was as if her mother, too, had the gift, so well could she penetrate her husband's follies. Along with Geoffrey's note to her father informing him of Cashel's yearly arrival in the neighborhood had come a curt letter from his houseguest Lord Iveragh, stating bluntly that he recalled Mr. Delamore's interest in Iveragh's string of Thoroughbred broodmares, which were currently up for sale upon the closing of his racing stable. Lord Iveragh was at Mr. Delamore's convenience, if he wished to discuss the matter.

Her father cleared his throat. "I'm sure there'll be no talk of horses at table," he said smoothly, and then added, with an ill-advised spurt of honesty, "At all events, not when the ladies are present."

Mrs. Delamore made a face. "I thought as much."

"Well, my dear," he said mildly, "if you see fit to rescind an invitation that I've already proffered, I'm sure I'll stand behind you."

"Already proffered—Frederick, you didn't!"

"I'm afraid I did. I saw Geoffrey this morning, and Iveragh, too, on my usual rounds. I must say, he didn't seem such a dreadful fellow to me. Quite the gentleman, really."

Once again, Roddy kept her amusement to herself. Her father was as contemptuous of Iveragh as her mother, but when he saw a chance for some profitable horsetrading, the opportunity overcame all scruples.

Mrs. Delamore bowed her blond head, touching the bridge of her nose with her fan in an attitude of suffering. "For Geoffrey's sake," she mused unhappily, "I suppose I must endure it. But I dread the talk."

"Well, he's Cashel's guest, after all," her husband said in a deliberately jovial tone. "I hardly think the county can cut *you* for his lamentable presence in the neighborhood."

"Perhaps not." Mrs. Delamore sighed, and looked up at her daughter. "But I won't have Roddy present. You may go down to your cousin at Thirsk."

Roddy came alive at this threat to her plans. "I won't! I'm not a child, if you please. And I've already made Lord Iveragh's acquaintance." A wave of dismay emanated from her father at this announcement, but Roddy ignored it. "'Twas at the races, a month ago. I liked him very well."

Her mother looked at her sharply. Roddy knew she had used strong ammunition, for her family never took her opinion of a stranger lightly. She smiled at her mother, trying to appear very reassuring and adult, and was rewarded with an immediate relaxation of concern.

"Did you really, darling? Are you sure?"

Roddy nodded, feeling like a charlatan, since she had no more idea what went on in the dark recesses of Lord Iveragh's mind than her mother did. But he had come, and she was not about to be sent into exile at her cousin's for the duration of his stay. In the past month, she had thought of him often, and it seemed almost prophetic that the Devil Earl was an old friend of Lord Cashel's.

"I'll call on them tomorrow, then," her mother said briskly, "and have it over with. You may drive me, Roddy, if you wish."

∽

September sunlight flashed in and out among the garden trees as the chaise rattled past the courtyard walls of Geoffrey's Moorside Hall. A tug and twitch, a soft word, and Roddy's gray mare swung between the stone pillars, into the yard bright with crimson vines against cream-colored stucco walls—those walls she had always coveted for her own. Such plans she'd had, for additions and improvements, changes that would have suited Moorside Hall as little as the childish dreams she'd nourished of molding Geoffrey himself into a horseman and farmer, instead of the man of pen and parchment and political passion that he was.

It was as well, really, that the truth had been forced on her. She and Geoffrey would not have suited: he with his honor and idealism, and she with her arguments and challenges. Often she'd annoyed him by her ability to see the other side of some question to which he'd applied his strict ethical principles. She'd tried to understand, but the realities of human will and weakness meant more to Roddy than philosophy. His vague and pliant bride Mary was by far the better choice for him—as Roddy would have known years ago, if she had not let her own longing blind her to the truth.

Stupid. Her gift was no proof against girlish folly.

So… she had given him up. She wished them happy.

Liar.

Oh, foolish, selfish, stupid liar.

A stable lad ran out to hold the horses as Roddy and her mother disembarked with the aid of Geoffrey's ancient coachman. Roddy felt the tall green-and-yellow ostrich plume bob gaily and precariously above her hat as she stepped down, trying to be as light as possible. She brushed surreptitiously at the front of her calico morning dress, and hoped that the green gauze veil trailing down from her hat didn't drag as it felt it did, for the windows of Moorside's drawing room looked directly out onto the front drive.

They found the house cheerful with early-afternoon sun and a small gathering of neighbors come to welcome Lord Cashel and his lady to their second home. Geoffrey's eyes lit with pleasure at Roddy's entrance—and she was a fool again, going breathless and hopeful for a moment, hardly noticing the flow of surprise from the other callers, who seldom saw the Delamores' daughter in public. Though no one had ever exactly said so, it was generally believed among the county families that Roddy was "high-strung," and suffered "nerves."

Geoffrey came forward, all tall and hawk-handsome in that way that made her heart sink, maneuvering neatly around the ample girth of the local baron's widow who sat in the place of honor. But long before he kissed Roddy's gloved hand with a polite touch, she knew the truth. His pleasure was not really centered on her, but on the fact that someone of an age with his young wife, who was sitting shyly alone in the corner near the fire, had at last arrived.

Roddy found a smile somewhere in her disappointment and went immediately to Mary after greeting the baron's widow, which earned Geoffrey's great goodwill. He then proceeded to forget all about her, except in the frequent moments when he glanced their way to ascertain Mary's degree of contentment.

In a small and pleasant gathering, Roddy knew well enough how to cope with her gift. It was a matter of concentrating on one person at a time, and letting the thoughts and emotions radiating from the rest fade to background. Like the babble of simultaneous conversation, the jumble of individual mentalities blurred easily into an indistinguishable mass. The occasional stronger thought would pop into her head: Mrs. Gaskell's affront at the flippant mention of her favorite card game Preference as "Pref," or Lady Elizabeth's growing impatience that tea had not yet been served; but mostly Roddy was able to control her gift and center her attention on Geoffrey's wife.

Thus she knew, long before Mary marshaled up the courage to speak of it, that Geoffrey was expecting an heir come spring. Roddy knew, too, that Mary was somehow upset with Geoffrey, and worried about him. *If only*, Mary kept thinking, and *I wish he wouldn't*, but her preoccupation with the coming baby drowned out anything clearer than a vague jumble of politics and meetings. Roddy saw no harm in those things, which had been Geoffrey's passion all his life, and tried her best to ignore the privacies that inevitably flitted through the other woman's mind.

It was boring. Roddy sat there and cooed over Mary's impending happiness and played cruel games, like saying that Allen was her very *favorite* name for a boy and then exclaiming over the delightful and amazing coincidence that it was also Mary's. And Katherine was so pretty for a girl. Mary thought so too? How singular!

Silly, Roddy thought, in deliberate meanness. *Sweet, silly birdwit. Oh, Geoffrey.*

Why can't I be like that?

The flow in the room changed. Roddy felt it, from her position facing away from the door, felt the pleasantries evaporate and curiosity take their place. A jolt of pure disgust soured the Irish girl's sweetness. Roddy looked around.

Not one of Geoffrey's callers, except for Roddy and her mother, had known of Cashel's guest beforehand. For a suspended moment, admiration for the fine, athletic figure in the doorway was universal. Then Geoffrey said, "Iveragh. Come in."

Attitudes changed. Instantly. The poorly concealed reactions of shock and affront made Roddy angry, though whether for Geoffrey's sake or for the earl's, she did not know. She reached out instinctively to take Mary's hand in support, but the other girl withdrew it in a wave of shame. The clear spurt of furious revulsion Mary felt for her husband's friend was impossible for Roddy to ignore.

She slid her hand back into her lap. She hadn't known how it would be—that among gentle society the Devil Earl was truly a pariah. Already some of the callers were standing up to take hasty leave, as if even an introduction would taint their pristine reputations. She watched him return her mother's greeting with a graceful, easy reply, and wondered if he was even aware of the antagonism which surrounded him.

He gave no sign of it, though she was certain that he was. How could he not be, when half the room was preparing for a sudden exodus? They only hesitated because the baron's widow and Mrs. Delamore, first and second in precedence, had already acknowledged their introductions. True, Lady Elizabeth had done so only because she had taken a moment too long to make the connection between Iveragh and the infamous Devil Earl, but Roddy's mother was determined to show that she, for one, was willing to extend approval to Lord Cashel's guest. She said something to Iveragh about the invitation to dinner, loud enough for the rest of the room to hear, and one or two of the others relaxed enough to reseat themselves.

Roddy could not keep her eyes from the earl as he followed Geoffrey from one chilly nod to another. Iveragh answered each with an unperturbed civility which appeared to Roddy to be far more well bred than the thinly veiled hostility he received in response. If he had really come to Yorkshire because of her, she thought, he must wish now that he hadn't.

"Your Ladyship," he said to Mary as they came at last to Roddy's corner of the room. "Good afternoon. I trust you had a pleasant morning's walk to town?"

"Quite, thank you," Mary said curtly, and Roddy had from her hostess the fleeting, agitated vision of a refusal to be driven into the village that morning by her husband's unvalued acquaintance.

Roddy was frowning at that when Geoffrey took her hand and transferred it to Iveragh's. "Miss Delamore," Geoffrey said gravely. "May I present Faelan Savigar... Lord Iveragh."

"I'm honored, Miss Delamore," the earl said, and Roddy found herself transfixed once again by coal-rimmed eyes of the clearest, strangest blue. He lifted her gloved fingers to his lips and pressed a firm kiss there without taking his eyes from hers. She swallowed. The spur-of-the-moment notion that had possessed her in Newmarket now seemed to border on insanity. Had he actually come to court her? There seemed to be a question in his glance, but without her gift, she trusted nothing. Still, if she could not fathom Iveragh's thoughts, she could be perfectly certain of the chilling emanations of disapproval from the rest of the company as he lingered a split second too long over her hand.

It made her angry. What right had they to hold their noses in the air? Every one of them had some scandal in the closet, and though Roddy was a little unclear on exactly what Iveragh had done to earn such dislike, it could hardly be worse than some of the secret desires Roddy could have told about the most respectable matrons present. In a mood of challenge, she smiled back at Iveragh and said warmly, "Oh, but we've met before, I think—and not so long ago! Have you forgotten?"

A shock wave of consternation swept through the room at her comment, but Roddy saw only the earl's face. It changed at her words, fleetingly but unmistakably, just a slight widening of his ice-blue eyes, a warming of the skeptical set of his mouth. Somehow Roddy knew it was a rare look that he gave her. "You're quite impossible to forget, Miss Delamore," he said softly. "I didn't know but what you might have decided to forget me in the interim."

"Not at all, Your Lordship." She was well aware of the double-edged nature of her words, and her heart sped a little in conspiratorial excitement. "I believe I said at the time that I hoped I might see you again."

"So you did." He turned to Lord Cashel, who was handing Mary up from her chair. "Yes, of course, Geoff, go on. You've done your duty manfully."

Geoffrey nodded, and then looked back at the two of them as Mary turned away. "Dragons," he muttered, under cover of a cough, which reinstated him somewhat in Roddy's estimation.

Iveragh stood back a little, turning partly toward the window as if, having finished his conversation with Roddy, he was interesting himself in some activity outside. She sat staring down at the handkerchief in her lap, far more aware of his silence beside her than of the busy hum of thought and conversation that emanated from the rest of the room.

Even so, his low address startled her. "You astonish me, Miss Delamore. Are you not dismayed?"

Roddy cast a glance up at him, and found that, to all appearances, he was still staring out the window. She took his cue, and bent her head before she answered softly, "I don't know what you mean."

"Don't you? I should think it would be obvious that your entire acquaintance has taken me in extreme dislike."

"It's no concern of mine what they think of you," Roddy retorted.

He stiffened perceptibly. "I beg your pardon," he said. "Of course it's no concern of yours."

The sudden hardening of his tone made her glance up again, realizing he had misinterpreted her offense. "I meant," she said quietly to his dark profile, "that what these people may think of you does not affect my own opinion in the least. I shall draw my own conclusions, Your Lordship."

He was silent for a moment, and from the corner of her eye she saw his hands tighten behind his back. He said abruptly, "Do you still wish me to call on your father?"

Roddy felt her cheeks turn rosy. Somehow, what had been shamelessly easy in the clothes of a stable lad became excessively brazen in a respectable drawing room. But the more she had thought about her plan the more plausible it had seemed: he needed her money, and she wanted a family and a home of her own. A marriage of convenience, to the only man with whom she could possibly hope to live. She twisted the handkerchief slowly into a ball and nodded her head.

He let out a harsh breath, whether in relief or dismay she could not tell. She felt his eyes on her, and looked up. "For the life of me," he murmured, "I cannot understand why."

At that, she glanced involuntarily across the room toward Geoffrey and his wife.

"Ah," the earl murmured. She turned back to find him watching her. A faint smile twisted his lips. "I see."

"Roddy, my dear—" Her mother's voice rose above the others, recalling her daughter to the time. A half hour was more than enough for a morning call. Roddy rose, and managed a nod toward the earl, which pleased several dowagers who interpreted its self-conscious brevity as coldness. The earl bade her good day without apparent emotion, and in a flutter of farewells she found herself back out in the fresh chill of the autumn afternoon.

❧

He came to call on her father two days later. The pretext was the broodmare sale, but Roddy had her heart in her throat as she stationed herself on a low bench, hidden by a hedge outside the open window of her father's study, to listen. If she had been able to summon the concentration in her excitement, she might have witnessed the conversation through her father's eyes and ears, but that took more discipline than her pounding pulse would afford. It was eavesdropping, plain and simple, but it seemed a minor trespass in a case that concerned her so dearly.

The conversation was at first painfully polite, but as her father warmed to the topic of horses, he became increasingly jovial and confiding. That was part of his technique, a way to assess and soften up the opposition. Old horse-trader that he was, he did not understand that there was another deal in the offing, and so did not question his success at bargaining down a judge of horseflesh who was clearly as knowledgeable as himself. The dance of wits was long and complex, and when it ended with a handshake on the purchase of the mares at a price exactly short of a steal, Roddy's father chuckled expansively.

"A drink on it, m'lord?" he invited, in a mood of supreme tolerance. "I've a fine cognac at hand."

Iveragh agreed, and they subsided into the familiar male small talk that Roddy had heard a thousand times before. Nothing remotely related to herself was mentioned, and she had the unhappy thought that Iveragh might be planning to take his time and approach the subject on some later visit. Unfortunately, it was clear to Roddy that her father's friendliness was only a temporary result of the horse trade. He had no intention of meeting privately with the Devil Earl again in his lifetime.

A short silence fell, of the kind which heralded the end of the discussion. Roddy had almost despaired of her plans when Iveragh spoke unexpectedly.

"Mr. Delamore," he said in a calm voice, "I'd like to ask your permission to pay my addresses to your daughter."

"Sir?" Her father was flabbergasted out of his mood of self-satisfied tranquility. "M' *daughter?*"

She could almost see the earl's dry smile. "Your daughter. Roderica. I should like to court her."

"But—" Mr. Delamore could find no more words.

"I'm sure this seems precipitate."

"Precipitate—" It was a dumb echo.

"Perhaps you should sit down a moment, Mr. Delamore."

Roddy put her hand over her mouth to press back a giggle. What abominable aplomb! It overset her father almost as much as the unexpected topic of conversation.

For a full minute, silence reigned, while her father struggled to cope with this unexpected announcement. Then he said, in a sinking voice, "But you don't even know her."

"Of course I know her. We were introduced at Moorside Hall. But I had met her before that."

It was spoken quietly, without emphasis, but the implication burst on her father instantly.

"Newmarket," he exclaimed with a groan. "For God's sake, Iveragh, you're not so lost to compassion as to bandy that about. It was a lark, a stupid lark. I beg you, man—you wouldn't ruin her by spreading such—"

"I have no intention of hurting her," the earl interrupted coldly. "In any manner."

The words sent a trickle of gratified warmth through Roddy, but her father flared in righteous indignation. "Don't get your back up with me," he snapped. "If you don't mean to hurt her, I suggest that you keep a respectable distance. I won't have her made into scandal-broth on your account."

The short space of silence suggested to Roddy that the earl was controlling a sharp retort. After a moment, he said mildly, "Will you give me leave to explain my intentions, before tossing me out on my ear?"

Her father cleared his throat. The earl's calmness of manner soothed him in spite of himself. He said gruffly, "Go on, then. I haven't all day."

"I ask only that you allow me to court her. If she dislikes my attentions, of course I will not press my suit. You'll be thinking of my situation, and my reputation—I'll tell you bluntly that neither is particularly good. I have just a few months ago been put in control of my estates in Kerry, which were held in trust until my thirty-fifth year. I find them a disaster. If I can't raise considerable capital in a short time, a writ of forfeiture will be served on every acre of arable land in the lot. The entailed property alone is too poor to support the house, which is already in a state of ruin." The earl paused, and then added, in a different tone, "I can offer your daughter an ancient name. Nothing more, except my pledge to do everything in my power to use her portion to create for her a comfortable home out of Iveragh, and to see to her happiness with my whole heart and mind."

Those final words took both Roddy and her father by surprise. She felt herself flushing even in her hiding place, unsure of how to interpret the earnestness behind the phrasing. It was mere verbiage, she warned herself. Any man might have said as much to the father of his intended bride. And Iveragh was a consummate actor—that was already clear to Roddy.

Her father harrumphed uncomfortably. "Plain speaking," he muttered. "Plain speaking, indeed."

"I've said no more than you could discover yourself with a minimum of effort. My financial circumstances are unfavorable."

"Then perhaps you'll tell me what is favorable about this proposal," Mr. Delamore demanded. "I fail to see where you come by the audacity to make it, myself."

The earl said nothing. Roddy pressed her hands together, envisioning a lifetime of spinsterhood. If only Iveragh would say that he already knew she was willing—her father could never deny her anything that she truly wanted.

She should have dropped hints earlier. If her father sent the earl away now, Iveragh's stubborn pride would not permit him to ask again. He was suffering already, if she understood him at all. The humiliation of admitting his destitution to a stranger must be agony. And to have nothing at all to offer, no word to say in his own favor—it was more than a man should have to bear.

She was suddenly, hotly, determined that she would have him. One way or the other. He needed her, which was something new and precious in her life. If her father refused the earl, she would find some way to contact him. They could escape to the border and be married there. A hundred wild plans filled her head, distracting her from the confrontation at hand. Her father's voice jolted her out of fantasy as a sudden recollection struck him.

"Have you been dallying with my daughter behind my back?" he asked angrily.

"I have not." The ice in Iveragh's voice would have frozen hot coals.

"She said she liked you." Her father made it an accusation. "Did you put her up to it? If you've compromised her and then forced her to prate about some affection between you to gain my approval—"

Say yes, Roddy begged the earl silently. *Say you've compromised me.* Her father was certain to knuckle under to that, even if he were mad with rage. Calling Iveragh out would only ruin her publicly. Marriage would be the only answer.

But Iveragh seemed to have lost the quick wit he'd displayed earlier. He said, quite gently, "I have forced her to nothing, Mr. Delamore. Nor will I ever."

"Then why in God's name would she say she liked you?" her father sputtered. "M' daughter's no muttonhead. She must know full well what you are."

"I confess," the earl said, "I am as much at a loss as yourself. Perhaps you should ask her."

"Eh?" Mr. Delamore had subsided into a concentrated review of exactly what he remembered of Roddy's declaration concerning Iveragh. She lifted her chin in renewed hope at the conclusion that leaped into his head. "Good God, man," he exclaimed. "Are you in love with her?"

Roddy bit her lip in the long pause that followed, afraid that Iveragh would miss another golden opportunity. But this time the earl took his cue. In a strangely subdued voice, he said, "It's quite possible that I am."

Beautifully done, Roddy thought triumphantly. Just the right touch of self-doubt and conviction. Her father snapped up the bait. "Damme, if that ain't a leveler!" He chuckled. "The little vixen. She never told me."

"I wouldn't have thought she knew," the earl said dryly. "I'm sure I've never discussed it with her."

Roddy's father gave a hoot of laughter at that admission. She heard his chair scrape as he stood up. "Court her, then, by God!" he cried. "By all means, press your suit!" And for the rest of the brief visit, he continued to break into chortles of wicked amusement each time he thought of how this hardened rakehell was in love with his daughter, and didn't even think she knew it.

Three

Roddy sat plucking at a seam on the green velvet couch in the music room while her parents poured out objections and warnings. Her father's impetuous permission to Iveragh had been instantly dismissed by her mother as an act of insanity. Under Mrs. Delamore's chilly stare, the joke had seemed not quite so amusing to Roddy's father either, and now both of them joined forces to instruct Roddy on how to repulse her unwanted suitor.

"You must not let him single you out tonight before dinner, my dear," Mrs. Delamore said. "If he approaches you, you must draw someone else into conversation immediately. Your father or I will come to your aid as quickly as we can in that instance. Now—I've rearranged the seating at table, so that you will be between Lord Geoffrey and the vicar. Iveragh I shall keep at my side, since your father seems so ill equipped to deal with him."

"Matty!" Mr. Delamore exclaimed in hurt accents. "My responsibility as head of this family—"

Her mother turned a jaundiced eye upon him. "Your responsibility, my dear? Indeed yes, I would think that would include protecting your only daughter from ruin, but I see that it only extends as far as making bargain purchases of horseflesh."

He flushed crimson. Roddy lifted her chin. "Don't blame Papa." She amazed herself with the calm decision she managed to put in her own voice. "I *want* Lord Iveragh to offer for me. I suggested it to him myself. If Papa had refused, I would have eloped."

Two pairs of horrified eyes fixed on her as her parents absorbed this unexpected blow.

"Eloped!" her mother said in strangled accents, and promptly burst into tears.

Mr. Delamore looked as if he would have liked to do the same. Roddy bit her lip, dismayed at the hurt she had never meant to cause. She had thought they would be glad to have her gone. Her gift gave her no divine omniscience: there were levels and levels in the quicksilver shift of mind and emotion, but right now there was only anguished disbelief. "Mama," she said, and all the steadiness had left her voice. "Don't cry. Of course I won't elope—not now. But you must understand I want to be married. You and Papa can't look after me forever. I need a family of my own. All my happiness depends on it."

Mrs. Delamore buried her nose in her handkerchief. "We *can* look after you forever," she cried in a muffled tone. "We want to!"

Roddy squeezed her hands together in distress. "Oh, Mama!" How could she say that a lifetime of unfulfillment in her parents' home stretched like bleak winter before her? She was a burden to them, however loving their intentions. A burden to anyone who knew of her talent. They loved her as they would have loved a unicorn in their midst. Careful of the magic. Of the sharp and certain truth.

And yet she was human, her needs and fears the same as theirs. She was not different. Not in her heart. She longed to be useful and necessary for her own sake. Not like Aunt Nell, sheltered and protected, imprisoned in her indulgent family for all of her life.

"*Iveragh.*" Roddy's mother could barely speak past the sob in her throat. "The things they say of him—"

A multitude of sins were rumbling about her mother's mind, too incoherent for Roddy to catch more than a flash of mistresses and duels and dishonored maidens. Roddy frowned, remembering Lord Iveragh's face in the moonlight, and how quickly it had changed from despair to cold pride.

"Mama," she said with gentle firmness, "I of all people should know that what people say isn't always the whole truth."

Her father looked up from where he had been breaking a quill into fragments at the writing desk. He stared at Roddy a moment. "Do you know the whole truth in this case?" he asked suddenly.

It was Iveragh's declaration of love that he meant. She met his eyes and committed herself beyond recall. "Yes," she lied. "Yes, Papa, I do know it."

Her mother made a pitiful sound of protest. Her father narrowed his eyes. "And have you told *him* the whole truth, miss?"

It took all of her determination to keep her face raised to her father's. "He understands everything."

Not exactly a lie. She didn't dare admit that her gift had failed with Iveragh, for she knew her only hope was to convince her parents that she had seen some redeeming quality in him that everyone else had missed. Lord Iveragh knew all he needed to know. With him, she was a normal person instead of a freak, and she saw no reason ever to let him think otherwise. For that one virtue she was willing to excuse him any number of indiscretions.

"Everything, Papa," she repeated, with extra firmness.

Her father's lips tightened. He stared down at the desk and struggled. The decision shifted and wavered in his mind, tossed one way and then another. He'd spoken to Geoffrey, quizzed the younger man mercilessly, and received not only anxious reassurance, but a written letter of recommendation as well. "A man of integrity," that letter had said. "A noble friend." There was no mention of Iveragh's reputation, Iveragh's insolvency. Nothing but Geoffrey's high-flown phrases of assurance and commendation.

Her father thought of the look on Iveragh's face as he made his offer. Pride and hard truth, with no sly insinuations. Not a simpering dandy with a weakness for the card table; no one had accused the earl of that vice. And only just come into his inheritance—*at thirty-five, by God, long after a man ought to be allowed control of his own affairs. Found it ruined—some nitwit trustee, no doubt. A shame, a damned shame, ill luck that any man might have. But my daughter... my daughter... my precious curse. Our poisoned blood. Nell and Jane. Oh, God... Nell and Jane. A wasted life and a broken one.*

He looked up, and Roddy saw herself then as her father saw her. Against the background of dull velvet and leaden sky, she was a fragile, golden fairy-creature: all hope and future promise, innocent and wise and utterly confounding. His joy and his burden. It was beyond him, the right answer, and he knew it.

I love you, he thought, in helpless silence. *Let it be as you want.*

Roddy slowly let out the breath she'd been holding.

Mr. Delamore rose from behind the desk. He rested his hand on her mother's shoulder and looked down at her huddled form. "Come, my dear," he said softly. "We cannot keep our bird in the nest if she wants to be free." He stroked her hair, the shining blond that was paling to gray. "Let us give her this chance at happiness with good grace."

Her mother only wept harder, and hot tears pricked behind Roddy's eyes. "Papa—" she said brokenly, hardly knowing how to put it into words the warmth and misery in her heart.

Mrs. Delamore wiped inelegantly at her eyes. She crossed to Roddy and sank down beside her, pulling her close. Neither spoke—there was no need. Roddy knew clearly how much her mother wished her happy, and how much Mrs. Delamore feared for her only daughter's future. There was no need to look deeper, to the tiny place that might wish Roddy well and gone. A long time it had been since that day in Mama's bedroom. Long enough to forget.

If a lifetime was long enough.

"Don't worry, Mama," Roddy whispered at last. "I know this is what I should do."

Her mother made a small sound, and stood up as quickly as she had sat down. She walked from the room without a word.

Roddy's father cleared his throat. He spread his hands self-consciously. "You've grown up too fast for us, you see."

Roddy stood up. Stifling a sniff, she reached on tiptoe to kiss his cheek. "Best of my friends. I love you, Papa. I shall love you both forever."

❦

No more was said of shunning Lord Iveragh. If her parents were not enthusiastic, they were at least silent on the subject. That was guilt, that silence. It was fear. Beneath the rush of unhappy objections there was a tiny, tiny flame. A faint breath of relief. With Roddy gone, their lives would be different.

Easier.

She closed her mind to that hurt and threw herself into impossible dreams of the future.

For the dinner party, Roddy's maid helped her dress carefully in her newest gown, with its bodice of pink-and-silver-shot India gauze and white mull skirt embroidered with bouquets of the same dreamlike colors. The dress fell softly from the ribbon tied beneath her small breasts, trailing behind her as she walked. She twirled in front of the glass, so that the pearls which rested on the pale skin below her throat shimmered with reflected candlelight. Her bright hair gleamed with its own luster, framing her wide gray eyes with wispy curls.

No stablehand tonight.

No beauty, either. She knew there was a way about her; an aura that caught and held attention. She knew what she was not. Not pretty. Not sweet. Not delicate. She was not a daisy on a summer day, but instead the wind that blew it. People looked at Roddy the way they would look at a blue rolling storm on the horizon. And when she looked back, they faltered and turned away.

Down the curved stairs she went alone, past the high walls lined with Delamore stallions in gilded frames, one above the other, a century and a half of breeding blood and bone and the will to run. The moment she entered the drawing room, she felt her mother's unhappy protest over the dress. But the vicar had already arrived, and Lady Elizabeth was just stalking ponderously through the front hall in the footman's wake, so no word was said about the low neckline and slender silhouette of the India-gauze gown. Just behind Lady Elizabeth, Lord Geoffrey's party disembarked from their carriage.

Roddy watched from the door, first Lady Mary and then

tall Geoffrey, and then a blankness, the sweep of a black cloak behind them. Iveragh. Her heart did a curious little half-beat. He always seemed to have that effect: that when she saw him she was so intent on deciphering his thoughts that no one else's intruded on her consciousness at all. It would have been a relief, except the uncertainty was as nerve-racking as knowing too much.

Lord Iveragh in evening dress was at his most elegant and intimidating yet. Roddy found herself staring at the rose-patterned carpet on the drawing-room floor, just as people did when they spoke to her, afraid that if she raised her eyes she would meet his. That possibility sent her heart into the greatest agitation. He was here; he had her father's permission to address her, and suddenly she could think of nothing more frightening than the idea of marriage to a total stranger.

He made no move toward her. He lingered near the door, talking horses with her father. Roddy carried on a distracted conversation with the vicar, who thought she was painfully shy.

As Roddy listened with half an ear to the vicar's description of his fall garden, she let her gaze drift over Geoffrey's lean figure clad in brown satin. She wanted to smile at him and look him in the eyes, but he would not let her.

Roddy had noticed that evasiveness more and more over the past few years. It had been the first real hint that she could expect nothing from him. Like Great-Aunt Jane's husband, Geoffrey had grown increasingly uncomfortable with the witchy gray eyes of a Delamore female. He was more happily occupied now with a warm perusal of the parlormaid's swelling bust as she leaned over to relight a candle that had sputtered out on the table next to him. When she straightened up, he gave her a smile and a half-wink, and the images in his head would have made her blush twice as pink if she could have read them as Roddy did.

Roddy watched the small exchange with resigned exasperation. Though Geoffrey loved his wife with a commendably rarified sentiment, as far as Roddy could tell he'd never felt an instant's remorse for keeping up his lady-killing ways as a married man. It was one more reason, Roddy knew, to be sure that he and she could never have suited. Women were the one thing which seemed to Roddy to have fallen through a particularly large crack in Geoffrey's moral platform. In fact, it had been the chief despair of her young life that she herself was the single female whom he considered in a completely sisterly light. Beneath his honest charm and modesty, Geoffrey was the closest thing to a libertine that Roddy personally knew.

"And what do you think of the Irish question, my lord?" The vicar addressed Geoffrey politely, when the blushing maid had departed.

Geoffrey forgot the buxom Yorkshire girl immediately. "The Irish question?" He spoke with a calm courtesy that was completely feigned. The subject brought a turmoil of excitement to his mind, but to Roddy's confusion it seemed to have more to do with the revolutionary government of France than with Ireland. *Representation*, he was thinking, and *human rights*, topics dear to his philosopher's heart. They were subjects that never failed to give Roddy a headache when she tried to follow his reasoning.

"Have you had trouble with the malcontents on your estate?" the vicar pursued. "I understand there've been most savage acts perpetrated on innocent people."

"No." Geoffrey smiled, his golden eyes cold. *United Irishmen* flitted in and out of his head before he spoke again. "We haven't had the least sign of unrest. But then, I try to treat my tenants liberally. Not all landlords agree with that approach."

"I heard that somewhere in Ulster a squire was found impaled on a pike made by his own smith." The vicar envisioned that discovery with a gleeful shiver. "The culprits were tarred and hanged, I do believe, and good work of it, if I say—"

"How long have you known Lord Iveragh, my lord?" Roddy interrupted.

She had meant the question only to change the subject and stem the rising tide of Geoffrey's fury at the vicar. The instant jumble of memories that tumbled through Geoffrey's mind was unexpected, so vivid and various that she could make nothing of them. But out of the multitude, one vision dominated—a strange, distorted memory of water flashing, choking... panic and then deliverance: a bruising grip and a boy's face very close, strained in desperate effort beneath streaming dark hair.

"Since our school days," Geoffrey said, glancing at her and then away. To Roddy's surprise, it was a subject that made him vastly more uncomfortable than Irish politics. He didn't even want to think of it, but his attempts to concentrate on something else did not hide from Roddy the knowledge that he knew Iveragh had come to Yorkshire with the purpose of courting Roddy. It embarrassed Geoffrey to have brought his friend for such a purpose, and in some way that wasn't clear to Roddy, it violated his rigid moral principles. But whether the unease had to do with Iveragh's reputation or some twist of Geoffrey's own, she could not tell.

"Oh," Roddy said, putting mild surprise in her tone. "I wonder that you've never mentioned him before."

A single word roared through Geoffrey's mind—a blast of wind that came and vanished. He shifted in his chair, focusing on the pearls that gleamed at Roddy's throat. But she had caught it, that single word, and suddenly she wished she hadn't.

Murder.

Plain and unvarnished. She stared at Geoffrey, willing an explanation, but he was concentrating heroically on his wife now, thinking of her pregnancy and her clearness to him, subjects guaranteed to chase everything else from his mind.

She sat back. It had shaken her.

Iveragh a murderer?

No. Geoffrey's scruples would never allow him to bring a murderer into their house and allow the man to court the daughter of one of Geoffrey's oldest friends. Murderers were ragged outcasts, not elegant Irish peers. Murderers were hanged, by honest gentlemen like Geoffrey.

And a gentleman's way to commit homicide was on the field of honor.

Roddy frowned.

It made little sense. Geoffrey had no disgust of dueling, as long as his strict code of ethics was upheld. In fact, Roddy well knew that he would not hesitate at violence when his principles were at stake. He was a man of action as well as pen, though one might not think it to see his aristocratic figure disposed as it was now in a prim shield-back chair.

No—an honest duel would not affect Geoffrey so. Perhaps it had been a dishonest one.

She glanced up for the first time toward the dark figure that dominated the far side of the room. As tall as her father, and more perfectly built, Lord Iveragh stood with his head bent attentively to Lady Elizabeth's desultory conversation. He appeared to be fascinated by every phrase that dripped from that lady's rouged lips, nodding occasionally, and even smiling once. It was just as that unexpected expression touched his hard mouth that he raised his eyes and looked straight at Roddy.

She was caught, with no possible excuse for staring at him except that she was staring at him. The astonishing contrast of light blue and dark jolted her, as it always did, with a physical sensation. He held the smile, faintly, as if waiting to see if she would return it. But before she could command her lips to move or her face to turn, the butler announced dinner.

Lord Iveragh looked away, offering his hand to Lady Elizabeth. Whatever the prevailing opinion on his morals, certainly no one could fault his manners. Roddy could feel Lady Elizabeth warming to his easy courtesy, and was suddenly and absurdly jealous of the fat old woman who entered the dining room on his arm.

Dinner was interminable. If any one of Roddy's four brothers had been at home, she might have found some enjoyment in contrasting their polite exteriors with the piquant personal opinions she was sure they would hold of such a dull and distinguished company. But they were all gone, Charles and Miles down to Oxford, and Mark and Earnest off to hunt grouse with a friend in Scotland. It was Earnest, the eldest, whom she missed the most. This tepid dinner gathering could have used a spike of his dry and pointed humor.

Seated at the far end of the table between Roddy's mother and Lady Elizabeth, Lord Iveragh carried on a charmingly innocuous conversation about some recent production at the reopened theater in Drury Lane, a topic that set both ladies at ease and convinced Roddy that he was himself an inspired performer. In his role of amiable gentleman, he reminded her of a great lazy black cat masquerading as a tame canary.

After dinner, when the men had finished their brandy and rejoined the ladies, he sought out Roddy for the first time. As she watched him walk toward her, the dinnertime illusion of domesticity disappeared. He seemed no longer a canary, but an untamed cat again, a natural predator with strange, light eyes.

She moistened her lips, trying to shed the uncomfortable feeling that it was now *she* who represented the canary. He stood just beside and a little behind her, a location that somehow, without words, claimed and branded her as his personal territory. The vicar, who had been heading for the seat next to Roddy nearest the fire, took one glance at Iveragh's cool smile and veered off for another part of the room. Roddy felt a gulf form between the pair of them and the rest of the guests, an intangible wall that even her parents seemed loath to cross. She looked up at the earl and felt as if she were alone with him.

He said softly, "I've spoken to your father."

Roddy nodded and fixed her eyes on her hands, unable to force her tongue to move.

He stood still a long moment, and then reached out and stroked the nape of her neck, a feather touch that made Roddy stiffen in surprise. She did not dare look up at him, but sat rigid, hoping that the movement was not visible to the rest of the party. No one was looking their way; everyone was covering curiosity with determined conversation, as if by mutual agreement they had decided to pretend that Roddy and the earl were no longer in the room. Iveragh's hand moved down her spine, leisurely, a bare tickle of warmth that made her breath come shallow and quick in a way that she'd never felt before. She sat paralyzed, telling herself that it was outrageous, preposterous—that he should be standing in her parents' drawing room with all the dinner guests and caressing her as if she were a tavern girl.

"Will you be my wife?" he asked, in a tone so low it was hardly a breath.

Roddy felt herself suffuse with color. A mistake, she thought frantically—it was all a mistake. She could not marry this man. Fear was not an emotion that often plagued Roddy, but it closed in on her now with an icy grip. What did she know of him? Nothing. Less than nothing. Blind, deaf, and dumb she was, without her gift to aid her. Naive and ignorant, unable to distinguish fact from fancy. She had made him a hero in her mind, a proud man bearing the weight of his misfortune with dignity, but what was that image to the purpose? He might just as well be—was *sure* to be—what everyone else thought him: a dissolute cheat unworthy of the title "gentleman."

His fingers paused in their feather movement. She felt them float above her shoulder, barely touching. Waiting. She realized that she was holding her breath. The moment seemed to stretch out painfully, and still she could not speak. Finally he moved, lifting his hand as if in withdrawal, and the cool place where his warmth had been was suddenly more than she could bear.

"Yes," she said clearly, and looked up at him. "I would be honored."

His face had been grim, his eyes intent on empty space as he waited. At her words, his bright glance flicked toward her. His expression changed, and in that moment Roddy was glad of her answer.

He lifted his head as he spread his hand over her shoulder. His fingers pressed possessively into her skin. His voice, low and carrying, caught the attention of everyone in the room. "Mr. Delamore," he said. "Your daughter does me the kindness of accepting my hand in marriage."

It was hardly a conventional announcement. Lord Iveragh met the stares with a level gaze. Roddy wished she could slowly sink through the floor. His touch seemed to turn cold—a result of the hot blush that spread up from her breasts to her face. The wave of consternation and dismay that emanated from her parents and their guests made her want to turn away and bury herself in the earl's hard arms, as if there she might find protection from the others' horror.

Why had he done that? He should have waited, told her parents in private, allowed them time to accustom themselves before they had to face their friends.

But she could guess why. He was afraid that she would change her mind. Or have it changed for her.

And he was right.

Given time to think, she would have grown cowardly. A day of reflection, and she would have found all the reasons to hang back. She was afraid. The future seemed to fall away from before her like a black pit. Yet his hand was firm on her shoulder, and his body a solid reality at her back. Trust me, that comforting presence said. Lean on me.

She managed an uncertain smile.

Geoffrey stepped forward while the rest were still frozen in astonishment. "Congratulations," he said, and reached for Iveragh's hand. Geoffrey's surface warmth did not match his true feelings, which were a confusing mixture of relief and guilt. *The cause*, he was thinking as he bent to brush a light kiss to Roddy's fingers. *The cause, poppet. I'm sorry.*

Roddy blinked up at him, and he recoiled instinctively at the direct look from her unsettling silver eyes, turning away to focus on Mary again. Lady Cashel came forward at his glance, and offered her good wishes in a subdued voice. Roddy realized at once that if there had ever been a possibility she and Mary might become friends, that event was impossible now. The Irishwoman's antagonism toward Lord Iveragh hung about her like a dark fog.

The earl received their approbation gravely. Roddy leaned a little toward him as her father approached.

"Roddy," he said, not even glancing at Iveragh. "This is truly what you want?"

Though the earl's deliberately public declaration had made denial all but impossible without hideous embarrassment, Roddy's father was fully prepared to speak out if she showed the slightest doubt.

She placed her hand over the earl's, a theatrical gesture, and one that made her intensely aware of the hard strength in the fingers that rested so lightly on her shoulder. "It's what I want, Papa."

He glared at Iveragh. In a savage undertone, he said, "Take care of her, damn you. Or you shall answer to me."

She felt the tiny quiver that went through the earl's hand, as if he might have clenched and unclenched it. "Of course."

Her father stepped back, and Roddy looked beyond him in trepidation. She dreaded her mother's response more than any other. Mrs. Delamore was standing stiffly, still staring at her daughter and the dark intruder who had claimed her as a wife. Her mother's anguished helplessness brought hot tears to the back of Roddy's eyes. *Please, Mama*, she pleaded silently. *Please understand.*

Pride came to Mrs. Delamore's rescue. She waged an internal battle of grief and rage, but nothing of it showed on her face. She went to Roddy and kissed her cheek, managing a smile that was brittle with despair. "Be happy, my dear," she said too loudly.

The other guests all left as soon as possible after offering their own congratulations. Lady Elizabeth and the vicar were desperate to start passing the word to the neighborhood, and Lord and Lady Cashel were uncomfortably aware of Mrs. Delamore's barely controlled emotion. Lord Iveragh stayed only long enough to ask if he might call on Roddy in the morning.

She nodded shyly to the request, still feeling the imprint of his hand on her shoulder like a brand.

❧

Roddy had never known anyone who had been engaged before. All of Geoffrey's courtship had taken place far from Yorkshire, and there were no girls of Roddy's age in the neighborhood from whom she might have gleaned the proprieties. Her mother had chosen to ignore the situation. She was avoiding her daughter, as Roddy well knew. In one way that made things easier, but no tearful reproaches also meant no advice, and Roddy was left to choose her own line of conduct toward her new fiancé.

She met him alone in the small parlor the next morning. A smile was more than she could manage, but she held out her gloved hand politely. He did not take it. He stood in the doorway and looked at her, with a far steadier gaze than she herself could command.

"Good morning," she said, trying very hard not to look down before those frost-blue eyes. She forced her lips into an awkward curve. "I'm… glad to see you."

He raised his dark brows, and faint humor touched the firm line of his mouth. "Brave girl." He stepped forward and took her gloved hand, bowing over it with smooth grace. "Would you be so courageous as to drive out with me?"

She looked up into his face and realized with surprise that she really was glad to see him. She felt like a spooky colt let out for the first time alone—fascinated by new sights and sounds and liable to bolt at the merest shadow.

"I should like that," she said. "I'll go speak to Papa."

He let go of her hand. "Ah, yes. Papa."

She left him standing in the parlor. The interview with her father was brief, for Roddy was determined to block her parents' fears from her mind. She wasted no time in the hopeless task of convincing her father that Iveragh was not going to attack her the moment they were out of sight of the house, but simply stated firmly that she was going for a drive, and might not be back for luncheon. Her father took one look at the stubborn set of her chin and agreed. As Roddy exited he was making hasty plans to stay out of his wife's sight for the remainder of the day.

Lord Iveragh handed Roddy into the phaeton and took up the lines. The crisp morning air and the fresh eagerness of the horses raised her unsteady spirits to the point of inebriation. A bubble of giddy laughter escaped her as the whip tapped the back of the nearside gray and the carriage rolled into motion with a gentle jolt. Appalled, she popped her hand over her mouth and tried to make the giggle sound like a cough. The earl slanted a look toward her at the sound, but said only, "Which direction?"

She raised her parasol against the sun with a nervous snap. "Have you visited the East Riding before, my lord?"

"Never," he said. "My name is Faelan."

"Faelan." She tested the exotic sound of it on her tongue, the way he said it with an Irish lilt—*Feylin*. It called up thoughts of mist and mountains and wild places. "Faelan Savigar." She hesitated, and then said diffidently, "It's certainly fierce-sounding."

"Faelan is Gaelic for 'wolf.'"

"Oh."

He gazed solemnly out over the backs of the trotting horses. "Fortunately, my second name is Vachel."

"Oh?"

"That means 'little cow' in Old French."

"Oh."

"They balance each other out, you see."

Roddy looked down at her gloves. "Not exactly."

He turned his disturbing blue eyes upon her. "Some young ladies are afraid of wolves."

She fiddled with the cloudy-glass handle of her sunshade.

"Are you?" he asked gently.

Roddy stole a glance and found him watching her. "A little," she said, in a burst of honesty.

The phaeton drifted to a stop at the end of the driveway. He smiled. "Then I suggest you pick a direction in which we won't meet up with any. East or west?"

Roddy swallowed her confusion. It seemed that they were carrying on two conversations at once, and she was not at all sure if one was not entirely in her imagination. "East," she said, trying to sound brisk and unconcerned. "I'll show you a surprise."

The horses arched their fine necks and leaned against their traces, and the carriage wheeled out of the drive.

Four

RODDY SPENT THE FIRST QUARTER HOUR OF THE DRIVE watching the wind flutter the silk of her parasol and trying desperately to think of topics of conversation. It was a new and imposing problem. With her gift and her small circle of family and close friends, subjects of mutual interest had always been easy to find. Several came to mind now on which she might have spoken quite knowledgeably, such as the weather and the horses and the price of wool, but none seemed to hold out much hope of amusing the Devil Earl.

When at length she hit upon a topic, she was so relieved to break the silence that her question came out with an excess of enthusiasm. "Will you tell me about Iveragh, my lord?" She caught her breath, furious with the way her voice quavered upward. "What it's like, I mean," she added, which only made her sound worse, as if she'd thought he was too stupid to understand the first time.

He glanced at her. "Iveragh." His mouth twisted into something like a smile. "Not yet, I think. I wouldn't want you to break our engagement before we put the contract in writing."

Roddy peeked at him, looking hopefully for a sign that he was joking.

He tilted his head and raised one eyebrow. "Tell me about yourself instead."

"There's little to tell about me," she said apologetically. "I've never been to London."

"Ah." He nodded, gravely enough, but she suspected humor in the odd set of his jaw. "We shall remedy that, if you like. But it's you and not London that interests me. What do you do with yourself, when you aren't dressed up in breeches and battling grooms?"

Roddy bit her lip. "I suppose I shall never live that down."

"No, I don't suppose you ever shall." He grinned at her, an expression so unexpected that it seemed to go straight to her heart and make it thump madly. "You've a damned graceful way of unmanning an opponent. You can rest assured I'll remember it to my grave."

She shrugged, to cover her agitation. "One is obliged to learn self-defense, with four older brothers."

His rich laughter wound around her thudding heart and seemed to squeeze it even harder. "Good God, I hope you never tried that trick on them." He rolled his eyes heavenward in mock terror. "I'll take care around you, my dear. I hope you haven't a short temper."

"Not really. Only—I dislike to see animals abused."

"I see." He glanced at her again, with laughter still warming his deep blue eyes. "Tell me about your father's stable."

The question was as surprising as it was welcome. Under the steady encouragement of his smiling interest, she found herself launched on an enthusiastic description of her father's training methods and breeding techniques. It must have been an hour, but it seemed only a few minutes later when she glanced up at the horizon and caught her breath.

"There it is," she cried, and pointed with her parasol as the phaeton bowled out of a steep chasm and onto a rise.

The horses clattered to a stop. They had been on an indifferent road, surrounded on all sides by nothing but sky and sheep and the gray-green bleakness of the moors.

"The sea," Faelan said.

It had appeared as if by sorcery. A moment before it had seemed that the moors would go on forever in their brooding beauty, but now sea gulls mewed in the cloudless sky, and a sapphire horizon stretched away beyond the sheer cliffs. On a headland in the distance, the crumbling skeleton of a medieval abbey crowned the scene. They sat in silence for a full minute, and then he said simply, "I like your surprises."

To her profound annoyance, Roddy found herself blushing again.

"Does the road go past the ruin?" he asked, when she did not respond.

"Yes. In another mile or so."

"Good. We can stop there to eat." He urged the horses forward. "Are you hungry?"

"Well—" Roddy hardly knew what to say. Surely he didn't think there would be food available at the deserted abbey?

"Well, what?" he mocked, smiling at her hesitation. "Look in the hamper, then, and see if there's aught to be tempting you. It's under the seat."

By the time they reached the abbey, she had examined and enthusiastically approved the contents. While Faelan saw to the horses she took it upon herself to spread the cloth and arrange the cheese, smoked salmon, and crusty bread on a convenient block of stone. She was working diligently, if inexpertly, to open the wine bottle when he returned.

He lifted the bottle out of her hands, and with one deft twist freed the cork. Roddy had seated herself on the block next to the food, facing the water. He sat down in the grass beside her, leaning against the roughly dressed stone and stretching out one boot-clad leg as he poured the wine. In exchange for the offered glass, Roddy handed him a makeshift sandwich. They ate in a comfortable silence. It was pleasant, to have someone nearby and yet not intruding on her thoughts. The horses were content with their feedbags. A light breeze from the sea fanned her cheek and the egret feathers on the bonnet she had set aside, but all else was quiet. Even the gulls had deserted them, too wild on this empty coast to accept a handout.

She finished her sandwich and stared around her at the quiet ruins. A melody came unbidden to her lips, the kind of haunting air she loved. She hummed it softly, liking the way the wind carried her notes away as if to please some fay sea creature drowsing far out on the shimmering waves.

She realized, with a small shock, that she was happy. Her fears and doubts had faded into pleasant attention to the numerous small sensations that interested her. In the cool autumn day, there was just a trace of heat from the man at her side, the slightest warmth where his shoulder rested half an inch from her knee. She felt it even through her light wool skirt. Against the background of cerulean, his hair seemed very black. It made her think of his eyes and their blue beneath thick charcoal. She watched his hands idly as he poured another glass of wine. The fingers were long and perfect: strong, rather than refined.

He was, she thought smugly, a handsome man.

The idea made her lips curve upward. She had to remind herself firmly that theirs would be a marriage of convenience. He needed her for her money, not her person. Those fine hands had undoubtedly caressed far more beautiful women than Roddy was sure she would ever become. After their wedding, he might even decide to go back to his mistresses.

A depressing thought. Not that she'd expected eternal devotion from him, but it would have been nice to…

But no, that was mere fantasy. She wanted children, and proper management of the money and estate that would be their future. That was enough. He could keep all the highfliers he liked. It was, she told herself, one of the specific advantages of marriage to the Devil Earl—she would know no more than he chose to tell her.

He slanted a look at her, and held up his glass. "To my bride," he said unexpectedly. "May you always be as happy as you were a moment ago."

Before Roddy could summon a reply, he finished off the wine in one swallow and stood up. "Walk with me." He held out his hand. "We need to talk."

His fingers curved around hers, giving her little choice but to obey. He did not let her go as he began to walk, but tucked her hand into the crook of his elbow, a move that seemed so natural to him that she thought again, gloomily, of the women he must have known.

"What is it?" he asked suddenly.

Roddy looked up at him in startlement. "I beg your pardon?"

He stopped and turned, and once again she was caught by the vivid blue of his eyes. "Why do you frown? I'd hoped you were enjoying yourself."

"Was I frowning?" Roddy made an effort to lighten her expression. "I'm sorry. Of course I'm enjoying myself."

He took her arm again and moved on. "Good. I like it when you smile."

"My lord—"

"Faelan."

Roddy took a breath. "Faelan—there's really no need for gallantry. I realize full well that you've offered for me because of my portion, and I'm well satisfied. You don't have to pretend affection when we're alone."

He stared out at the water. "Don't I? How practical you are, Miss Delamore."

"You may call me Roderica," she said generously.

"I would far rather call you Roddy, as Geoff does. May I have that honor, or is it reserved for"—he paused, and then said with an odd quirk to his mouth—"old friends?"

"I'll never be properly dignified if everyone calls me *Roddy*," she protested. "It sounds like a stableboy."

"Ah, but I have a special fondness for stableboys. I'll call you Roderica until we're married, if you like. After that, I shall consider it my prerogative to choose what suits you best."

They walked in silence for a while as he led her aimlessly among the tussocks of dried and windblown weeds. Finally she said, "You wanted to discuss something, my lord?"

"Yes." He reached down and pulled a late-blooming wildflower, a ragged thing with tiny, colorless petals, and gave it to her absently. "We both know the advantages to me in this match." He lifted his head to gaze at the horizon. "I'd much like to know what advantages you see for yourself."

Roddy looked down at the brittle stalk in her hands. "That's difficult to explain. Is it so important to you?"

"It is," he said.

"I want a family, my lord. Children."

He tilted his head, probed her with a glance that was as hard and quick as blue metal. "Forgive me if I seem vulgar, but I can assure you that there are any number of men who could give you children. My... talents... in that area are hardly unique."

"Nevertheless," Roddy maintained bravely, "I feel that we shall suit."

He gave a humorless laugh. "What illusions are you laboring under, child?" He stopped and turned to face her. As he met her eyes, his brows drew downward. He reached out and gripped her shoulders in a savage shake. "Has no one told you about me?" he demanded. "God's mercy, will your friends let you do this blindly?"

Roddy held his fierce gaze on the strength of willpower alone. "If there's aught to tell, my lord, I would rather hear it from you. As a man of honor."

His hands fell away from her as if she had singed him. "*Honor.* There's a piece of drollery. Half the world would tell you I can't even spell it."

Roddy said nothing. *I will not let him frighten me*, she promised herself, watching gamely as he tore another autumn weed from the earth and ripped the plant into tattered shreds. There was violence there, in the restless fingers that made quick work of destroying a wildflower. He dropped the crushed pieces as if they were nothing. "Shall I tell you, then?" His voice was harsh. He looked at her and then away. "Ahh... those eyes of yours. You scare me, little girl. Old... young..." He laughed, a distorted sound. "A man might fear Athena in all her wisdom never saw as much as you."

Roddy pressed her hands together behind her back and swallowed. She kept her gaze resolutely from his face.

"Where shall we start?" he said, with a lightness that was chilling. He took her arm and turned her toward the sea. "With my most recent sins, I think. I remember them more clearly. You'll forgive me if I give you a summary rather than an accounting—thirty-five years of corruption might be too much to stomach at one sitting."

"My lord—"

"Just lately," he went on, as if she had not spoken, "I have seduced the third daughter of George Compton of

Asherby—her name is Jane, I believe, but I can never keep all these Marys and Janes and Elizabeths straight in my mind. She is to bear my child—so you see, Roderica, you have indeed selected a man with fertile seed. That should put to rest any fears you might have entertained on that score. This Jane..." He paused, as if searching his memory. "Ah, yes. I've blackmailed her father into paying her keep for me at the remote hunting lodge where I will continue to visit her until my carnal desire for her is glutted. When that time comes, I plan to cast her off entirely, but of course I shall continue to insist that her father pay me well to keep the secret to myself. He holds a sensitive government post, you see, and has five more unmarried daughters, unfortunate man. I believe they have put it about that Jane has died of smallpox."

The painful grip of his fingers on her arm belied his conversational tone of voice. She could almost feel bruises forming beneath her jacket and blouse.

"A representative example of a scheme that I've found to be successful over the years," he added. "I shall not bore you with particulars. Suffice it to say that I've ruined no fewer than eight innocent maids and sent them all to walk the streets of London while I pocket their parents' hush money."

His stranglehold on her arm had begun to cut off her circulation. She twisted one hand about the other, trying to ease the tingling. He showed no sign of noticing her discomfort, but forced her along with him on his slow and terrible stroll. "Yes," he said casually, "I quite excel at extortion. I'm also in the habit of manufacturing false evidence concerning the many indiscreet young bucks who frequent certain houses in the City. It's shockingly easy, I fear, to bribe servants into the wildest of tales—stories which could ruin a man's good name for life. Occasionally the game becomes more challenging, for a few of these young men are quite courageous. Even rash. They have the effrontery to face me down in a public place and accuse me of blackmail. They challenge me to meet them, and naturally I accept—how could a man of honor do less, my love? And you have called me a man of honor, have you not?"

She opened her mouth to put an end to the bitter words, but he quickly cut her off. "I don't care for duels myself," he said, in a careless way. "But I assure you I am an excellent shot. I always aim to kill on the field of honor, my dear. A clever way of discouraging the practice, don't you think? I fancy I would have faced challenges without number had I been so foolish as to go lightly on my adversaries. I'm proud to say I've dispatched three young men of promise and valor and still escaped the displeasure of the law, although I believe my feats are common knowledge in the highest circles. Alas, there is no proof." He made a sound of disgust. "Otherwise, I make no doubt, I wouldn't be in a position to offer you my hand—as a man of *honor*." His hold on her loosened, so suddenly that she took an unbalanced step away from him. He let her go, with a sardonic, sideways glance. "Frightened, little girl?"

"No." Roddy stood rubbing her tingling hand. "I think you would like me to be."

He raised his dark brows. "You don't believe what I've told you?"

"I—I hardly know what to believe, my lord." She was floundering, and missing her talent painfully. What had seemed like freedom a few moments before now felt like a prison with blank, unbreachable walls. "I cannot think you have killed men for nothing."

His smile was sour and hard. "It's always for nothing that men are killed, my sweet child."

"I don't believe you've shot any young men over trifles," Roddy said resolutely. "You wouldn't even race your horse when I told you he might die."

His blue eyes narrowed. He inclined his head in a slight, chilly bow. "Ask Cashel," he said. "He has acted second for me. He may also tell you that an accusation of blackmail is no trifle."

She stiffened at the steel in his voice. "I will." She was glad to hear that her own words only quivered a tiny bit. "Geoffrey will tell me the truth, even if you won't. Have you more tales to frighten schoolroom misses?"

His face became a mask. "Many," he said curtly. "I think the most celebrated of them must be the rumor that I murdered my father when I was ten years old."

If Roddy had never perceived the same word flitting through Geoffrey's mind, she might have stopped herself from instinctive recoil. But self-discipline came too late. The earl saw her start, and a smile of acid satisfaction twisted his mouth. He lifted her chin with one finger. "My lovely innocent. Will you let me kiss you, little girl? I would dearly like to do so."

It was a challenge, a gauntlet thrown down to cover what had gone before. He had made himself out to be a monster, and he dared her to accept him still. She could make no conscious choice; she half believed and half did not. Yet she raised her face to his in a move that must have been an invitation, for his bitter smile suddenly faded.

He stared down at her, his face bleak and still as a winter sky. With a low moan, more like pain than pleasure, he pulled her toward him, trapping her hands at her sides. His mouth closed hard on hers. Cruel and yet gentle, harsh but tender; a confusion of sensations enfolded her. His punishing demand forced her head back, and yet his arms were there to hold her, to cradle and caress her.

He kissed her mouth, her cheeks and eyes, and then took her mouth again and kissed her until darkness swam in the back of her brain. He tasted like the wine they had drunk. Deep and drowning. Intoxicating.

"Curse you," he breathed as his mouth moved in a rough trail over her exposed throat. "You'll haunt me all my life— you and your damned witching eyes." His teeth closed on soft skin, and fire bloomed in the pit of her stomach. With an urgent move, he pulled her hips against his, as if he could make her part of him by force. Roddy found that she wanted the same, and answered him in kind, her body arching close; her hands seeking warmth beneath his coat and shirt.

She found the heat she sought. A hoarse sound escaped him as her fingers burrowed under his waistcoat and splayed across his back where taut muscle and hot, smooth skin lay under a shirt of thinnest lawn. He moved away suddenly, a quick, rejecting push, as if her touch burned him. Her hands fell free. Then, before she could even moan in protest, he had pulled her back into his rough-gentle embrace, sliding his hand to the nape of her neck and trapping her cheek against his shoulder. He held her tightly, too tightly to move; so tightly she could feel the faint tremor in his palms. She resisted a moment and then rested there, listening to his harsh breath, feeling the beat of his pulse and her own, while his hand and his lips moved softly in her hair.

"Little girl," he whispered against her temple. "It's not too late. Tell me you won't marry me."

She thought of what he'd told her, in a voice that mocked itself. She thought of what she wanted. A life of her own. A family.

Love.

A day ago, an hour—even a minute—she might have obeyed him. But the taste of his mouth on hers, his arms around her and his warmth beneath her hands...

Roddy shook her head without lifting it from his chest.

He groaned softly, and held her closer. "God help you. God help you. I'll do my best, but there's so goddamned little I can give you."

This is all I want, she could have said, but she knew he would not heed her while this dark mood held him. She rested in his arms, closing her mind to doubt. She would deal with what was real, not rumors. What she could see with her own eyes. He hated the man whose sins he described, whether that man was himself or a creation of vicious gossip. Of that much she was certain, and it was enough for now.

❧

They were halfway back to Roddy's home when the pastured mare's distress came to her like a dog's howl on the wind: distant and distorted at first, gone for a moment, then closer and sharper as the phaeton moved on at a brisk pace.

She said nothing of it, having nothing logical to say to someone unaware of her talent. Instead she searched, her eyes focused hard on the horizon for the first reasonable moment when she could say she had seen the horse. She only hoped the animal was in view of the road. Pain rendered her gift deceptive, overcoming distance with intensity, driving all closer consciousness into background. And this pain was increasing by the moment, expanding into something she'd never experienced before. She could not tell how far away the mare might be, or even in which direction.

As the discomfort grew she cupped her elbows and squeezed, clenching her teeth and closing her throat against the moan that rose in unthinking response. She wanted to move as the mare did, wanted to cry out under the swelling strength of the anguish that gripped her. The carriage rolled on. The torment increased. Roddy dug her fingernails into her arms. She had not held back to protect herself, leaving her full gift open to locate the horse. Too late, she realized her mistake. By then the pain was beyond controlling, beyond any barrier she could possibly raise. Merciless. She would have screamed with it if there had been air in her lungs to move.

"Are you all right?"

The question seemed to come from far away. As the phaeton jolted to a halt she lifted her head and stared at the man beside her, hardly knowing who he was. Her lips would not form words. He asked again, more sharply. She felt as if she were splitting in two, trying to answer and trying to push away the pain. She looked at him and past him, desperate for words, for a way to explain what was inexplicable. A dark blur took shape in her watering eyes—the mare, black against the faded green in the shadow of the far hillside.

She pointed, which was all she could manage of sense in her torment. He turned.

"Help." Her voice came out a croak. "Help."

His gaze swung back, dark brows drawn low over a bright question. She felt his hand close hard and urgent on her arm. "Are you ill?"

"Not me." She shook her head, wild with the pain. "The mare."

He let go, looking again toward the hill. And then moved, leaping out of the phaeton with an oath.

Roddy gathered sense and strength and scrambled after
him. He went over the wall in one easy vault, but Roddy
stumbled back from her attempt in a tangle of hampering
skirts. Her legs threatened to collapse under her. She gathered
her skirts and tried again, her throat choked with sobs of
effort and pain and frustration. She was halfway across and
falling back when his strong hands closed at her waist. He
dragged her over and lifted her down, setting her feet without
hesitation in the mud that had already ruined his boots.

They both ran. The horse was laid out flat on the rocky
ground in a hollow of the hill, her legs stiff and restless with
distress. The pain had eased for a moment to something duller,
but Roddy knew it would come again. It hung over her like
a robe of chain mail, dimming reason to disorder. Faelan
snapped, "Careful," as she came too near a flailing hoof.

"Hold her head," he ordered, with an authority that penetrated the blind and unreasoning urgency in Roddy's brain.
She obeyed him, unable to think farther through the haze.
The mare jerked with fear as Roddy went down on her knees,
but habit and instinct brought the right music to Roddy's
tongue, the ageless soothing croon to comfort animals and
babies. She bent over the mare's head and rocked and sang a
lullaby in the velvet ear, keeping one hand free to gather the
animal's soft upper lip into a pinched fold, a trick that always
worked at home to deaden pain and terror.

"It's breech," Faelan said, from a thousand miles away.
"We'll have to make her stand."

Roddy looked up in blank stupor, saw him shirtless and
bloody, and still made no sense of it. The mare groaned and
twisted. Roddy whimpered. She bent her head as another
wave of dark agony rolled through her mind.

Faelan grabbed her hand and hauled her to her feet. He
drew her roughly toward him, gripping her chin and forcing it
up. "Don't you dare faint," he hissed, shaking her head as if to
drive reason into it. "Stay with me. You stay with me. Hear?"

Roddy stared up at him, breathing hard. Her eyes searched
for focus and found it in his, blue light in the darkness. She
swallowed and nodded.

He released her, glaring at her hard a moment, as if he thought she might fall. Roddy pulled anger out of the pressing pain, a tonic for her wits. She bared her teeth in something like a smile. "All right," she panted. "All right. So let's get her up."

Between them, they did it. With Faelan's shirt for a halter and his strength for a crutch they prodded and pulled and coaxed the mare to her feet in the short intervals between contractions. He made the horse and Roddy walk, both of them, and if the mare tried to lie down he slapped her hard on the rump with a stick.

He was adamant in his purpose. When the stick lost effect he began to yell, to wave his arms in the mare's terrified face. Her eyes rolled white as Roddy dragged at the horse's head and stumbled on, thinking dimly that he would probably take the stick to her, too, if she faltered in her job of leading.

Walk and walk. Walk and stumble and walk again. The pain came in huge tearing waves, rising and falling and rising to a higher peak each time. It seemed to go on forever. Never in all the years in her father's stable had she been present at a breech birth, but in the rational part of her mind she knew Faelan was right in his insistence. The moment had to be postponed, as long as possible, and then, when it came, completed in a frantic rush.

That was how it happened. The mare went down with a heavy grunt, pulling Roddy into the sweep of straining agony. Roddy closed her eyes and bit her lip until she tasted blood. The smell of sweat and horse and fear filled her nostrils. The mare breathed in great moaning gusts. The pain mounted and the world dissolved, one long excruciating moment in which the mare was screaming and Faelan was shouting something and Roddy could not tell human sound from animal. She felt blackness closing and the liquid salt of tears in her mouth.

Then it was over.

It left her as weak and wobbly as the newborn foal that Faelan scrubbed with the shirt Roddy had dropped.

She watched him, too drained to think. When he'd finished, seen to the mare and foal both, he left the tiny bundle of legs and nose and came to where Roddy was crumpled at the exhausted mare's head.

He held out a hand to her. She took it, letting him pull her to her feet, and leaned on him as he led her a few yards away to a patch of grass.

He drew her against his shoulder, hard and warm, and she focused for the first time on the fact that her dress was in ruins and his shirt far beyond recall.

She thought vaguely that she ought to be embarrassed. Instead, she was only tired. She rested her cheek on his bare skin and watched the age-old tableau unfold before them as the mare lunged to her feet and turned to inspect her new foal.

A creature of the moment, the mare was. The pain was forgotten already, fading and dulled in the new interest of this appealing little fellow that smelled like herself. She began to lick the tiny creature, pausing often to look up at Roddy and Faelan with mild and protective suspicion.

Roddy found words in her thickened throat. "Thank you," she said to her muddy toes.

He looked at her sideways. She thought there was a lurking smile at the corner of his mouth. "I thought I'd lost you once or twice."

She kept her eyes down. "Your boots are ruined, I'm afraid."

He bent one knee and leaned over to inspect his formerly polished footwear. "Salvageable. Which is more than I can say for my shirt."

The foal splayed out one leg and fell back. Roddy saw Faelan's half-smile widen.

"I'm—" She searched for a way to say it. "I'm glad you knew what to do."

He shrugged, his eyes on the mare and foal. "Whose are they?"

"I don't know."

He glanced at her, and let out a breath of amusement. "You are a wonder, Miss Delamore."

"Am I?"

"You feel it, don't you?" he said. "What the horses feel."

The blood drained from her face. "What—what do you mean?"

"At Newmarket with my stallion. And just now." He shook his head at her look of horror. "I've known one other who could do the same. It's a damned God-given gift. You knew about the mare long before you saw her."

"Of course not. I—"

"The devil you didn't. You looked like death by the time we stopped." His hand closed on her arm as she started to rise in panic. "Don't run away."

She tried to relax, tried to act easy. "I wasn't feeling well for a moment," she said. "That's true. It was the salmon, perhaps, and then the—all the excitement. I'm better now."

He looked at her again, a long, deep, speculative look. Roddy managed to hold her gaze steady beneath his.

"I'm sorry I wasn't much help," she said.

For a moment she thought he would say more, but then his smile broke into a sudden grin and he splayed his fingers through her hair, pushing her head down in the kind of affectionate shake that her father gave her brothers. "You kept her walking, little girl."

Roddy smiled too, then, a little shakily. "I thought you'd smack me with that stick if I didn't."

He nodded. "So I would have." He pulled a stalk of dry grass and stripped the grains from the stem, biting carefully into one. He spat it out with an expert puff. "Volunteer wheat. What's that doing here?"

Roddy looked at the stalk in his manicured hands, those strong hands that were stained now with blood and dirt. At his once perfectly laundered shirt, sacrificed without a thought. She thought of him tending the mare, with moves expert and certain and not at all fastidious. She sat up and looked at him. "You're not a rake," she cried. "I believe you're a bloody *farmer*!"

His blue eyes crinkled in humor. "Watch your language, child. Do you think the one mutually excludes the other?"

"I'm sure I don't know what to think," Roddy muttered.

"I'll tell you what I think," he said, reaching out to drag her against him in a hard hug. He kissed her ear, and then her mouth when she turned in confusion. Colors were pinwheeling behind her eyelids and breath had almost failed her before he let her go. He gave her a smile that made her toes curl in her muddy boots, and then flicked a gentle finger across her cheek. "I think that we shall suit, my love."

&

A week later, Mark and Earnest returned empty-handed of grouse.

"Not that we should grouse about it," Earnest said, which was something Earnest *would* say, when Roddy ran out to meet them amid the bustle of baggage and servants in the drive. He gave her a bear hug that lifted her off her feet, so that blond hair flew in her eyes and she couldn't tell if it was hers or Earnest's; a hug as warm as his feelings on greeting her.

Mark was not so cheerful. He was determined, in fact, to grouse loudly and long about the poor shooting. In view of his temper, Roddy reserved her great news for later, and joined with her parents in demanding an account of every boring and wasted day of shooting.

The silence on the subject of her engagement held through dinner and after. Every time Roddy's father worked himself up to speak, his throat would go dry and he'd take another sip of wine or sherry or whatever happened to be at hand, until finally he forgot what it was he'd been trying to announce and went to sleep in his chair by the fire.

It was long after the household had retired that Roddy gathered the courage to tiptoe to Earnest's room and knock softly on the door.

He was still awake, as she'd known through her gift, awake and sitting in a dressing robe reading by the light of one candle. He closed the book and smiled when he saw her. "You've come to congratulate me," he said. "I deserve it. 'Twas devilish hard to miss my shot every time Mark did."

Roddy set her candle down and went to stand beside him, leaning over to give his short queue a playful tug. "A noble effort."

He put his arm around her and chuckled. "Base self-interest. It doesn't do to plague Mark when he's carrying a loaded gun."

A memory of Mark's angry frustration rose in Earnest's mind, and Roddy marveled at how amusing their hot-tempered sibling appeared, in the midst of a tantrum, through his elder brother's eyes. Earnest looked up and caught the smile that quivered on her lips. He grinned, making the picture in his head more and more absurd, distorting poor Mark's imaginary features until both of them burst out laughing.

"I think I shall go into print," Earnest said.

"And have your life forfeit in ten counties," Roddy predicted. "I know what pictures you'd draw of all our neighbors."

"Perspective, my dear sister. A simple matter of perspective. As I'm sure you well know."

Earnest was the only one who took her gift so matter-of-factly. She was silent a moment as caricatures of half the local personalities formed and changed and vanished from his fertile and energetic mind.

"Earnest," she said shyly, "I wanted to tell you something."

He abandoned his amusing meditations in an instant. "And what might that be, love?"

She twisted her hands together. "I'm engaged to be married."

For a moment he just looked at her, his mind a stunned blank. Then the thought and the words erupted simultaneously. "Engaged! To whom?"

She pulled away a little. "I don't suppose you know him. He's one of Geoffrey's friends."

"Engaged," Earnest repeated. "I never thought you—" He stopped, but the completion of that sentence was clear to Roddy.

"I know," she said, and pulled away entirely. She went to the window and tugged nervously at the heavy damask drapes. "My talent. But you see—I want—" She dropped the curtain and turned. "Oh, Earnest, my gift doesn't *work* with him! It's just like normal people."

"Doesn't work." He frowned at her. "Are you certain? That's never happened before, has it?"

"No. But I'm certain. There's nothing. He's like—I don't know. Silence. With everyone else it's a babble, and I have to work to keep them out. When I'm with him… I don't have to try. I can't feel him if I *do* try. It's wonderful, Earnest. So peaceful and calm."

"Who *is* this fellow?"

"He's an Irish peer," she mumbled quickly, as if by speaking too fast she might somehow slide over the truth. "Lord Iveragh."

"*Iveragh!*" Earnest's dismay hit her like wall of falling bricks. "You're joking!"

"No, I—I'm not. And I know what you must have heard of him, but—"

Earnest had lunged to his feet. "Heard of him! Holy hell, girl, are you raving mad? The man's a killer!"

"I don't think—"

"Does Papa know of this?"

"Yes, he—"

"Why didn't he call me back?" Earnest flung himself into pacing the room. "I could have told him—oh, God, oh, God, how did he let this happen? Has a contract been written yet?"

Roddy summoned a trembling breath. "Last week. And Faelan isn't a killer. I mean—they were honest duels, and fair, and they were forced on him. Geoffrey acted his second."

"*Faelan,*" Earnest sneered. "It's Faelan, is it? The bloody bastard—I suppose he knew just how to twist a pretty child around his finger! I suppose he asked you to call him *Faelan*, and he called you *my love* and *darling*, and expected you to fall down at his feet. Has he kissed you?"

Roddy drew herself up. "That isn't your affair."

"Roddy." He caught her arm. "He's a murderer. He killed his own father in cold blood."

She twisted away. "That's not true!"

"The devil it isn't. I suppose he told you that, too."

"He said it was a rumor. And why wasn't he hanged, if everyone is so certain he's a murderer?"

Earnest waved his hand. "Because his mother got him off somehow. The deluded woman stands by him to this day. She's the only reason he's received anywhere in London, and she won't hear a word against him."

"Perhaps she's right."

He took her by the shoulders and shook her. "He wants your money, Roddy. Don't you see that?"

"Of course he wants my money," she cried defiantly. "He's going to lose his estate without it."

"*Why?*" Earnest pleaded. "Why marry him? There are any number of gentlemen who—"

She struggled out of his punishing grip. "You know why, Earnest! I *told* you! My gift—"

He looked at her for an arrested moment as the piece he had forgotten fell into place in his mind. Then he threw back his head with an ugly laugh. "Like a damned stupid ostrich. You can't see the evil in him, so you think it isn't there."

"He isn't evil. He's Lord Geoffrey's friend."

"Yes. And a worse judge of a man than Lord Geoffrey I'd like to see. His Lordship's damned notions of loyalty will be the death of him one of these fine days."

"Just because—"

"Just because Geoffrey's some kind of bloody philosophical saint, you don't have to send yourself to perdition by the same road. He thinks Iveragh saved his life when they were a couple of scrubby schoolboys; that's why Cashel holds with the man. It was some boating accident... *ancient* history. The last decent thing Iveragh ever did, and it happened before I learned to walk. You weren't even a gleam in Papa's eye, you little twit."

"You don't understand."

He sat down heavily. "No. I don't. Roddy, I can't let you do this. For all we know, the next we'd hear of you after you went off with Iveragh was that you'd fallen from a sea cliff and been killed like his father was."

Roddy caught a chilling vision along with those words, of a body tumbling from a cliff—a man's body, that twisted and changed to her own. She shoved away Earnest's horror. "*Stop it.* You're being ridiculous. I hope I'd not be so poor a wife that Lord Iveragh would feel he had to push me off a cliff."

Earnest bent his face into his hand. "I can't believe Mama and Papa have agreed to this."

"Well," she said, "they have."

"And when is the wedding to be?"

She hesitated, wary of another outburst from him. "The banns are already posted. The ceremony is to be in two weeks, when Fae—when Lord Iveragh returns from London."

"Oh, God," he said, his voice muffled. "Roddy—don't do it. There must be any number of ways to break the contract. His character alone—"

"I'm not concerned with his character," Roddy said sharply. "Don't you see, Earnest? *My gift.* How can I make you understand what it means to find someone who isn't afraid of me? Who doesn't flinch when I look at him? Maybe I am an ostrich, but that's better than being an outcast all my life!"

Earnest looked up in sudden suspicion. "Does Papa know your talent has failed with Iveragh?"

She set her chin. "No, he does not. And you won't tell him, Earnest, because if you do, I'll run away with Iveragh. I swear to God I will."

He stared at her, judging the seriousness in her stony expression. "Yes," he said slowly. "Yes, I see that you will."

A sudden trembling took her lower lip. "Just wish me happy, Earnest," she whispered. "Please."

He stood up and drew her into his arms, closing his eyes in anguished defeat. *Oh Roddy*, he said in silence. *I do. You know how much I do.*

Five

AN EARLY WINTER STRUCK ON THE MORNING OF THE WEDDING, leaving the parish church frigid with the first deep snow of the season. Even the crush of guests did not warm the gray stone walls or the chilly air. In her stiff white muslin gown, Roddy's toes were cold and her fingers were frozen around her nosegay of satin ribbon and evergreen, but her face burned with shamed agitation as she walked down the aisle under the prurient interest of everyone present.

The general opinion was pregnancy. The hotly debated topic was *who*—Lord Iveragh himself, or some undergroom whose get the earl would claim as his own in order to gain control of Roddy's portion. Odds ran heavily in favor of the groom, since Iveragh had been known to come into the country only a bare few weeks before.

Still, there was wild speculation about the man who stood silently waiting at the front of the chapel beside Geoffrey. Tall and fiercely handsome, black hair and black cloak and eyes as blue as the sky beyond a soaring hawk—Faelan's unholy allure was as strong in church as without. As she walked toward him Roddy was treated to some lascivious inspirations from the imaginative ladies of the East Riding concerning her future husband.

The images made goose bumps of cold and fright stand out on her arms. She reached Faelan and would not look at him. Only his solid warmth, so close as they turned to face the altar, made him seem human to her at all.

His voice, that rich and seductive voice that she had almost forgotten in the three weeks since she had seen him, repeated the vows with steady certainty. Her own words quavered pitifully, as fleeting as her frosted breath. It was suddenly becoming real, this ceremony. She stood there and thought: *What am I doing?* Every warning, from her father and mother and Earnest—from Faelan himself—all came back and tumbled around in her head until she thought she would crumple to the floor where she stood.

Faelan touched her arm, and suddenly it was already over, already too late to change her mind. He took her hand and worked her glove free. The ring slid onto her trembling finger, as smooth and cold as the closing of a trap.

Without the support of his offered arm, she doubted she could have made the walk back down the aisle. She looked toward her family as she passed, and saw not a flicker of the discomposed emotion beneath those unmoved faces. Even her mother did not cry, too frozen in unhappiness for tears.

It was Roddy who wept as the door closed on the carriage. In the cold light of dawn that morning, she'd visited the stables before she left home, fed her old pony an apple in small pieces, so his worn-out teeth could manage it. She'd gone to all the rooms in the house and the secret places in the garden where she had played as child, gathering precious memories amid the bare, silvered branches.

She pulled her woolly cloak about her and pressed her gloved hand to her mouth to conceal its quivering, staring very hard out the frosted window until the sight and sound of the guests was far behind. It was done, irrevocably, and she felt as if she had leaped from Earnest's imaginary cliff and now fell through the air, a long, slow fall, with time in plenty to remember every fear and regret.

Faelan was watching her, she knew. Just watching, from his place by the other door, which made her want to cry harder. Because she was afraid. Because he was a stranger still and maybe did not understand what it was to leave the home and family that had been her shelter for nineteen years. Maybe he had never loved anyone, and never could.

The future unrolled before her, empty of affection and laughter: no brothers, no parents, no familiar network of minds and hearts to envelop her in comfort and security. She marveled that her lips had moved to say the words that bound her to him. The folly of it, the utter folly... she would never find happiness by leaving behind all she had ever known and loved. Her need for freedom now seemed a crazy dream, with no connection to this reality of a ring and a promise and the unknown man beside her.

Her head drooped, nodding listlessly with the motion of the coach as the long ride dragged on. Faelan was silent, and Roddy found she had no voice to speak. Even the rattle of the wheels was muffled by the new snow that covered the frozen road. The interior grew dim with late afternoon, and her clasped fingers seemed very white in the gloom.

An unexpected movement caught her eye in the twilight. His hand touched hers, covering the pale shape with another, larger one, entwining their fingers in a gesture that was no less intimate for being muffled by two layers of kidskin. He remained silent. He did not even look at her. Though he pressed his palm to hers steadily, she sat still, afraid to misinterpret. It was so strange, to have that touch and not be certain of the thought behind it. She wanted comfort, but she was not sure, not brave enough to turn to him and lay herself open and find that she had been wrong.

"Regrets?" he said, his voice soft amid the darkness and the creak of the wheels on fresh snow.

Roddy looked up at him. She nodded.

He smiled a little. "Honest child. You'll shame me into respectability."

She moved her hand uncertainly, and his hold tightened, just enough to still her.

"Roddy," he said, with a note in his voice she had never heard before, "I want you to forget your regrets. For tonight. Tomorrow you may take them up again. I won't blame you. But you've given me back my home, little girl. You've given me another chance. For that..." He stopped, and his fingers closed harder on hers. He said fiercely, "God—there aren't words to make you understand what that means to me. I want to show you." He lifted her hand and pressed it to his lips. "For tonight—forget what I am, forget what you know of me. Let me make everything perfect. This one time. Before the world comes back to haunt us."

She stared at her hand in his. Gratitude. It was not what she had wanted, but anything... anything that would fill this terrible void...

"I'll try," she said.

"Thank you."

The relief in his voice surprised her. He sat back, but kept her hand in his lap, and held it there for all the long ride to York.

❧

Firelight sent huge shadows against the low ceiling of the inn's best chamber. Roddy watched them move and listened to the occasional creak of the floor under Jane's busy feet. A simple mind Jane had, with no room for fine speculations on gentlemen's reputations. To Roddy's maid, a man was at worst a brute to be endured and at best a mild annoyance. Jane's thoughts as she hustled Roddy into the bedroom, clucking around her as she changed out of the wedding dress and into a taffeta gown, were divided between sympathy that Roddy would have to suffer a woman's duties and the hope that those duties would soon result in another child for Jane to fuss over. The maid said nothing of either, though, and kept her moon-shaped face neutral. *Won't do to frighten the girl*, she was assuring herself. *Only make things worse.*

Such grim presentiments made Roddy's knees feel a little shaky. Deliberately, she called to mind another opinion, this one held by a scullery-maid: the one who seemed to be caught so often in the pantry by one of Roddy's brothers. *She* had no quarrel with male importunities. She was proud of the fact that she had introduced each of the Delamore boys in turn to the delights of love. Standing there with Jane fussing about her gown, Roddy felt her face grow hot as she recalled jumbled pantry scenes that had leaked into her awareness, try as she might to block them.

In the midst of these agitating reflections, a light knock on the door made both Roddy and her maid stiffen. Jane stood upright from buttoning one of Roddy's lacy cuffs, pursed her lips, and stalked resolutely to the door.

A stalwart young girl entered, carrying a tray, followed by the innkeeper's wife with another. They arranged the dishes on a round table near the fire, lit new candles, and then retired. With one hand on the door, the innkeeper's wife paused and looked at Jane. "If you please, I've been asked to see you to your room, ma'am. If you'll come with me now?"

Jane's face went blank, covering her instant affront at this thinly veiled order. But its source was obvious, and she obeyed, leaving the room with her jaw set and her eyes glued resentfully to her feet.

Left alone, Roddy stood staring into the fire a moment, and then sat down. Her hands felt cold, and though a pleasant smell drifted up from the covered dishes, all appetite had left her. She poured herself a generous portion of wine and stood up again, wandering restlessly around the room.

The bright reflection of her hair in the dressing-table mirror made her stop. She turned, frowning critically at her image in the candlelight. There was nothing there to surprise her, nothing different from what she had seen reflected in the minds of her parents and brothers and friends all her life.

She was not beautiful. She wasn't even pretty. She was... intense. Contradictory. Her hair shone dull gold and angelically curly, but her eyebrows were two dark wings that tilted upward, like the faces on the demons carved in the chapel at home. Her chin was too pointed, her mouth too apt to smirk, and her eyes—well, her eyes weren't the kind that lovers liked to gaze into for dreamy hours. There would be no lazy afternoons in a hidden bower for her. When men looked at Roddy, they didn't see an attractive woman. They saw themselves, and it was an image that none seemed to care to focus on for long.

She lifted the silver goblet and drank greedily, hoping the wine would warm the chill from her fingertips. At a sound from the door, she jumped, and the empty vessel fell with a soft thud onto the carpeted floor. She stooped to pick it up.

When she rose, he was there.

In a full-length dressing gown of midnight blue, he seemed to Roddy to be inordinately tall. As he reached back to close the door behind him, the robe fell carelessly open, revealing a shirt unbuttoned at the throat, a sprigged waistcoat, and pale breeches above soft ankle-boots and plain silk stockings. Roddy moistened her dry lips, determined not to let her voice squeak.

"My lord," she said, and sketched a formal curtsy.

He gave her a slight bow in return, then stood looking at her, his dark brows raised and his lips pressed oddly together. "Shall we dance?"

Roddy blinked up at him, and saw belatedly that he was joking. She made an effort to smile which didn't quite work.

"Perhaps we'd better eat," he said.

Roddy nodded. She sat down in the chair that he held for her. The heavy odor of warm food and his lingering presence at her back made her stomach squeeze uneasily. When he pulled his own chair close to hers, she felt positively ill with fright.

There was a tureen of soup, from which he served them both. Roddy sat staring down at the clear broth, unable to even lift her hand and pretend to eat. Her insides seemed to press upward into her throat. It was a panic that fed on itself: the more she tried to calm her fear, the more terrified she became. She could not even have said what she was afraid of. Strangeness. Change. Him. Herself. Not *knowing*.

That was it. The uncertainty. Her life had been ordered and comprehensible, without surprises. She'd been hurt some-times—by Geoffrey's withdrawal, by his loving someone else—but she had always been sure.

Now, cut adrift, she was drowning in doubt. Faelan had said to forget what he was. For tonight, just one night, to forget. But she could not forget; she didn't know what he was. A dark man with eyes the color of the sky. That was all she saw.

He looked at her, returning stare for stare. "Eat your soup," he said.

Like a chastised child, Roddy picked up her spoon. She had thought she could not eat, but the first salty taste of broth slid easily down her throat. She took another sip, and began to feel slightly better. When he tore off a piece of bread and offered it to her, she took it. The familiar, crusty smell and blandness comforted her. Before she realized she had eaten the whole chunk, he was offering her another.

Roddy accepted that, too, and their fingers touched in passing. His eyes met hers. He smiled.

Roddy smiled back, shyly.

She looked down immediately, but the brief contact had been reassuring. If she could smile at him, surely she could take the next step. It was like crossing a stream on a fallen log—the more nervous she felt, the harder the task would become. She took a deep breath and made herself relax enough to face the boiled pudding.

He uncovered a roast duck after she had finished half the pudding. It was odd to be eating without footmen to carve and serve, but she was glad of the change. It saved her the strain of keeping up appearances in front of strangers. Faelan served, after a fashion, by slicing a bite of fowl and crisp skin, and offering it to her on the two prongs of his own black-handled fork.

Roddy looked uncertainly at the tidbit. He waited, and after a moment, she did as he seemed to expect: took it gingerly into her mouth from his fork.

He made a low sound, a kind of masculine purr of approval from deep in his throat. It seemed to vibrate along Roddy's spine, and she swallowed the bit of duck too fast. She groped for her wine, and took a gulp. When she emerged from behind the goblet, another bite of duck was waiting for her.

Roddy took that one, too. And the next. The fire popped and hissed. Her fingers moved restlessly in her lap, clasping and unclasping. Something in the simple act of accepting food from his hand hinted at deeper things: yielding on levels not so safe and simple. The room seemed to be growing hot. The duck disappeared, shared in this intimate way, and then he pared an apple and cut it into neat cubes. Not even the fork intervened then: the fruit passed from his fingers directly to her lips. His thumb brushed her cheek. The touch seemed incidental, but his eyes were half closed and his mouth curved faintly upward as he offered her another bite.

The intensity of his look disturbed her. She turned away a little, refusing. The goblet of wine was a welcome relief against her heated skin: the cool metal, and the liquid slipping down her throat.

He touched her cheek. With a light, steady pressure, he made her face him again, and she set down the goblet with reluctance. She would not look up; she focused stubbornly on the bite of apple, as if that might make the disturbing figure behind it disappear. She closed her eyes and took the fruit, wanting anything that might cool the warmth that suffused her face. The juice ran sweet and chill on her tongue, mingling with the mustier taste of burgundy as she swallowed. Then there was another taste, another feeling—a shock as his hands gently cupped her cheeks and his lips closed over hers.

His tongue slipped between her teeth, seeking the apple-rich flavor that lingered there. Roddy stiffened, raising her arms as if to push him away, and found in the confusion of the moment that they only curved around his shoulders instead. She felt very queer, light-headed and heavy at the same time, so that her hands seemed too much to lift once they came to rest against his neck.

He drew his open palm down the column of her throat, bending to follow the touch with kisses. She held her breath. Her hands closed reflexively, kneading the powerful muscles beneath his robe, and he made another low sound of approval.

In the candlelight, his black hair had taken on glints of red and gold. It brushed her cheek and lips softly, as soft as his fingers as they slid around her neck and worked the fastenings at the back of her gown. Each satin button came free with a tiny tug, down and down, until his hand had reached her hips and the gown hung open the length of her spine.

"Sweet," he murmured against her throat. "Sweet wife." His fingers slid beneath the gown and moved lightly on her skin, warm in the chill air. Panic flooded her. She arched her back, trying to retreat, and found her breast pressed against his hard shoulder like an offering. She jerked away and sat up stiffly, breathing in frantic little gusts.

He let her go. The slight smile had left his face; he leaned back in his chair and gazed at her, with a faintly quizzical look. "You're afraid of me," he said.

Roddy bowed her head in misery. Yes, yes—she was afraid. She knew her duty; she tried to be brave, and yet when he touched her like that it seemed that her body was no longer her own. This stranger, this man whose mind was closed to her; he made her muscles hot and weak just by looking at her. He could control her. She could feel it, though he did not exercise the power yet.

He moved away a little and turned back to the table, pouring himself another goblet of wine. He took a sip, watching her over the rim.

She wet her lips. "I suppose you think I'm being ridiculous."

"Not at all." He set the goblet down. "I pride myself on my ability to terrify children. Are you going to cry?"

"Of course not."

"Oh." He sighed. "That's usually the best part."

Roddy sat up with dignity. "Pray do not laugh at me."

His lips twisted only slightly. She stared with narrowed eyes at the offending mouth, daring him to break into a smile. After a moment, the peculiar tightness left his lips and he returned her look with perfect gravity. "We seem to have reached an impasse," he said. "I fear I shall have to ravish you."

Roddy looked down.

"It's really rather fun," he said. "I predict you'll like it."

She bit her lips.

"As long as you don't giggle," he added. "It's considered quite a faux pas at such a moment."

Roddy stood up abruptly and turned her back, finding it necessary to avert her face. She shoved her loosened gown up onto her shoulder.

"I wish you wouldn't do that," he said. "You have a very pretty back."

She felt like a row of bowling pins, being knocked down one by one. The gentleness in his voice was devastating, but his demon-smile meant nothing. Just so he might have smiled at one of those gentlemen's daughters he'd accused himself of ruining, and for that look the girl would have given away her body, her soul… everything she had. Roddy could understand that. The pull was something beyond reason. Only her doubt, her knowing so well that a face could hide the intent beneath, kept her from melting into him like a snowflake into fire. She could not read faces, not without her gift to aid her. But the lure was stronger than the doubt. Far stronger.

"*Don't*," she said when she heard him move, and the word came out harsh with her own confusion.

There was a silence behind her, a void she could not fathom. At last, he said, "You're making me wonder, little girl. Do you have some reason to avoid your husband's touch?"

Roddy stiffened. She gripped her hands together. "You know what I'm afraid of. It's just that I've never…" She swallowed hard. "I've never… *you* know."

"Never?"

The skepticism in his voice mocked her. She whirled on him. "Of course not."

His eyes met hers, a shock of chilly blue. "You've never been with Geoff?"

"*No*," she cried. "Whatever makes you say such a—"

He was on his feet. He caught her to him before the furious words were out of her mouth. "Shh," he murmured. "Hush. I'm sorry."

Roddy stood stiff in his arms. "That was unkind," she said to his shoulder.

"I'm sorry," he said again. His voice seemed strained. He bent his head, pressing his cheek to her hair. "I suppose I've never been jealous before."

A funny tight place curled in her middle. "Jealous," she whispered. Her fingers moved uncertainly in the folds of his robe. "Of me?"

He did not answer. He held her tighter. She missed her talent with unprecedented fierceness.

"I've never been with anyone," she said. "Not like this."

He groaned, rocking her softly in his arms. "Forget I said it."

She laced her hands together behind his back, tentatively allowing her weight to rest against him, and spoke into the muffling robe. "It's what everyone else thinks—that I *had* to marry, and it made no difference whom."

"It's not important."

"It is." She bent her head, staring down at the play of light and shadow in the entwining folds of their robes. "What you think is important."

"Ah, Roddy," he said in a hollow voice. "I'm only a man. I can't see why you've done this—thrown yourself away on me. I've tried to think of reasons; I've tried every logic I can imagine, and it all comes down to one. God knows, I'll be happy enough with another answer if you can give it to me."

"I need you," she said simply. "And you need me. There's nothing more."

His harsh breath ruffled her hair. "Sweet Jesus... an innocent. Don't you know, little girl, that whatever you say can be proved or disproved before this night is over?"

Roddy had a general idea of what he meant, from Jane's disturbing thoughts. There was pain involved, Roddy was certain of that: the memory of sharp, tearing hurt from the maid's mind was what had frightened Roddy most of all. But then, how often had Jane gone into wailing hysterics at a scratch that Roddy hardly noticed? People were different. Jane was a lady's maid, not a girl who'd grown up falling off horses and out of trees and into ice-cold streams all her life.

Roddy lifted her face, looking steadily into his eyes. "I know it."

He turned his head, staring into the shadows with a baffled grimace. "I'm half afraid to find out." He looked back at her, and the grimace deepened to a sneer. "Behold, the libertine—unmanned by the chance that his wife's a virgin. I suppose if you're pure, I shall have to abandon my chivalric fantasy of saving a lady in distress." He shook his head. "And even if you're telling me the truth, no one else will believe it. Any child of ours who arrives in the next ninemonth will be labeled a bastard."

Roddy stiffened. She whispered, "No," but the word was weak with her sudden realization that his prediction was all too accurate.

"Oh, yes," he said. He brushed a wisp of gold back from her cheek. "What did you expect, little one? That the world would be any more trusting than your own husband? I was willing—" He paused, and looked hard at her. "I still am willing, if all this pretty innocence is some ill-advised play at gammoning me, to recognize any child you carry as my own. I'll kill the man who calls me a liar, but no one will be so stupid as to say it to my face. My delightful reputation as an executioner protects you that far, but it won't bridle loose tongues behind our backs."

The calm way he stated his violent promise made her fingers tighten nervously together. She said stumblingly, "Perhaps I won't—perhaps we won't—"

"Have a child so soon?" He raised one dark brow, and murmured, "Perhaps not." His hand slid down her back, where the unbuttoned gown still parted beneath his touch. Roddy felt his body tauten as he bent to nuzzle her hair. "But I plan to give the matter some attention."

She held her breath as his lips moved softly, bringing a melting heat to life in her loins. Slowly, tentatively, she allowed her weight to rest against him. It felt so good; so very good to stand there pressed against his solid, living warmth. She did not want him to go away. Not now.

"I suppose I must seem very strange, to want to marry you," she whispered.

"Very," he said.

"Don't all the ladies find you irresistible?" She was only half teasing.

He stroked her hair, pressing her closer to him. "They've generally stopped short of the ultimate sacrifice."

Roddy refrained from asking him if he had forgotten all those hapless gentlemen's daughters. The more she knew him, the more she questioned their existence. They were rumors. Silly, vicious, stupid rumors, made up by idle minds in malice. He could not have hurt anyone, this man who smiled and touched her with such aching gentleness.

She drew a circle with the flat of her palm on his shoulder. "My lord," she said hesitantly. "Shall you ring for the servants?"

It was surrender, that shy suggestion, and his slow smile said he knew it. He reached out without letting her go and pulled the bellrope beside the mantel.

When the domestics arrived a moment later to remove the dishes, Roddy was seated demurely in a chair, and Faelan stood with one shoulder against the mantel, gazing down into the flames as if a particularly fascinating scene lay illuminated there. The stout maid fumbled with the dishes, preoccupied with hefting her heavy tray and estimating how late the innkeeper might want her in the kitchen. Before she left, the door opened again, to admit the innkeeper himself, bearing a cut-crystal spirit decanter and one glass on a silver salver. Without lifting his eyes to either of his guests, he arranged the tray on the table and shepherded the maid out ahead of him.

The fire sent red highlights through the amber liquid as Faelan poured for himself. Roddy watched, curious and edgy. Between four grown brothers and her gift, she thought she should have known more of these things, of what was to happen next, but in truth all she had gleaned from the pantry was a confused blur of excitement and hungry, uncivilized pleasure. Such currents—such enticing, alarming power: when she looked at Faelan she wanted to submit, and when she looked away she did not.

His movements were insanely slow as he replaced the stopper and lifted the glass. Over the rim, he looked at her, and Roddy's throat went dry.

The glass sparked in the light as he set it down. "Come here," he said. His voice was hypnotic. Roddy felt the pull of it, the sensuality that hung tantalizing around him like a fog. She obeyed without thought, without conscious effort: one moment sitting primly in the chair, and the next standing before him like a captive pawn.

He smiled, a lazy glitter, and touched her lower lip with his forefinger. Her tongue moved instinctively to catch the drop of liquid he left there, and encountered the burning sweet taste of sherry. He bent to her, followed the trace of her tongue with his, invading a little and withdrawing. As she stood with her lips parted, he anointed them again with sherry, outlining their shape with the tip of his finger and then the warm sweep of his tongue. He drew a tiny circle of sherry on the soft skin below her ear, and Roddy found it increasingly hard to breathe as he followed the droplet with flickering kisses.

She moved restlessly when he straightened, glancing up to find that he had lifted the glass of sherry again. He did not sip at it. Instead he grasped her hand and guided the tip of her finger into the cool liquid. Roddy caught the hint instantly, but she stood still, not quite able to translate thought into action.

He waited, holding the glass steadily under her hand. Roddy cast down her eyes and then raised them. Looking straight ahead, she was on a level with the open collar of his shirt. She stared at him a long time, seeing his even breath and the beat of his pulse. Slowly she lifted her hand and touched the shadowed hollow at the base of his throat. When her finger came away, a clear drop hung there, begging to be collected. She leaned forward, and scooped up the liquid with the tip of her tongue. He tasted of salt and sherry. She felt again for the glass and repeated the process, this time lingering a little to explore the flavor.

His deep moan vibrated beneath her tongue. He raised his free hand and rested it on her hips. "Roddy," he murmured. "Help me undress."

The third drop of sherry she'd transferred had begun a provocative trickle downward toward his chest. It disappeared beneath his shirt. Someone's fingers—hers, her own—began to work at the buttons, opening them, one by one, following the errant drop lower. His skin was smooth and dark and warm in the shadows. She fumbled with the more difficult frogging on his waistcoat, pushed that and the shirt aside to find the drop of sherry vanished in a light curling fleece of black hair.

From there, everything seemed to move under some strange force, a will outside herself, that wanted more, that wanted to see the firelight on the curve of his skin, to touch the hidden contours. She eased the robe and shirt off his shoulders, arms upraised and reaching... how tall he was, how much larger than she. Beneath her hands he was hard and soft, a contradiction that cried out for exploration. On tiptoe, she spread her palms across the broad, bared skin of his shoulders, and looked up into his eyes as he stood immobile under her touch.

He was smiling, his devil's smile. Her own lips curled upward, fierce with new pleasure. So *this* was what it was, and she had been afraid.

No longer. The shirt and robe dropped to the floor, and he stood in front of her with his body outlined in flames: beautiful, beautiful, like the tiger she'd seen once, a wild thing that patiently suffered her touch. He let her look, let her gaze and her hands drift over him, and when she stroked certain places his eyes closed, and his throat rumbled softly with that animal sound.

She leaned over and kissed the base of his neck, tasting the lingering sting of sherry. His hand slid around her as she moved, from her hip to her buttocks, his fingers spread to press her into the unfamiliar male shape of him. He sought her mouth, not gently, forcing her body to curve and bend for him, until the loose mass of her hair brushed softly on the small of her own bare back. The taffeta gown was half fallen down, trailing off her shoulders. He let her go suddenly, moving back, and the gown dropped to her waist, held up only by his arm around her hips. There was nothing underneath, but she stood as still as he had, protected from the chill of the room by the hot flush his steady gaze brought to her breasts and throat and face.

Would he think her pretty? She looked up into his face, hopeful and scared. Too small, too awkward and coltish—*little girl*, he called her, and she burned with the shame of not being good enough. She was afraid her difference showed somehow, that he would recognize it and turn away in disgust.

And that, suddenly, was a thing she could not bear.

"Roddy." His voice was a low melody. "You're lovely, little girl."

Her lowered eyes flashed up, the way other people's did when she read their true hearts and let it slip. He touched the tip of her nose with his finger, leaving a drop of sherry to hang perilously. "Don't ever grow up, sweet child. Play with me."

The drop was dangling, a funny tickle. She reached out her tongue and tried, unsuccessfully, to catch it.

He laughed. He swept her up, carried her with gown dragging to the bed, bounced her into the thick down, and kissed away the drop on her nose. His body came beside her, sinking down the bed so that she rolled against him, her feet all tangled up and bound by the gown.

With one quick twist he reached down and freed her, sliding his hands up the naked length of her legs. She drew in a startled breath at that intimate touch, but he was laughing still, silently, his eyes crinkled in a way that made him look much younger. Roddy squealed and giggled breathlessly as he found her ticklish places. She jerked away, but he rolled over and held her down, ruthless, nipping and nibbling until she wriggled beneath him and tried to retaliate. It was like a romp from the old days with her brothers, when they had tumbled together in the grass and each vied to outwit the other. In this contest, Roddy was sadly outgunned, but she struggled gamely for the upper hand.

Then his movements changed, slowed, and he returned to the places he had teased with a different intent. Roddy lay quiet, breathing hard, her muscles relaxed from the merry tussle. The close contact was a pleasant sensation, the weight of his leg across hers warm and right. When his hand slid downward, stroking the tender skin of her inner thigh, she closed her eyes and arched a little toward the delightful touch.

His fingers skimmed up and down, and up and down, and then passed lightly over the soft down between her legs. She drew in her breath as he stroked that secret place. A throbbing grew there, a need that she could not quite define. She wanted to move, to somehow encourage him, and she pressed up blindly beneath his hand. He bent his head over her breast, still sliding his fingers rhythmically down and up across the place that had grown tender and damp and so responsive that when his mouth closed over her nipple her whole body jerked with the leap of sensation.

She tilted her head back into the pillow, giving up to the sweet, hot pleasure that sang through her limbs. Her hands moved aimlessly, seeking in ignorance until they followed the path of black hair downward to the band of his breeches. When she touched him there he groaned and shifted himself hard against her hip. She reached out, reasoning that if his hands on her could give such ecstasy, then she could do the same for him. She fumbled, meaning to unbutton buttons, but he trapped her hand against the pliable doeskin and pushed her fingers away.

"Patience, little love," he said hoarsely, bringing her hand up to kiss her knuckles. "I don't want to hurt you too much."

Roddy blinked, having forgotten all about that part. Her body tensed, and he gathered her close.

"Only this first time," he said. He stroked her arm and kissed her shoulder. "Only this once. I promise."

She looked up into his eyes, and thought that if he'd promised to bring her the moon on a platter of silver stars, she would have believed him. "I don't care if you hurt me," she whispered.

His thick lashes lowered at that, his fingers digging into her skin as he lifted her and bent to suckle and tug at her breast. She ran her hands down his muscled arms, spread her fingers across his chest, and then moved them persistently downward again, into the heat where his body half covered hers. He made another sound, a short, impatient growl of defeat, and this time his hand lingered when he brushed hers away, tearing at buttons and ridding himself of the soft barrier that contained him.

He shifted above her, seeming much larger suddenly, a smooth slide of hard body between her parted legs. She began to be afraid again, trembled with a little scared-excited shiver of anticipation. On his elbows, he leaned over her and kissed her, forcing her lips wide, holding his weight back so that all she felt was the unfamiliar thrust of maleness against the heat between her thighs.

She arched in unthinking response, pulling at him with her hands on his hips, rubbing her body against him with moves that sent sweet agony up and down her limbs. It didn't hurt; it was wonderful; she couldn't stop, though she heard him breathing ragged protest.

He moved suddenly, pulling away from her hands, and then his weight came down on her as he reached to find the place he had stroked and drive himself swiftly into it.

She did hurt, then. A little. It was surprise and pleasure and pain, and a flinching back she could not help, because she had expected much worse. His entry met no barriers that she could feel, no stab of tearing membrane as she'd imagined, but only a faint burning stretch that turned quickly to a hotter fire as her body awoke and accepted his gladly. She relaxed, opening to him, feeling foolish and glad at the same time to know her timid fears had proved groundless.

But he did not move. She lay still beneath him, not sure of what would happen next, half afraid that it was over while this excitement still sang in her blood. Tentatively, she reached up and curled one hand in his hair in wordless question.

He lifted his head, and the expression on his face made her throat tighten. "My lord—" she whispered in dismay, unable to understand the sudden dark fury in his eyes. "My lord—" The question came out an anxious croak. "Have I displeased you?"

Without answering, he pressed into her as he watched her face. Slow and hard, and that *did* hurt, so that she bit her lips and tried to hide it, for fear that it was her flinching which had angered him. "My lord," she said desperately. "'Tis not so much pain. I only thought—I was a little afraid, because I thought it would be more. It hardly hurts at all, my lord. Truly."

He just looked at her, and she'd never felt so helpless in her life, pinned and possessed by this man who defeated even her gift. She could not conceive what he might be thinking behind those eyes, and worse, his body in hers made her hardly care. She arched her hips and shivered with eagerness even as he frightened her.

He answered her movement with a harder pressure. She saw the anger waver in his eyes, the intent go hot and unfocused. He gripped her shoulders and drew away and rammed again, filling her with short, deep thrusts. She whimpered under the pleasure-pain, closed her eyes and threw her head back, felt his breath harsh on her throat as he kissed her.

"Damn you," he rasped. "Damn you for a liar. Or an innocent babe."

Roddy did not understand. Her mind would not focus on words. The sentences made only a jumble of sound as he buried his face in her hair. She saw nothing but his shoulder, a glaze of sweat and firelight that moved as he did, with his weight and his drive that dragged her upward on sensation. "God help me," he groaned in her ear. "It doesn't matter. It doesn't matter now."

Nothing mattered to Roddy now. Nothing but him. Her breath was gone and her body was exploding. She clutched at him, at his arms and his back and his hips, frantic for something she could not name. She made a sound—a long, low, inhuman moan that rose from deep within her throat as he met her seeking. Her legs spread and her body rose, arching and straining to his surging thrust, until she cried out in fright and pleasure as the tremors racked her limbs.

Then she was in his arms, sobbing for air, cradled and kissed and covered with his scent and her own in mingled warmth. She collapsed back into the curve of his arm, limp and stunned and absurdly sleepy.

She raised her lashes to find him looking steadily down at her. There was cool speculation in his blue eyes, and for one terrible moment she thought he was still angry. Then his gaze drifted down to where her breasts still heaved quickly as she worked for air. He watched. After a long moment, she saw the taut line of his mouth relax.

"Good," he said, with his devil-smile. "You liked that."

Roddy tried to stop panting. She swallowed and took a deeper breath. His grin was infectious. She tilted her chin up and giggled.

Yes. Oh, yes. I liked it.

And she liked it still when he lay on his side, his arm around her, curving her body close into his. She liked the feel of his chest rising and falling against her back. She liked his hand moving over her skin, its rhythmic stroke a drowsy beat that seemed to guide her into sleep. His low voice barely reached her through the haze when he asked in a soft and oddly intent voice, "Do you ride your horses astride, little girl?"

It seemed a funny question, not at all what she would have thought he might want to know. "Only to... race," she mumbled, struggling to hold herself out of sleepy mists. "Don't tell..." She yawned, slurring the words. "Don't... tell m'mother."

"No." He pulled her a little closer into the warmth of his body. His breath stirred her hair as he added softly, "I wouldn't tell."

She relaxed against him. "Faelan," she whispered, half conscious and drifting. "Faelan. I love you."

His hand paused, but she was already sliding down the dark hill. In the fuzzy edge between sleep and waking, she dreamed that his mind was open to her, and thoughts echoed through and around and between them both.

I love you. I love you.

I love you, little girl.

Six

THE COUTURIÈRE THOUGHT SLOWLY, IN SIMPLE WORDS, BECAUSE she had to translate from French to awkward English before she spoke. Such concentration gave Roddy a headache. She let her mind go fuzzy as she stood amid pins and ribbons, which was a way to block not only the dressmaker's lumbering thoughts, but also the crush of humanity from the city outside. London was noise and emotion, a confusing babble. Roddy found her talent dulled, blunted by the countless thoughts and voices that jumbled together into the city's tumult.

Slowly, she was learning how to cope. How to relax and think of the chaos as something like the wind: a natural force, an elemental energy that would flow around and past her if she let it. But it sapped her strength to maintain the balance. All the other changes: new life, new place, new people; they all combined to wear her soul down to exhaustion. There was only one refuge in the tempest—Faelan—and she clung to him with desperate vigor.

He had given Madame Descartes strict instructions. The demure young ladies of the city were wearing shapeless, high-waisted gowns of luxurious fullness, made of yards of shirred material that puffed at the sleeves and below the bodice. It was an effect that Roddy was sure her mother would have approved.

The new Countess of Iveragh, however, was to dress with no such becoming modesty. The gowns that Madame had created for Roddy were at the forefront of fashion. Flimsy tubes of sheer muslin, low-cut necklines, and tiny sleeves evoked Mediterranean sunshine rather than the English winter. Her pastel-colored slippers were no more than shaped pieces of silk with ribbons that wound up around her calves, and the matching gloves did nothing to hide her body or warm her skin. When she walked down the cold marble stair to where Faelan waited in the lofty salon, she felt that the heat of her blush alone must raise the chill of the room ten degrees.

Madame fluttered after, trying to give an appearance of calm sophistication as she searched for words to explain Roddy's shortcomings.

"The hair," she said quickly, "the pretty blond, it will cut, yes? To be—to make the curl. Now—too long, you comprehend? Short you want. Curls. But the figure—" She grinned slyly at Faelan. "Very pretty, eh, monseigneur? Very straight. Perfect."

"Perfect," he agreed, and smiled at Roddy in a way that made her heart contract and her knees go liquid.

For a week she had gone about with such wobbly knees, and they were not all the result of long days in a traveling carriage. A hundred times a day he touched her, or smiled at her; a caress in passing, a kiss on the nape of her neck as she bent over a letter to her parents or strained to read by the light of a wavering candle.

And at night… oh, God, at night there was a whole world she had never known existed. He taught her; he made her body sing with pleasure. So now, when he asked her to dress in these scandalous fashions, she felt she could not refuse. She wanted badly to please him.

Turning in the clinging gown, she peeked uncertainly at him over her shoulder. "Do you like it, my lord?"

He glanced at the couturière, and the woman responded to the silent command without hesitation, gathering up the net she had been about to suggest for a veil and disappearing back up the stairs toward the bedroom.

After she was gone, Roddy waited nervously, searching for some sign of approval, all too aware that Madame Descartes had considered Roddy's coloring hopelessly unfashionable, with her slash of black brows against golden hair. Dark tight curls were the rage: dark hair and coolly classic features, not Roddy's strange combination of storm and sunlight. After trying seven different styles, Madame had thrown up her hands in frustration and sent Roddy for viewing in the gown she had on, having never before encountered a face that could not be complemented, a face too striking to be softened or improved by the dressmaker's art.

The moment of waiting dragged into a small eternity. Roddy stared at Faelan's boots in despair, certain that he must think she wasn't even suitable to be presented in public.

When the apprehension became unbearable, she hesitantly raised her eyes.

He was smiling at her, a slow, sensuous smile that might have meant anything. It made her breath stick in her throat. Beneath lowered lids his gaze traveled from her toes to her hair, lingering at her hips and breasts and mouth.

"A witch," he said. "My golden witch."

Roddy moistened her lips in dismay. "A *witch*, my lord? Madame Descartes did say I was... difficult, but I hoped—"

"Come," he interrupted and held out his hands. He looked down at her as she obeyed him, sliding his palms up both sides of her neck, caressing her chilled skin with warm fingers. "Don't let Madame trouble you."

She held his gaze, feeling his spell creep around and inside her. His fingers spread, his thumbs pressed upward under her jaw. The kiss was slow, heady, the way he had taught her. "In Ireland," he murmured, "they'll see you for what you are. One of the *Daoine Sidhe*."

She frowned in confusion. "Deena shi?" The strange syllables made an unfamiliar slur on her tongue.

"The fairy folk." His gaze wandered over her face. "The people who live between day and night, and drink the dew that's neither rain nor river nor spring nor sea." He caressed a lock of gilded hair. "The Shining Ones."

She looked up into his azure eyes, and thought that it must be he who lived between dark and light, like a demon prince. "My lord—" she whispered. "Do I please you, then?"

"You're mine." The soft, certain words sent a shiver of wild music down her spine. He bent his head and brushed her mouth and cheek with his lips. "You're mine," he murmured against her skin. "And you please me."

❧

London was empty this time of year, he told her, which made her want to giggle hysterically. Empty? The city nearly crushed her, a multitude of thoughts and feelings so enormous it had a kind of monolithic life of its own, surly and intense on days when the wind blew sleet and cold, and lighter-hearted, bubbling, on a sunny winter day like this—the first one on which she and Faelan had ventured forth from the house.

They walked, because after the jolting trip from Yorkshire Roddy was heartily tired of carriages, and in her light dress and cashmere shawl she preferred some exertion to keep her warm.

She could not avoid glancing back at the house as they strolled across the broad courtyard toward the iron gate. The dwelling was as rich as—far richer than—her expansive home in Yorkshire. A proud, princely house, with a double row of tall windows capped by elegant pediments. She counted the top row, and doubling that figure came to the impressive number of twenty-two windows on the front facade alone. Then there were the stables and the carriage house, set to either side of the square court, and behind it all the garden which she had seen from her bedroom window, stretching five times the length of the house to the next line of magnificent buildings beyond. Inside, there was no sign of reduced circumstances in the light and expensive French furniture or the intricate plasterwork upon the walls. She forced her gaze away from the mansion and found Faelan watching her.

"My mother's house," he said, in that tone he used sometimes, that seemed to Roddy ominous in its utter indifference. "You needn't fear that the rest of family is as destitute as I."

Roddy made no comment, but thought darkly that "the rest of the family" must enjoy a fine income, given the quantity of servants and the quality of the interior appointments and the fact that Banain House, as the majordomo had informed

Roddy with pride, was kept open at all times, even though Her Ladyship traveled in great style ten months of the twelve.

A fine income, for the mother of a man who had stood within a hairsbreadth of losing his estate to debt and taxes.

Her Ladyship was traveling now; no one knew just where, or particularly cared. The generously paid servants functioned with the same efficiency under the majordomo whether the mistress was at home or not. They had their opinions on Faelan—unbounded respect for his authority and considerably less for his morals—and a sharp curiosity about his new bride. But they hid all that behind paper-board expressions, and treated Roddy with perfect solicitude.

As Faelan had predicted, the huge square outside the mansion's walls was nearly empty, the manicured geometry of flowerbeds frozen in winter brown. A milkmaid, her buckets balanced from the yoke across her shoulders, hurried toward the far corner. Across from Banain House, a young gentleman on horseback had stopped to bargain over a brace of rabbits. As the vendor haggled to raise the price, his two slender hunting dogs sat eyeing the fat, dangling hares in a quandary of canine optimism and restraint. When the sale was made and the rabbits changed hands, the dogs looked after the departing rider for a long, disappointed moment before they obeyed the vendor's whistled command and bounded away.

"Where is everyone?" Roddy asked, confused by the solitude of the neighborhood and the great press of humanity she felt through her gift.

"Gone home to the country, I imagine," Faelan said.

"But I thought—the city—" She frowned in consternation. "There must be more people *somewhere*."

He gave her a glance, a blue flash of amusement. "Are you lonely?"

"Of course not. Only I expected more people."

"I fear my company wears thin."

Roddy looked down at the pavement. "Not at all, my lord," she said with shy warmth.

She was rewarded with the press of his hand on her arm. He stopped and smiled down at her, so close that their frosty breaths mingled. "Careful, little girl. I may be forced to show you to what good use an empty street may be put."

It was like a fever, she thought weakly as she raised her eyes to his. Like a sickness, the way he made her heart pound and her limbs shake and her mind forget everything she had been taught in her lifetime. "My lord," she said faintly, "you may show me anything you like."

His hands slid to her waist, drawing her against him. He kissed her, there in full view of the hundreds of blank, staring windows, warmed her cold lips with his heat and delved deep in her mouth for the answering warmth. Roddy lost herself in him. It was cold and he was warm, warm with a fire that passed anything she had ever known. His body was hard beneath the winter clothes. She knew how it would feel against her skin. How firelight would dance on his bare arms and chest and make his eyes seem like ice and flame...

It was her shawl that broke the moment, sliding from her shoulders as she pulled her hand from her muff and lifted her arms to twine around his neck. Roddy herself hardly noticed the chill on her bared skin, but Faelan instantly let her go and retrieved the fringed cashmere. He wrapped her in it once again and resumed their walk with a faint smile playing on his hard lips.

"Now," he said, "we shall go and find you more agreeable company."

To Roddy's country-bred legs, the walk through Cavendish Square and across broad, unpaved Oxford Street to the octagonal center of Hanover Square was no great journey. She was glad to keep a brisk pace, for the soft shawl was only moderate protection against the cold. There were more and more people about as they approached the business districts of the city, but beyond Hanover Square, Faelan veered off from the southerly direction in which they had been going and headed west. They came to another great square, and while Roddy politely expressed her admiration for the impressive prospect, Faelan kept his hand firmly under her elbow, steering her without pause toward a particular doorway.

Messrs. Gunther, read the scrolled sign above the lintel. *Confectioners.* Posted discreetly beside the door was an advertisement from the *Times.* "Messrs. Gunther respectfully beg to inform the Nobility and those who honor them with their commands, that they are able to supply CREAM and FRUIT Ices. Also all sorts of Biskets and Cakes, Fine and Common Sugarplums."

"Ices!" Roddy said with a shiver as a boy held open the door and the proprietor hurried forward from inside.

Faelan grinned and pushed her gently through. "I prefer the sugarplums myself."

And so he did, Roddy found.

She watched in astonishment as Monsieur Gunther, recognizing Faelan on the instant, hastened to bring out all sorts of sweets, in jars and stacked on plates and spread across big metal trays. "A cup of chocolate for Mademoiselle?" he asked, and at Faelan's brief nod the boy scurried to set up a table and a pair of chairs. A moment later Roddy found herself seated in front of a steaming cup of dark, foamy cocoa and a pastry, while Faelan plunked himself down enthusiastically at her side and proceeded to demolish every confection in sight.

"Long walk," he said, when she eyed him incredulously. As he finished off an apricot tart, she half expected him to lick his fingers like some mischievous boy, but Gunther was already holding out a snowy napkin.

Roddy nibbled at an éclair and tried to control a giggle. She loved watching Faelan, the way his dark lashes lowered and his eyebrows drew faintly together as Gunther displayed a new tray and Faelan deliberated on his next choice, and then how one Satan-black brow snapped upward comically when he burned his tongue on the tiny cup of chocolate.

"Try this," he offered, holding out a cream cake. "Gunther is incomparable."

The hovering proprietor's expression did not change, but Roddy could feel him swell with pride. It made her want to laugh, to find that the Devil Earl was one of Gunther's most frequent, and favored, customers. What would her family and all those other doubters think now, if they could see Faelan's adolescent delight in sugarplums?

She had hardly finished the éclair when he sighed and surveyed the table, where her one lone little cream cake was all that was left of the imposing array. "Are you finished?" he asked, when she made no move to pick up the cream cake.

Roddy nodded.

He gave her cream cake a lingering look. "I suppose that's more than enough," he said reluctantly. As he stood and offered his arm to Roddy, he glanced at Gunther. "I compliment you on the cream cakes. I rather like those."

"Do you indeed, my lord?" Gunther was as pleased as any housewife at the mention. "A little experiment of mine. Adding a bit of aniseed to the dough, and then..."

Faelan listened gravely to the full account of how the cream cakes had come into existence. When Gunther had finished, Faelan drew Roddy in front of him. "Lady Iveragh," he said in mock formality, "you have just been introduced to the finest pastrycook in England. See that you remember him."

Gunther's startlement at this oblique wedding announcement was kept rigorously concealed. He made a humble bow. "I beg your forgiveness, Your Ladyship. I'd not had the honor of hearing of His Lordship's marriage until this moment. Allow me please to extend my most sincere best wishes for your happiness."

"Thank you. Your fare was delicious." Hidden from Faelan, she gave the baker a quick wink. "I believe I'd like to take that last cream cake with me, if you please."

"Of course, my lady." Only the faintest quiver of his lips betrayed him as he wrapped the cake in paper and handed it to Faelan. Her husband gave the small package the same kind of wistful glance that the vendor's dogs had given the brace of rabbits. Roddy met Gunther's eye, and a flash of merry understanding passed between them.

"And perhaps, Gunther," she added, "you would send round a dozen of them to Banain House."

"Immediately, Your Ladyship," he said.

Roddy felt an odd little thrill of pleasure at the first domestic order she had placed in her married life.

She turned to find Faelan's mouth twisted into a wry smile.

"You'd best not humor me," he said. "I'll eat all twelve of them before dinner."

"Thirteen." She tapped the little package in his hand.

"Wise of you to offer it, my dear," he said judiciously. "I'd have had it out of you one way or the other."

Gunther held the door open, and Roddy gave him a special smile as she passed. He only nodded, all humility, but he had caught her meaning. He could count on Lady Iveragh's patronage for the indefinite future. As Roddy slipped her arm in her husband's and turned down the walk, a new and amazing thought passed through the confectioner's mind. He stood looking after them.

Why, I believe she loves him! he mused. And then: *Poor child.* Roddy blocked the baker from her mind.

The last cream cake was long eaten by the time they reached Pall Mall. There they found a generous portion of the huge populace that Roddy felt through her gift, the bustle of carriages and strolling shoppers. It was a good-humored crowd, easy to bear, and Roddy went wide-eyed along the famous street, more impressed by the elegant shopwindows than by the prince's new colonnade of Ionic columns that screened the facade of Carlton House. She had little interest in the silk and muslin displays, but the infinite variety of clocks and watches and carved walking sticks and tea caddies and intricately decorated snuffboxes fascinated her.

Her nose was pressed as hard as any beggar child's against a window to look at a large ormolu-and-enamel item that somewhat resembled the turret of a castle—though no castle had ever boasted those gay colors and that gilded peak—when a stranger paused behind her. "Whatever is that?" she asked Faelan, without turning from the window.

It was not her husband who answered. "A music box, my child," a new voice said gaily. "And a jolly fantastic one, at that." As she looked around she found the newcomer's name in the curious glance of another passerby. *His Grace of Stratton.*

Roddy blinked at the first duke she had ever seen, and found herself measured, judged, and labeled in a glance as one of Iveragh's whores.

She went scarlet, but Faelan was already introducing her. "Good afternoon, Your Grace," he said calmly. "May I present my wife, Roderica?"

It was His Grace's turn to go scarlet then. He wasn't nearly as clever at covering his shock as Gunther had been. His double chin jerked and quivered as he choked, "Your—" He caught himself, and after a moment of struggle managed, "—Ladyship! I'm honored." His corset creaked as he straightened himself and bowed. "Honored indeed. Well, well, Iveragh. This is a sh—a surprise. I daresay you've made no announcement. I just now gave my compliments to—" He stumbled, thinking of whores again, and then took another tack entirely. "Lovely music box. Lovely. Perfect wedding gift. Come in, my dear, and you shall have it!"

He reached for Roddy's arm. Faelan moved at the same time, an odd, sudden move that he stopped before it was completed. *Jealous*, the duke thought, catching the significance before Roddy did. *By God, he doesn't even want me to touch her!*

To the duke, Faelan's unexpected possessiveness was even more of a shock than his marriage. *The peculiar devil, what's he care? Never did so before. Damned money-match, bound to be. Girl with funds and in trouble—no bloody reason to get on his high horse over her. Pretty chit, in an odd sort of way.* The duke smiled at Roddy. *Try my own luck, after she drops the brat.*

"Your Grace," Roddy said, moving toward Faelan and just out of the duke's reach. "I couldn't possibly allow you to do such a thing." She stared at him, to let the double meaning of that sink in, and then added, "It's far too generous of you."

"Far too generous," Faelan repeated coolly, tucking her hand into the comforting crook of his arm. She stood as close as she could easily manage without appearing to hide behind him. He added, "If you'll excuse us, I'm afraid we have an appointment with Mr. Skipworth."

"Skipworth?" The duke glanced toward the shop and saw the sign. *Blake and Skipworth. Jewelers and Watchmakers.* "Ah, yes—of course. Do go on. I'm only in town for a sennight, myself, and not time for a bit of pleasure in it. Give your mother my devoted service. Good day, Your Ladyship. Honored. Most honored."

He walked away thinking: *Oh, Liza, Liza, Liza, this business will sink you!* And then, with a hint of malice: *What devilish luck, that I should be the one to tell it!*

Roddy supposed that Liza was the duchess, and turned her attention to the more pleasant prospect of visiting the jeweler. The duke's disagreeable reaction to Faelan's marriage seemed better forgotten.

The head salesman of Blake and Skipworth, who had witnessed with interest the attention of the Duke of Stratton to the shopwindow, hurried forward to greet Roddy and Faelan. Though the salesman did not recognize Faelan, any acquaintance with His Grace the Duke was reference enough. When Faelan gave the man a glance and asked in a quiet, authoritative voice for Mr. Skipworth, the young man did not even hesitate, but dispatched an underling on the instant to fetch Mr. Skipworth from his office in the back.

"Her Ladyship would like to look at music boxes," Faelan said to the tall, angular gentleman who appeared from the depths of the shop with a skeptical lift to his white brows.

The words "Her Ladyship" worked magic with the doubting Mr. Skipworth, and Roddy and Faelan were ushered into the private room without delay.

"I believe you were interested in the one displayed in the window," the salesman reminded her. "I'll bring it directly."

"And some others," Faelan said placidly. "Less... *gaudy*, perhaps."

"I understand completely, my lord." Mr. Skipworth nodded wisely. "We'll be happy to show you a wide variety."

"*Gaudy*, Faelan?" Roddy demanded when the jeweler had gone to hasten his salesman. "Unique, I should say."

Faelan lifted one eyebrow. "Gaudy," he repeated firmly.

"Unique," Roddy replied with spirit.

He only smiled, and stood back to allow the salesman past with his weighty burden.

The turret-cum-music was a wonder. It played "God Save the King" in the keys of A and C, and when the music began, six little doors around the tower popped open to reveal tiny figures of dancing lions and unicorns, just like on the Great

Seal of England, that spun clockwise in A and counterclock-wise in C. The seventh door opened to extend a snuffbox mounted on a golden foot: a tiny human foot, with four perfect toes and one large, misshapen one.

It was certainly unique.

Faelan watched the demonstration without comment. Since he had suggested it, Roddy listened politely to the other, smaller boxes put forward for her approval, but she had already made her choice. When Faelan picked up a delicate sandalwood box that opened to play a pretty contredanse and display only an empty bed of red satin, she thought that he was teasing her.

"No, no, that one isn't gaudy enough," she cried. "I like a great deal of color."

He set the sandalwood box down.

"I like this one," she pressed, winding the key of the turret again.

Faelan glanced at Mr. Skipworth, and the jeweler withdrew with a silent nod, certain that he had sold his musical prize. When "God Save the King" had played through twice, once in A and once in C, Faelan reached over and snapped the center door shut. The music stopped.

"Roddy," he said quietly. "I fear this unique object may come with a high price."

She gave him the smile that she always gave her father when she wanted some special trinket. "Oh!" she said in a teasing tone. "Can we not afford it, my lord?"

"You can." He met her eyes with a level gaze. "To my great and eternal embarrassment… I cannot."

All her joy—her thoughtless, childish mischief—vanished on the instant. She stared at him. "My lord…" Her voice faltered and faded, unequal to the magnitude of the mistake she had made.

In the fraught silence, he smiled faintly and brushed her cheek with a gentle fist. "It wouldn't be a gift, you see," he said softly.

She turned away and snatched up the sandalwood box. "This is the one I want!" She opened it and held it up and stood listening to the metallic tune while the satin went to a scarlet blur of shame and remorse. "I'm sorry," she whispered. "I'm so stupid."

He took her shoulders and drew her back against him. "Don't cry, my love. It isn't worth tears."

She shook her head and turned into his arms, holding the music box tight between them. "I c-can't help it. You've been so g-good to me, and I—"

"Hush." He lifted her chin and brushed moisture from beneath her eye with his thumb. "One more teardrop and I'll go into hock to buy that damned monstrosity."

Roddy giggled wetly. "It is awful, isn't it?"

"Ungodly," he said with feeling.

She sniffed and took the handkerchief he offered. When Mr. Skipworth came back into the room a few minutes later, she held up the sandalwood box with a tremulous smile. "Isn't it lovely?" The tears threatened to spill over again. "Oh, my," she exclaimed. "I think I'm going to c-cry!"

Mr. Skipworth thought he was, too, when he saw which of the two boxes she had chosen. But he rallied and called her a person of exceptional sensibility, and asked the salesman to usher her back out into the showroom while Mr. Skipworth "conversed" with His Lordship. Roddy went, clutching her prize, and paused at the door. When Faelan looked up, she thought her heart would burst at the tender smile he gave her. "I shall treasure it *always*," she said fiercely. "Forever."

Faelan and Mr. Skipworth's "conversation" took somewhat longer than Roddy had expected. She was still waiting ten minutes later, glancing desultorily over some bracelets the salesman had brought out, when another customer came into the shop.

Roddy might not even have looked up, but the woman entered with her mind obsessed by Faelan.

Roddy's breath stopped in her throat. She dropped the bracelet she was holding and turned... to confront her husband's mistress.

Liza.

The face and the name from the duke's memory came together, and with them the certain knowledge of who she was. It was in Liza's mind clearly, and it had been in the duke's too, though Roddy had not understood the image at the time.

She was different from Roddy, opposite in everything, older, wiser, full-bodied—a dark burgundy to Roddy's clear spring water. As she entered the shop her sable-brown eyes were looking for Faelan, thoughts hard behind dark velvet. She knew of his marriage—the duke had told her—and she was burning.

Just at that moment the door to the private room opened, and Faelan stepped out with Mr. Skipworth.

"Iveragh!" Liza cried, going forward past Roddy as if she weren't there, although Liza knew perfectly well that the slender girl—*the veriest schoolroom chit,* Liza thought viciously—was certain to be Faelan's bride. "How glad I am to find you still here! Stratton, that old rogue, has just been telling me the wildest tales—"

Faelan took her outstretched hand and brushed it with his lips. "Mrs. Northfield," he said. "I hadn't expected you to be in the city at this season."

"The admiral is on shore leave," she answered with magnificent nonchalance. "But are you married indeed, my lord? And this is your bride—what a lovely child!"

Roddy stood miserably, damning her gift. It was all so subtle, so delicate. She would never have known without her talent. They carried it off in flawless style, Faelan and his mistress, introductions all around and the most civilized of conversation. It made Roddy sick inside. He was perfect. No slip, no seams, no single clue that he felt anything more for Liza Northfield than he would for a passing acquaintance.

The grand Liza herself was not quite so cool. There was a faint, betraying flush on the creamy skin revealed by the *décolletage* beneath her filmy mantua. Her voice was a trifle higher than it should have been, concealing spite as she smiled at Roddy with the kindest of smiles.

Roddy returned the greeting, not quite overcoming the awful dryness in her throat that made her voice come out all wrong.

"I'm delighted," Mrs. Northfield said. "The admiral and I have been putting forward eligible young ladies these ten years and never once would this paltry fellow do his duty." *Because I held him; because he craves me; all those other silly chits—nothing. Like you, my dear. Like you. You'll never hold him.* "Wherever did you find her, my Lord Iveragh? In the country, I'll be bound. You were always one for unearthing diamonds from the rough."

"My family is in Yorkshire," Roddy said, getting determined control of her voice.

"Yorkshire!" Mrs. Northfield slid a gloved hand up behind her ear, tucking back a curl. She sent a glance under heavy lashes toward Faelan, preparing to go for Roddy's throat. "And what a pretty milkmaid it is! I fear our city ways may curdle her cream."

There was a pause. Faelan said, "I shan't allow that to happen."

Mrs. Northfield smiled at him. "Of course. You're the very man to guard such innocence."

"In this case."

"Indeed." A new thought came into Liza's mind, a new interpretation. *Silly dupe, stupid mouse, he never means to keep you. The others—that Ashley girl, and the little Traherne bitch— just the same; do you think he cares? The streets, that's where you'll be, along with that besotted Ellen Webster—he'll grow sick of your face as he will of hers; he'll be rid of you. The same, just the same, like the others...* She looked at Roddy with veiled speculation, pleased and aroused by the image of ruined innocence.

Roddy realized then what drew this woman to the Devil Earl.

It was not the Faelan that Roddy knew, not the blue eyes and rare laughter. It was the other side: the darkness. The seducer and destroyer of foolish young girls. The black image in a dawn mist. The killer. His mistress clung to him for a taste of that power, to be taken as a virgin again and again: mock struggle, imagined pain, a shadow-lover's lifeblood soaking slowly into the ground. An image passed through Liza's mind, a stab of purest lust as she imagined Faelan, just come to her bed from a duel.

Roddy stood very still. She had to concentrate to keep her fingers from allowing the music box to slide from her hand. She did not want to know these things. Liza Northfield *believed* in Faelan's sins; she reveled in them. She even had names for the innocent victims Roddy had convinced herself were only figments of society's twisted imagination.

"The admiral," Faelan said. "May I call on him tomorrow?"

Triumph exploded behind Liza's brown eyes. She closed her full lips and smiled. "He has orders to Gravesend," she purred, in a voice softened with false regret. "He leaves me this very night, I fear. At ten."

It was a signal between them, that question and answer: an appointment as clear as a handwritten note.

"At ten," Faelan repeated. "I'll be sorry to miss him."

Liza smiled at the confirmation and shrugged prettily. "The sad case of a sailor's wife. Left alone for nights on end." She gave Roddy a pleasant nod. "You won't have such a burden, of course, my dear. Now—I must go and see that the admiral has a proper supper before he leaves. Such an honor to meet you, Lady Iveragh. Do call on me at the earliest. His Lordship can give you the direction."

Roddy watched in silent misery as her husband's mistress walked serenely out the door, making plans for what she would wear to their assignation. *The blue silk*, she was thinking. *It slides off the shoulder and breast so—*

Roddy pushed the conclusion of that image away with frantic haste.

It was no use telling herself that it made no difference. A week ago, she might have managed it. A week ago, she had made a marriage of convenience, trading her money for the chance to create a life of her own. But she found now that she did not want a life of her own. She wanted Faelan, the Faelan she knew, the one who smiled at her and called her lovely and stroked her softly as she fell asleep.

She stared down at the carved lid of the music box, her spine stiff with helpless fury. Fury at Faelan, at Liza, at herself—at her own stupid, childish hopes. She'd been prepared to limit her demands, to accept his faults and his lovers, or at least pretend they didn't exist. But he'd cheated; he'd been different from the start. He was an actor, a fraud, a fake.

And he'd made it so achingly easy to love him.

Seven

THEY RODE BACK TO BANAIN HOUSE IN A HACKNEY. RODDY said she was tired and didn't care to walk. For the sake of her pride, she tried to keep a pleasant face, but every time her eyes fell on the package that contained the music box, they wanted to fill up and overflow. She spent the greater part of the ride staring resolutely out the window away from Faelan.

The worst moment was when the hackney swung up to the doorstep of the great house and Roddy had to bear his warm touch on her arm as he helped her from the cab. One part of her wanted to turn toward him and throw herself into his arms and beg to be told that it was not true, that there was no deception in him, that the things he had said to her and made her feel were real, not pretty lies. The other part of her wanted only to get away, to escape this city and go back to what she had been, simple and protected and sure, with her gift to guide her between truth and falsehood.

A footman held open the door for them, and Roddy entered to a familiar and unexpected touch in her mind. *Geoffrey!* She did not need the majordomo's announcement to know Lord Cashel waited for them in the drawing room. She barely paused to allow a footman to open the door before she rushed past. She ran to her old friend and took his hands. "Oh, Geoffrey," she cried, and to her utter horror the tears escaped control and her hands closed on his lapels and she found herself sobbing against his elegant shirtfront. "Oh, Geoffrey, I'm so glad you're here!"

"Roddy, Roddy—what in God's name…" He held her away from him and then looked beyond toward Faelan in dawning anger. "What's the meaning of this?"

Roddy pulled away at that, realizing what she had done. She pushed off Geoffrey's hands as if they burned her. Oh, God—what a mistake, what a stupid, infantile blunder, to shame her husband and herself by letting Geoffrey see her like this!

She summoned a false and brilliant smile and exclaimed, "Oh—how *could* I make such a cake of myself as to cry? I'm sorry, but it's been such a wonderful day—we took a walk, and I've seen everything, and my lord has bought me the most beautiful m-music b-box—" Her voice cracked again, because Geoffrey's first interpretation of her emotional behavior was the same condemnation she had heard from everyone else. Pregnancy. "I think I should go up and change," she said, desperate to escape. "Will—will you be staying long, Lord Geoffrey?"

He shook his head. "A moment only, to speak to Faelan." He hesitated, and *meeting* flashed through his mind, colored by some desperate need to keep his purpose concealed. "A matter of business. I'll be joining Lady Mary this evening, to catch the Dublin packet."

"Oh." Roddy found that her friend's sudden arrival and desertion made her more miserable than ever. Secret meetings, politics—he had no time for one confused girl in the great swirl of human affairs. She wished he had not come at all. "I'm sorry," she mumbled.

He took her hand and gave it a special squeeze, the kind of guilty gesture that her father often made. Her outburst had baffled and upset him, and sparked a protective anger. "Roddy," he said, drawing her close in anxious affection. "You're certain you're all right, poppet?"

She leaned on him, comforted a little by his honest concern. From the circle of his arm she looked toward her husband. Faelan held the music box in his hand, staring down at it.

"Yes, of course, Geoffrey," she said, barely above a whisper. "I'm perfectly well and happy."

"I'm glad." He took her remark as truth, because his conscience preferred it that way. "You know you can depend on me, love," he added, in a voice of caressing warmth. "For anything."

She stood away from him. "Thank you," she said shyly. "My lords... may I be excused?"

Faelan glanced up. His face held an expression she had never seen before: blank and vicious at once, as if he looked at her and saw something else, far beyond, and whatever it was made him murderous. "Yes," he said. "Go on."

That was all. Not a touch, not a word or a look of affection. Not even "please."

She spent the remainder of the afternoon huddled on a bench in the farthest reaches of the garden, alternately promising herself that her husband was not worth a single tear and then weeping over crushed hopes like the silliest babe. It was well after dark before she returned to the house, driven by the cold to desert her refuge. Her steps were slow and reluctant as she slipped in through the side door by the vegetable garden, knowing through her gift that the hall from the servants' quarters was empty.

It was London, she had decided. London was to blame for it all. It was the press of the city that unbalanced her, made her into a vulnerable, romantic idiot when she should have been wise and cold.

She had known what Faelan was, and stupidly allowed herself to forget it. She had been foolish, this past week, to interpret his attentions as anything more than well-bred politeness. And the humiliation of meeting his mistress in public—he could hardly be blamed for that. No one could have foreseen such a coincidence. He had handled it in the only possible way. With faultless discretion.

What could I expect him to do, Roddy asked herself, *stand out on the street and renounce the woman?*

Even his assignation—Roddy couldn't even object to that. She was not so naive. Faelan was a man, a sensual, vital man—it was in every move he made, the way he kissed and touched and held her. After the sophisticated life he had led—that she had known perfectly well he had led—she could hardly expect him to be satisfied with her untutored caresses.

She had vowed to herself that she would not object to his infidelities, and meant to keep that vow. It was to be a marriage of convenience, not love.

But she had her own pride. Stupid she had been, there was no doubt of that. Helpless fury and hurt filled her when she thought of how she had melted for him, had given gladly what he could come by so easily elsewhere. She was his wife, but she did not have to be the pliant, panting wanton he had made her. Things would change now.

His heart was not engaged, and she'd been a fool to entangle hers. And the first step back to rationality was to extricate herself from the drugging influence of his lovemaking. He could go to his mistress, with Roddy's blessing. Let him spend his passion elsewhere, and not drag her down into that net of blind unreason.

I wanted children from him, Roddy reminded herself fiercely. *Not love. Let him go to his precious Liza for his kind of love.*

As Roddy entered the main hall she met Minshall, the majordomo, emerging from the library. He did not see her at first, being absorbed in the direction scrawled elegantly on the envelope in his hand. *Mrs. Northfield. Number 8 Blandford.*

He tucked the note into his pocket, made a mental note to inquire before dinner when His Lordship would want the carriage, and looked up. It was only his years of training that kept him from showing his guilty start.

"My lady," he said, since she stood in the dim, candlelit hall apparently waiting to speak to him. "How can I be of service?"

"His Lordship—is he in the library?" she asked hesitantly.

"Yes, my lady. I might add that he has instructed me to put back dinner an hour, since you've been walking in the garden later than usual."

An hour! Faelan would have to hurry if he were to meet Mrs. Northfield at ten. But perhaps it was only Roddy's dinner that had been postponed. "Am I to eat alone, then?" she asked.

Minshall was surprised. A trace of pity touched his mind as he thought of the note in his pocket. "His Lordship did not mention it, my lady. In the absence of orders to the contrary, I assumed that you would be dining with him *en suite* as you have been. I will inquire, if you like."

Roddy moistened her lips. "Perhaps you'd better do so. He mentioned to me that he might be… going out tonight."

The majordomo looked at her more closely, noting the slight puffiness around her eyes. *Poor child*, Minshall thought. *Damn him—can't he wait? It's a bleeding shame if he's let her guess.* Aloud, the manservant said, "I shall speak to him, Your Ladyship. Do you wish to join him now?"

Her throat went suddenly dry, but she managed a nod. The majordomo scratched lightly at the door and then held it open for her.

Faelan was far across the huge, dark room, in a wing chair by the fire, the reflection of the flames dancing off the polish on his crossed boots. He turned his head at Minshall's restrained cough, and stood up without setting down the drink in his hand.

"Your Ladyship," he said, in that tone that told Roddy nothing. "Good evening." Silhouetted by the fire, his face was too shadowed to reveal his expression.

Roddy went resolutely forward, followed closely by Minshall, who placed a chair and fire screen for her. She sat down. After a moment of silence, Minshall said softly, "The dinner arrangements are to be as usual, my lord?"

Faelan looked up from his contemplation of the glass in his hand. "Put back an hour, Minshall. I just told you, did I not?"

The majordomo bowed, reminding himself that the lord had a right to sound as if Minshall were slightly lacking in wit. "Yes, my lord." He hesitated, trying to decide if he had a clear answer or not, and then added, "Her Ladyship had expressed a question as to whether or not you would dine with her."

From the startled half-turn of Faelan's head, Minshall surmised smugly that His Lordship had never intended otherwise. A rake and a reprobate the earl might be, but he had manners enough to dine with his new bride.

Faelan said, a little abruptly, "Do you not wish it, Lady Iveragh?"

Roddy was caught, unable to repeat her fib that Faelan had told her he was going out, and with no other excuse for why she would question the established custom. "I have a touch of the headache," she improvised, "and thought perhaps I should go to bed directly."

He looked toward her, his face profiled by shadow and fire. After a moment, he said, "I shall eat in the dining room, then, Minshall. Her Ladyship will have a tray sent up."

Minshall bowed again, turned to go, and then paused. "I beg your pardon, my lady. Did you intend the cream cakes to be served this evening?"

She looked down at her hands in a flush of misery. "Yes," she said in a small voice. "If Lord Iveragh would like them."

"I would," Faelan said, in a warmer voice than he had used before. "Very much."

The majordomo nodded and left the room, thinking that it would have been most indiscreet to inquire about the carriage just at that moment when his lord was looking at his lady with that rare smile softening his dark features.

Minshall might have been fooled by a smile, but Roddy was not. Not any longer. When Faelan came to stand beside her and brush his fingers along the curve of her throat, she knew it for the sham it was. But her pulse began to pound under the light caress.

"Do you require assistance to your bed, my lady?" he asked softly.

She moved away from him a little. "No, thank you." Her voice was slightly breathless.

The fire popped, flaring. Faelan curled his fingers and withdrew them.

"Did you enjoy your sojourn in the garden?" he asked. The warmth had receded from his voice, replaced by an odd, taut note. "I noticed that you didn't return to bid Godspeed to Lord Geoffrey."

Roddy heard the irony in his tone, but she was too agitated by the things that she wanted to say to resent it. She said unsteadily,

"Geoffrey understands. It would have made me cry again, I think." She cleared her throat, and added in a firmer tone, "I wished to speak to you."

He sketched a bow. "I'm at your service, Your Ladyship."

The faintly insolent formality made a hard task harder. She could find no words to say what she intended.

"What did you wish to speak to me about?" he prompted after a moment.

She clasped her hands together. Her brain seemed slow and stupid and her tongue stuck in her mouth.

"Are you situated comfortably?" he asked, when the silence had stretched again. "There's nothing wrong with your room?"

"No." Roddy knew he was mocking her. "Of course not."

"Some problems with the servants?" he taunted gently. "A difficulty with your pin money? You want a music box, perhaps. Come, my dear, you needn't be afraid to speak to me."

"Faelan." She took a breath. "It's about our—circumstances."

"Ah."

"With respect to each other," she added.

He walked back to his chair and set his glass down on the little table. "I'm not certain I understand you."

"It's just that... I've been thinking. About our marriage, and—and our, um... our relationship. Our married relationship, I mean. And I believe, my lord, that it's my duty to..." Her voice almost failed her, and she squeezed her eyes shut. "—To... submit... to you—when necessary—for the purpose of having children, but as to what... what we've been..." She swallowed, and said in a desperate rush, "My lord, I don't think I can bear that anymore!"

She opened her eyes and looked toward him. The faint smile had vanished from his face. He stood and stared down at the glass beneath his hand. "Roddy," he whispered. And that was all.

"Please don't be angry!" She was half frightened by the way his palm tightened over the fragile crystal. "I can't expect you to change your—your way of life, I know! But I thought that if you realized... if I made you aware... that I would perfectly understand and approve if you should... prefer to go elsewhere for... your pleasure..." Her voice trailed off in mortification.

He did not say anything. He only stood rigid for an excruciatingly long moment before his fingers curled around the glass. With movements that were more stilted than his usual easy grace, he poured himself another drink from the decanter on the table. He took a swallow, and turned to her. "I am to go elsewhere," he repeated coolly. "I collect I am also expected to extend to you the same... permission?"

Roddy blinked in shock. "No, my lord. I wouldn't—"

"No," he agreed, with dangerous mildness. "You wouldn't, my dear. That I assure you." He finished the drink in another swallow and took a step toward Roddy. She flinched back a little, afraid of how her body might betray her if he chose to exercise his lethal magic. He stopped, his blue eyes quick to catch the tiny movement. "I beg your pardon. I misunderstood. I am to go elsewhere and leave you in peace."

"Yes!" Roddy came to her feet. God, how she hated this—how she wanted him to hold her and stroke her hair and kiss her until she could not stand. But there was Liza. There was Liza, waiting for him. Roddy turned her back. "Leave me in peace!"

There was silence behind her. And then: "For how long?"

Forever. Never. Oh, *now*, she thought helplessly. *Love me now.* She opened her mouth, but no words came out past the knot in her throat.

"Second thoughts, little girl?" he asked bitterly. "Have your *regrets* caught up with you this afternoon?"

She flinched at the sneer in his voice, not knowing how to answer.

The silence stretched, dark and painful. After a long time, he asked harshly, "Are you thinking of divorce?"

Roddy gripped the arm of the chair and shook her head.

"Good," he said softly. She heard his footsteps, long strides toward the door. He stopped, halfway there, and looked back at her.

"Good," he said again, out of the shadows. "Because I warn you, my love. You may talk of peace, but I'll hold you by force before I'll let our marriage be dissolved."

❧

She lay awake all night listening for the carriage, but if it came or went in the court below her window, she did not hear, or feel any stirring among the servants through her gift. Alone in the great, cold bed—alone for the first time since she had left her home—she stared at a shaft of moonlight between the bed-curtains as it drifted across the other pillow.

Regrets. She had a hundred of them. A hundred thousand. Regrets tumbled around in her head and lay next to her on the bed and piled chin-deep against the windowpane watching for a carriage.

"Did your regrets catch up with you this afternoon?" a demon-voice whispered through her waking dreams. "Regrets," the walls answered as she twisted and turned and tangled in the bedclothes. "Your regrets. This afternoon." The night echoed with the words. "This afternoon. This afternoon."

She knotted the pillow and buried her face in it.

What did he mean by that?

Liza. He might have thought Roddy knew the truth, that Liza was his mistress and he meant to keep her. He might have meant that Roddy had been warned. "Say you won't marry me..." It had been her choice, for better or for worse. And now her regrets had caught up with her.

But he had been so angry. Since that moment she had turned in Geoffrey's arms—

Roddy sat bolt upright in the bed.

Geoffrey.

A crystallized vision burst in her mind, of that moment when the Duke of Stratton had reached for her and Faelan had moved to stop him. The same look—it had been the same look on his face: a primeval rage, come and gone in an instant, too quick for Roddy in her inexperience to see. But the duke had caught it, and known it for what it was.

Roddy struggled out of the bed, pushing back the curtains to find the first chilly light of dawn in the room. She dressed by herself in her country clothes—flannel undergarments, a warm woolen calash, and sturdy wooden pattens over her shoes. The house servants were just awake and beginning to stir, but when she reached the stable she found the horses all fed and the undergrooms already at work slapping the circulation into their charges' coats with braided wisps of straw.

She smiled good morning at the head coachman, and complimented him on a well-run stable. "Quite as excellent as my father's," she said generously, and defused his astonishment at finding the new young mistress unannounced in the stableyard at dawn by engaging in a detailed description of how her parent's famous operation began each day.

By degrees, she led him into a discussion of the daily routine of the Banain House stable, and finally found an unobjectionable place to insert a question about which horses were used when the carriage went out after dark on such a chilly night as last.

She did not even have to use her gift to interpret his ready answer.

"Oh, that'd be Dogs and old Charlie, m'lady. They go on great guns in the cold. Blest if the two of 'em warn't disappointed when the House sent round last night to say that His Lordship wudn't a-going out after all like Mr. Minshall 'ud thought. They gets an extra measure of oats if they go in the dark, and they do know it, m'lady. Animals is smarter than some people thinks, as you needs must know, ma'am, bein' so familiar with Mr. Delamore's stable an' all."

Roddy blinked at the beefy coachman. *Faelan changed his mind. He didn't go to Blandford Street.*

And he was jealous of Geoffrey.

"Without a doubt," Roddy agreed joyously. "Without a shadow of a doubt, Mr. Carter. I'd better go back inside now. Good morning to you."

The great entrance hall was empty when she slipped off her pattens and tiptoed in. At the far end, the door to the library stood partly open, and through her talent the soft voices of the two people inside were clear in her head.

"'Twere here when I come in, mum!" a young and anxious maid was saying. "I fetched you, mum, on the quick—I didn't do it, on my grave! I never done nothing but opened the door and went to trim the candles, and I saw it then, mum. I come right away to find you!"

"Fetch a broom, then!" It was the housekeeper, flustered and trying to hide it. "'Tis plain you didn't break the thing. But for pity's sake, clean it up and have it out of here."

"Yes, mum." The maid scurried for the door. "Yes, mum."

Roddy drew back into the wide doorframe of the drawing room as the housekeeper and the maid came out in the hall and disappeared in silent servant fashion behind the curving stairs.

After they had left, Roddy set the wooden clogs down and moved toward the library door. She did not want to. She knew what she would find; what the two servants had seen that had put them into such a flutter of dismay. She went halfway into the room and stopped, her eyes fastened on the white marble hearth and the cold ashes within.

Shards of broken crystal covered the stone, flashing prisms of color in the red light of the rising sun. Across the dark wood of the mantel, a vicious scar showed raw and pale above the broken neck of the decanter that had struck it.

But worse, far worse, was what lay smashed among the dead coals.

Her music box.

"M'lady," said a horrified voice. The young maid hurried into the room with her pail and broom. "Oh, m'lady, I beg your pardon, but I didn't do it. Mrs. Clarke, she kin tell you, m'lady."

Roddy slowly tore her eyes away. "Of course you didn't do it."

The maid stared at Roddy, and then ducked and began to sweep vigorously at the broken pieces. The girl knew she was not supposed to speak to the young mistress unless spoken to, but in her fright her mouth would not be still. "I'll have it gone in an instant, m'lady. 'Twere a terrible accident His

Lordship had," she explained breathlessly, stooping to retrieve the music box. "A terrible, terrible accident—"

"I'll take that," Roddy said, holding out her hand.

The maid looked up. "Oh, my lady," she said in a stricken whisper. "It is yours?"

Roddy did not answer. She did not have to. The girl laid the charred and broken remains of the music box reverently in Roddy's hands.

"I'm sorry, m'lady." The maid's voice was soft and miserable. "I'm so sorry. Such a pretty box..." She raised her eyes, and they were glittering with tears. "I'm sure it were an accident, m'lady. His Lordship—he wouldn't... oh, mum—such a pretty, pretty box."

"Yes," Roddy said.

And they both knew it had not been an accident.

The maid finished her task hurriedly. With a quick, anxious curtsy, she scuffled away toward the door. Halfway there, a frightened "Oh!" escaped her, and she dropped into another panicked curtsy, clattering her pail loudly on the floor. "Beg pardon. Beg pardon, m'lord," she squeaked, and slid out and away into the nether regions of domestic safety.

Faelan stood in the hall just outside the library door, looking over his shoulder, frozen in the motion of pulling on his gloves.

In the slanted light of dawn he might have been a vision: an illusion of heaven and hell, perfect and beautiful and macabre in his dark cloak and his eyes like ice burning.

His gaze was fixed on her hands. Her fingers closed on the broken box in sudden protectiveness, as if he might stride across the room and snatch it away from her and fling it back into the fireplace again.

"My lady," he said, lifting his eyes with a faint, grim smile. "Perhaps in the future, you'll remember your belongings when you retire."

He raised his gloved hand in half-salute and was gone, leaving behind only the booming echo of the great front door.

Roddy pressed the box closer, not caring that it had been cracked and broken beyond repair. She would keep it, as she'd promised. Forever.

Because if he was human and not marble; if his heart and his mind were flesh and blood—then he said hurtful things because he was hurting.

And he hurt now because she had the power to wound him.

Eight

SHE KEPT REPEATING IT TO HERSELF.

He's jealous. He's only jealous.

He didn't go to Liza.

But neither did he come home. Not until long, long after darkness had fallen and the city lay in heavy sleep. In the distance a watchman called three o'clock, and as Roddy sat in the library in the chair Faelan had used the night before, she could only stare into the fire and imagine a small carved box among the flames.

She had sent Minshall and Jane to bed, but the little maid, Martha, insisted on sitting up to keep the fire as long as the young mistress was awake and waiting for her lord. Roddy could not have borne Jane, or more particularly Minshall, who had his notions of where His Lordship might be, but Martha was too innocent—or ignorant—to suspect that Faelan had gone after all to his paramour. Poor Martha dozed off in her corner dreaming of robbers and cutthroats. Between the two opinions, Roddy was not entirely sure she didn't wish for Martha to be right. Faelan, Roddy was certain, could handle any number of mere criminals.

A woman like Liza he could handle only too well.

At half past three, she felt the first touch of movement amid the sleeping streets. The horses in the stable stirred, and then the sound of metal shoes rang in the empty court. Martha snuffled and sat up with a start, looking at Roddy with round eyes.

"Go to bed now," Roddy said softly. "He's come."

Martha jumped up and added a log to the fire, relief and reluctance warring in her mind. Soft voices drifted from outside in the quiet, and then came the sound of booted feet on the stone steps. The maid hesitated at the library door, then took hold of all her courage and drew herself up, like a rabbit preparing to defend her single nestling from the approaching fox. "It may be I ought to stay, m'lady," she said, in a voice that shook with the enormity of her own rashness. "Beg pardon, ma'am, beg pardon, but... His Lordship's temper—"

"Go on," Roddy said. She smiled as best she could manage. "I shall be quite all right."

Martha's resolve failed her at the sound of the front door opening. She bobbed and gasped, "Yes, m'lady," and fled.

Roddy stood waiting alone by the fire.

She felt no steadier than Martha. Roddy hardly even knew why she had waited up for him. If it had been in some tenuous hope that she could somehow make things back into what they had been, that dream vanished the moment he appeared in the doorway.

He stood there, the same cloaked and unfathomable image she had seen in the dawn. Only this time—this time he did not raise his hand to her and pass on. Instead, he stepped over the threshold and pulled the door softly shut behind him.

It took all of Roddy's self-control not to take a step backward away from him.

It was Liza's Faelan that Roddy saw. Black night and flame. Hellfire and ice. When he smiled at her, she went cold to the tips of her fingers.

But somewhere, deep, there was an answering flame in her. She would not have run from him if she could have made her feet move.

"Waiting?" he murmured.

Roddy swallowed. She nodded.

"I'm here," he said softly.

It was an invitation and an order... a vortex that dragged her down into the blue depths of his eyes.

"Where have you been?" she whispered.

"Visiting." His gaze held hers. "A friend."

Liza.

Roddy looked at the floor.

"I have your permission, have I not?" The words were gentle. Horrible. He made a careless motion of his hand, as if beckoning a servant. Come here, that meant, and like a servant she obeyed, moving out of the warm ring of firelight into the shadow.

A trace of cold night air hung about him, a faint breath of smoke. She had expected perfume—Liza's perfume—but instead there was something else... something familiar. A sudden and disparate memory of the fields at home in Yorkshire leaped into her mind.

She forgot it in the next moment.

He held out his hand, palm downward. "Lady Iveragh," he murmured. "Will you help me with my gloves?"

She wet her lips. This was punishment, she knew. There was banked anger in that steady hand, in every cool and controlled move he made.

She reached out, and worked the black leather off his long fingers. She looked down at them and felt tears prick her eyes as she thought of where he had been, whom he had been with. His hands were so beautiful, so strong and perfect. Why did it have to be this way? Why couldn't he be hers alone?

He curled the glove in his fingers and brushed her cheek with the soft kidskin. "Your Ladyship," he murmured mockingly. "Did you miss me today?"

"Yes." It was barely audible.

His hand slid downward, his thumb tracing her throat. "In the absence of other company." The light chill of his touch warmed as it rested against her skin. He raised her chin slowly with his fist. "'*Poppet*,'" he said, repeating Geoffrey's endearment with a trace of derision. Faelan stared down into her eyes, direct—the only one who ever did so. "Gods, the man must be blind."

He drew the black leather slowly upward, shaping her brows, her mouth and jaw. Her heart began to pound in anticipation. She tried to remember her pride. She tried. She did not have to let him touch her like this, not when he kept a mistress who would do the same. As his wife, she had only to allow him his rights if he demanded them. She should be cold, for the sake of her sanity. She should be stone.

But instead, she was all melting heat and weakness.

He saw it. He smiled, as a wolf would smile at its cornered quarry. "Can you bear this?" he asked as the glove fell carelessly from his fingers. His hands slipped beneath her shawl. He cupped her breast with his bared palm and caressed the swelling tip beneath the fabric of her gown, bending to her, pressing his mouth to the tender place below her ear. "Can you suffer my touch?" he whispered harshly.

Roddy tried to speak, but her body was aching for his familiar torture. The sound came out a reluctant moan.

His other hand slid around her hip. She heard his breath quicken, a warmth in her ear. "You lied," he sneered softly. "You lied when you said you don't want this."

She turned her face into his neck, trying to dam the words. *Yes. Yes, I lied!* Her mouth opened against his skin, defying her will, and she pressed hard to stop her lips from speaking.

"Roddy," he groaned as her teeth scored his skin. His grip on her tightened convulsively. He tasted male and smoky, and smelled of outside: of winter grass and frost. Cold and clean, no lingering trace of the city or Liza upon him. He pulled Roddy closer, between his hard thighs, crushed her against him with a strength he had never used before. "Tell me." He dragged her head back. "Show me how much you dislike what I do."

Roddy's throat closed as she stared up at him. His eyes were dark, his mouth still curved in that slight, awful smile. Fell he looked: fell and wild, and fit to murder anyone. If there was pain behind his words, she could not hear it. There was only the sudden pain of his lips claiming hers, sweet and brutal, an ache that sparked fire and flamed down her spine.

It was hopeless. It no longer belonged to her, this body that arched in pagan answer to his touch. Murder or mistress—she did not care. Only Faelan mattered. Only his heat and his mystery, and the demon-blue glitter of his eyes.

His mouth moved on hers with a punishing demand. The gentleness she had known before from him had vanished. He dragged her down with him to his knees, moving with ruthless ease to tear away her shawl and loosen her dress.

The muslin gown was easy: a ribbon here, an eyelet there, and his hands and his mouth had access to all of her. She felt the chill of night air on her skin, and shuddered with more than the cold as he pushed her down beneath him. The cloak swept around them, a black river of cloth. With his dark-gloved hand, he shoved the loose hair back from her temple and forced her chin up, bruising her lips with another kiss.

His mouth and his weight pressed the air from her lungs. She shifted, struggling, but he slid his bare palm down her shoulder and trapped her beneath him. "Don't fight me," he said, his breath harsh against her skin. "You'll never win."

She met his eyes and saw the inevitable. He meant to take her now in cold anger, with nothing of affection or laughter between them. As he had destroyed her music box, he wanted now to destroy the pleasure he had given her, to shatter those precious memories with something else.

Her lips parted in dismay. She did not want him, not like this, and yet her body responded, arching upward when he circled her nipple and caressed it with his thumb. He made her feel him, every inch of him, pushed her legs apart and lowered himself between them, pressing her bare buttocks into the silken rug. A sound escaped her, a small moan, half protest, half desire, as he forced her hips to move against his in seductive rhythm.

He lifted his head at the sound. His palm slid over her breast, coaxing another panting whimper, while his smile and his eyes taunted her for her weakness. "You're mine after all, aren't you? I can hold you with this."

Roddy could have wept for the derision in his words, but instead she only proved them by tilting her head back and offering herself for more.

He moved aside suddenly, taking the cloak with him, so that it slipped from her leg and her naked thigh shone pale against the black cloth. His gloved hand brushed down her skin, a dark shadow on silver. Before she could gather her wits, he lifted himself and knelt over her, his hands sliding beneath her hips. His tongue traced the path that his fingers had discovered, and Roddy lost the last thread of reality.

He squeezed her buttocks and pressed her upward under his mouth, while her body seemed to turn to water, to flow and burn and writhe. Her breath was gone, and all her strength; she could not help the way her throat contracted, making little gasping whimpers. His tongue reached inside her, and her hands clawed at his shoulders. A cry began in her chest, that familiar long moan that expanded into sound like the blossoming explosion in her body.

She hated her weakness, and wanted more. She wanted *him:* in her, around her, rising with her as she strained and ached for the thing he had set to spark. He lifted her, his tongue penetrating deep, and like a flash of powder the spark erupted. Her body convulsed. She cried out and reached for him in blindness and need.

"Open your eyes." He caught her hand at the wrist with a wrench that made her obey on the instant. "Look at me," he said fiercely. "Do you pretend I'm your precious Geoffrey when I touch you? Look at me, *cailin sidhe*, and call me by name." His mouth hardened in bitter irony. "There's power in a name, little girl, and I've given you mine."

She gulped air and stared up at him as he loomed over her. Like a cornered animal, she knew that she was lost if she looked away now. He would take that as proof, as fuel for his fury: that she thought of another when she writhed with passion in her husband's arms.

With his demonically beautiful face so close above hers, she half feared for her life if she faltered.

Colleen, he had called her. She knew that simple Irish word. But the other, she remembered, meant something else entirely.

Dark and light. Magic. *Sidhe.*

"Faelan," she whispered, holding his gaze with desperate steadiness. She raised a trembling hand and touched his cheek. "Faelan. 'Tis you I want. None other."

His fingers loosened on her wrist. A change came in his darkened face, a slow focus, as if her words had been spoken in some half-known foreign language.

She watched her spell work, watched the anger waver in his eyes, and found her small magic a two-edged sword. For another phrase swelled into her throat, something with a power of its own to make her tongue move. "I love you," she said, and could have killed herself for that mistake.

She turned her face away, as if that might somehow blunt the words. They were folly, those words. Spoken to a man who might not even exist, who might be nothing but an actor's well-played part.

"You love me, do you?" He caught her cheek and turned her. The savagery had faded from his hard features, but his eyes were still as light and cold as winter frost. "Little girl," he mocked. "You love this—" He moved his hand between her thighs, and Roddy drew in her breath. "You love the devil's touch, *cailin sidhe*. Not the devil."

She could not say that he was wrong. She could not even think when he stroked her like that.

"Save your affection for those children you want so much," he recommended, moving away abruptly. "I have my talents, but you're a fool to think the way I make you feel has aught to do with love."

She had said the same thing to herself, over and over, but the self-scorn in his voice gave the words a sudden new meaning. He sat up, yanking at the lacing on the cloak, and tossed it across her as he turned away.

She pulled the scratchy softness up over her shoulder. Its smell made her think of the winter pastures at home again, and when her hand came away a tiny clod of earth fell from the folds. She turned on her elbow, frowning, and picked up the fragment. It dissolved into dust between her fingers.

Faelan was staring into the fire. Roddy lifted her hand and sniffed at the lingering traces of soil. "Faelan—" she asked softly, "where have you been?"

He gave a short, harsh laugh. "Breaking ground in a damned frozen field," he said without turning. "Would you believe that?"

As if to emphasize the absurdity of his claim, the far-off voice of the watch cried four past midnight. Faelan slanted a look toward her, with a faint lift of dry humor at the corner of his mouth. "The field was in Bedfordshire."

Roddy blinked. It had taken them nigh on a full day's driving to reach London from Bedford on the trip from York. "Why?" she breathed.

"Because," he said, with that self-mocking sneer, "I felt the need to break something. Soil comes much cheaper than music boxes, my dear." He paused, and then looked back at the fire. "I'll buy you another."

Roddy blinked, and realized suddenly that she had just gotten the best apology over the destruction of his gift she was likely to get. After a moment, she asked carefully, "You have a friend in Bedfordshire?"

"Several."

"But that's who you were visiting so long—a friend in Bedfordshire?"

He massaged the back of his neck. "If you'd call opening five acres with a plow and a pickax visiting." He threw her a challenging look. "And where did you think I'd gone?"

"To Mrs. Northfield."

For a long moment, he just looked at Roddy, and then he said, "You're remarkably acute, little girl."

She glanced down and shrugged.

"Who told you of Liza Northfield?"

"No one. I guessed."

She found her chin jerked up by a firm hand. "You guessed! And gave me *permission* to keep her? For God's sake, you stupid, brainless chit—was that what you were about?"

She pulled away from him. "Don't call me that."

Her escape was halted by his hard grip on her bare shoulders. "Tell me the truth. How did you find out?"

"You sent her a note." She hadn't meant for him to hear the accusation in her voice, but it came out clearly.

"It's customary," he said in a cold tone, "when terminating an arrangement." He shoved her away. "But you wouldn't know that, would you? I doubt you've sent one to Cashel."

At that, Roddy lost her last shred of patience. He had led her on and left her alone and made love to her and frightened her to death, and now he had ruined what gladness she might have felt over Liza's dismissal with a shaft that was worthy of a sullen schoolboy.

Roddy scrambled up, clutching the cloak to her breasts. "Perhaps *I'm* a brainless chit," she cried, "but you're a—a—" Words failed her in her fury. "A *muttonhead!*" she spat, for want of a better epithet. "I'm not half so childish as you and your vile temper and your absurd jealousy and your damnable pride! Geoffrey is my *friend*. He's not my lover. Have you forgotten that I was a virgin on our wedding night? Have you forgotten that? My God, I never even knew how to kiss before you happened along! I was a virgin, a nice, proper, innocent, stupid little virgin who was just naive enough to think she'd fallen in love with her own husband! And if you have a heart any bigger than a—than a—" She struggled for a suitably vile comparison. "—a piece of *pea gravel*, then by God you'd better say so right now, because I'm going back home tomorrow!"

She shut her mouth then, because her lower lip was quivering alarmingly, and stood glaring down at him with her hair tumbling free and the cloak dragging folds on the floor at her feet.

After a long moment of silence, he drew one knee up and leaned on it. "No," he said softly, "you're not."

Roddy stiffened. The words were even, unemotional, but there was a new gleam in his eyes as he surveyed her. "You're *laughing* at me," she wailed.

He raised his eyebrows in perfect innocence.

"Damn you," Roddy shouted. "It isn't funny." She pulled the cloak around her shoulders and started for the door, too angry to avoid the obvious trap. His arm swept out as she passed, his fingers tangling in the cloak and catching one bare ankle. Roddy stumbled and stopped. "Kindly unhand me," she said, in her best haughty tone, which was somewhat strained by the necessity to make little hops on her free foot to keep her balance.

He tugged lightly on her ankle. "Come here. Your mutton-headed husband wants his cape back."

"Cretin," she said scathingly. "Numbskull. Lackbrain. Clodpole. Let go of my foot."

He did not. He only looked at her with that quiver around the corners of his mouth.

"*Bastard*," she hissed, which took care of the quiver. His blue eyes narrowed.

"Goose," he said, and gave a hard pull which brought her toppling down in a tangle of cloak and legs. Before her shriek had died away, he had pinned her beneath him on the floor. "Greenhorn," he said, very close to her face. "Has no one ever told you not to call a spade a spade when he's got hold of your foot?"

She pressed her lips together in frustration, but Faelan ignored her wriggling attempts to escape. Instead he cradled her face between his hands and ran his thumbs over her cheekbones. "Roddy," he said. "Listen to me. Listen to me now, for I'll only say this once, my love." He waited, watching her until she had stilled, and then bent to brush her mouth with his lips. "You weren't a virgin on our wedding night," he said softly.

She froze. "*What?*"

Instead of accusation, there was apology in his voice. "Not that I could tell." He kissed her again, his mouth moving gently on her parted lips. "Forgive me, little love," he whispered. "I'm a bastard indeed, for doubting you."

Roddy stared up at him and drew in a savage breath. "You... are... *impossible!*" she said between her teeth.

"No," he murmured, exploring the corner of her mouth and cheek with light kisses.

She tried to push him away. "Get off me."

He said, "No," again, this time to her temple and her hair.

She threw her head back. "I shall go stark, staring mad," she groaned.

"Then we'll be a pair."

"Yes," she whispered, thinking in despair that if he changed again so swiftly she would be fit for Bedlam. "We'll be a pair."

He pulled the cloak around her and took her with him as he rolled onto his back. With his hands on her shoulders, he held her above him. "Make love to me," he commanded, and then arched his head back and moved against her hips. "Please."

Roddy closed her eyes. That one word was magic. *Please.* It made her want to hold him and hug him and melt into wax. It did not even matter that he still wore his boots and his traveling clothes while the dark warmth beckoned and flamed through her limbs. She worked just enough buttons to reach him, and shivered to his groan of pleasure as she sank down on his waiting hardness.

The way his exposed throat tightened and his eyes slid closed in response sent a surge of excitement through her. She leaned over, spreading her fingers across his chest, gathering fine linen into her fists. She feathered kisses down the line of his jaw, running her tongue over the faint, scratchy stubble and then the soft skin beneath his ear. He turned his head, giving her access, and raised his bare hand to cup her breast. When he ran his thumb over the sensitive tip, her whole body tautened around him.

"Ah... God—Roddy." His voice was hoarse. He gripped her waist, holding her down as he rose within her. Roddy welcomed him, reveling in the way her slightest flexing sent pleasure or agony or something like both chasing across his fire-lit features. Between her thighs, the soft doeskin breeches radiated his heat as if it were his own skin she touched. She held his face between her hands and kissed him the way that he did her: hard and deep and fierce, as if she could reach his hot center and drink the fire.

He moved strongly beneath her. His hands slid down and grasped her buttocks. He tore his mouth away and drove upward, breathing hard, pulling her down again and again to meet him. When Roddy spread her legs to accept him more fully, he groaned her name, twice and then three times, as if he were dying and she could save him.

She arched her back and leaned over, basking in her power to bring him to this. Her mouth curved into a wicked smile.

"Not Roddy," she whispered. "*Cailin sidhe.*"

He answered, a shuddering moan that turned into a cry as his fingers dug into her skin and his body stiffened and burst into hers. His harsh sound of ecstasy filled the room, mocking the French tables and gilded chairs: a wild primitive music in the civilized hall.

Roddy rested on his chest, feeling the dampness of sweat through his linen shirt. The sound of his heart and his ragged breath were all she could hear as she lay against him. Without raising her head, she reached up and traced his jaw, following the firm curve of it blind, down to his chin and up across his lips.

He kissed her fingers, his breath warm and heavy on her skin. She smiled ruefully into the darkness.

Fit for Bedlam.

Or wherever else he might care to lead her.

Nine

FROM SOMEWHERE, MINSHALL HAD FOUND FLOWERS. RED anemones, purple-veined tulips, and white narcissi, forced in some nurseryman's succession houses, lay scattered over papers on a polished table in the blue withdrawing room. Roddy placed another tulip in the tall Florentine vase she was filling, and watched with resignation as the flower drooped awkwardly and then fell out of the vase, taking two anemones along.

She wasn't very good at flowers.

Unfortunately, though Minshall had brought her the floral offering with a gloomy face, underneath his surface expression had been every expectation of pleasure and praise. Roddy hadn't had the heart to suggest that any maid in the house could do a better job of arranging. She picked up a spray of narcissus and gave it a dubious frown.

"Lovely," came Faelan's low voice from the open doorway.

Roddy half turned, and smiled at him over her shoulder. "You're too gallant, sir," she said. She glanced back at the sagging cluster in the half-filled vase. "Or you have a good imagination."

His boots made no noise on the carpet as he came toward her. He caught her shoulders and pulled her back against his chest, twisting her chin up for a hard, lingering kiss. "I have an excellent imagination, *cailin sidhe*," he murmured, sliding his hands down from her waist to her hips. "My memory isn't wanting, either."

The forgotten narcissus dangled and fell from fingers that grew too weak to hold its weight. Roddy leaned against him, feeling his shape all down her spine and along her thighs. It was as well, she thought hazily, that she knew all the servants were busy at distant tasks. When he touched her like this, all sense of shame and decency vanished.

It was then, while he caressed her bare shoulder with his lips and molded her body to his, that she felt the intrusion.

The mental touch was peculiar. Unfamiliar. She tensed, and in another moment Faelan had realized her resistance. His head came up in question just as the unmistakable sounds of arrival filled the courtyard outside.

His blue eyes narrowed beneath their thick brush of lashes. He bent and kissed her earlobe. "Later," he whispered. "Later."

He was standing behind her with one hand on her arm—the always-possessive touch—when the front doors thundered open. The sound of a feminine voice echoed through the hallway and into the drawing room.

Faelan let go of Roddy.

"Faelan, my love!" the woman cried, sweeping into the room with a footman in her wake. "You can't guess where I've been these two months! And who is this child? Ah, I do despise this miserable house." She let the servant take her rich cloak without a break in her flow of words. "The drafts, I declare, nothing could be worse. With the exception of Iveragh, of course. *Nothing* could be worse than Iveragh. I have been to the Lakes, my dearest boy. Who did you say this young person was?" Her vivid blue eyes rested for a split second on Roddy and then passed over. "Ah, Keswick—you would adore it! I have bought a house, the most precious cottage; you must pack and return with me on the instant. Your Uncle Adam insists. Of course, I knew he would; he dotes on you, Faelan dear..."

The stream of words flowed on without a pause. Roddy stood, nonplussed, staring at this slender, olive-skinned matron with shadowed eyes as blue as Faelan's. Her movements were quick and jerky as she pulled off her gloves and moved about the room, examining each table and chair, picking up figurines and turning them over in her hands as she talked without ceasing. The words obscured her thoughts from Roddy, obscured even her identity. In her restless circuit of the room she came to where Faelan stood and raised her hand to be kissed. There was a momentary pause in her monologue, and he bowed over her fingers.

She smiled up at him coyly. "Not even a hug, my only son? But no, you would ruin my hair, and Tilly worked for an hour—*two* hours—to dress it." She looked at Roddy. "What do you think? Too much height, I told her. Make it *au naturel*, I said. Like yours, my dear. How pretty and unusual you are. But no, my Tilly says, it's not for you, ma'am. I must have height, she says. Well, so it will be. What *is* your name, my dear?"

Roddy kept her eyes downcast. "Roderica," she said hesitantly.

"I knew a Roderica once. No, I did not. That was the name of Clara Walters' great-aunt. Or was it her spaniel? My lamentable recollection. Have we met? I declare, I cannot recall your surname, child."

"Savigar," Faelan said in a still voice. "The Countess of Iveragh."

"The Countess of Iveragh." She turned toward her son. "You must be married, then. My congratulations. My warmest regards." She turned back to Roddy and gave her a perfunctory embrace. "When did this happy event take place? I see that I've rusticated far too long. And Adam must be told, of course. He'll be delighted, I assure you. But why did you forget us, you naughty boy? Do ring to have my room prepared. I must have a nap."

"Your room is ready, m'lady." Minshall appeared in the doorway, not showing a hint of the haste with which he had rushed to the drawing room when he heard his mistress had arrived.

"You are a treasure, Minshall. I shall retire directly. Send Tilly up. Has the fog been so horrid all week? I declare, it wants to hang in the very drawing room. I shall not stay above a fortnight, I dare swear; I won't be able to abide it. But you don't think she's a trifle young for you, Faelan? I suppose it's all the crack just now—child brides…"

She left the room still talking. Roddy could hear her voice echoing as it drifted away up the stairs.

Silence hung in the study, thick as the dowager countess' fog. Faelan had a strange look—too neutral; his dark features set in unnatural calm.

"Allow me to present my mother," he said at length. "I'm sure she's honored to meet you."

Roddy stood in silence. She could think of nothing to say. Above her the dowager countess' presence whirled, a giddy torrent of nonsense, unsettling in its very banality. It was as if the marriage of her son and the drafts in the house occupied equal importance in her mind, and neither of them very much.

After a long moment, Roddy managed to say, "She seems an excellent person."

His mouth drew taut in a humorless smile. "Do you think so indeed?"

❦

They sat at opposite ends of the polished table, Faelan and his mother, with Roddy at a place in between. The huge room sent back every little chink of silver in echo and made the few words spoken sound hollow and strange.

The dowager countess ate with the same jerky restlessness with which she moved. Roddy had begun to see a pattern. The older woman was either talking or silent. She never conversed. Just now, she was silent, her mind a babble. The dowager countess' thoughts darted up one path and then another, meeting blank walls and doubling back, twisting down narrow strands of logic, ballooning into volumes of nothing, chasing some thought about the initials on the silver and then envisioning the whole room washed in a metallic gleam with a focus so powerful that Roddy saw the room that way herself for an instant. She attempted to ignore the chaos, careful never to meet the other woman's eyes, concentrating instead on the flavor of the food in her mouth and the way the candles reflected in the crystal and on the shining wood.

Her control was flawed, for if Lady Iveragh's glance happened to light on the same image, Roddy's hard-fought barriers were no match for the intensity of the doubled vision and she found herself dizzy and sick with the peculiar sensation of seeing the epergne on the table from two sides at once. It was a problem that she had not experienced since childhood, before she had learned the rudiments of control over her talent.

"Where will you live?" the dowager countess asked suddenly. "You won't take her to Iveragh. I'll speak to Adam about a house in town. It will have to be leased, of course. Perhaps he can raise your allowance. You're a sad wastrel, my dear, but I'm sure I can convince him—"

"You needn't convince him of anything." It was the first time Roddy had heard Faelan interrupt the countess. "Adam is no longer my trustee."

Lady Iveragh picked up her wineglass and set it down again. Twice. "I suppose you mean that silly agreement you insisted upon. Really, my dear, you know Adam only went along because it seemed to mean so much to you. It can't possibly change anything."

"Yes." Faelan smiled bitterly. "A sop to my pride, there's no doubt. But the fact remains that Adam relinquished part of the trust. Iveragh is fully mine now. Debt and all."

"Exactly my point. Adam tells me there's not a bit of income to be squeezed out of the place. Not without *mounds* of money to be invested first."

Faelan ran his forefinger over the intricate pattern on a sterling-silver knife. He said slowly, "Nevertheless, that was the bargain I chose. You and Adam keep the money, and I hold Iveragh."

"'Keep the money.' Really, Faelan, what a vulgar way to talk. I'm sure Adam—"

"Adam will do well to stay out of my sight," he said, in a tone so soft it chilled Roddy down to her toes.

The countess waved a vague hand. "How dark it is in here. Ring for an extra candelabrum, Faelan. I'm sure I don't know what you mean about Adam, my love. Have you and Adam had a disagreement? I won't have quarreling between my two favorite men, you know. My brother does his best for you. Think of the years he's spent looking after your interests. All those trips to that godforsaken place since your father—"

"*Don't.*"

The word hung in the air. Roddy stopped in the motion of lifting her fork. She stared at her plate, afraid to look right or left. In spite of her efforts, the soaring agitation in the countess' mind leaked through Roddy's weakened barriers, muddier than ever in its increased turmoil.

Very quietly, Faelan said, "You won't speak of my father again."

"Faelan, I can't imagine what's troubling you this evening. Not speak of your father—why ever shouldn't I? I'm sure he was a fine man. An excellent man. I've missed him sorely." She glanced at Roddy without ceasing the quick movements of slicing a cube of cheese into tiny pieces. "This Stilton is a trifle dry, don't you agree? I pray you never know the agony of raising a son alone, my dear. Particularly a boy like Faelan, wild as he always was. After his father was killed, he—"

They both looked up at the violent scrape of Faelan's chair. He stood at the head of the table. "That's enough."

The countess gave him a pleased look, as if she had just noticed him standing there. "Have you seen Lord Geoffrey, dear? Minshall told me he had been here. What a charmer that boy is." She smiled at Roddy. "I declare, I fell in love with him when he was ten years old. Has Faelan dared to introduce you? He'll not be anxious to do so, I imagine."

"Lord Cashel is an old friend of my family, ma'am," Roddy said, keeping her eyes from where Faelan stood at the head of the table.

"Oh—then you'll be as much in love with him as all the other girls. He's a slyboots, is my Lord Cashel. I do believe he's stolen the heart of every young lady my poor Faelan ever cared for. But you're the exception, aren't you? I can't tell you how very grateful I am that a girl has finally seen my son's true worth. You'll hear rumors, my dear, but don't give them a thought." She smiled up at Faelan. "We've survived those vile stories for years, haven't we, darling boy? We don't pay them the least mind."

Roddy said, "Of course not, ma'am," in a thin effort to neutralize the dowager countess' tactlessness. His mother might be unaware of the tension in Faelan's still figure, but Roddy was acutely conscious of it. She caught a swift thought out of the jumble in Lady Iveragh's mind and pursued the topic. "Tell me about the house in Keswick, ma'am, if you please. I've never been to the Lakes."

"Call me *mamá*, my dear—do." The countess gave Roddy a charming smile. "Keswick is fabulous. The most adorable little town right on the lakeshore. My house—it's naught but a cottage, I assure you. I shan't be able to keep more than a half-dozen domestics when I'm in residence. But that's the fun of it, dear. One is so intrepid and isolated…"

She rambled on, and after a few moments, Faelan looked at the plates and glasses before him. He sat down. His hand curved around his wine goblet and he emptied it. A footman was there to refill the glass twice before Lady Iveragh had said everything she had to say about the "cottage" in Keswick.

"I'm sure we can find you something just like it," the countess said. "I shall set an agent on it immediately. We can all go back together, though I shan't have room at my house for you both, I fear. There's a delightful inn where you could stay while you look over the available properties." She squeezed her hands together. "Oh, 'twill be such fun. The lakes, the mountains—I tell you, there's nothing to compare with it."

Faelan said, "Iveragh surpasses it. A thousand times."

His mother laughed. "Nonsense. Iveragh is a wilderness. You won't take poor Roderica there—I shan't allow it." She turned to Roddy. "Stay here, my dear, if you don't care to come with me. I shall be back before Whitsuntide, and then we will have such a season! We'll soon remedy this awful boy's oversights." She shook her head and put out her hand toward Roddy. "Not even an engagement ball, my poor darling child! He should be whipped, for marrying you in this slipshod fashion. Why—where were you wed? I wouldn't put it past him to have carried you off to Gretna Green!"

Faelan looked toward her with an arrested expression. He set his goblet down and said, "We were married in the Delamores' church in Helmsley. The records are in perfect order. You may be sure that I'll make certain everyone is aware of that."

The dowager countess sighed. "I'm vastly relieved. I hadn't wanted to say anything, you know."

Though his mother did not speak of them again, the rumors about Faelan seemed to be troubling the dowager countess far more than she admitted. Amid the agitated tumble of her mind, *seduction* whirled around with thoughts of blackmail notes and dueling pistols. *Ellen Webster*, she thought, and *her brother*, and suddenly there was a quick vision of a killing— whose, Roddy could not tell.

But there was no fear in the countess' mind for Faelan.

"I'll be leaving town tomorrow," Faelan said, with a slight nod to the footman who stood behind Lady Iveragh with a dish of bonbons and crystallized fruit. The servant offered the dish to the countess.

Roddy looked up at her husband in startlement. He smiled at her, and added, "For a few days only."

She opened her mouth, about to offer to accompany him, but before she could speak she received another shake of his head, as faint as the one he had given the footman. Roddy bit her lip and looked down at her plate.

"For several days, Faelan?" Lady Iveragh's mind flooded with relief, but none of it showed on her face. *Ellen Webster*, she thought again and again in wild, tangled threads of reason. *Time. Speak to her. Brother… brother. Money. Dead.* "And where are you going, love? Will you be back by the fourteenth? You needn't hurry, I'm sure; Roderica and I will spend the entire time shopping. And don't worry over the cost one instant. I know you haven't a feather to fly with, but I shall pay for everything. Everything." She glanced at Roddy. "It will be a pleasure, my dear Roderica. A pleasure. When did you say you would be back, Faelan?"

"In four days, perhaps. Not before."

The dowager countess gave a nervous little clap with her hands. "Excellent. We shall have such fun. Some jewels for Roderica, I think, now that you're married. And hats—I have the most marvelous milliner. We won't miss you at all, Faelan,

I assure you. I suppose you're going into the country to look at cows, or some such thing."

"Yes," he said evenly. "I am."

Lady Iveragh began to laugh, a sound that started with a giggle and ended in mad hilarity. "Cows," she sputtered. "Oh, my son. My poor, poor boy. Cows!"

He tapped slowly at the crystal globe of the wineglass as his hand rested against the stem. "I don't wish for Roddy to wear jewelry not of my choosing," he said, lifting the glass to his lips.

The dowager countess smirked at Roddy. "He *wishes* to be a bully. But you shan't be browbeaten, my child. As soon as he's well and out of sight, we may do just as we please."

"It might please you to spend your time packing," Faelan said, without lifting his eyes from contemplation of his glass. "Roddy and I shall leave for Ireland as soon as I return."

❦

Roddy woke in the midst of a nightmare. She came to confused sense with a cry of fear in her throat, a scream that emerged a choked whimper, and then Faelan's voice murmured and his arms wrapped around her, soothing, warm and solid and real in the darkness.

She turned into him, pressing herself against his bare chest, breathing in hard gasps. Her heart seemed to have sunk deep in her belly with the jolt and dive of transition to consciousness. *It wasn't real*, she thought in relief. *It wasn't real.*

Faelan smoothed her hair. "All right?" he asked softly.

She drew a breath and pressed closer, nodding beneath his hand.

His arm tightened around her shoulders as she shivered and clung to him. "Silly child." He spread his fingers through her hair and his lips grazed her temple. "I'm here."

Roddy voiced her agreement in a tiny, heartfelt sound of gladness. It was too dark to see him, but she heard the bedclothes rustle and felt his body shift as he turned on his back and drew her against his shoulder. She buried her face in the hollow of his neck and stayed there, breathing his deep scent and feeling the smooth warmth of his skin against her cheek. Her heart was still beating savagely. She could not hear his, but she could feel his steady pulse beneath her fingertips.

In the darkness, he traced the bones of her hand with his forefinger. "What frightened you?" he whispered. "Does the devil walk in your dreams, little girl?"

She raised her fingers and found his, lacing their hands together. "I don't know. I dreamed…" She frowned, searching for the images, but there was only an echo, a sense of monstrous horror and fear and loss that was vanishing by the moment under the light caress of his thumb against her palm. "I don't know. It's gone now."

He moved again, drawing his arm from beneath her head and rising on his elbow. In the dark, his slow search for her lips encompassed her cheeks and forehead and eyes. "Roddy," he breathed. She felt his arousal grow hot and hard against her thigh.

She reached for him, sinking gladly beneath his weight as he moved across her. *The devil*, she thought, and knew that she did not care if he haunted her dreams. Not as long as he fired her body and heart and held her safe in his arms.

❧

Faelan went away, but the nightmares remained. Over and over Roddy woke to the sound of her own sobbing whimpers during the first night he was gone. But the dream-demons always slipped away the moment she came awake, leaving no clear memory, nothing but the sleeping city like a great weight around her.

She missed him desperately. With Faelan she could sleep in oblivion, cradled in his dark, silent peace. In his absence she found herself defenseless. She lay wide awake in the shadows and thought of him: how he had looked on his blood-bay mount; how the horse blew frost and pranced in the dawn chill; how Faelan had smiled at her as she stood forlornly at the top of the front steps. "Four days," he had promised.

Forever.

She sat up in the bed and reached for her robe, finding no refuge in sleep this night. Bad dreams she'd had often in her life, sometimes her own and sometimes others'. She knew already that these dreams that plagued her now were not her own.

Her slippers were cold and stiff as she thrust her feet inside. She hardly knew what she intended, but it seemed impossible to lie back down among the bedclothes and give herself up to the dreams. Awake, her talent focused and controlled, she felt only a faint whisper of the troubled mind that raked nightmares through her sleep.

She slipped out the door, into a hall black with shadows, feeling her way with her hands and her memory. Her feet scuffed softly on the marble floor, the only sound in the sleeping house. Down one hall, turn right, down another, while the source of dreams drew stronger and closer.

She stopped outside a bedroom door. Since the night before, Roddy had been certain of the identity of the tormented dreamer. Her gift only confirmed what logic alone made an easy guess. The dreams had come with Faelan's mother.

Roddy glanced around the dark hall, and found one point of reference in the blackness. At the far end of the corridor, a huge, round window showed the cold glow of the night sky beyond, silhouetting the spidery network of mullions that rayed outward from the center. Using the pattern for a mental anchor and clutching at her barriers like a soldier's shield, Roddy carefully and slowly opened her talent to the dreams.

It was like leaning out over the edge of a cliff. The depths of fear dragged at her, pulling her down into someone else's horror. She hung on to the double vision, the image of the window that glittered in starlight, while the dowager countess' demons twisted and flowed and reached out from the depths with murderous fingers. They had faces, those monsters, they had eyes like blue coals. They wanted her with them, far down in the dark; they howled with frustration and madness. One came up, reaching, growing larger and stronger, wrapping hands of iron around her wrists and filling the night with a screaming curse as it fell back and dragged her down...

With a wrenching effort, Roddy focused on the window and pushed the vision away.

The hall seemed to ring with silence as the dream-voices vanished behind her mental wall. She stood there, breathing hard, and a moment later heard whimpers and a low cry from beyond the closed door. A nearby consciousness sprang suddenly to wakefulness at the sound—the maid, Tilly, who had been wrapped in deep, insensible sleep on a cot in the same room.

She roused herself with the patient aggravation of long habit. *Now, now—I'm coming*, she thought grumpily. *Where's the bleedin' bottle? There... candle, no candle...*

Several colorful curses directed at the negligent house-keeper occupied Tilly's mind as she stumbled out of bed to her mistress' side. Roddy heard the maid speaking sharply to the dowager countess, and knew she had grasped the sleeping woman's wrist with a hard pinch to wake her.

Lady Iveragh reacted with a short, sharp scream, and then the moans and mutterings of a half-conscious brain.

"Your medicine, m'lady," Tilly said. "Here's your medicine. Sit up now and take it, and then you can sleep."

The words were spoken with the brisk, cruel comfort of a hardened nurse. Like a child, the countess held on to Tilly and obeyed, still half sunk in the dregs of nightmare.

Roddy waited. Tilly shuffled back to her cot, asleep almost before she pulled the bedclothes up. For a while Lady Iveragh ran from imaginary horrors, and then the laudanum did its work. Her mind eased into a soft, silent void.

The dreams were gone. Roddy walked back to her own room, certain that now she could sleep undisturbed.

But when she lay down, no sleep would come.

She could not sleep, knowing that the demons that haunted Lady Iveragh's dreams all wore her own son's face.

Ten

"NOT HERE?"

Geoffrey's voice rose a little, a dim reflection of the anger and consternation in his mind. He threw his hat and coat at Minshall and strode into the drawing room toward the pianoforte. *Son of a… I told him stay put—damn him, damn him—*"Where is he?" Geoffrey snapped as Roddy's music came to an abrupt stop.

She lifted her hands from the keys. In the face of his heated emotion, her answer seemed absurdly mundane. "He's gone into the country," she said. "To look at some cattle."

"Cattle!" Geoffrey stared at her. "Do you expect me to believe that?"

Her spine stiffened. She had never encountered Geoffrey like this: his unfailing courtesy and charm lost in a whirl of thoughts that bordered on panic. "I'm sure I don't care what you believe. It's what he told me and Lady Iveragh."

He turned sharply. "The coun—" It suddenly occurred to him that Roddy was now the countess, and he cleared his throat. "The dowager countess is at home?" *Pray God she doesn't see me*, he was thinking. *That woman has a mouth like—*

"Would you care to speak to her?" Roddy asked in dulcet tones—a small thrust in retaliation for his shortness and reticence.

"No!" He stood up again. "No, I—Don't disturb her. I'll need to write Faelan a message. Could I ask you to deliver it—" He hesitated. He was thinking causes and meetings again, and how to reach Faelan with news of new dates. *Iveragh* leaped into his head: an image of wild mountains, of distance and a desperate need of Faelan. "Privately?"

Roddy fingered the ivory keys and lowered her lashes, reaching for the truth behind the turmoil. "If you tell me what this is about."

"I can't, poppet," he said quickly. "I'm sorry."

She didn't have to ask again. The question itself provoked a train of thought in his mind that was as illuminating as any spoken answer he might have given her.

Guns. Geoffrey's head was full of them. French guns for the United Irishmen, smuggled through the wild western lands of Faelan's estate on the Iveragh peninsula.

Roddy's fingers clattered discord on the smooth keys. Philosophy and debates were one thing—but guns…

Only a lifetime of caution kept her from crying out her horror. She sat very still, groping for a question, for a way to find out more without arousing suspicion. She made herself relax her hands, and said in her mildest voice, "Can you not? Do you think my husband has kept what you're doing a secret from me?"

He froze in his restless pacing.

"I'm fully aware of the circumstances," she added in blithe dishonesty. "You needn't be afraid to speak of it to me. And a spoken message will be much safer than a written one, will it not?"

Disbelief, confusion, and anger chased one another across Geoffrey's mind. "He's told you? For God's sake—there was no reason for that; no reason on earth!" He paced to the fireplace and glared into the mirror above. *Damn the man; him and his deal*—He slid a glance toward Roddy's reflection. *Ah, poppet*, he thought, with pain and guilt in his eyes. *I shouldn't have gone along, but there wasn't a choice. He'd have it his way or not at all.*

A memory stood out sharply in his thoughts—Geoffrey trying to explain to Faelan how perfect Iveragh was for the smuggling; how much it would mean to the cause. And Faelan, impatient, unimpressed by Geoffrey's speeches. *Self-centered bastard*, Geoffrey fumed even now, *try to talk to him of freedom and all he wants to do is plant potatoes.*

Roddy stared down at the keys, washed in the flow of Geoffrey's feelings for Faelan: half affection, half fury, and then an anomalous recollection of some birthday spent entertaining three courtesans—a clear image of Faelan's ironic smile as he presented the ladies, like a gift, knowing Geoffrey's more earthly passions. *Damned cold devil*, Geoffrey thought ruefully. *Call me a softheaded fool one day and lie down and die for me the next. So where is he now, curse him?*

Geoffrey glanced at Roddy, and the guilt came surging back. *Oh, God, I'm sorry, poppet. He wanted you. He wanted you and I needed Iveragh...*

Roddy sat frozen, her insides contracting like the swift, sickening drop of flying with a fast horse off a steep bank. She saw the implication of his thoughts clearly.

They had made a bargain, Geoffrey and his friend. In return for Iveragh as a smuggling base, Faelan had gained what should have been impossible for the ill-famed Devil Earl: the sanction of a trusted family friend to ease his way with Roddy's parents.

Roddy curled her fingers together into a tight ball in her lap. A bargain. As if she were a sack of flour. Something with a market price.

She set her lip and looked up at Geoffrey. But he had forgotten her already, lost in his internal agitation. The smuggling had gone awry somehow, the guns were stalled at Iveragh, and Geoffrey was terrified that Faelan might move ahead too soon with plans to revive the estate. *Too much activity—the house, the guns... bloody informers, too risky to start repairs—*Geoffrey's mind went black with rage at the threat. *Some bastard—make himself rich off our blood. Sweet Mary, 'twould be so easy. So damned easy.*

At that, Roddy's rigid spine went weak with sudden fear for her husband. If these rebel guns were discovered on Faelan's estate, it would make no difference whether he was personally involved or not. He would be implicated far more deeply than Geoffrey.

"Give me the message," she said. "I'll find him."

He turned toward her. "Do you know where he is?"

"No. But I'll find him."

"Tell me where to start. I can move faster—"

"And draw ten times the attention. No. Give me your message and go away, Geoffrey. Get out of this house, and don't you dare try to contact him again. What if someone's watching you? I'll wager fifty people know of this stupid little game, and I wouldn't trust a one of them."

Geoffrey saw the force of her argument all too clearly, but he still clung to the idea that Roddy, as a member of the fragile and benighted female sex, should be kept ignorant of weighty masculine concerns. With a care that might have made her laugh at some calmer moment, he struggled to frame a message in his mind that would inform Faelan and still hide as much as possible from Roddy.

His efforts were pointless. Roddy used her gift with ruthless effect to glean what she needed to know. By the time he said, "Just tell him to contact me, and not to start work," Roddy was fully aware that the guns might be held up at Iveragh for the next month while the Irish militia bivouacked and held maneuvers on the only road in the district. She also knew that the rebel lieutenant who had commanded the smuggling operation had taken to his deathbed with an inflammation of the lungs, that Geoffrey's unfamiliarity with the countryside rendered him helpless, and that a parson in Ballybrack who was altogether too curious about ghosts stood in danger of his life if he persisted in nosing around the abandoned mansion at Iveragh.

"All right," she said. "I'll tell him. He was planning for us to go as soon as he returned."

"*Don't*," Geoffrey ordered, appalled at this new possibility. "For the love of God, don't let him take *you* to Ireland. Tell him you want to stay in London. That you want to shop, or that you're sick or—" *Pregnant* flashed through his mind, but he said "tired of traveling" instead.

"I can manage," Roddy said, a little testily. Lord, was everyone from the Duke of Stratton on down obsessed with babies?

"I'll wait in Gravesend with Mary. The White Lion. You may tell him that, too—and have him post down there on the instant," *damn his hide*, Geoffrey finished silently.

"Do you want me to keep him here or post him to Gravesend? Or perhaps I should just wrap him up and mail him directly to Newgate."

Geoffrey gave her a look of banked fire. "It's no joke, Roddy. No joking matter at all."

"No!" she burst out. "And who dragged us into it?"

He flushed. "I never meant for you to be involved," he said in a low voice.

"Nor poor Mary either," she added bitterly. "I suppose you think you have her safe and innocent, and never think what would happen to her if you should be—" She bit her lip. "Well, never mind that."

"Roddy—"

"Never mind!" She was tired of talking. Even before he spoke, she felt the headache coming on that always did when Geoffrey tried to explain his political ideals. He was already marshaling reasons and imperatives to convince her of his rightness. She stood up, closing the conversation by dragging at the bellpull. "You should go now, if you wish to avoid Lady Iveragh. She'll be down for luncheon any moment."

He stood frowning at her, robbed of his explanations as she walked vigorously forward, spreading her hands to shoo him as if he had been a stray chicken. He went, secretly a little intimidated by this new and commanding side of his young friend. Roddy stood in the hall and watched him leave, his figure just as tall and dashing and romantic as it had always been, and wondered how she had ever imagined she could live with Geoffrey for the rest of her life.

Guns.

They hanged people for less than guns.

She took a deep breath and turned to Minshall. "Come into the withdrawing room. I need to speak to you."

The majordomo followed Roddy without hesitation. Minshall, along with Martha, had become one of Roddy's conquests. They were people she liked, even beneath their surface: good, honest, uncomplicated folk. She'd had a whole stableful of such admirers at home in Yorkshire. She knew exactly how to charm them, and didn't mind using her knowledge, since she wanted very much for them to like her, too.

She turned as he closed the door. "Lord Cashel has brought me news of some urgency. Do you know where I can find Fae—" She stopped, catching in time Minshall's opinion of informal address before the staff, and finished, "my Lord Iveragh?"

She had expected to cause some discomfort with the question, since she was fairly certain that if Faelan hadn't elected to tell his wife exactly where he was going—except into Hampshire and Dorset—then he probably hadn't given the majordomo a detailed itinerary, either. But the amount of discomfort that welled up in Minshall's kindly mind was far more than she'd anticipated.

The manservant didn't think Faelan had gone into Hampshire at all. Minshall's thoughts went instantly to Faelan's departure. *North*, he thought. *No valet and no baggage and heading north.*

Roddy might have discounted that oddity as merely the direction of some errand Faelan intended to perform before he left London, but Minshall knew better.

The dowager countess had told him that Faelan kept a house in Islington.

The particular purpose of this house brought a faint blush to Roddy's cheeks. Mrs. Northfield figured prominently in the majordomo's thoughts, and he was most anxious to protect Roddy from any hint of his suspicions. He said in answer to her inquiry, "I believe I can locate him, my lady. What message shall I transmit to His Lordship?"

Roddy hesitated. Faelan might have met his mistress at this mysterious house in the past, but Roddy was certain he hadn't gone there for that purpose now. Liza Northfield, Roddy was sure, had been honorably retired.

Perhaps he had gone to Islington to meet a business associate, or to collect important papers. Her father was always dealing with papers of one sort or another. Men, Roddy knew, took a great delight in creating documents and carrying them around and about to be signed and discussed and amended. Faelan's lack of baggage was a bit more inexplicable, until Roddy had the happy thought that perhaps he intended to pack up whatever clothing he had kept at this house and remove it for good.

"I'm afraid I must speak to him myself," she told Minshall.

"Then I shall send to him to return immediately."

"No." Roddy looked Minshall straight in the eyes. "Just tell me where you think he is."

Pelham Cottage, came her answer, as clear as words. Aloud, he said, "I'm really not certain *exactly* where Lord Iveragh might be, my lady. I can only send a boy to inquire in the direction I believe His Lordship has gone."

"Oh." Roddy forced herself to sound disappointed. "That seems unlikely to answer. Perhaps it would be better simply to wait until he returns."

"If it's a matter of urgency—"

"Oh, 'tisn't that important," she said, and then added in a confiding voice, "I've a notion Lord Cashel exaggerates a bit sometimes. I've known him all my life, and I have an idea this is just one of his little teases. We'll wait until His Lordship returns." She strolled to the window and made a great show of looking outside. "It's another lovely day, is it not?" She gazed a moment, and then turned back to the majordomo with an air of sudden decision. "Have the phaeton brought round, Minshall. I'm going for a drive."

❦

Three hours later, with Martha for a guide, Roddy was on the turnpike to Islington. She had no expectation of finding Faelan at Pelham Cottage. After all, his purpose had been to look at cattle in Hampshire and Dorset, and he had promised her he would return within four days. He would hardly have loitered about Islington with such a demanding schedule as that before him.

What she did hope was that he might have left word of his next destination at the cottage. Trotting up the pretty tree-shaded street that bordered the banks of New River, she slowed the phaeton in front of an inn and came to a stop.

Martha—who considered being chosen above Jane to accompany the young mistress on this expedition an honor akin to a seat in Parliament—jumped down cheerfully to obey

Roddy's request for directions. A few minutes later, replete with lemonade and instructions, Roddy sent the horses again to a trot. The phaeton rolled on through Islington village. Just past Hybury Place, a lane branched right, as the potboy had predicted, and at the end of it a neat stone house sat amid trees laden with unplucked October apples.

As if their arrival had been awaited, a groom ran out to take the horses. She felt his shock of surprise as he glanced up at Roddy. *'Nother lady?* His brow wrinkled in disgust. *Be havin' a dashed great harem in there.*

The groom's dark musings gave Roddy a moment's pause. She suddenly wanted to hang back, to question and explore before mounting the steps of Pelham Cottage. But Martha was already bouncing up the gravel walk to ring the bell. Roddy glanced dubiously at the groom, who had turned his full attention to the horses, and then followed Martha.

The front door opened a crack before they had reached it, and then shut again in their faces.

Bewildered consternation radiated from behind the solid oak. *A lady! Oh, me—oh, Lor'—oh, Father in Heaven, what's to do?*

Martha beat enthusiastically on the door knocker, but whoever was standing in the entry had no intention of opening the barrier again. The only answer was a renewed surge of agitation from the other side. Martha raised her sturdy hand to knock again, but before the brass clashed against the door, the hidden personage behind it had an inspiration. *One of Miss Ellen's friends*, the unknown servant decided, and swung open the door.

A young and pretty maid peeked from behind the heavy oak, and lost some of her newfound composure when she could not recognize Roddy's face.

Martha stepped into the silence. "'Tis Her Ladyship, the Countess of Iveragh," she declared loudly, thinking with scorn that this flighty little thing hardly knew her business. "You'll be letting us in?" Martha added, with scathing sarcasm.

Instead of obeying, the young maid simply froze in horror. Martha used this opening to give the door a violent push, which took the maid hanging on to it stumbling back into the entry hall.

"Your Ladyship." The little maid dropped into a curtsy and simply stayed there, too terrified even to rise. Her mind was an agitated litany: *Miss Ellen, poor Miss Ellen, oh, what's to be done now? The countess, the countess herself—Oh, she'll be here to ruin us, this lady; she'll be makin' Miss Ellen a fine spectacle, draggin' her home by her heels. And me job—Lor', me job's gone for good, helpin' Miss Ellen run away—like I'll go to prison, or be flogged to an inch...*

Before Roddy could say a word, the girl began to cry. She was so far past rationality that in the face of all appearance and logic, she did not even question the notion that Roddy was Faelan's mother. To the maid, there was one Countess of Iveragh, and one only.

Another presence, a burst of female eagerness, distracted Roddy from the maid's frenzy. She looked up to see a young woman in an elegant morning dress descending the stairs. In her flurry of excitement, the girl still had the sense to concentrate on holding the rail on the narrow staircase, and as she bent to watch her feet, her dark, crimped hair shone with deep oily highlights in the latest fashion. She looked up as she neared the bottom step. Her eagerness dissolved into surprise.

Who on earth—? The girl stopped uneasily on the lowest step, a beautiful doe-eyed vision, taking in Roddy's expensive clothes and maid in one glance. "I'm sorry," she said quickly. "I'm afraid you must have the wrong house."

From somewhere out of the depths of shock, Roddy found her voice. "This is Pelham Cottage," she said slowly. She stared into the other girl's lovely dark eyes, and felt a rush of furious jealousy that was like nothing she had experienced over Liza Northfield. "Miss Ellen Webster?" she asked, in a voice that wanted to shake with rage.

The young woman stiffened. "Who are you?"

Very deliberately, Roddy said, "Faelan Savigar's wife."

The revelation had all the impact she could have wished. Miss Ellen Webster stood immobile, her mind unable to cope with the announcement. *Wife*, she thought in horror. *Wife*.

Then her hand tightened on the banister. "You're lying," she hissed. "Leave here at once."

Roddy eyed her coolly. "I think 'tis you who should leave. I'm afraid my hospitality doesn't extend to tolerating Faelan's mistresses."

"*Mistress!*" Miss Ellen flew down the last step and grabbed Roddy's arm. "I'm no more his mistress than you're his wife! Get out, before he finds you here, or I shan't answer for the consequences!"

Roddy pulled free of the other girl's grasp. "Nor I," she said.

Her coolness increased Miss Ellen's panic. "Get out!" she cried, while her maid curled into a ball on the floor and sobbed harder. "*Get out!*"

Roddy laughed. Out of the searing pain of this new betrayal sprang a malicious mischief, a need to antagonize this girl with the lovely face and ugly thoughts. "Is he expected so soon? I'll wait, then."

She started for the stair.

"You can't!" Ellen clutched at Roddy's arm again. "He's going to marry *me!*"

Roddy stopped.

Ellen's mind was near hysteria. *He's coming,* she was thinking wildly. *His note—the money. He'll come to me. Not her, not her—He'll marry me—*

Roddy whirled on the other girl. "You've had a note from Faelan?"

Ellen stood back, her lips pressed together in mulish silence that shouted *Yes* to Roddy.

"What did it say?"

Meet him. Money. Elope. "I've had no note," Ellen snapped. "And I wouldn't speak of it to you if I had. I want you out of this house, else I shall have you thrown out."

Roddy stared at her, focusing her talent full on those delicate eyes. "What did the note say?"

Ellen set her full lip against speaking, but her mind couldn't help reviewing the lines she had memorized in her joy. *My Darling little girl, my love… fortune enough now for us to be happy together… whatever you wish shall be yours…* Through Ellen's eyes, Roddy saw the bold, familiar *F.S.* in signature. *Happy together*, Ellen thought again, with a hazy image of Faelan kissing her: a chaste, virgin's kiss that was nothing like what Roddy knew of him. *Happy together. And rich.*

Roddy had fallen from a horse once, flat onto hard-packed ground. This was what it had felt like—her ears rang and she could not get her breath, could not think or feel or move. Martha took Roddy's hand, murmuring words that made no sense to her. "Come away, mum, don't pay that slut no nevermind." It might have been spoken in words or might have been Martha's thought. Roddy was too stunned to know the difference. She followed Martha in a numb silence, out the door of Pelham Cottage and down to where the groom still waited in helpless puzzlement, not even knowing what to do with the horses.

It was only when she was seated again in the phaeton that she remembered why she had come. She sat still a moment, feeling the smooth leather between her fingers and the light, restless tugs of the horses at their bits.

Damn him, she thought. *Let him hang.*

❧

She was still in that mood three days later when he returned to Banain House.

She'd reasoned, in that time, that he was not actually planning to elope with Miss Ellen Webster. Perhaps Miss Ellen Webster had been led to believe so, but Roddy did not think Faelan was so stupid as to hope that Roddy's father would stand by and allow his son-in-law to abandon his wife and still keep her money.

And it was the money Faelan needed.

Roddy had known that, but she seemed to keep forgetting it. She let him lead her on and cajole her, kept playing with him a game at which he was a master and she was a dupe.

The same as Miss Ellen Webster. Poor Miss Ellen Webster. Much as Roddy hated the girl, she would not have wished on her the ruin that Faelan must have in mind.

Even the dowager countess knew. She worried and fretted and thought of Ellen constantly. As constantly as Lady Iveragh thought of anything. She never seemed to get very far in her logic. Roddy avoided her mother-in-law to the point of rudeness, eating in her own room and spending hours in the garden, keeping her barriers firmly in place. At night she lay awake until she was certain Lady Iveragh had taken her medicine and lay in dreamless sleep.

By the time her husband returned, Roddy was exhausted. She'd been lying in bed, trying to stay awake and escape the dowager countess' dreams by reading the most riveting book she could find in Faelan's library. But Volume Three of *Theory of the Earth; or, an Investigation of the Laws Observable in the Composition, Dissolution, and Restoration of Land upon the Globe* did not help much to keep her from drifting into the countess' nightmares and tumbling back. She jolted out of one to find the demonface turned tender and smiling as Faelan leaned over and touched her cheek.

"You're up late, little girl," he said softly, and eased the fallen book from her hands as he sat on the edge of the bed.

Roddy just looked at him. She felt her insides all knotted up and hurting, and knew nothing would come out of her mouth but a sob if she tried to speak.

He tilted his head. "You've been crying."

It wasn't true; she hadn't been, but at his words the tears welled up and made his face go to a blur of shadow and candlelight.

"Roddy," he said, and moved to take her in his arms. "Don't touch me," she cried. "And don't lie. *Please* don't lie to me anymore!"

He sat still, watching her. She realized she was probing wildly with her talent, but there was nothing there to guide her.

After a moment, he said, "Tell me what's happened."

"You know. She must have told you!"

He frowned. "I've just returned. I've spoken to no one."

Liar! her mind cried. *I hate you!* But she drew in a great, shuddering breath and spoke. "Geoffrey came. About the guns. I needed to find you, and I—I asked Minshall. He... told me about Pelham Cottage. So I went there. I went there, and I found..." She bit her lip, and said in a whisper, "Ellen Webster."

He turned his head at the name. Just a little. Just enough for Roddy to be certain that it meant something.

"Ellen Webster," he repeated softly. His lashes lowered, and he stared into the shadows, frowning faintly. "Dark-haired? And beautiful?"

"Very beautiful," Roddy said. Her voice was harsh and crisp, but it broke a little on the last syllable.

"Yes. I remember her."

"Remember her! Oh, God—" Roddy couldn't contain a sob. "Faelan—"

He glanced at her sideways. For a moment she read nothing in his face. Then his eyes focused on empty space with the arrested intent of a man hearing distant music. Like a shadow the change came, the darkness she was growing to know too well. His lips curved upward a little, into the grim smile of one of Lady Iveragh's dream-demons. When he looked at her again, his eyes were the blue of flames dancing deep in the hottest fire.

"Miss Webster. She was at this... Pelham House." He stood up, a sudden, violent move that belied the controlled tautness in his voice. He moved from the bedside to the dressing table and stood, staring at himself in the mirror. "I suppose you found that I've had a lover's correspondence with her, and she was expecting me to carry her away."

No regret. No remorse. "Do you think nothing of it?" Roddy cried. "To lie to me? To her? To ruin that poor girl, for your own..." Her lips twisted in disgust. "Did you enjoy her, Faelan? Have you told her the truth yet—that there'll be no elopement and no wedding and no money? Or do you plan—"

"Roddy," he said. "I warned you of this."

She had opened her mouth to add more bitter words. At that, she closed it.

Yes. He had warned her. And she had not believed him.

She hid her face in her hands and moaned. It was as if something had died. Something had: all her faith, all her hopes. She had gambled and lost. The Faelan whom she loved did not exist. There was only this silent man who offered no justification or reason for what he had done, who only said, "I warned you."

She moved suddenly, sliding off the bed without looking at him. Her bare feet hit cold wood, but she did not wait to find her slippers.

He caught her before she reached the door. His fingers dug cruelly into her arms, but the instant she jerked to a stop, his grip loosened. He held her, lightly but firmly, his chest not quite touching her back. "Little girl," he said, in a ragged voice. "Don't leave me now."

She stood rigid, refusing to answer. Refusing even to acknowledge that he held her fast.

"I need you," he whispered.

If he had tried to kiss her, tried to use the power that he had to make her body melt and burn, she could have resisted. She could have imagined him with Ellen Webster—a picture guaranteed to act like ice water on the fire. But he did not.

He only held her, with a faint, faint trembling in his fingers, and waited for her answer.

It's all an act, her reason warned her.

And: *He needs me*, her heart replied.

Against all evidence, all sane judgment and common sense… the barely perceptible tremor in a man's strong hands.

She did not give in to him. But neither did she pull away.

An eternity later, his touch slowly relaxed. She stood still as his palms slid upward, skimming her arms, outlining her shoulders, and then smoothing her hair. It was not a lover's touch—it was more like a child's: searching, memorizing, asking reassurance. *I need you*, that light, tentative contact said. *I need you*.

"They say I murdered my father," he said. It was hardly a whisper.

Her knees felt they would buckle beneath her.

"Did you?"

His hands stopped their restless motion. "Roddy—" She waited. She could not even hear him breathing. When she turned, he was staring into nothing.

"Did you?" she repeated.

"I don't remember." He looked at her. "Roddy, I don't remember."

Eleven

"I'VE NEVER HEARD OF PELHAM HOUSE," FAELAN SAID TO THE shadows on the far side of the room. "I've never written to Ellen Webster. But she was there. I don't doubt she was there. Waiting for me." His lips curved in the feral imitation of a smile. "You have a choice, you see. Your choice of a husband. A villain or a madman."

Roddy kept silence. The bitterness was on him, as she had felt it once before on a high Yorkshire cliff above the sea. He turned away and walked to the window, yanked open the velvet curtains, and threw the sash wide.

"A full moon," he sneered as the cold air poured inward. "Shall I howl?"

"Faelan—"

He gripped the curtains with an inhuman laugh. "Faelan! God, how fitting. Wolves do howl, don't they? Wolves and lunatics." He stood there, breathing harshly. Then he clasped his hands hard around his head and slid slowly to his knees, his fine, strong fingers white against the black of his hair. "Lunatics," he whispered. "Oh, God…" He leaned on the sill. "I don't remember. Roddy—I swear it, I swear—I don't remember."

"It doesn't matter," she said: a stupid thing, because she knew nothing else to say. She only stood there, with the wind blowing her gown in soft billows around her.

He came to his feet in a sudden, lithe move and began a restless circuit of the room. His slanted look back toward her held watchfulness: the mingled distrust and hope of a half-wild animal, lost and hunted and longing for shelter. "It matters," he said in a voice that was cracked. Driven. "After my father..." He paused, and then took a shuddering breath and spoke with unnatural calm. "After my father was killed, they sent me to England. My mother told Adam it was Iveragh. She said that place would drive anyone mad." He gave a hollow chuckle. "Dear Mamá. She's afraid of me. She hates being in the same house with me. I suppose she thinks I'll push her over the stair rail some night in a frenzy." The moonlight caught the blue glitter in his eyes. "I've thought of it, by God—watching them drain Iveragh dry. Like a pair of vampires."

There was savagery in his voice, and a kind of challenge. See what I am, he seemed to be saying. I hate. I want to hurt the ones who've destroyed what I love.

"So they sent me to school," he said—not to Roddy, but to the bed, the chairs, to anything that was not alive. "And things began to... happen. Animals. Beneath my window, in the morning—they'd find..." He stopped in front of the dressing table, looking at something dark and far away. After a long moment, he said roughly, "Mostly cats and hares." He spread his fingers wide. "They'd pull us out of bed and line us up, all in our nightshirts and barefoot—and God, it was so cold. I was always last, I had to stand there while they went down the row... and they would come to me... they knew it... the way they looked at me..." He stared at his image in the mirror. "The others were all white. All clean. And they made me the last; they went down the whole row every time, even when I was standing there... all spotted with it—on my shirt and my hands... and they held up the animal, and they asked me..."

His voice trailed into silence. The night wind blew in the window, lifting the curtains and ruffling his hair.

"I always told them no," he said suddenly. "I didn't do that." His mouth grew taut and dangerous, and with a move so swift that Roddy had no time to interpret it, he swung his fist in a backhanded arc and slammed it into his reflection.

The glass exploded in the silent room. Roddy jumped back, her eyes squeezed shut, and opened them an instant later to see him close his bleeding palm around the shards in his hand. "I didn't do that," he repeated in a strangled whisper. "I couldn't have."

Roddy moved. There was a panic in him, in the way he tightened his fingers until she was sure the glass must be driving jagged edges deep into his hand. He stood motionless, but she sensed a breaking point, a violence that threatened to erupt in far more than the destruction of a mirror. With the same instinct that had aided her in calming a stricken mare, she went to him and touched his shoulder, slid her hand through his hair, and drew him into her arms. He was stiff a moment, resisting, and then an instant later he leaned against her. The shards fell tinkling to the floor. He turned his face into her body with a rough, clinging move, as if to hide what she might see.

She waited, smoothing his hair down over the high, stiff fold of his neckcloth.

"I should have told you," he said. His voice was peculiar and thick against the gown. "I tried to. But I just… wanted to go home. You were the only way left. When you looked at me—those eyes of yours—" He shifted, moving away from her, but not far enough to break her touch. "You're so damned wild and lovely," he said. "I just couldn't let go. When I saw you with Cashel—" The name choked in his throat. "That bloody whoremongering hero—my friend, the only one who's stood at my back, knowing what I am…" His hand tightened around her hips. "I wanted to murder him for touching you. I wanted to put a bullet through his damned noble brain, and then—God—you came to me and said you didn't want me… and, Roddy… I was afraid of what I might do. I didn't sleep; I went off, as far as I could, and I never let myself sleep until I was sure that Cashel must be out of the country."

He pushed her away and slid his fingers around her wrist, turning her palm upward and staring down at the bright smear of his blood on her skin. "I've loved three things I can remember. Iveragh and Geoff. You. If ever I hurt any one of them—" He closed his eyes, and with a gentle, terrible certainty, whispered, "In the name of God—I'll kill myself."

She gazed up at him, and realized something in that moment: how Geoffrey's loyalty to Faelan was an ideal of the mind, of reason and philosophy, while Faelan counted his honor in more primitive terms. In lifeblood and love. No elevated sentiments. Just a quiet, deadly promise: *If I fail you…*

Madness. It had a horrible, improbable logic. It explained a score of things. But the shock of his admission blunted feeling or response. Once before, she had felt this way—long ago when a favorite dog had died. Dry. Emotionless. Unable to accept the reality when she had seen the beloved brown eyes close forever. Instead of the weeping hysteria it seemed she ought to feel, she found that a brisk, numb practicality directed her movements and her words.

"Sit down," she said. "Of course you'd never hurt me. 'Tis you who're hurt." She lifted his bleeding hand and reached for one of the towels that hung beside the dressing table, wrapping the cloth firmly around his wounded palm. With the other towel, she brushed broken glass from the needlepoint bench-cushion, pushing the wicked shards onto the floor as if they were so much insignificant dust.

She looked up into his eyes and splayed her hand on his chest, exerting just the slightest pressure to urge him onto the bench. For a moment, she thought he would resist. His face was tight and strange. Beneath her palm, his chest rose, making her vividly aware of the leashed power under her hand.

He held her gaze an infinite moment, a battle of wills that Roddy was afraid to lose. She summoned concentration, put all the force of her mind and heart behind her talent. It was a look that would have penetrated fathoms deep in any mind but his.

He stared down at her, a long uncertainty. Then, with a sudden rush, the air went out of him. The taut, wild look faded from his face. His thick eyelashes fell. When they rose again, it was as if he saw her anew, as if they were both different people from the ones they had been an instant before.

The corner of his mouth tilted upward. He murmured, "*Cailin sidhe*. Is this the Evil Eye?"

Roddy relaxed. The panic was gone, then, the black spell broken. In the flood of relief at finding reason in his eyes again, she adopted a cheerful, deliberate normality. Better to ignore it all for now, to pretend it hadn't happened. "Quite possibly." She leaned forward and gave his chin a kiss. "Sit down and tell me about your cows while I dress your hand."

In silence, she searched for handkerchiefs and pins to secure a makeshift bandage. She had no desire to call Jane. Morning would be soon enough to explain the mirror. Roddy filled the basin with water from her pitcher and dipped a bit of linen into the clear liquid.

Faelan held up his hand when she had finished her dressing. He inspected the broad, red patch soaking through the lace with a grim smile. "Not very effective, I fear. Bits of fairy moss and moonbeams might have done better work, *cailin sidhe*."

She smiled briefly, relieved that his humor held, along with the fragile pretense that nothing was hideously wrong. She hesitated a moment, and then said, "I went to Islington to find you because there's a problem with Geoffrey's guns."

"Ah," he said carelessly. He left the bench and sat down on the bed, beginning to unbutton his coat. "Those slipshod French. Have they forgotten to include the powder and ball?"

Faelan was obviously not a starry-eyed Irish patriot. Roddy frowned at him. "It doesn't worry you at all, to have illegal arms smuggled through Iveragh?"

He looked sideways back toward her. "Just what is this problem?"

"They can't be moved for a month. Geoffrey wants you to postpone your work."

"A month be damned! I gave him until the twentieth of October. That was yesterday."

"The army is camped in the district. Geoffrey's men can't get through on the road."

"Christ!" Faelan threw his head back and moaned. "Spare us the Irish army. Buffoons blocking clowns on the road out of Iveragh. For God's sake—must Geoffrey's fine strapping rebels have a highway paved with gold? There're other ways across the mountains."

"The local lieutenant has taken ill. Geoffrey says no one else knows the country."

Faelan pried at the heel of one boot with the toe of the other. "I do."

She looked sharply at him. He bent over and yanked the boot free.

"Faelan—"

He sat up. "Are you packed?"

"We can't go yet."

"The devil we can't. We leave tomorrow."

"But Geoffrey said—"

"Damn what Geoffrey *said*. If he came after me, it's because he needs me to clean up his mess."

Roddy opened her mouth to protest, and closed it. She stared at him as he worked on the second boot. That hope *had* been in Geoffrey's mind. Underneath all the panic.

Faelan tossed the second boot after the first. "What did you think—that he ran back here just to save my hide? 'Don't start any work.' What the deuce difference would work make? I was hardly going to bring in King George to start draining the bog."

He pulled off his coat. Roddy stood watching him, chewing on her lower lip. His sprigged white waistcoat followed the coat onto a chair. As he began to unbutton his shirt she said, "I think you should stay away from there."

He looked up from loosening his cuff.

"I'm afraid for you," she whispered. She rubbed her flannel gown between her thumb and forefinger. "I know why you did it. The bargain you made, to let Geoffrey use Iveragh."

Faelan raised an eyebrow. "My Lord Cashel seems to have developed a bad habit of running on at the mouth." He watched her a moment, his gaze drifting down to where her fingers worked at the gown. He reached out suddenly and drew her toward him, pulling her between his knees. "Do you hate me for it?"

"I suppose… you had no choice."

He rocked her gently side to side. "Are you packed?"

"Yes."

He grinned and caught her chin, drawing her down to his mouth. His shoulders were broad and warm beneath her hands. He kissed her lips, then her throat and breasts, his fingers cupping their weight through the gown. With a low growl, he pulled her close, burying his face against her. "Between French muskets and you, I know who had the best end of the bargain."

She arched a little as his hands slid down and his thumbs followed the curves and hollows of her body to the joining of her legs. "Faelan," she said, "I want to talk about this."

"We're going." He didn't look up from his provocative exploration. "Tomorrow."

"Can't we even wait—" She drew in a quick breath, and forgot her train of thought as he found the tender, sweet warmth between her thighs. "Faelan…"

She leaned on him. While his hands pleasured her below, his tongue circled and flicked over her nipple, a rough, tingling delight through the flannel gown. His legs closed against her and he lay slowly back, dragging her inexorably with him until she had to sprawl with her full weight on him and the hard evidence of his intentions pressed into her belly. She lay there, feeling each breath that he took lift her, as lightly and easily as a leaf.

He could be a killer. There was that much power in the hands that ran over her hips and loins, in the shoulders and smooth torso beneath her. He smiled at her as she looked down at him, no madness in his face, nothing in those eyes but the depths of the sky and a faintly wolfish, male anticipation. It was as if that moment by the mirror had never been.

She found herself glad—too glad—to forget it. She focused instead on the other question he had made her forget so easily. "Why do we have to go so soon?"

His thick lashes lowered in indulgence. "I want to be there on November Eve."

"Why?"

The hesitation was slight, just a flick of his gaze to some unfocused point behind her ear and then back again. His smile turned into a wicked grin. "You'll see." He wrapped his arms around her and rolled her onto her back, propping himself on his elbow as he leaned across her. Golden hair fell in a cascade from his bandaged hand. "*Cailin sidhe*," he said, playing with a strand. "You'll see."

✎

Before dawn he was up, like a child on fair day. Roddy woke to the mutter and mental groans from the powder closet of a valet rung out of bed and put to work shaving before he had the sleep out of his eyes. She buried her face in her pillow, thinking that Faelan might not have trusted the man with a razor if he'd known just how violent the poor fellow felt about his rude awakening.

Jane bustled into the room, in just as foul a mood as the valet. She stopped short of shaking Roddy out of bed in order that everyone might suffer together, but the maid didn't hesitate to rattle the tea tray or slam the wardrobe door a shade too loudly. She walked around to Roddy's side of the bed, and suddenly her early-morning grumbling blossomed into shock.

"Gracious Lud! What's this—"

Roddy sat up, coming full awake with an unpleasant jolt. She glanced at the glittering shards that covered the floor and the bloodstains in the washbowl and on the discarded linen. "Oh—yes!" She struggled to gain command of herself, searching frantically for an explanation. Finally she faked a yawn as she flopped back down into the bedclothes. "'Twas an accident, Jane." She affected a bored drawl. "I couldn't get one of those ridiculous hairpins out of my hair, and I was so furious I just—threw my brush. I never thought it would come *near* the mirror."

Jane rushed to the bedside. "La—you didn't hurt yourself, m'lady? I'll ne'er forgive m'self if you've taken a cut and it goes inflamed. Lawks, what would I say to your dear mother? You might have called, m'lady, by all that's holy, you might have—"

"Oh, I'm not even scratched!" Roddy exclaimed quickly, seeing Jane descending upon her purposefully. "'Twas His Lordship who—"

Before the sentence was even completed, Roddy realized her mistake. Jane—no admirer of His Lordship—recoiled in immediate suspicion. She glanced again at the mirror, and back at Roddy. *Drunk*, Jane thought in quick disgust. *Drunk and breakin' things again.*

Roddy had forgotten that the earlier incident of the music box and decanter would certainly be common knowledge in the servants' quarters. She felt herself blushing for her lie, and Jane noticed the flush with growing fury. Ever since the maid had been told that the trip to Ireland was imminent, she'd been gathering spite against the earl. Stories of Iveragh, begun by the dowager countess and embellished by Tilly, had grown to frightening proportions. *Live in a ruin*, Jane fumed. *Happen the roof'll cave in on me. Happen t' place'll be haunted.* She darted a venomous glance toward the closed door of the dressing room. *Happen that black devil'll murder us all in our beds.*

"Jane," Roddy said sharply. She sat up and frowned at her maid. "Bring my dressing gown. And call the charwoman to clean this up."

"Yes, m'lady." Jane dropped a quick curtsy and obeyed. Roddy stayed abed until the mess was cleared and a new mirrored dressing table brought in from a guest room. Jane fussed about, taking things out of drawers and rearranging them, and then helped Roddy into her dressing gown and followed her to the vanity, beginning to brush Roddy's hair without a word.

After a few silent moments, Roddy said quietly, "I know you don't want to go to Ireland."

Jane's hand didn't pause in its even stroke. She was long accustomed to Roddy's uncanny understanding. "No, m'lady," she said, and shut her lips tight.

This was her stoic act, but Roddy had no patience with it this morning. "Then you shan't go," she said.

That time Jane's hand did falter, but Roddy countered the maid's relieved misunderstanding immediately. "I'll go without you. You may return to my mother."

Instantly, Jane reversed her stance. "I'll do no such thing, m'lady! Why, I'd ne'er go back and tell your sweet mother that I left you to that—" She stopped her tongue in time, but Roddy knew the rest well enough. Jane began brushing again, refusing to meet her mistress' eyes in the mirror.

"I shan't tolerate disrespect for my husband," Roddy said softly, and nearly stopped there, for Jane was already crushed by such unfamiliar harshness as an open reprimand. But Roddy had made up her mind. She said as gently as she could, "You can't go with a glad heart, Jane, and therefore, you shall not go at all."

"M'lady—"

"No." She finally met Jane's eyes in the glass, and felt the shock and quick recoil in the maid's mind.

Jane bowed her head and began to brush vigorously. There were tears pricking her eyes, but her lips were pressed together desperately tight.

"I'll send a letter to my mother," Roddy said, addressing Jane's greatest fear. "You may be sure there'll be nothing but praise in it."

"And who will take proper care of you, m'lady?" Jane asked stiffly.

"I shall take Martha."

"Martha…" For a moment, Jane could not place the name. Then her bosom swelled. "The *chambermaid?* Oh, m'lady, I couldn't—"

A sound at the dressing-room door forestalled further argument. Faelan strode into the bedchamber. He stopped behind Roddy and gathered up a thick fall of her loosened hair. He said nothing about the new dressing table. He did not even look at it. With a smile that held no hint of the night before, he lifted the curling strands to his lips. "Laggard. You aren't dressed."

Jane withdrew, silently. She was suddenly quite glad to be given a reason not to go to Iveragh. His Lordship in the shadowy candlelight looked like Satan underlit by hell.

Roddy found it was easy to respond to him, to pretend to go on just as they had. Far easier than acknowledging the darkness that underlay her airy words. "As it isn't even dawn yet, my lord, you're fortunate to find me awake at all."

"Your time of day, *cailin sidhe*. I'll go down to the garden and bring you back a cup of fairy wine."

Roddy made a face. "Strong tea would be more the thing."

She looked at him in the mirror. His teeth flashed white in a lecherous grin. He bent over and crossed his arm beneath her throat, forcing her chin up for a deep and lingering kiss. For just a moment, his forearm pressed too hard into her windpipe, and then the kiss broke and she could breathe again. "Good morning, little girl," he murmured, resting his forehead on his encircling arm, trapping her with him into a small, close world. She could feel the cool dampness of his cheek against hers and smell the lingering tang of shaving soap. His arms were heavy and warm on her shoulders.

I love you, she thought, with a sudden fierceness. *You are not mad. You cannot be.*

He turned his head and took a deep breath in the mass of her hair. His arm tightened for just a moment, and then he straightened and stood back. "We leave at half past nine," he said, starting for the door.

Roddy looked after him, surprised. "But your mother won't be up."

"Will she not?" He smiled wryly. "I'm prostrate with grief over that circumstance."

He did contrive to look a little guilty, which made Roddy laugh. He went out the door with an answering grin.

Three hours later, in her traveling dress, Roddy was helping herself to eggs and deviled kidneys from the sideboard in what was whimsically called the "small" dining room, a silk-hung cavern that Roddy estimated to be the size of one of her father's horse barns. The sun was full up and streaming through the tall windows. In the morning cheerfulness, the scene with Faelan the night before seemed like a dream, and just as easily dismissed. She filled her plate and rang for tea, sitting down and beginning to eat without delay, since it was already quite close to the time declared for departure.

In the courtyard below the windows, all was calm and organized haste, the last-minute loading of trunks and adjusting of harness, the eagerness of four fresh coach horses and the soothing, nonsensical babble of experienced grooms with their charges. Faelan was there, standing at the top of the front steps, not giving orders, but just watching—Roddy knew that because the earl's presence made the head coachman especially careful and efficient with his orders.

Roddy sensed the stranger before anyone outside noticed him. The blast of emotion was like an unexpected summer storm—a gust of anger from a distance, then a growing rumble and the electric shock of hysterical fury so close that it made her start. She stood up quickly and went to the window. A tall gentleman strode across the gravel yard, a figure who had not lost his gangling, youthful gait—or whose walk was rendered jerky and awkward by his agitated state. His eyes were pinned with malevolent hatred on the carriage emblazoned with Iveragh's crest, and his thoughts overrode every other.

Run, will he? Bastard—bloody, stinking bastard—Kill him. Cut his rutting heart out and let the pigs eat his—The young man saw Faelan, and the mental litany lost coherence and exploded into rushing images of violence and obscenity. He almost broke into a run, but a last shred of rationality made him hold on to his pride. He stiffened to a measured tread, heading for the steps of Banain House with white face and set lips.

Roddy ran out of the dining room and into the hall. She reached the front door and stepped out just as the stranger halted at the foot of the wide limestone stairs.

The bustle in the courtyard had come to a stop. "Iveragh," the young man hissed, in a tone that rang in the suddenly silent yard. "Name your friends!"

Roddy saw only Faelan's profile. He did not move, but it seemed to her that he changed, grew dangerous and still, staring down at the other man as a great baleful wolf would eye the terrier snarling at its feet: in contempt and affront and the certain knowledge that one slash of its yellow fangs would send this puppy broken and dying out of its path.

"I have no friends," Faelan said softly.

It was an insult, that departure from formula, and the young man lost his battered wits. He took a half step onto the lowest stair and cried, "Name them, you blackhearted son of a bitch, or I'll shoot you where you stand."

He moved to reach inside his coat, but the heavy coachman was already on him. The pair fell back a disorganized step, struggling.

"Let him go." Faelan's voice cut the sound of the scuffle and the morning air. "There'll be no killing."

The coachman obeyed that commanding tone by instinct. But he gave his captive a little shove as he was released, a reminder that there was force standing close behind. The coachman judged a man by the way he treated his horses, and the Earl of Iveragh had the servant's unreserved devotion. *No killin'*, the coachman snorted to himself as he eyed the intruder. *Damn right.*

Through her gift, Roddy felt the stranger's furious humiliation: all the power of that slight, scornful curl of her husband's lips to make the younger man feel the blighting shame of his now-disheveled coat and hair. He was near tears, this angry gentleman, half hysterical with the force of his hate and fear—a fear which only made his hate the greater, for it made him despise himself.

"Mr. Webster, I collect," Faelan said calmly.

"You may keep our name out of your filthy mouth." Mr. Webster's blustering words shook noticeably, but he refused to acknowledge it. "Do you deny my right to demand a meeting?"

Faelan smiled lazily, but Roddy saw the slight narrowing of his eyes and the way his jaw grew taut. "Your rights are a matter of complete indifference to me, Mr. Webster."

The young man struggled for some rejoinder that would convey the intensity of his threat, but could only find sense enough to shout, "I'll have satisfaction!"

"Satisfaction for what?" Faelan asked silkily.

My sister! Mr. Webster's mind howled. *I'll kill you!* But he kept his mouth closed in front of the servants. His eyes flicked to Roddy and registered a gentlewoman's dress, but his thoughts were all on Faelan's perfidy. He mastered his voice and said harshly, "For your presence at the house called Pelham Cottage these four nights past."

"I'm afraid that you're misinformed."

Mr. Webster shook off the coachman's hands. "And you're unspeakable vermin." He spat on the step below Faelan's boots. "Come down, Iveragh, and let me spit in your face if you're afraid to meet me honorably."

An unearthly silence filled the courtyard, and suddenly the young fire-eater was frightened of what he had done. He thrust his chin out and looked up at Faelan, defiance and terror quivering on his lips.

"Mr. Webster," Faelan murmured, "I'll not murder a promising gentleman such as yourself for the sake of your lying whore of a sister."

Mr. Webster lunged forward, but the coachman was there to hold him before he took a full step. "You—" He almost choked on his emotion, and then screamed, "You filthy, blackguarding fiend!" He drew a sobbing breath and gasped, "The law will give me redress in this!"

Faelan moved for the first time, descending the steps and jerking Webster's chin up with a black-gloved hand as the younger man stood pinned in the coachman's burly grip. "I daresay it might, if you cared to place your sister's name on a level with mine." When Faelan's hand came away there were red marks of pressure on Mr. Webster's smooth cheeks. "I advise you to resist the temptation. Your sister is lying to you, my friend. I have any number of witnesses who can testify that I was in Hampshire until yesterday noon."

Webster half stumbled as the coachman let him go. For a moment he almost threw himself at his adversary's throat. But pride and a sudden doubt saved him from another useless defiance. *She told me; she named you—conniving, slimy son of a bitch—witnesses! And Ellen—*A vision of his sister displayed to public ridicule in the courts and in the press made bile rise in his throat.

He drew himself up. Somewhere in the frenzy of hate and defeat he found the only recourse left to him: a gentleman's weapons. He slid a look of pure loathing from Faelan's boots to his face, and then settled that contemptuous gaze deliberately on the hand that had touched him.

"Permit me to take leave, then." His lip curled with venomous hauteur. "I wish to return home and *bathe*."

Twelve

FAELAN SAT SLUMPED IN SILENCE, HIS EXTENDED LEG SWAYING slightly with the roll of the carriage. He had not said a word for four hours. They were nearing Gravesend; Roddy knew so because the coachman, perched on the box and sharing a rug with Martha—who was hogging it—was thinking warm thoughts of mulled ale and a meat pasty.

Roddy hated the silence inside the vehicle. She hated the way Faelan had changed, from the laughing devil of the morning to this grim remoteness. There was a violence to the set of his mouth, a vacant and haunted look in his eyes that frightened her.

This morning it had been easy to be sure of him. He had seemed so much the man she loved. The man she wanted him to be.

But now...

She watched him from the corner of her eye, phrasing and rephrasing empty words of comfort—words mocked by the questions that burned through her mind.

Ellen had lied, she had made it all up.

But I know that she didn't.

He was in Hampshire. He has witnesses.

But she had a note from him.

"'My Darling,'" that note had said, "'My Darling little girl.'"

Oh, God, he is not mad. I would rather he was lying.

But she looked at him, silent and dark and unmoving, and saw again the inhuman tension that marked his mouth and eyes.

She remembered what he had done once for her in a dim-lit, rocking carriage, and she reached out her hand and touched his. He turned his head at the move, looking down at where her glove overlay his own. For a moment, she thought he would pull away, but then his large hand shifted. He gripped her fingers in a fierce and awkward squeeze.

She returned the pressure of his hand. "I believe you." She spoke just loud enough to be heard above the sound of the wheels.

He smiled, bitterly. "Believe me? Believe what?"

"You never went to Ellen Webster. You were with me last night. You were in Hampshire before that. And if you have friends there who can prove—"

"Witnesses?" His laugh was short. "If you believe that, you're as easy as young Webster. I can't produce any witnesses, my dear."

She felt her heart drop in her chest.

He released her hand and turned away to the window. "I went into Hampshire… anonymously, shall we call it that? It was a business convenience. I was interested in the auction of a particular lot of breeding stock, and—" The line of his mouth deepened. "To put it politely, there are those who won't deal with the Devil Earl."

She felt a surge of wifely indignation. "Won't even sell you cattle?"

"I fear not." His winter-blue gaze slid toward her. He said softly, "You see, I killed the consignor's son."

Roddy stared at her hand, still resting on the seat between them.

"You needn't worry for your husband, my love," he said with cold irony. "I shan't be forced to flee the country. It was a long time ago, and neither the seconds nor the doctor have ever talked. My reputation is of some effect in these matters."

The carriage jolted over a rut. Roddy shifted and grabbed the strap, seeking that small stability in a world that seemed to have lost all balance.

"But you were in Hampshire," she said doggedly. "*You* know that."

"Does it exonerate me?" His look mocked her. "Yes—of course. If you've been to this Pelham House, it must be in the city. Therefore I must be certain I haven't been there recently."

She dropped her eyelashes in discomfort.

"I'm greatly relieved," he said dryly. "I'm sure I haven't a broomstick fast enough to carry me between Salisbury and London in the space of a night. But then, perhaps I only imagined I was in Salisbury. One can have such odd fancies sometimes."

She frowned. "Don't be ridiculous. If you were there, you were there."

"Ah. While at the same time Miss Webster dallied somewhere in London with a man she mistook for me."

Roddy pretended to look out her window, not wanting him to see the doubt in her eyes. She knew—oh, she knew—that Ellen Webster would never have mistaken another man for Faelan. "She just thought you would come," Roddy said sharply. "She had that silly note, and she thought..." Roddy waved her hand helplessly, lost between what she knew of Ellen's thoughts and what flew in the face of all logic. And the note, the note itself—

"Can you recognize my handwriting?" Faelan said suddenly.

Roddy jumped, caught out in her own speculation. She gripped her hands together in her lap and shrugged. "I doubt it," she lied. "I haven't seen it often."

"Did you see the note?"

F.S. burned before her eyes, the telltale slash and curve of letters like none other, and no figment of Ellen Webster's imagining. "No," Roddy said. "I didn't see it."

He was silent a moment, and then said in a different voice, "So you think she was lying?"

Anything, *anything* to keep from facing the alternatives.

"Yes," she said with feeling. "I'm certain of it."

She felt his eyes on her. To refuse to meet that look was to admit her doubt. She thought of him the night before, standing amidst the glittering remains of the mirror, his body taut with a perilous vibrancy, like a thread stretched within a hairsbreadth of its strength. Against that floated better memories: his laughter, precious in its rarity, and his kisses, just as priceless in their abundance.

She could doubt him and lose him for certain. Or she could go on hoping.

The choice was so simple that it surprised her. She lifted her eyes and smiled into his, a fierce smile, made of loyalty and determination in place of pleasure.

He did not answer it at first. Then the carriage rolled again, leaning her toward him and away. He caught her as she swayed and drew her hard against him. His arms curved around her shoulders and under her breasts, crushing her back into his chest as he bent over and buried his face in the curve of her throat. He said nothing, only held her until the tightness of his embrace made foggy insensibility hover at the edges of her vision. She said his name, faintly, and gasped a quick breath when his hold loosened.

He moved back, pulling her with him into the corner of the rocking coach, so that she sat in his arms, her spine braced against his chest as he took her hands in his and locked their fingers together. They sat so for a long time, not speaking. Finally he pulled one hand away a little and caressed her skin above her glove.

"Roddy," he said softly. "Do you know why I refused Webster's challenge today?"

She wet her lips. *Please*, she thought. *Please don't say because he was right.*

"Don't you?" he repeated.

She shook her head.

He wrapped his hand around hers and squeezed. "Because, *cailin sidhe*—I didn't want to get shot."

Roddy frowned, defeated by that simplicity. She turned a little, just enough to give his lips access to her ear. "Has that never stopped you before?" she whispered.

His low laughter kissed her skin with warmth. "No. That's the irony of a duel, little girl. The man who cares the least for living has the steadiest hand."

They sat with Geoffrey in a private parlor in the White Lion. Mary had been banished, and Faelan stretched out in a chair with a brandy cupped between his hands. Geoffrey drummed on a marble tabletop, glaring meaningfully at Roddy, his fingerprints marring the polish that gleamed in the late-afternoon sun.

Roddy stood up, a move which pleased Geoffrey, and positioned herself firmly in front of her husband, a move which did not have the same lightening effect on Cashel's mood.

"My lord," she informed Faelan with regal politeness, "you may wish to know that I intend to be placed in complete possession of any and all facts concerning smuggling and other acts of treason that might affect your health and well-being." She took a deep breath at the end of this speech, which she had been memorizing an hour since, and added, "*I am not leaving.*"

A faint, familiar twitch played at the corner of Faelan's mouth. The light from the high, small window made a reddish halo around his cropped black hair. "Then you shall stay. By all means, let us have no secrets between us."

"Here now," Geoffrey protested. "I won't have Roddy involved in this."

Faelan raised his dark brows and fixed his friend with a look that Roddy dearly wished she might learn to emulate. "Your concern does you credit, I'm sure. But the sentiment is a bit belated, don't you think, Geoff?"

Geoffrey frowned, as much at the unexpected sight of Roddy laying her hand trustingly across her husband's shoulder as at the pointed rebuff. Geoffrey stared at them a moment while Faelan drew Roddy against him, and then a slow smile touched Lord Cashel's classical features.

"This is a cozy picture," he said. "I should have known you'd talk her out of the sulks."

Roddy lifted her own eyebrows, trying to glare him into submission as Faelan had. She had even less success. Though Geoffrey looked away, his smile turned into a grin.

"Down, poppet. You could kill at thirty paces with those eyes."

"Which is likely more than you can do with your smuggled muskets," Faelan said. "Are you going to tell me your woes, my friend, or shall we sit here all night discussing our female companions?"

A brief, provocative vision of Geoffrey's latest chamber-maid flashed into the other man's mind at the words. Roddy blushed, disturbed by the easy way in which Geoffrey could forget his high-minded love for his wife at the mere recol-lection of a tempting tavern wench. But Roddy had begun lately to develop a new insight into her old friend. Geoffrey did not forget Mary, exactly. It was more as if his feelings for his wife existed on some different and separate plane from the urges of his body. He loved Mary as he would love a work of art or a graceful sonnet—in that ethereal realm of reason and philosophy where Roddy, grounded in emotion and human passion, had never been able to follow him.

Modest, perfect Mary was worthy of such spiritual love, but Roddy found herself wondering how the two of them had managed to conceive an heir.

"Poppet," Geoffrey said, in a last effort to be rid of her, "I know Mary'd like your company. She's been... restless, you understand—cooped up here at an inn for two weeks."

This polite reference to Mary's condition was calculated to appeal to Roddy's feminine instincts, instincts that Geoffrey grossly overestimated. She was saved from a tart answer by Faelan's arm tightening around her waist.

"She'll stay," he said. "I want her here." He drew a frayed footstool up with his toe and crossed his booted ankles comfortably. "Get on with it, Robespierre. The revolution won't wait all day."

Geoffrey took that shaft with an equanimity that surprised Roddy. She would never have been so rash as to ridicule Lord Cashel's political ideals. He only shrugged, giving up on evicting Roddy in the face of Faelan's stated desire, and launched into a detailed explanation of the situation.

It was much as Roddy had told Faelan before. The guns were hidden in the great house at Iveragh, and the road out of the isolated estate blocked by the militia. Geoffrey had received even worse word since—his stricken lieutenant had died, and the rebels were without local leadership. Rumors of the guns were already spreading, and the army was showing signs of dangerous curiosity. A simple murder of the archeologically minded parson in Ballybrack would no longer be enough to protect the secret.

Faelan listened to that, and more, in silence. Roddy tried to keep her expression controlled, hiding her horror at Geoffrey's matter-of-fact talk of killing. As easily as he violated his marital vows, he seemed to have forgotten that the parson in Ballybrack was a human being, with hopes and dreams and loved ones, instead of just a negative numeral in the great equation of liberty.

Geoffrey finished, and no one spoke for a long moment. Faelan took an idle sip of his brandy. "You've been landing in Saint Finian's Bay?"

"Aye. You know the spot."

"As does half the loyal militia, I'm sure." He smiled down into his glass and shook his head. "You may be about to catapult us all to freedom with rhetoric, Geoff, but you're a damned poor hand at reality. Did you never think to appoint a second in command?"

In Geoffrey's response to that comment, Roddy saw a glimpse of the strange camaraderie that made these two disparate men friends. Instead of the affront Roddy had expected, Geoffrey sighed and said, "God knows, you're right about reality. Morley *was* second. I was to be there myself, if this blasted militia situation hadn't developed. I suppose I should have appointed a third and a fourth, and a fifth as well, and you don't have to say it—I damn well know you would have, and I wish you'd have handled the whole thing as I asked you in the first place."

"You flatter me," Faelan said mildly. "And I thought I was only good for raking stables."

"Planting potatoes, I think it was." Geoffrey grinned, unashamed, exerting his charm as easily as he breathed. Roddy was amazed to see her husband smile back—a slow, deep smile that lit his eyes and changed his face.

"What would I be," he said softly, "without you to rescue, my friend?"

Geoffrey shrugged, hearing only Faelan's cynical humor where Roddy heard much more. *I've loved three things I can remember*, Faelan had said… and one of them was Geoffrey.

She bowed her head and closed her fingers on her husband's shoulder, feeling the smooth texture of living muscle beneath his coat. It frightened her, to see that light in his eyes, to watch the unreserved curve of his lips. She knew what love meant to him now. She could lose him, to the ideals of a man who thought nothing of murdering an innocent parson in Ballybrack.

"We'll need a ship," Faelan said, the smile vanishing as he turned to business. "Contact the O'Connells at Derrynane this time—tell them you'll be wanting to land a small orchestra there… just a harp and a few violins. Four white horses of impressive size and high action, the worse-tempered the better. A score of the most elegant rebels or Frenchmen you can scrape together, and a dance partner for each one. Full ball dress for the dancers," he added tonelessly. "Preferably a quarter century out of style. Wigs and powder and all the paste jewelry you can muster."

Roddy and Geoffrey stared at him, both convinced he had lost his senses.

He met their incredulous looks with a particularly demonic grin. "Have I ever failed you, Geoff?"

Geoffrey, having created the muddle, kept his questions to himself and shook his head.

"November Eve." Faelan stood up, kicking the stool back into its earlier position. The corner of the rug flipped back under one mahogany leg, revealing a clean, smooth spot in the dented floor. "Have the horses concealed at Cahirciveen before dark; the musicians and dancers and the gun carts—manned and ready to load—at the great house at quarter till midnight. Your guns will be past Blackwater Bridge by morning." He turned to Roddy and offered his arm. "I've ordered dinner for eight. Will you and Mary join us here?"

"Certainly." Geoffrey was miffed at the glaring lack of any explanation for Faelan's weird requests, but he was chary of his friend's uncertain temper. That Faelan could save the guns

Geoffrey never doubted, and he had no desire to jeopardize the commitment by crossing Faelan's mood. *Let him have his fun*, Geoffrey thought. *And get back to his damned potatoes.*

Roddy hung back a little as Faelan started for the door. "My lord," she said. "I'll join you in a moment, if you please."

He paused, looked at her and then at Geoffrey. The warm grip on her arm loosened. "Of course," he said, in a chillingly neutral voice. Before she could make up an excuse—a word with Mary, or some other reason to linger alone with Geoffrey—her husband had opened the door and shut it behind him.

She stood frowning at the heavy wood, sure that he had jumped to old conclusions. It made her angry, to realize even a moment alone with another man was enough to spark his jealousy, when she had reason enough to believe he had spent four entire days ravishing a besotted *débutante*. She said sharply, "I'd like a word with you, Lord Geoffrey."

Geoffrey had been deep in trying to puzzle out Faelan's peculiar plans, but the tone of her voice made him look up quickly.

Roddy grimaced at his cheerful response. It was outside of enough, she thought, to have a murdering rebel bent on high treason turn to one and ask, "What's to do, poppet?"

"I've found out that Faelan keeps other women," she said boldly, hoping to jolt clear truth into his head by her brazenness.

It didn't work. Instead of dwelling on Faelan's sins, Geoffrey immediately took Roddy herself to task. "Good God, madam," he said stiffly. "That's no fit topic to bring up with me."

Roddy tried to catch his eye, but he would not look at her. He turned away to the writing desk. *Little hussy*, he fumed. *Knew she'd never make a proper wife. What the devil can he want with musicians?* Already lists of possible recruits were forming in his mind, and he reached for a pen and inkwell as he sat down.

"Geoffrey," she said urgently. "People say that Faelan—"

"Gossip," Geoffrey said absently. As far as she could tell, he believed that himself. He began writing names. "Don't listen to tattlemongers, Roddy. That isn't like you."

She made a small huff of frustration. "*Geoffrey*," she snapped, "Faelan told me why you wrote Papa that letter of recommendation about him."

Geoffrey sat up. A wave of guilt swept him, and then a memory of Faelan's arm around Roddy's waist. He shrugged, setting his moral unease aside. "It seems to have turned out well enough." He looked up, not quite straight into her eyes. "There are higher causes that we have to obey sometimes, Roddy. Things that override individual claims on our duty."

She had an idea what her husband would have said to that. With only slightly more politeness, she murmured, "Spare me the lecture, please," in her best imitation of Faelan's razor-sharp smoothness. Geoffrey's surprise gave her a moment's heady power, and she plunged on. "I want to know... Geoffrey, I need to know, is Faelan... do you think that he's perfectly"—she broke off, struggling to frame the question, afraid to put it into words—"in control?" she finished, unable to keep the scared quiver from her voice.

Geoffrey stood up so suddenly that the chair tottered on two legs and then fell back into position with a loud thump. "What are you saying?" he asked, in a voice of deadly challenge.

The instant defensiveness was both reassuring and frightening. "Faelan told me he doesn't remember things," she blurted. "His father, and—"

"Of course he doesn't," Geoffrey snarled. "Damn you, have you been pestering him about his father? Leave off, Roddy—I warn you. That's over; years gone, by God. Do you think I'd have written your parents that letter if I'd thought there was the slightest danger to you? He promised me—he vowed he'd never hurt you. It was an accident, Roddy. An accident that he's better off forgetting. Lord, he's lived with it all his life—can't you let well enough alone?"

Behind the words was a turmoil of emotion, of anger and loyalty, and beneath it all, a twinge of fear that drove the aggression. Geoffrey believed what he was saying, because he was afraid not to believe it.

She opened her mouth to speak again, but Geoffrey grabbed up the paper he'd been using, without even sanding the ink. "I'd best be dressing for dinner. As would you, my lady." He gave her a chilly nod as he passed her for the door. "Faelan and I will be busy enough without your meddling. I'd advise you to go shopping with Mary tomorrow, and refrain from bothering your husband with foolish questions."

❧

Roddy pulled the bedclothes up under her chin, wondering if she would spend the night alone in this lumpy bed. The sheets were clean enough, even if their rough surface tended to rub raw on the tender skin of her cheek and ear.

Thinking of those sensitive spots made her think of Faelan, of his lips, his breath soft and seductive on her skin, and the cold distance he had maintained through the long and uncomfortable dinner.

Roddy wished she had done as Mary, and pleaded a headache. It was apparently a good enough excuse to avoid sitting down with the Devil Earl. During the meal Faelan had refused to discuss his plans for the guns, and those plans were all Geoffrey thought about, so conversation was slow and desultory. Roddy had left them immediately after dessert—hours ago.

She turned over and stared at the candle, burned down nearly to its holder. A slow dribble of wax made a puddle on the table, a liquid pool that gleamed like gathered tears. She felt her own eyes go hazy, and her throat filled. In spite of all the rest, in spite of Ellen Webster and Liza Northfield and the horrible fear that Faelan was not... *right;* in spite of it all, the worst was to lie in this bed alone and want him.

The candle went to a bright prism of color, gold swimming with blue and red and green. She sniffed, hearing the forlorn plop of a tear on the stiff sheets. *Damn him, damn him.* Everything that should have destroyed her faith only seemed to drag her deeper into love than before.

Below, the sounds of the taproom had long since subsided. She heard footsteps down the long corridor, coming closer—pausing at the door to the anteroom of their suite. So... he would stay there, on the narrow bed in the outer room provided for husbands who preferred—for whatever reason—not to sleep with their wives.

But after a moment she heard him move again, coming closer down the hall. The click of the door handle was loud in the silence.

Roddy drew in her breath as the door swung open and the faint light of his shielded candle made dim new shadows in the room. When she looked he was standing in the doorway with darkness behind him and a decanter and glass in one hand. She waited, but he came no farther. She sat up at last, and whispered, "Faelan?"

"I thought you would be asleep," he said softly.

"I waited for you." Her voice sounded small in the wide, misty ring of candlelight.

"Did you?" He lingered in the door. "Did you indeed." There was an odd ambivalence in his stance, as if he could not decide whether to enter or withdraw. He seemed to be inordinately interested in the carving at the foot of the bed; he spent a full minute staring at it without speaking.

Finally Roddy said, "Will you come to bed, my lord?"

His light eyes flicked up toward her. She felt the gaze like a physical touch, gathering in her tousled hair, caressing her face and shoulders and breasts. She moistened her lips, letting them part in an invitation she was barely aware of.

His mouth curved in a bitter smile. "How eager you look," he said. "Is Lord Geoffrey occupied elsewhere?"

Her eyes went wide, with shock at first, and then with dawning anger. He set down the candle, turned, and shot the bolt home on the door. She watched him as he strolled into the room, the candlelight painting contours of dark and light on his face.

"I fear your rebel prince has found a willing chambermaid," Faelan said. He sat down on the bed, and Roddy caught the sweet whiff of alcohol on his breath. "A mite more buxom than you, my dear. I'm afraid you aren't quite in Geoffrey's usual style."

"I believe you're drunk," Roddy said.

He grinned, his eyes glowing demon-blue. "Do you think so?" The long black lashes swept downward, a slow perusal of her breasts that made the blood rush to the surface of her skin. "But drunk is so much better than insane, don't you agree?"

He shifted, setting the glass down on the table with careless force and pouring a generous splash of amber liquid. He held the glass up in a mock toast. "To honesty, my love. I shall stay here and keep you an honest woman, and you shall make sure I remain an honest man. I should be distressed to wake in the morning and find that I'd murdered my wife and my only friend."

"Nonsense," Roddy said sharply. "Is this because I stayed a moment to talk to Geoffrey?" She glared at him with her chin set. "Whatever do you think, that we arranged some tryst to cuckold you and Mary under your very noses? Give us credit for some discretion, my lord, if you give us none for simple honor."

His lips curved without humor; he downed the shot of whiskey in one swallow. "Ah, but I know to a fine degree where Lord Geoffrey's honor begins and ends. If he wanted you, he'd have you if you were willing."

"Well," she said stoutly, "I'm certainly not." Which was somehow better than admitting that Geoffrey harbored no desire for her whatsoever. Faelan's obsessive jealousy was insulting, but it was just a little gratifying, too. The way his blue glance traveled over her and left and returned again with renewed intensity made her throat tighten in anticipation.

"You loved him, did you not?" Faelan poured himself another whiskey. "You married me for children, as I recall."

Roddy thought of Geoffrey and his plans to murder the parson. "Perhaps I loved him once. I don't think I knew him very well."

As the words left her lips she realized how true they really were. She'd had access to Geoffrey's mind, but she'd never known him. Even with her talent, she'd never seen past the surface of fine ideals and reason to the man beneath. On his visits to Yorkshire, there had been no chance to see how his philosophy translated into action. In all the years she'd known him, she'd never even learned of Faelan. Yet she was finding now that her husband had been a central figure in Geoffrey's life for far longer than she could claim to have been so. "Not well at all," she added pensively.

Faelan's vivid eyes met hers. "This talk of murdering the rector... that shocked you, did it not?"

Roddy blinked, taken by surprise at the insight. She nodded.

"I thought so." He ran his hand idly along the shape of her leg beneath the covers. "He's Protestant, Roddy. Do you know what that means?"

She frowned, trying to guess what he was hinting, and finally looked at him in blank question.

"It means," Faelan said, "that the rector is not only a kind and honest old man—which he is—but that he sends his men out by night to steal the tithe corn from the Catholic leaseholds."

Roddy tilted her head. "Tithe corn. I would hardly call that stealing," she said.

His hand moved upward, skimming her cheek. "You may say so to the babes in arms who go hungry for it. Or the tenants who can't meet their rent and face eviction."

"But a tithe, my lord. Only one-tenth—"

"No. One pound sterling an acre on potatoes and wheat. Five shillings on hay. And even for those who can spare it, there's enough bitterness in their hearts to murder any number of kindly parsons. You don't know, Roddy; you can't imagine... 'No Catholic may sit in Parliament,'" he recited, his voice going to a soft, legalistic singsong. "'No Catholic may be a solicitor, gamekeeper, or constable. No Catholic may possess a horse of greater value than five pounds. Any Protestant offering that sum can take possession of the hunter or carriage horse of his Roman Catholic neighbor. No Catholic may attend a university, keep a school, or send his children to be educated abroad. No Catholic may bequeath his estate as a whole, but must divide it among all his sons, unless one of those sons become Protestant, where he will inherit the whole estate.'" His recitation trailed off, and his long eyelashes lowered, as if he were seeing something far away. "I was almost a man before those laws were amended. The Relief Acts are two decades old, but no one forgets. No one forgets wrongs in Ireland."

"But Geoffrey isn't Catholic," she said.

He lifted one eyebrow. "How very observant you are,

my clever little wife. There's the rub. What shall we make of this glorious rebellion of Geoffrey's—a fight for liberty or a religious war? His peasants with their pikes and pitchforks don't know the difference, I assure you." As he spoke the candle flickered, light glancing off his elegant cheekbones and the muscled line of his throat where his cravat had been loosened. Roddy watched him, the way his look grew distant and intent, and his dark brows drew together as they had when he was bent on helping Geoffrey out of his muddle. "And just how this sacred freedom will fill their bellies is a thought that seems to trouble no one."

"I think," she said softly, "that it troubles you, my lord."

He looked back at her and shook his head, the frown in his eyes turning to a cynical smile. "Of course. Me and my potatoes." He finished the last of his whiskey and set the glass aside. "But cow dung and crop rotation are so dull, you see. There's not a stirring speech to be had among them."

Her fingers crept across the blankets and settled over his. "They aren't dull to me," she said. "I'll listen to your speeches."

"*An Argument on Behalf of Turnips in the Rights of Man*," he proclaimed lightly. "*Subsistence Before Independence.*"

She drew a light circle on the back of his hand. "I'm hanging upon every word."

"Further eloquence seems to have deserted me." He lifted her fingers and bent his lips to the base of her palm. "Perhaps you'd like a demonstration of some other talent."

His caress was cool and practiced. She felt his reserve still, the dark part of him she could not know. But he dragged her down, as he always did; he knew what he could do to her. He took her hands and spread them wide against the bed, bent to her, and shared the hot taste of whiskey as his tongue probed between her trembling lips.

Her body arched beneath him, seeking through the bedclothes, wanting his weight, his hands on her breasts. She would have reached for him, but he pinned her wrists and lowered his head, nuzzling aside the plunging neckline of her gown, exploring until his mouth found the taut, waiting peak of her bared nipple and pleasure shot through her groin. Her throat worked soundlessly; her body twisted and begged. He took her to a peak of agony, of exquisite, flaming need, and left her there on the brink of explosion.

As she moved beneath him, her breath short and straining for more, his lips traveled upward to the curve of her ear.

"There's still this," he whispered, above her tiny, panting moans. His fingers tightened in cruel possession on her wrists. "You still belong to me, *cailin sidhe*."

Thirteen

"Hobbies," Faelan called them, but Roddy would have given the surefooted local ponies a prouder, sweeter name to match their setting. The road that skirted the wild peninsula of Iveragh between the mountains and the sea was new, but Faelan had chosen older ways, overgrown paths that wound in and out of valleys and clung to the sides of cliffs where the waves rolling in from the Atlantic echoed an eternity below. They traveled in a blowing mist, she and Faelan and one extra pack pony, a fog that made the rocks to their left no more than a mass of slightly darker gray and the pitch to their right a single step into nothing. But the ponies never faltered; they placed one hoof in front of the other, heading home, passing wild grass and furze dripping with gleaming mist in the hopes of the oats they were sure would be waiting.

It seemed to Roddy that the fog thickened with each mile, as if they were heading into the far unknown reaches of the earth, leaving life and land and frail humanity behind. She found herself oddly pleased with the notion. Somehow this atmosphere was magic, a shining cloud out of which the most fantastic of dreams might coalesce. There, if she looked hard enough, she might see the golden towers of a castle in the distance, or feel the mysterious flutter of an angel's wings. She felt, if she would only listen, that someone sang to her through the shifting prisms of sunbeams in the vapor.

Fog had only been fog in Yorkshire. It had never felt like this.

She had caught Faelan's fever, it seemed. She loved Iveragh already. Ever since they had left Dublin, this place had pulled at her, an eagerness that was physical, that had made her as impatient as her husband with the gliding trip down the Grand Canal from Dublin. The new inns along the water had been lovely and well kept, and the green and gold countryside moved past in stately beauty beneath the late-autumn sun, but it was all a transitory picture.

Something stronger called them, even though the weather, the quality of the inns, and their mode of transportation had worsened with each change. In Tullamore the canal ended, and the hired chaise could not seem to go fast enough on the smooth, uncrowded roads. Through Roscrea, to Limerick and Castleisland, where they had abandoned Martha and chaise and baggage and mounted good Thoroughbred hunters. Even those were temporary, though, for when they had arrived at the little town of Glenbeigh in a dismal rain, Faelan had traded one hunter for three hobbies, and sold the other horse on the spot. After one night in a tiny inn where the bed smelled of mice and the chimney smoked too badly for a fire, Roddy had been happy to set out on the road to Iveragh.

She shifted in her stiff sidesaddle, careful not to throw the balance of the shaggy pony beneath her. Ahead, the mists around Faelan's dark figure glowed red-gold with the lancing fingers of sunset. They began a rapid, sudden descent, and Roddy swayed with the sliding steps of her pony. She began to smell the sea, very close. A dog took up deep-throated singing somewhere a long way ahead.

The sunset had faded to murky evening by the time Roddy could make out the string of whitewashed houses with slate roofs through the gloom. More dogs joined the first, and the ponies broke from their wild path onto the lonely main road to a sonorous bugling that bounced off the cottages and the invisible hills.

Faelan halted before the second house. No one came out to greet them. The stone cottage was empty, its windows gaping curtainless and the roof sagging, but Roddy was aware of people all around in the others, of mild suspicion and greater curiosity. Through her gift she could interpret emotion and image clearly, but the native language added a confusing element, as if she were holding a conversation in which she could understand only every second or third word. She let the ribbons of thought roll past her without concentrating, too stiff and weary to deal with her talent, or even wonder very hard what Faelan planned to do next.

Something strange, she was certain. It was November Eve. Tonight, if he kept his word, Geoffrey's guns would somehow elude the Irish militia.

So far, she had not even seen the Irish militia. She'd seen nothing but mist and Faelan's back all day, except when they had stopped to eat and rest. He hadn't said much then, but his face and eyes had told her volumes.

Tension was there, anticipation and intensity. She closed her eyes, remembering how he'd taken her the night before, in the squalid room in Glenbeigh: fiercely and silently, deeper in himself and farther away than he had ever been, and yet demanding as if he could not taste her or feel her or pull her close enough.

He dismounted now, and walked back to where she sat, damp and tired, with her hood pulled up against the fog. From her perch on the pony, her eyes were just on a level with his. She could see the dew that clung to his heavy lashes, while his eyes seemed to take on the color of the coming night.

"Wait here," he said. He looked at her a moment, and then suddenly reached out and slid his hand roughly behind her neck, drawing her against him for a long and heady kiss. He stood back, and a hint of the wolf-grin touched his lips. "That should give them something to talk about." He caressed her cheek lightly. "Keep your face down, little girl, and don't pull back your hood."

So she sat, while he disappeared into the house. A moment later he was back and they started off again, this time with a little more force applied to the round, patient ponies, who thought it was high time to put an end to the day.

It was full dark, but the mist was already luminous with the promise of a harvest moon. The ponies plodded on down the road between the wet gleam of slate shoulders, until Roddy felt the sudden, agitated touch of a human mind. A few moments later she sensed horses, at the same time the ponies pricked their ears. Her mount raised its head with a little huffing whinny.

The answer was shrill and far away. The distance surprised her. After London and Dublin and populous places, in this deserted land her talent seemed far more sensitive than she recalled.

The ponies went along a little faster then. Faelan turned off the road at some landmark Roddy could not fathom, and led the way down a steep gully where the moonglow did not follow. She clung to her saddle as the pony stumbled and felt its way by sound and smell, nose to tail behind the others.

The man they approached was nervous. His unease had increased since he'd heard them coming, which made the horses he tended restless. Vague pictures, ghoulish and creeping, insinuated his braver thoughts. He kept repeating an Irish word to himself, and Roddy finally matched it with an image of a half crown—the tie that kept him to his post in spite of growing panic.

Faelan said something, very soft, and suddenly her pony ran into the one ahead and stumbled to a halt. Roddy waited, puzzled, sure that the man and his horses must be very near now. It seemed that she could hear the muffled beat of agitated hooves ahead.

They stood there for a full minute in utter silence. And then a howl rent the night—a sudden, inhuman peel of sound that made the ponies shy and Roddy gasp and clutch the saddle and the reins and anything else she could reach as her heart leaped into her throat and stuck there in pounding terror. The sound had come from just in front of them; it couldn't have been a foot from Faelan, she was sure. But just as she was opening her mouth to call out to him and hauling her pony around to flee, he hissed a sharp order that halted her, more from its tone than from the unintelligible words.

The truth struck her at the same moment that she realized the man ahead had lost his battle with his wits and fled. *Faelan* had made that sound, Faelan himself, and now he was on the ground and striding toward her, half dragging her off her mount. "Help me," he ordered near her ear. "Calm the horses—can you?"

He was already stripping the pack pony; he took her wrist and pulled her past the frightened native animals toward the sound of thumping hooves. Silver-white shapes swam into view: the other horses, locked in the traces of a bulky carriage and threatening to kick free in their panic.

Without having to think, Roddy began to sing. It was as if the music came to her from the misty air, a strange sensation she had no time to contemplate as she eased up to the frantic beasts. Their ears pricked toward her; the one in the lead which had been trying to rear settled down with a suddenness that was eerie. Roddy moved toward it, took its shining white head between her hands, and felt the soft muzzle against her cheek. The song drained out of her, and a moment later she could not even remember what she had sung.

Faelan's laugh behind her made her turn. "You're home now, little *sidhe*," he said. There was exultation in his voice. She heard him come up to her shoulder and felt something soft pressed into her hands. "Put that on, and get inside. Hurry, or we shan't be in time for our ball."

The thing in her hands seemed to have a luminosity of its own; she held it closer to her eyes and saw that it was made of silver thread that caught the moonlight and held it as the mist did. A veil. It draped open into a full-length mantle, a clinging sheen of light.

She heard the creak as Faelan mounted into the driver's box and hurriedly yanked off her cloak and hood. Beneath it, the white gown that Faelan had insisted she wear that morning took on a new significance. With the silver mantle over her shoulders and her hair freed from the hood, she felt like a sliver of moonlight herself.

She thought suddenly—giddily—that she would like to dance, but the horses were backing and reversing under her husband's hands. With a small cry, she ran for the door of the carriage and scrambled inside.

Cobwebs engulfed her hair, and she almost jumped back out again. She lost her chance when the carriage moved forward into jolting motion, and she fell against the seat, coughing on the sudden cloud of mildew and dust that rose up around her.

She clawed at the sticky web in her hair, bringing curls all down in a tumble around her face. The night wind blew in the open windows, tangling the golden mass further, but at least it carried the cobwebs away and cleared the mildew from the air. A strange excitement filled her; she grasped the windowsill and put her face to the rough breeze, watching the dark shapes of trees race by. The coach came up out of the gully and topped a rise. The trees disappeared, and the fog began to break, so that the carriage seemed to fly above a landscape made of light and shadow.

Far too soon for Roddy, the vehicle began to slow. Outside, the mist had gone to moving clouds. She could see the mountains now, huge and black, with the rolling bogs spread out at their feet. A deep night scent rose from the low places, and in the darker crevices, pale blue light hung like wispy lanterns of imagination.

Beyond the bogs an incandescent sheet of silver lay, and more mountains beyond that: the sea, and distant, mysterious lands, islands and brooding hills where clouds ran like fleeting, silent stags.

The carriage rattled to a stop. Roddy peered out. A stranger stood on the road, an old man in an ancient footman's uniform, looking up at Faelan with a toothless grin.

"Senach." Faelan's voice blew to her on the breeze, soft, half laughing and affectionate. "God's blessing on you. Will you drive Finvarra and his lady?"

In the moment before the old man spoke, Roddy realized that her talent had deserted her. She frowned, focused, and found the old man as mysterious to her as her husband. But Senach's obscurity was not like Faelan's; not a blank wall, but a well of nothing that seemed to drag her in. Even the minds of the skittish horses had disappeared into that infinite depth. The more she tried to concentrate her talent, the more she felt the pull. Her fingers clutched at the window frame, her thumbs digging into the moldering upholstery that hung in fat tatters from the door.

"I'll be greetin' Finvarra's lady first," Senach said, in the melodic English of the countryside.

He turned his eyes toward the carriage door. Roddy had no idea who Finvarra was, but she had a strong impression that she was the lady in question. She took a nervous breath, remembering Faelan's gentle greeting, and tried to convince herself there was nothing to fear in this strange old man who wore servant's clothes and held himself like a royal prince. She fumbled for the door handle, and let herself slowly down.

She stood just outside the carriage, with the wind lifting her hair and the mantle into a shimmering fall of light. The horses were still; not the stamp of a foot, or the jingle of harness. Only the wind, faint and playful, that blew their white tails as it blew through her hair.

She found herself moving, a few steps that took her near the old man.

Senach touched her face with his fingertips, lightly, so lightly that the touch, too, might have been the wind. His eyes were pale, like Faelan's, but emptier. Sightless. She stared into them, and it was like looking into the depths of a bottomless lake. There was fear for a moment, the dizzy sensation of falling, and then he smiled, with a smile that took her up like a dreaming mother's arms; like a lullaby, soft and safe.

"Lassar," he said, and turned her toward the carriage with his spidery touch. "God bless. I'll carry ye safe home."

Faelan came down from the box, leaving the horses as if they were stone statues. He opened the door for her, and climbed in after. As Roddy settled gingerly back in the musty seat, he drew the silver veil through his fingers. "Lassar he's named you." Faelan's touch was warmer, firmer than the old man's. "*Flame.* I like that."

"He's blind," Roddy said.

In the dark, Faelan's lips in her hair felt like swallow's wings. "Do you think so?" he asked complacently. "I've never been certain."

The carriage moved into a smooth, forward rock. Roddy clutched at Faelan's hand. "But he's driving!"

"He knows the way."

"Faelan!"

His arms came around her, restraining her plunge for the door. "Ho there, little *sidhe*—we're safe enough with Senach. Haven't you recognized a kindred spirit?"

She stiffened in his embrace. Her voice came out a little shrilly. "I don't know what you could possibly mean. I've never tried to drive a coach-and-four blindfolded, I'll tell you!"

His grip stayed firm across her shoulders. The swaying carriage brought their bodies together, and he kissed the top of her head. "No. But I'll wager you could, if you tried."

"Of course not—" She broke off, and looked sideways at him in the dimness. A sudden terror gripped her, that he knew; that he had guessed her secret. She stared into his eyes, light blue in the moonlight from the door, and searched frantically for the telltale fear and disgust, the awful knowledge that had destroyed her great-aunt Jane's life and marriage long ago.

She did not see it. In the changing shadows, he was as impenetrable as ever, but the smile that curved his fine lips seemed warm—almost proud.

"*Cailin sidhe*," he murmured. "Do you remember when we helped the mare? I told you then, I knew a man who felt what you feel. Senach can see through the animals' eyes, if he can't see through his own."

"That's crazy," she said, and meant it. Never before had she encountered someone else with her talent, and she found she was as unprepared to believe in it as any ordinary person would have been.

He laughed. "Ah, but we're home now, little girl. I think everyone is a little mad in this place."

Roddy gave him a startled look.

"Yes," he said, in a taunting voice. He took her chin and forced her close, his lips brushing and exploring her skin.

"Were you hoping I was sane? I've seen you with that hope in your eyes, little girl. But we can't be sane—not tonight. It's November Eve, *cailin sidhe*, when mortal folk stay home in bed and Finvarra and his lady ride a coach with four white horses on their way to dance with the dead."

She wet her lips and said, "Finvarra?" in a dry whisper.

"The King of the Fairies of the West, my love." His arm tightened around her, and his lips caressed her mouth. "Will you dance with me tonight?"

Her breath seemed to be coming very short and fast; her heart thumped louder than the horses' hooves. It was fear and confusion, but it was something else besides: the night and the moonlight and the wind that rushed past. Like wild music, it hummed in her veins, and sparked a chill of pleasure as Faelan slid his hand beneath the silver cloak and explored the shape of her breast.

The touch on her skin was solid and human, in spite of his words. It reassured her. She leaned against him, pressed into his flesh-and-blood warmth. There was some purpose in this, she told herself. There were Geoffrey's guns and the militia, things all too real and dangerous. She could not afford to give in to the fancies that seemed to fill the air around them.

King of the Fairies, indeed. She reached up to his cheek and gave him a hard pinch, and told him to stop roasting her.

"Ow!" He jerked his head away. "Good God, woman, I'll steal your luck for that."

Roddy laughed, relieved to hear the common teasing in his voice. He grabbed her and dragged her closer and growled, "I'll carry you off to Tir-Na-Oge and hold you prisoner in my castle."

"Good!" she said, muffled in his black cloak.

"You'd like that, would you?" She felt his low chuckle, a vibration against her cheek. "You're hopelessly fairy-struck, I fear."

She lifted her head, just enough to see his face: his blue eyes like the glowing mist, his dark brows and lashes as black as the mountains. "So I must be," she said, speaking lightly. It covered the truth in her words, she hoped.

He touched her temple, spreading his fingers through her hair. "It will serve you well enough tonight." His thumb grazed her brow. "Those eyes of yours—keep them high, my love, and don't look down before anyone you see."

Then, as if that had been the most natural advice in the world, he sat back and turned his face from her, pulling out his pocket watch and holding it toward the window to read.

She had no notion of what time passed, and didn't ask. The road was smooth, eerily so, as if they traveled on the path of the moon she saw shining across the silvered water. The bulky hills rose and fell beside them, brooding shapes that matched the mystery of the islands and headlands across the bays: some sharp and small, some broad and long; all dark, all silent, all patiently waiting as the carriage flew along under a blind man's hands.

Her first warning of the militia was an agitated shout, a demand to halt that Senach ignored, and then the crack of musket fire behind them. They were among people, almost before she could realize that her gift still eluded her. The carriage did not slow at all; it picked up speed and flashed by figures silhouetted against the lurid spark of campfires. There was more shouting, more gunfire, and then her talent struck her with a vengeance, dragging her ahead to where a sentry stood frozen in the road and watched the white horses bear down on him.

She felt his terror; it washed into her own, and she tried to pull away, to force it back, for she feared she would be with him when the horses ran him down. But the images engulfed her. She saw with numbing clarity the animals' flared nostrils and red eyes of reflected fire, heard the thunder of hooves and wheels, felt the shaft of horror as the soldier stared up into Senach's fixed and glassy gaze. The militiaman's body moved somehow, his limbs reacting to what his mind could not comprehend: that the coach that exploded through their camp had a blind man at the lines. The soldier abandoned his duty and threw himself aside. The last she felt of him was the solid, painful impact of his face and shoulder with the dirt at the side of the road, and then her gift was gone again.

They were in empty country, so suddenly that she found herself still clinging in panic to Faelan's sleeve beneath his cloak. She let go of him, though it was an effort. The road was rougher now, and the carriage began to tackle a slight rise. Faelan took out his timepiece again.

He put it away and grinned at her. "A quarter till midnight," he said, and yanked once on the signal bell. "We'll give them time to catch up."

The horses slowed to a trot, then a walk. Roddy sat with her arms and ankles tightly crossed, trying to convince herself that Faelan actually had some rational plan. The more she thought of the hot exhilaration in his grin, the more it seemed to border on mania. When she considered the whole situation—a blind driver, a mad rush through an armed camp, the half-wild talk of fairy kings—it seemed that he was far less than sane.

Not even this pause made sense. Why plunge through the militia like avenging angels and then slow down to wait for the pursuit?

She stared at his dark profile against the moonlight. And while she stared she began to hear music. It came, a fair, faint sweetness, there and gone, and there again. Faelan did not move, but the horses picked up a trot. Their hooves filled the air with muffled thunder, and she thought she had imagined the distant tune.

But she began to hear it again—in snatches, in small, strange moments of suspension, as if for an instant the horses' feet flew instead of struck the ground. The haunting melody grew louder. Beyond Faelan's profile the sky took on a lighter glow.

The carriage leveled out and then dipped into a valley where a tangle of vegetation blocked the view. Roddy had opened her mouth, ready to force out a half-formed question, when the coach rose again and made a sharp right turn. The encroaching bushes fell away like dark, frightened sheep, and then, on the hill above them, she saw it.

A house. A huge house, stark black against the shimmer of underlit clouds. Tall, symmetrical windows lined the long facade, spilling cold light into the lingering wisps of fog. She grabbed at the rotating seat as the carriage swung left again. The mansion disappeared from view. When she saw it again from her own window, the source of the glow in the clouds above the structure was unmistakable.

The mansion had no roof. No curtains graced the stark windows; no sign of habitation softened the grim spires of crumbling chimneys. The place was a skeleton.

And yet light shone out of the dead windows like the weird blue fire of the boglands, and strange music played, and vague silhouettes danced and turned and curtsied in the hall.

In Roddy's conscious mind, she had reasoned out the trick. This mad scene was all staged, a play made of darkness and superstition, to scare the militiamen into staying safe by their fires while Geoffrey's rebels moved the guns from the mansion into the mountain passes.

And the ghoulish diversion worked. It worked too well. In the deeper reaches of Roddy's being, she felt a chill such as she had never known before.

November Eve. The night the fairies danced with the dead.

The carriage drew up before the great doors and came to a halt. In a black sweep, Faelan was on the ground and turning back toward her, holding out his hand. She took it, stepped down, and looked up at her husband.

If ever she had thought to imagine Finvarra, the King of the Fairies of the West, it would have been Faelan in that moment, with the wild moon in his eyes and the music behind him and the luminescence that touched him like a crown of living light.

"Lassar," he said. "*Cailin sidhe*. Welcome home."

She looked beyond him to the great, gaunt, haunted ruin. Home.

Oh, God, she thought. *God help me.*

Fourteen

SHE SUPPOSED, MUCH LATER, THAT LEGENDS BEGAN WITH LESS. A hundred years from now, they would speak of Finvarra's ball, and the way the hills had echoed with fey minuets and glittered with the ghostly torches of the departing guests. The way a man feared to look over his shoulders to find the source of footsteps behind him. The way a force of one hundred gallant West Country militia had known better than their foolish officers to interfere with fairy business.

Three men, a captain and two lieutenants, came to grief that night while trying to investigate. One was found in the morning by the little lake in the bottom of a mountain coum, having fallen, the broken condition of his body told, from the cliff eight hundred feet above. The second—what was left of him—was buried near the clear spring where wolves, so the official report stated, had sprung upon him. The unofficial whisper was that there had been no wolves in the barony for decades; that he had been torn to pieces by something far, far worse—while his horse, like the others, had wandered home unscathed.

The third man, the captain, had come riding up just as Roddy descended from the carriage. His loud hail was more indignant than frightened, but when Faelan took no notice of him, only guiding Roddy toward the moss-covered stairs, the soldier's voice faltered a little. At the top of the steps, Faelan paused, turning back.

The officer's horse was dancing under a tight hand as the man looked over his shoulder behind him. "Armstrong," he'd shouted, amid the drifting music and the fog that had begun to roll in thick fingers up from the glen. "Logan!"

There was no answer, no pair of armed, red-coated riders at his back. He swore and faced the house again, spurred his horse forward where it seemed loath to go. "Your name, sir," he demanded.

Faelan smiled. The mist hung about his head, gleaming from the light behind. "I have many," he said. He held out his free hand. "Will you join us?"

Unable to come closer without mounting the steps, the captain hesitated, and then swung impatiently off his horse. The animal shied as he did so, reared and tore the reins from his hand. The captain's urgent soothings were useless: while the carriage horses stood, carved still as white marble, the soldier's mount twisted backward, bucking as if to dislodge a devil from its back, and plunged down the hill into the fog.

Faelan stood unmoving, smiling still with that strange knowing smile.

The captain swung toward them. With the same startling, crystalline impact that Roddy had experienced on the ride through the militia camp, she felt her talent return. The captain's disconcerted anger and chagrin throbbed in her head. He strode up the steps and confronted them.

"In the King's name," he snapped, "identify yourself."

Faelan laughed. "Call me the east wind," he said lightly. "My lady's name is Flame."

The soldier frowned nervously. He could barely see Faelan's face against the pale light from within the open door. "What nonsense is this?"

"The east wind," Faelan said, in a voice that tangled with the music floating past them. "The demon wind. It blows tonight."

In spite of himself, the captain glanced toward the east, where the mists slid up from the dark below.

"Join us," Faelan said again.

His hand closed on Roddy's arm. She turned with him, driven by the hard grip on her elbow, the only thing that seemed real in the whole unearthly scene.

Beneath the arched doorway, leprous with black lichen, shadowy figures danced to the ancient music in the hall. A faint haze silvered everything, made the dark corners darker and the candlelight deathly pale. Without Faelan's hand on her, propelling her forward, no force on earth would have made her join that spectral company, with their faces paste-white and their mouths painted murderous red, and the elegance of five decades past streaked and moldering on their bodies.

But she, like the dumbfounded captain, was swung up in the haunting dance. Faelan bowed, dragging her down in a curtsy when she would have stood gawking at the burned-out shell. Three stories rose above them, open to the lowering sky, and dead vines crawled where fine curtains should have hung. Roddy felt the brush of lifeless fingers at her back, and then—as Faelan's punishing grip controlled her start—saw the rotting silk that draped in tatters along the walls, swaying as the dancers passed like the strands of a drowned maiden's hair.

She danced, clinging to the reality of Faelan's bruising touch. The captain's rising panic was at one with her own; she could not separate them, or bring her mind to focus on the knowledge that this was all an illusion made of night and fog. When a wordless gentleman with a wooden smile pressed wine into the officer's hand, Roddy tasted the sweet, convulsive gulp he took to rally himself. A lady's cold fingers touched his hand, and Roddy felt the same chill pass down her spine. She glanced that way, seeing his partner from two minds at once: from Roddy's view, a beauty like a winter night, all frozen stars and stillness, while in the captain's befuddled brain the lady's face was skeletal and strange, too difficult to comprehend in the gleaming, mist-tricked light.

The room began to sway then, to rotate slowly around her head. From a distance, she saw the captain's scarlet coat begin to blur, and felt the buckling of his knees. Caught in his mind, she stumbled too, hanging on to Faelan's arm for one dizzy moment before the soldier crumpled—slowly, slowly—so slowly that it seemed a more fantastic dream than any that had gone before. She saw him for one instant, a red pool like bright blood on the ballroom floor, and then the shadows claimed her too, and darkness closed around her.

❧

She woke to the cool breeze on her face. Her body seemed disconnected from her mind; she had to fight to open her eyes, and her fingers would not move when she bade them.

Someone spoke. It was an important voice, one she thought she should know. "She's stirring," it said. "Senach—God, thank God—will she…"

The voice swirled and faded. "…winter planting," it said the next time she made sense of it. "I've seed spuds coming in from Kenmare. Enough for tenscore cows'-grass. No more than that…"

She spun in and out of odd dreams: cattle and ghostly dancers and huge mountains of potatoes.

"…he's after wakin' up." Another voice spoke in a light rasp, like the touch of the wind on her cheek.

And, "Aye," said the first. "I can see him moving."

She struggled to hold her eyelids open; to find reason in this babble.

"Hush… hush…" The words were close, a warm breath in her ear. "Little girl, little love… be still."

She wanted badly to please that voice. For a moment she stopped struggling. The confusion in her mind began to sort itself, to separate and order. The dreams of walking ghosts belonged to another, she realized, and the stiff spine and cradled shoulders were her own.

"How do you feel?" the gentle voice inquired close to her ear.

The tone filled her with a flood of comfort and security. "You're so nice," she mumbled.

The support beneath her shoulders shook softly in silent laughter. "A vote of confidence."

Her eyes wrenched open at last, and shut again instantly against light that seemed blinding. The arms around her tightened.

"Rest awhile, little girl. Rest here awhile with me."

"No. Let her wake, m'lord. That's the way now."

Pain sparked through her limbs as she tried to move. She made a little complaining moan.

"Oh, aye, it hurts a bit, do it not? All night sleepin' on the hard cold floor."

Roddy opened her eyes again. Another pair, empty blue, stared into hers and through her. From his position several feet away, Senach smiled. The world seemed to right itself. Roddy drew her shoulder blades together and yawned. She shifted and sighed and laid her cheek against rough wool. For a moment, it was enough to know that the firm chest beneath her belonged to her husband.

She drowsed safely in his arms, listening to morning sounds. Somewhere in the distance a cow was lowing, and choughs called and sea gulls mewed, circling closer by. After a while she lifted her head and looked around.

They were in a broad place behind a low wall, very close, it seemed, to the sky. To both sides stretched a parapet that fell away to a great depth, forming a huge, sheer-walled rectangle of stone beneath them. The wild countryside lay in a sweep of olive-green and silver all around. Three stories below she could see the militia captain sprawled on the ruin's broken floor.

As they watched he dragged himself onto his elbows. Roddy frowned as memory began to return to her. She felt a little twinge of fear as she realized that once again she was alone in her mind; that neither Senach nor Faelan nor the soldier below was open to her talent.

That had not been true the night before. It had been the overwhelming power of her gift that had dragged her down with the captain. She blinked, staring at the officer's red coat as he sat up and looked around groggily.

"You drugged him," she said.

Faelan's hand came over her mouth with an impact that rocked her head backward. "Be still," he breathed harshly into her ear.

Roddy nodded, and he slowly released her. Senach remained gazing into empty air, with that seraphic smile on his brown and wrinkled face.

She could guess the soldier's confusion, the sensation of waking in an unfamiliar, unexpected place. Early sun warmed the cracked marble where specters had danced; a chough landed on a broad, bare windowsill and sidled along it, fluffing glossy black plumage with a coarse cry.

The captain had lost consciousness in a nightmare. He woke to morning peace and sunlight that mocked such macabre dreams.

It took him a long time to stand up. When he did, he tottered and fell back to one knee. He gathered himself and tried again, successfully this time. From their hiding place high above, Roddy watched with gradually warming sympathy as he blinked in confusion and cast a despairing look around. She saw him look down at his feet and then up at the tall, ruined walls. Faelan's arms flexed just slightly as the man's bleary gaze passed over their hiding place.

In time, something like reason seemed to direct the captain's movements. He began to look more closely around the floor. They could still see him after he stumbled out the great arched door, down on his knees in the overgrown drive.

"Looking for wheel marks," Faelan whispered into her hair. "He'll only find his own horse's prints—three hooves shod and the near fore missing."

She looked up, a question in her eyes, and he ruffled her disarranged curls.

"Success for our hero, little girl. There was a signal fire on the pass just before dawn. Geoff's guns made it across."

Finally, with a weary and baffled set to the shoulders beneath the red coat, the officer stood straight and rubbed his palms across his face, and then began the long hike down the hill toward the sea.

For many minutes after he had gone, no one spoke. At last, when Roddy thought she could hold back her questions no longer, Faelan's hold on her loosened. He pushed her back and gently kneaded the nape of her neck with his thumbs.

"Stretch the knots out, my love," he advised. "We'll break our fast on the way."

❧

It was an appropriate introduction to her husband's estate, Roddy thought wryly. A day of fog, a night of enchantment, and then a week spent camping out like savages under the shadow of mountain crags. When finally the three scruffy hobbies clipped into Killarney, she looked back at the mist-crowned cliffs and valleys with relief and vast regret.

They were beautiful, with a beauty that was an ache in the mind. She held them to her heart, those days with Faelan among the moody peaks, some tranquil with the mobile, melting mists; some grim with blue storm and bare rock. She had seen the land that her husband loved as she never could have from the well-sprung coach that carried her on her second, official, entry.

This second trip held none of the mystery of the first. "English," Faelan said of their mode of travel as they settled in under soft wool rugs. Which meant, Roddy began to understand, comfortable, efficient, and insulated. The mountains and bays were scenery, lovely subjects for a lady's watercolor that flowed past too quickly. The militia was respectful, unsuspicious—a mere pause on the road in which Roddy was allowed to venture forth from the carriage under a soldier's protection to view several small antiquities: a souterrain, a pillar stone, and a few rocks said to be early tombs.

Far above them on the mountainside she could see the dark outline of the great, ruined mansion. Faelan, strolling behind the anxious young militiaman who guided her among the rocks, seemed to take no notice of it.

Roddy wondered what had become of the captain who'd gone to the fairy ball.

"Why, look at that," she said, in a breathless, overblown imitation of a new bride. "My lord, is that the house?"

Faelan settled back against a boulder. "What's left of it," he said with a teasing smile. "I'll build you another posthaste, my dear."

"We had a fine scare a sennight past." The young soldier looked quickly at Roddy, eager to tell the tale, but torn between impressing her with the story and frightening a delicate lady.

"What was that?" Faelan asked as he pulled a snuffbox from his pocket and took an idle pinch. Roddy frowned at the tiny enameled box. She'd never seen Faelan take snuff before.

The question was encouragement enough for the soldier. "Lost three men, sir," he said importantly. "Well, two. Not from my company, m'lord, no, sir. 'Twas the Fifth; a captain and his lieutenants went up to investigate some lights in the hills, m'lord—on account of all the smuggling in these parts, don't you know. Not that Your Lordship would be apprehensive to them doin's, oh, no. But like that; there was some of their men as wouldn't go with 'em." He stopped, suddenly realizing that this refusal of duty hardly reflected well on the militia, and decided to concentrate on the ghostly aspects of the story. "Bein' 'twas November Eve an' all," he said, lowering his voice to emphasize the drama. "'Twas a wee bit eerie, do you see? There were talk o' ghosts, and a carriage, real as you or me, that run through camp like the divil out o' hell was pursuin' it. I didn't see that; I don't know as I believe that part, but I was there when they brung in that lieutenant's body, an' that was after bein' real enough, beggin' your pardon, m'lady. An' the captain, he come draggin' in, and he'd run plain mad—talkin' ghosties and white ladies an' such." The young soldier drew a breath, and said more heartily, "Colonel Burns—he put a stop to that. He sent his man downcountry quick. 'Twas makin' some o' the lads jumpy, do you see. Not me. I'm from Castlebar. But some of them as is thick with the local lads, they said 'twas the fairies. They said that mad captain was after describin' the king of 'em himself, an' the lady all in white his beauteous queen that he'd stole from her bed an' left a log in her place."

"Fairies," Faelan said. "Good God."

The militiaman laughed, a sound that did not quite cover his own uneasiness. "Oh, aye, m'lord. Oh, aye."

Faelan played with the enameled box. He slanted a look toward Roddy. "Do you have any more questions, Lady Iveragh?"

"No," she said slowly. "No, my lord."

He straightened, tall and easy, his dark elegance a sharp contrast to the fresh-faced militiaman from Castlebar. The soldier was preparing to offer his escort when Faelan stepped casually in front of him and took Roddy's arm for their return to the carriage.

A few miles past the militia camp, the new road ended. White-haired and patient, Senach stood waiting with a pair of fine hunters to carry them over the old track that mounted the forbidding hill ahead.

Roddy found herself uncomfortable. In the daylight, Senach seemed no more than an old, old man, but still he eluded and somehow seemed to interfere with her gift, drawing all consciousness into his silence. She did not want to meet his eyes, sightless though they seemed to be. He helped Roddy to mount, and brushed her hand with his feathery fingers.

"Ye cain't hear me, can ye, my lady? 'Tis no matter," he said softly. "'Tis a wee thing."

Roddy jerked her fingers away. "What do you mean?" she asked sharply.

"Ye know. Ye know me meanin', my lady Lassar." He patted her dappled gelding, and the animal bent to nuzzle his shoulder. "Remember the horses."

A peculiar panic rose in her, a fear of something she could not name. She looked up and saw Faelan and his mount already opening distance between them. "I don't——" She looked again at Senach, and his blank eyes caught hers for an instant that was an eternity.

She broke away. "Nonsense," she exclaimed. "Nonsense." She drove her heels into the gray's sides.

"Remember the horses," Senach called after, and the words lingered in the ocean air like an ancient, mocking curse.

She and Faelan came to the unpretentious slate-roofed house of their temporary hosts not long before sunset. Hidden beyond the great hill from the incursion of the new road, Doire Fhionain, the O'Connell family home, emanated welcoming candlelight and the sharp smell of burning peat.

It seemed a very human place amidst the wilds. The door opened the moment they rode into the yard, spilling light into the cool evening air, and a man strode out, tall—powdered and distinguished, like her father. He came directly to Roddy and reached to help her from her mount.

"Our fairy queen," he said grandly. He set her on the ground, and looked down his long nose at her. "Welcome, welcome, brave child. This villain has dragged you through half the county, has he not? Well, you've come to the right place now. Come in, then. Get you down, Iveragh, and come inside."

Three hours later, she sat at a long table laden with bacon and fowls and cabbage, with a large roast turkey on one side and a leg of mutton on the other. Boiled salmon, boiled cod, lobster, peas, potatoes… she closed her eyes, unwilling to take another bite.

The grand old matron at the foot of the table noticed the tiny gesture on the instant. Maire O'Connell raised her querulous voice and informed her son and the rest of the large company that it was time for a song.

In a great shuffle and thumping of chairs, they gathered around the fire at one end of the room. Roddy sat in the chair she was offered, keeping her eyes cast down. Her gift was overly sensitive, throbbing, caught in a confusion of Gaelic and English. Hospitality and distrust swirled around and eluded her. She could not tell who thought what, or why.

The tall man who'd greeted her thrust a glass of the fruity dinner wine into her hand as someone began to pluck random notes on the huge harp in the corner. Maurice, the tall man's name was. He smiled often. She noted, uneasily, that he was less glad to see Faelan than outward appearances indicated.

It wasn't a concrete thing: more caution than rooted dislike. No one was quite certain of this prodigal son. The divisions in Irish society began to sink into Roddy's consciousness. Catholic, this family was. It radiated from them—a creed, a way of life, as much as a religion. They began to sing songs and tell stories in Irish while proud, sharp-witted Maire guided the talk, gathering her family around her.

Roddy and Faelan sat alone amid the company. English. Landlords. There were older, darker memories of Faelan in Maire's and Maurice's minds. They remembered his father; remembered his death. They looked at Faelan and wondered, trying to match the boy to the man.

The others just looked, never having known the boy.

Roddy picked one fact out of the muddle of curiosity and Irish song. Faelan's father had been Catholic, too.

Which seemed an odd thing. A very odd thing.

The songs went soft and haunting. Roddy sat in her chair, held straight by will alone. Every muscle in her back cried out from the long ride in carriage and saddle. She closed her eyes and let the music fill her with its plaintive beauty. Behind her eyelids, a dream took shape—a lady in the moonlight, whose face was made of winter stars.

"Little girl." Faelan's voice was warm at her ear. She opened her eyes to find his hand on her shoulder. "You're exhausted. Go with Senach."

Roddy sat up with a start. "Senach—"

Faelan was making her apologies and pulling her bodily to her feet. He seemed to interpret her drawing back as simple weariness. When she saw Senach waiting at the door and began to protest, Faelan lifted her and carried her out in front of everyone, up the stairs behind the old man's measured steps. Faelan set her down at the top of the stairs and laid her hand in Senach's cool, thin palm. "Go on to bed. I'll be along when I can."

"But…" She trailed off, finding no words to express her fear. Faelan was halfway down the stairs when she called his name.

He turned, a touch of impatience in the set of his mouth. "What is it?"

Senach's fingers moved like spiders in her hand. She jerked it away. "Wait! I—Can't you come now?"

His frown told her no. "We're guests here, Roddy."

"I'll come back down, too." She took a step toward him.

"Go to bed," he said. "You look ready to fall down."

"Faelan." It was a plea, a cry for help. "Don't leave me."

He looked baffled. After a moment, he climbed the stairs and took her hand. "What is it, little girl? Lord, you're shaking like death." His arm came suddenly around her shoulder and he spread his palm across her forehead. "Pray God—No, you don't feel warm. Perhaps you ate something..."

She leaned against him. "Don't leave me," she whispered into his coat. "Don't leave me with Senach."

She felt his surprise in the tightening of his body. "Whatever are you talking about?" He put her away from him, and reached again to join her hand with Senach's.

In spite of herself, she flinched. "He's blind," she whispered. It was all she could say to explain her fear. He was blind, and yet he could see, and he sucked her talent away, down into a black vortex of silence.

Faelan looked into her face, and suddenly his mouth went hard. "You hold a good man's disability against him?" he asked roughly. "You think he can't take care of you, as well as I ever could? Go on, Roddy. You disappoint me." He glanced at Senach, still standing with a slight smile on his ancient face, as if nothing they said touched him. "You disappoint me, little girl."

With that, he turned away from her, and did not look back as he thudded down the wooden stairs and disappeared into the parlor.

Roddy stood still, frozen in misery and terror. When Senach touched her again, she clenched her teeth together to endure it.

"Ye might be freein' him," Senach said. "Ye might be."

"What?" Roddy said uncertainly.

"Ye could know him, if ye would do it. But ye be fearin'. Him and me."

His light contact burned into her arm. She was afraid to look up, afraid to meet his empty eyes. "I don't... I don't know what you mean."

"Oh, aye, child. Ye do know it. I'll be tellin' ye till ye listen." He stroked the back of her hand.

"I don't like this," she said brokenly. Tears of strain and agony blurred her vision.

"No. Ye won't look to me, like the folk dursn't look straight at you all your life. Folk know the truth. What they hear in their hearts, they dursn't say aloud. They look the other way, they do. But I be thinkin' ye've known all that."

"Please," she said. "Please leave me alone."

"Ah. Ah. Leave ye alone, will I? Leave ye in the dark? 'Twould hurt me to do it, an' ye alone there, all afeared."

His hand closed lightly around her arm, and he led her into the dark hall. They came to a door; without fumbling, he found the knob and opened it. Inside, a single candle illuminated the curtained bed and a fine Oriental rug.

Roddy stepped quickly inside. She wanted to fling the door shut in Senach's face, but from somewhere came a modicum of politeness. She turned, and mumbled a hasty good night.

"God bless," Senach said. "Trust be the key."

He closed the door.

Roddy stared at the wood and listened to his light steps down the hall. The man who knew her secret. The man who shared her talent. Who drank her gift and left her empty and alone.

Her soul was bared and open to another's mind. It was a fearful thing to comprehend.

Fifteen

IN THE DINING ROOM THE BREAKFAST WAS LAID OF REMNANTS from the night before: minced turkey and warm potatoes on the side table, and the men sitting down to a dram before their boiled eggs.

Faelan sat in his earlier place one chair down from Maurice. There was a touch of coolness in her husband's greeting when Roddy joined him there, but no one noticed except herself. If her husband had come to her bed and gone the night before, she never knew it. The talk was of wine and customs men, and a shipment expected that night in the little bay of Derrynane. She remembered Faelan, with a teasing glint in his eye, informing her before they'd arrived that their hosts were in the import-export business.

It dawned on her, belatedly, that this genteel, comfortable family were smugglers by profession.

"You've put us to shame now, Iveragh, with your grand fairy ball," Maurice complained. He spoke with good nature, but there was a question, a delicate probing, in his next words. "And a fine diversion it was, but a terrible waste, to my mind. To be movin' a lot of cold steel when I had a good cache of tobacco and spirits that was wanted by the lads in Cork a wee bit more than guns."

Faelan finished off his dram. "The bluff is yours to use again. Make it an annual affair." He smiled briefly at his host over the tiny glass. "You needn't worry that I'm going into competition."

Maurice inclined his head. He'd abandoned his powder this morning; his graying hair was dressed in rolls at the temples and clubbed back over his collar. In the whole room, Faelan was one of only two males who wore their hair cropped and free of curls or powder. *A la rèvolution*, someone in the company called it to themselves, and Roddy was puzzled by the significance such a minor thing seemed to carry.

"Will our good friends from Paris be following their guns?" Maurice asked.

Faelan shrugged. "I fear I'm not privy to their councils."

"Yet you move their muskets in the dead of night," said the young man with the cropped hair. His fair skin flushed a little. "With our help."

"I thank you for it." Faelan leveled his blue gaze on his questioner. "But 'twould be a mistake for you to think I favor an Irish invasion by your good friends the French. They're no friends of mine."

"Why, then?" Maurice asked quietly.

"The guns," Faelan said, "were an inconvenience to me. So I had them removed." He offered no explanations of how they had arrived in the first place.

The faint touch of arrogance in his voice did nothing to conciliate his hosts. Roddy sensed that they were puzzled. Although a week ago they had casually opened their small hidden harbor to land and dispatch Faelan's counterfeit fairies, he was still suspect in their eyes. He ran rebel guns with Irish flair, but he was English-schooled, Protestant; he fit no mold, and as a landowner he would wield great power in the district. Beneath the age-old traditions of Gaelic hospitality, they regarded him with all the respect and affection they might have felt for a loaded powder keg.

"'Twas only a thought of ours," Maurice said softly, "that a man with French muskets comes with the fleet close behind."

Faelan laughed without humor. "Ah, but *how* close—that's the thing you might wonder. The Frogs missed their chance in '96 when the headwinds kept them out of Bantry Bay. They missed it again this spring, when Britain lay helpless as a babe for weeks with her navy in the hands of mutineers." He sat back in his chair with his fingers locked and raised one dark brow at Maurice. "The east wind doesn't love the French, it would appear."

O'Connell decided to drop the subject. "Here," he said in a tone of melodramatic resignation, "we only wish to mind our own affairs."

"Just so." Faelan's glance took in the comfortable room and imported furnishings, the well-filled decanters of wine and spirits. "And you do it so well."

Maurice nodded in modest assent, ratifying the mutual, unspoken agreement to stay out of one another's business. In a sudden reversion to formality, he said, "We welcome Your Lordship, for as long as you and your bride will stay."

Faelan took a sip from his glass. "Thank you. But we won't impose on Mrs. O'Connell's hospitality for long. I have a lease that has fallen in—there'll be a house available as soon as we have our first eviction."

A quick, sharp tension thickened instantly in the room. Faelan looked around with no visible emotion at the suddenly hostile faces surrounding the table.

"You disapprove," he said dryly. "Do you think I would move my wife into a cottier's hovel? 'Tis Willis who'll be vacating."

"John Willis." Maurice sat up straight. "By the saints—do you mean that, man?"

Faelan's lips drew back in a wry half-smile. "Not by your saints, perhaps. But yes. I do mean it."

"And who's to replace him?"

"Myself," Faelan said simply.

They all stared.

"You mean to live there?" the flushed young man exclaimed. "I can't credit that."

Faelan looked toward Roddy, reaching across the corner of the table to take her hand. "Do you like this house, Lady Iveragh? Do you find it sufficient for your ease?"

"Of course," she said quickly, and hoped it was the right answer. The level of emotion in the room was running high, consternation and glee shifting too fast and wildly for her to make sense with her gift.

"Then you'll like the one John Willis has built for himself even better. He's a man who knows his worldly comforts, I hear."

She wet her lips. "But—my lord... you wouldn't turn a man out of his home—"

The young man snorted. "Aye. John Willis'll burn the place down first."

"Not if he wishes reimbursement for his improvements," Faelan said. "I'll give him fair price."

"Will you now?" The youth made a rude sound. "That's more than Christian, then. He can take his miserable pack of hounds and go hunt in hell and welcome."

"Davan." Maurice addressed his young cousin in faint reproof and looked at Faelan. "Have you other changes in mind, Your Lordship?"

"Yes." Her husband ran his forefinger around the rim of his glass. "The Farrissy lease is also at an end."

The approval that had gathered dissipated, gone in an instant at this news.

"He's a good man, Farrissy," Maurice said with careful neutrality. "A good neighbor with a promising family."

"And hunting a pack of skinny hounds the equal of Willis', I'm certain. No, Mr. O'Connell—I'll not support a crowd of petty gentlemen at their leisure, Catholic or Protestant." Faelan's mouth set hard as he returned his host's look. "Who leases my land will work it. Under my supervision. The countryside's poor enough—there'll be no subletting five-deep and living off the rents. As for Farrissy's promising family, I know that kind of promise. All to become priests, or schoolmasters, or French officers, no doubt."

"Honorable professions, my lord," Maurice said stiffly.

"Leeches. Living off beggarly peasants and giving nothing back but a sorry smattering of bog Latin."

"That's not the remark of a gentleman, sir." Offense pulled the lines tight across Maurice's cheekbones. "Your father had better manners."

Faelan stood up. Though his face remained cold and utterly neutral, Roddy could see the tendons in his hand flex. "Of course I'm no gentleman," he said softly. "I'm not my father.

I have no manners and no morals and no heart, but I have title to my land, and I'll make it produce. Those who choose to help me may stay and share in the results. The rest may find another place to pass the time. Be it in the alehouse or in the church, they'll have no support from me."

❧

Roddy was glad to escape the uneasy atmosphere of Doire Fhionain. Only the grip of tradition kept Maurice from bidding Faelan leave the O'Connells' roof that very day; tradition, and their host's determination not to lower himself to Faelan's level by putting a well-bred English gentlewoman out of shelter. But Roddy would rather have slept as she had the past week—on the ground beneath the sky—than endure the concealed animosity and the memories of Faelan's past that her husband's abrupt declaration of his intentions had invoked.

Faelan seemed insensible to the tension. As they rode out in the crisp morning, sea-cooled and sharp-aired, he was smiling the way he had smiled in Gunther's pastry shop: like a small boy let loose from hated lessons.

He led the way back over the high road they had taken the day before. At the top, he halted and swept his arm wide over the long valley spread before them, the magical country with the sea on the west and the misted mountain passes on the east. It seemed empty of human habitation, and yet full of some presence, some welcoming song that the mind heard, though the ear could not.

"Iveragh," he said, in a tone that echoed with love and pride. He looked sideways at her, and shrugged with a trace of self-consciousness. "There isn't much here yet, I know." The wind billowed his black cape as he reined his horse and turned to point down the ridge on which they'd paused toward a sheltered bay. "Down there—we'll build a pier," he said with studied casualness. "I think that will be the place, at any event; I have an engineer from Aberdeen coming in December to begin sketches."

He stared intently at the spot, as if he could see the pier in all its detail. "'Twill be next fall before it's finished, at that rate," he added suddenly. "I wanted the damned fellow sooner, but he's the best man in the field and in high demand. It took a king's ransom to draw him off at all."

The trace of impatience, the eagerness which he could not quite hide, made Roddy want to smile. "And what will we ship, my lord?"

"Butter," he said seriously. He pointed again, this time up to the east, where Roddy could see several small black dots on one hillside. "The native upland cattle yield fine milk-fat on this scant pasturage. I want to consolidate a herd for improvement, and do some careful crossing with English imports. If we could make some enclosures, isolate the dairy herd—cull out the poorer milk producers and cross them with English imports—luck might have it that we'd gain better hardiness in a beef cow, too."

"I see." Roddy kept her voice solemn, not wanting to break into his rising enthusiasm with her amusement.

"Those bogs across there," he went on without pause. "We'll drain them. I think we can have a good start on it before the weather turns. We'll have corn there next year, or hay."

"Yes," she said. "Of course."

"We'll increase tillage in that way, by reclaiming the bogs. I don't want to convert to grazing at the expense of crops. Particularly grain. Too precarious. There was famine in 1741—" He shook his head. "That's the other thing I want to start on right away. A mill. And storage enough for our surplus. I won't have my people starving. And I want to begin replacing the trees—" He motioned up the valley. "All those hills used to be forested. There's an old ironworks up there. I've thought of reopening it. We'd have to operate on imported coke until the trees are ready."

"Only a few decades, my lord," she murmured.

"Yes." He sighed harshly. "I don't know that I have the patience for trees."

Roddy chewed the inside of her cheek to control herself.

He gazed at the far hills. She lost her desire to laugh as she saw the bitterness come into his face. "If I could have begun planting when I first had the notion," he said, "they'd be fifteen years along by now."

She wished she could touch him, soothe away half a lifetime of frustration. "'Tis no matter, my lord," she offered softly. "The trees will be there for our children."

He looked toward her. His horse moved restlessly beneath him, closer to hers. He caught her hand in a hard squeeze. "Little girl." He raised her glove to his lips. "If not for you, there'd be no trees at all."

She smirked, to cover the way her mouth quivered with a sudden, silly weakness. "No. Nor children either, I should hope. Shall I beat you to the bottom of the hill, my lord?"

"Indeed not." His grip transferred instantly to her horse's bridle. "You'll break your neck." He grinned as the horses sidled. "And it's such a pretty neck, my love. I have plans for it."

Roddy felt herself blushing. "You seem to have plans for everything, my lord."

He let go of her horse. The animal moved forward, and he brushed her cheek as she passed. "But some," he said seductively, "can be executed so much sooner than others."

Roddy ducked her head and gave her mount a kick. They scrambled ahead of him down the long, green hill.

Riding with Faelan through the wild and lovely country, she found it easy to forget the antagonism that had erupted this morning. But as they approached the home of John Willis, Roddy began to lose her carefree mood. She glanced often at Faelan. He did not seem to be concerned about the coming interview. He did not even mention it; just rode easily down the well-tended side road and past the stone gates toward the house.

It sat among fine grounds, this house they were to summarily wrest from its resident. Roddy liked it, in spite of herself: it had a simple, pretty Palladian facade softened by a thick growth of vines that had turned scarlet in the autumn chill. A peat fire warmed even the high-ceilinged entrance hall, the coals burning in an efficient chimney that drew off all the smoke and still radiated a comfortable heat—a feat which the O'Connells' smoky fireplaces had not accomplished half so well.

Mr. Willis stepped into the hall with his hand outstretched just as the manservant was taking Roddy's cloak.

It was a welcome carefully contrived, Roddy knew, exquisitely timed to be gracious and yet unperturbed by His Lordship's visit. Under Mr. Willis' polite reserve was a turmoil of question and curiosity at this unprecedented "honor."

He was utterly unaware of Faelan's plans for him. Roddy realized that instantly, and it made her more miserable than before. She smiled painfully in answer to his greeting, hardly knowing how to act toward someone who was about to experience what seemed to her the most heartless act of cruelty. As they sat down in the pleasant drawing room amid gold velvet draperies and polished wood, she glanced at Faelan.

No manners, no morals, and no heart, he had said.

That was not quite true. The devil himself could not have been more smooth of manner as he accepted a glass of rum punch from his victim.

Mr. Willis was much younger than Roddy had expected, round-faced and boyish-looking, with fine brown hair tied back in a limp queue. Behind a pince-nez and a mild smile, his mind worked rapidly, assessing his guests and his interests. His hospitality held none of the emotion, the warmth and strong tradition, that characterized the O'Connells'. His actions were schooled and careful. It was necessary to be polite to his landlord; it was expected. And so he was.

They began with a discussion of Roddy and Faelan's journey, moved to the weather and the hunting, and the frightful lack of decent horses in the area.

"Since the Relief Act, there's not a nag to be had for under twenty pound," Mr. Willis said. "Why, I can remember my father speaking of the time, not threescore years ago, Your Lordship, when that Popish fellow—O'Leary, the one eloped with Eileen O'Connell—refused to give up his mare for five pounds when the sum was legally offered. They shot the man," he said with satisfaction, "but everything's changed now. They wouldn't do so now, and there's not a bag o' bones will hold a saddle to be gotten for love nor money."

"Yes," Faelan said, in that neutral way Roddy had come to know so well. "It's bound to be an inconvenience, when you can't have a man shot for overpricing his horse."

Willis laughed in honest humor. "Too true, Your Lordship. Only too true."

"I understand you think the same of my price for the renewal of your lease."

The other man came back to business with a jolt, but he recovered smoothly. "Ah—the lease, Your Lordship. We can discuss that at some other time. I should be loath to bore your lovely wife with farming matters."

Faelan set down his empty glass and sat back in his chair. In his polished boots and open coat, he was the epitome of the carelessly elegant aristocrat, a fine greyhound to Willis' plump country beagle. "I think we will discuss it now," he said softly.

Roddy's finger tightened around the cup of tea she held. She took a sip, and tried to keep the cup from rattling in its saucer.

Willis recognized the disadvantage of trying to come to terms with his opponent's young wife present. "Your Ladyship," he said. "If your husband insists—I'm terribly sorry to have no hostess to represent me. Perhaps my housekeeper might take you on a tour of the house... or would it be too cold for you to stroll in the garden?"

"Not at all." Roddy was happy to leave. Willis had hardly impressed her with his talk of five-pound horses, but he seemed no more than a plump gamecock in her husband's ruthless hands, and she had no desire at all to be in at the kill. She and Mr. Willis started to rise, but Faelan remained firmly in his seat.

"Don't desert us, my dear," he said. She caught the hint of steel beneath the silk. "This won't take a moment."

Roddy sat back down.

After a moment, Mr. Willis did so, too. Like two children caught misbehaving and called up for a lecture, they glanced at one another.

Mr. Willis recoiled a little from the first direct look into Roddy's eyes. She tried to smile, to show him that she, at least, was not so unfeeling of his situation. But then, he did not know his situation yet, and he took her smile and quickly lowered lashes as coy shyness. *Charming*, he thought. *Damned shame this devil's got hold of her.*

Aloud, he said with determined pleasantry, "You wished to discuss the renewal, then, Your Lordship?"

"Yes. I'm afraid the offer in your letter to me several months ago will be insufficient."

"Indeed." Mr. Willis glanced at Roddy. "Well, Your Lordship, I would have preferred to discuss this between us in private, but since you insist on coming to terms immediately, I'll say without ceremony that I can go to an annual rent of four thousand, and that is my absolute limit."

"I see. We won't be able to come to an agreement, then. Do you have any documentation on the net worth of your improvements?"

It was said so evenly and casually that Mr. Willis missed the point for an instant. Then his mouth thinned into a smile. He steepled his fingers and leaned back, tilting his head. "Your Lordship," he said. "You're unfamiliar with the area. Four thousand is an excellent offer, I assure you. You would look far and long and not find better. But I understand that you may wish to do so. Perhaps we could make an appointment for three weeks hence to further—"

"No. Thank you, Mr. Willis. I expect you will have long vacated by the time three weeks have passed. In fact, my wife and I will be looking forward to taking up residence here next Sunday."

"Faelan—"

He silenced Roddy with a flicking glance and spoke again to Willis. "You may not wish to move all your furniture on short notice. I'm sure Her Ladyship would be happy to look over anything you wish to leave."

"I shall do nothing of the sort!" Roddy's conscience overwhelmed her on hearing this last indignity to be forced on the hapless Mr. Willis. "I won't turn this poor man out of his home, and then come and look over his furniture as if 'twere at public auction."

"As you will," Faelan said moderately. "We'll fit the place out to your own taste, then."

"No." Having taken a stand, Roddy clung to it. "I won't live here, Faelan."

He had been contemplating the view beyond the windows; at that, he looked toward her. Only his bright, cold glance and the faint flaring of his nostrils betrayed any emotion at all.

"I'm sure this discussion is quite unnecessary," Mr. Willis said. "I confess—I had no notion that you intended to take up permanent residence. You're welcome here for as long as you wish, of course; I've a house in Kenmare to which I can remove—"

"Absolutely not. We won't put you out of your home." Roddy set her chin, in spite of the ice-blue warning in Faelan's eyes. It was he who had insisted that she sit through this farce; let him find that she was not so docile a creature as he seemed to think. To be a willing party to this barbarousness... it was impossible.

"You won't live here, my lady?" Faelan asked politely. Freezingly.

She took a breath. "No. Not even if Mr. Willis should remove."

"I'm sorry for it," Faelan said. And that was all.

Mr. Willis, trying to smooth the disagreement over, said placatingly, "No, no, the house is yours. I shall do quite well in Kenmare; it won't inconvenience me in the slightest. And I'm sure you'll be wanting to begin on something grander for yourselves."

"It appears my lady has her principles," Faelan said. "We won't be moving here, then. But I still expect you will vacate the house by Sunday."

"Your Lordship," Mr. Willis said, with the smiling patience of a man speaking to a small and rather dense child. "I feel certain that after you've a chance to review any other offers, you'll find this decision is precipitate."

"I don't fear that."

Faelan's certainty made Mr. Willis frown at him uneasily. "You don't have a better treaty, Your Lordship?"

"No."

Mr. Willis sat back in relief. "Then, sir, allow me to explain the local situation to you. The subtenants—their rents simply cannot be raised at this time. No Christian man could ask it. Any larger offer will cut directly into my own living, I fear, Your Lordship."

Faelan smiled. "Ah. We couldn't have that, could we?"

"I think you can sympathize with my position. It's a simple matter of arithmetic. I'm sorry, Your Lordship, but you will not get a better offer."

"And I won't move into this house," Roddy said. "So there's no need for this to continue, is there? Faelan, please. I'm sure Mr. Willis' offer is quite fair, and we can find somewhere else to live—"

"Oh, I intend to discuss that point with you, my lady," Faelan said. "Never fear. But you're right; there's no need to go on with this conversation. My decision on the lease is final. The old lease fell in ten days ago, and that Mr. Willis remains here at all is on my sufferance. If he and his belongings are still here past Sunday next, he can expect a visit from the bailiff."

Sixteen

FAELAN DID NOT SPEAK AS THEY RODE FROM THE HOUSE. At the end of the drive, he turned west, away from the direction they had come onto an overgrown track that seemed to lead up into the very mountains themselves. It reminded Roddy of the paths they had taken after the fairy ball. But then Faelan's face had been open and easy; he had pointed out landmarks and named each one; he had told her stories of ancient kings and laughed when Roddy swatted her shaggy pony for trying to take a nip out of her hat.

He wasn't laughing now. His hands on his mount's reins were unnaturally gentle and controlled, a sign, she feared, that an explosive temper was held in rigid check. He might not punish an innocent animal in his fury, but she had no certainty of what he might do to the blatantly guilty human party concerned.

She didn't speak, either, afraid to question their direction or intentions. *If we're going to evict Mr. Farrissy*, she thought miserably, *I believe I shall start to cry.*

They rode for a full hour in silence. Then, high in the hills, they descended suddenly into a brushy valley. She caught the first touch of unfamiliar minds at the same time she smelled the sharp tang of burning peat. It was a child's raw hunger and whimpering that filled the wretched stone hut huddling at the side of the path, a baby, not more than a year old, whose incoherent unhappiness overwhelmed any other thought.

Faelan halted and swung off his horse, greeting in her own language the black-swathed woman who came to the door. She looked at him and Roddy, her eyes red-rimmed from the smoke that wafted through the thatch and the open door, and crossed herself quickly. Faelan spoke again, and above the baby's misery Roddy felt the unfamiliar words form a sharp image of the great ruined mansion in the woman's head. She glanced from Faelan to Roddy. One moment Roddy was looking with her own eyes at Faelan's profile, and the next she saw him as a stranger, an image as dark and frightening as the ghostly great house itself.

Roddy's own presence made it worse. She saw herself as the woman saw her: richly dressed, smiling oddly, a wisp of gold flame with eyes that could kindle nightmares. The woman stood rooted to the spot on bare, muddy feet, emanating a mixture of awe and profound fear, and Roddy knew that the cottier woman was convinced her visitors were something other than human.

The woman stepped back, and began to beckon them urgently into the squalid hut. Her dismay, Roddy realized, was centered not so much on fear of the unknown as on her utter lack of anything to share or offer. Not to be thought niggardly or close was her greatest fear—this woman who had not even food for her crying child.

Faelan moved to follow without glancing back at Roddy. On her own, she scrambled from her horse, willing her nose not to wrinkle as she entered the dark hut.

Inside she could hardly see for the smoke and the watering of her eyes. But the sound of grunting snuffles and the dreaming dark mind of an animal alerted her to the sow and six piglets sprawled out in the corner. There seemed to be no furniture; the baby lay whimpering on the dirt floor amongst a pile of straw and rags.

Faelan said something in a kind tone, and bent over the child. There was nothing threatening in the gesture, but to Roddy's shock a shaft of sheer panic struck the woman. Her mouth dropped open, and her cry and Roddy's blended, halting Faelan in mid-move.

"Don't touch it," Roddy exclaimed. "She thinks—"

Roddy stopped, caught exposing knowledge she should have no way of knowing. Faelan straightened, his gaze passing from her to the peasant woman's frightened face.

"We scare her," Roddy said quickly. "Is it possible—I mean… she seems to think you might hurt the child."

That was not exactly what the woman thought. The fear in her mind was that Faelan was going to steal the baby; that the *sidhe* had come to take the little girl away to raise her as one of their own.

In a peculiar, spotty way, Roddy translated the unknown words through another's mind and images as Faelan told the woman that she had nothing to fear for her child. He moved away from the baby, and stood looking down at the pigs.

Instantly the woman scurried into the corner. She grabbed a piglet, ignoring the grunts and squeals to pull out the one she considered the finest, and thrust it into Faelan's hands.

He looked down at the wriggling creature, and a strange black humor curved his mouth. He turned to Roddy. She had no more choice than he about receiving the squalling, wriggling creature into her arms. "It seems we have a gift," he said, above the pathetic shrieks.

The sharp panic of the little animal and the dull hunger of the baby seemed to thicken the air in the hut until Roddy could not breathe. "Faelan," she said hoarsely, trying to hand the piglet back, "we can't take it! She has nothing, not even a scrap of bread for her child."

"Ah, you think you know the way of it all, don't you?" His mocking voice cut through the dimness. "You leave it, then. You leave this miserable suckling pig and let this woman lie awake nights for a year, fearing that the *bhean sidhe* will return to take her babe." He jerked his head toward the trembling figure, white-faced in the gloom. "Aye, she's afraid of us, little girl. You more than me. You look straight in her eyes and give her back her gift in the name of charity. Do that, and see how grateful she'll be."

Roddy stood still, gripping the piglet—knowing Faelan was right, that the woman was terrified the *bhean sidhe* would refuse her gift. The naming echoed in the woman's mind, a darker one than ever Faelan called her. *Banshee*, it was, the stuff of nightmares. Roddy meant to do good, to reach out and help, but the truth was always there to bind her. Forever different, forever to be shunned for the trace of strange power that clung to her. She could never be kind to this plain peasant woman. She could only be fearsome, a fell spirit to be appeased.

Her mouth thinned and quivered, and the blurring in her eyes was not all smoke. She hefted the scrabbling animal and turned away, slipping a little as her skirts trailed in the mud just outside the low front door. She reached her horse and stood there, unable to mount, unable to cry, unable to do anything but stand helplessly and clutch the filthy, unhappy piglet to her breast.

She heard Faelan behind her. He took the little animal under one arm in a grip that made it squeal even louder, and with the other hand boosted Roddy into her saddle. He handed up the piglet and left her. Without a word, he began to rummage in his saddlebag.

He brought out a half loaf of hard-crusted bread and some oatcakes. He tore the bread, and Roddy saw him slip a gold coin deep into the soft interior. When the woman came out of the hut to watch, he offered her a portion of the bread and oatcake, and leaned against a tree to eat the rest.

Roddy sat on her horse with the piglet and watched. Somehow, it seemed, she had gotten to be the villain of this piece: here she sat like some aloof princess with her royal booty while the two of them shared a companionable meal. Faelan ate all of his, but the peasant woman only nibbled at her oatcake. When she had eaten part, she nodded toward the hut and spoke. Roddy understood that she meant to ask Faelan if he would be pleased for her to share the bread with her baby.

He nodded assent. As soon as she disappeared inside the hut, he swung up onto his horse and nudged it toward Roddy. Grabbing her reins, he led her at a rapid trot down the brushy path and out of sight of the cottage.

Roddy had her hands too full of piglet to make any complaints or demands at the bouncing gait. They splashed across a deep, wide stream, and began rising steadily. When the path flowed into an overgrown road and took a switchback, she realized suddenly where they were.

Above them loomed the burned-out mansion, rising dark gray and skeletal against the hill. Faelan's horse broke into a canter and hers followed, demanding every ounce of skill she had as a horsewoman to hang on to the squirming pig and keep her seat. Faelan didn't seem particularly worried that she'd lose it, she thought grimly, and could not decide whether that was a compliment or an insult. Or just forgetfulness... although how he could forget this pig when it squealed as if it were being eaten alive she could not imagine.

They drew up before the great house, the horses blowing and the piglet kicking and complaining. Roddy could see the far hillside through the barren windows. Like a dead hand, a piece of rotting silk waved gloomily from the closest one.

"Will you shut that damned thing up?" Faelan snarled as the piglet's squalling echoed off the ruined walls.

Roddy was angry; she was exhausted from fighting the piglet and trying to stay on her horse; her ribs ached from the baby animal's thumpings; she was hungry, and she had the strong suspicion that it was her own lunch that had gone to feed the cottier woman while Faelan had stood calmly by and eaten all of his own.

"Oh, *yes*, my lord," she snapped. "Immediately!" She held the piglet out straight in her trembling arms and gave it a shake. "Silence, please! Or His Most High and Mighty Royal Highness will have you summarily evicted!"

He dragged her horse up and twisted around, his mouth tight and dangerous. "Don't tread on me, Roddy. You've damn well done enough today."

"What have I done? Sat by and watched you throw a man out of his living. Taken the food out of a babe's mouth because of some nonsense about fairies—"

"Get down." He swept the piglet out of her hands and dismounted with it under one arm. She watched him stride over toward the house and deposit the animal in one of the empty ornamental urns that guarded the broad, moss-covered steps. The piglet shrieked pathetically, its cries interspersed with the scrabbling sounds of its small feet on the stone. "God," he said. "Will it never be silent?"

"It's hungry." Roddy dismounted alone, though it was no easy task in her hampering skirts. "Like some others I could mention." From the cantle of her saddle hung a leather wine flask. She untied it and peered over the top of the stone vase, holding the mouth of the flask pinched closed until the piglet's anxious lips found a shape that promised nourishment.

The commotion in the urn quieted suddenly. The piglet took to the "imported" Spanish wine as if it were ambrosia.

Faelan swore. "Will you waste all our drink on that squalling beast?"

"I've gone hungry. I suppose you can go thirsty."

He paced over to where she stood looking down into the urn and pulled up her chin. "Hungry, are you? Surely such mortal weaknesses don't touch your charitable soul."

She jerked away. "The only food I begrudge is that *you* ate. You might have given her it all."

"She wouldn't have taken it that way."

"No? How convenient, to think so."

His frown grew black and deep. "I know these people," he said. "She wouldn't have taken it."

"If you know them so well, why did you tarry there at all? Could you not predict what would happen?" She lifted her eyes and stared hotly into his. "Behold—" she sneered. "A *fairy*, my lord. Come to steal a babe, or a swine, or whatever she can filch. I know what people think of me; how they dread to look at me, and turn away as soon as they can. 'Tis no different here, but only more honest." Her voice broke slightly, and she clenched her teeth and looked down to hide it. "*Banshee*," she said to the wine flask and the suckling pig. "Is that how they'll call me? Well, I understand the meaning of that, too, my lord. It takes no great knowledge of the people to guess."

A silence followed her bitter words, filled only by the

sniffling sounds of the piglet. Faelan turned away and crossed the steps; sat down heavily in the center.

"Yes." His voice sounded suddenly hollow and tired. "I shouldn't have stopped there. I was angry. I wanted to show you—" He broke off, frowning down at his boots. "Damn you. Why did you cross me with Willis?"

"I should think that was obvious. It's wrong, to put him out with nothing. I won't live in that house, and I won't live in this Mr. Farrissy's house when you put him out. I couldn't, knowing—" She bit her lip, and then said carefully, "*Imagining* what it would feel like, to lose one's home so suddenly."

"And how do you suppose that woman felt," he snapped, "when her husband died and Willis evicted her because she couldn't meet the rent?"

A furious response died on Roddy's tongue as the significance of his words dawned on her. "He put her out?" she repeated stupidly.

"Oh, aye—that he did, my dear. Along with a hundred others." Faelan rubbed his hands across his face. Then suddenly, harshly, he laughed. He took off his hat, leaning with one elbow on the highest step with his black hair curling and blowing softly in the wind. "So," he said. "What do you think of your new abode?"

Roddy blinked.

He waved his hat, taking in the ruined mansion in one sweep. "You've made your bed, little girl. This seems to be the only place now that we have to lie in it."

❧

Faelan, Roddy mused with a sigh, was most definitely not quite sane. From her position on the hill above the house, she looked down into the biting west wind on five weeks of progress. The structure had taken on a strange, comical appearance—half hairy, half bald—where the hastily erected roof framework had been covered temporarily with thatch that was now being removed to make way for the blue slates that had arrived by ship from Wales.

She drew her cloak up around her chin, holding MacLassar

under the warm folds. He gave a comfortable little series of grunts and settled down to sleep after his lunch of cow's milk and Spanish wine.

It was Faelan who had named the piglet. MacLassar—Son of Flame, for the way it had emerged from its first tumultuous bathing to follow doggedly at Roddy's heels and curl up at her feet on their bed of straw in the abandoned stable.

Roddy could see Faelan now on the roof with the other workers; he was easy to pick out, taller and broader of shoulder than the rest, his voice clipped and impatient as he issued orders and then moved to do the job himself if the laborer didn't respond fast enough for him.

He had absolutely no tact.

She remembered with wrenching clarity the day the tenants and cottiers had gathered at his invitation in front of the big house. They were all sorts, some plain and warmly dressed, but many in threadbare wool. A surprising number sat on good hunters, decked out in clothes as fine as any country squire's. They stood in a straggling half-circle facing the terrace and the house, with their hats in their hands so that the chill wind off the sea blew their hair in their eyes, waiting for Faelan to speak.

They were afraid of him. All of them. In some it was a conscious thing, as the cottier woman's fear had been—a peasant's belief in fairies and the creatures of the night. In others, mainly the ones on horseback, the fear was clothed in belligerent anger, in mental scorn and enmity. There were patterns there, secrets and self-interest, but the fear hung over it all like black smoke. They had expected an Englishman and a stiff and proper lady, but to a man what they saw was something else entirely. The devil and his fallen angel. A bad dream come to life.

Faelan just stood, watching the uneasy crowd in silence. He seemed to be looking at each man at his leisure, immune to the cold that made everyone else shiver and curl their toes in their boots and MacLassar huddle completely under Roddy's skirt. At length a rider kicked his horse forward and reined up in front of the weed-grown terrace steps.

"Will you be speakin', my lord," he demanded, "or keepin' us stamping our feet all the day long?"

Faelan raised his eyes to the man on the horse, a man whose sparse-haired pate wouldn't even have topped his lord's shoulders if the rider had been standing on the ground.

"Rupert," Faelan said pleasantly. "Rupert Mullane. I remember."

His pure, unaccented intonation rang out like a clear warning bell. Rupert Mullane gave a stiff nod in return for the recognition. He was secretly a little gratified to be remembered, but he knew better than to show it. "You've a marvelous head for names," he said ungraciously. "You might have come back and used it a few years past." He paused, and then added, "My lord," as if it were an after-thought, hoping his comrades appreciated his daring incivility.

"I was prevented."

Rupert would have snorted in disbelief, but even from a slight advantage of height, he did not quite have the nerve.

"Mr. Mullane," Faelan said. "If you would be so kind as to remove your mount..."

Roddy turned curiously toward the crowd, surprised to find that several were pleased to see Mullane dismissed so coolly. The approvers stood at the back, a knot of three, two strapping young men and an older one dressed in muddy shoes and worn leggings. Roddy focused on the oldest, who was half listening and half fretting about a milk cow that had dried up and the charge Mullane planned to make for a replacement. But Faelan's next words caught the man's full attention.

"Gentlemen," Faelan said, when Mullane had reluctantly backed his horse aside. "My intentions are simple. I plan to put this estate into full productivity. I have no interest whatsoever in your religious beliefs, your political affiliations, or the way you've always done things. In all matters concerning my land, I demand your unreserved cooperation. If you or your families are ill fed or clothed, you will come to me. In return for short-term assistance, you will plant what I tell you, when and where. Those who wish to participate with me in improvements to the estate may lease cattle from me at five shillings a head per annum. You will do things in my way, or you may expect that your lease will not be renewed. Are there any questions?"

Faelan, Roddy thought ruefully, could give his own mother lessons on insensitivity. Only the trio Roddy had noticed before, and a few others, turned to look at one another in disbelief at the astonishing generosity of the five-shilling offer. The rest were bridling visibly at Faelan's blunt demands.

Mullane was quick to capitalize on the fantastical sound of the scheme. "Five shillings, my lord!" He flung a grin over his shoulder toward his fellow riders. "He'll be runnin' us out of business, now!"

"Yes," Faelan said calmly. "I will."

Oh, God, Roddy thought, closing her eyes in despair.

"And just where would these cattle be hidin'?" a horseman at the far end of the gathering called. "Faith, I've no five-shillin' cattle for sale."

"Nor I!" cried another, and a round cheer of agreement went up.

Faelan shrugged. "Not yet, perhaps." He surveyed the muttering crowd. "Any other questions?"

"Aye! Will ye be upholdin' the tithe?" someone shouted, from far back and unseen.

Everyone quieted. That sudden silence was warning enough, but Roddy received the full force of feeling on the subject. The tenants might be divided over the five-shilling cattle, but here was an issue they would unite and kill for.

"What tithe?" Faelan asked, in that carefully emotionless voice Roddy had learned to recognize.

A babble broke out, shouts, and Mullane urged his horse forward. "To the damned Church of Ireland!" he yelled, dragging on his horse's reins until the poor animal danced and half reared in protest.

Roddy took a step backward, intimidated by the rising emotion. But Faelan's hand on her elbow stopped her as he faced the crowd. "I don't give a damn if you pay the Church of Ireland or the Church of Rome or if all your souls go to bloody hell," he shouted. "But don't look to the Devil Earl for salvation when you're starving to death. Not if you cross me now."

In the disconcerted silence that followed this speech, Faelan began to look to his tenants like the devil indeed. To hear him call himself by the title they'd used to vilify him for twenty-five years seemed to make the illusion concrete. Roddy realized that the Devil Earl had been something of an entertainment at a distance, like a child's shiver of pleasure over tales of ghosts, but in the flesh he appeared all too satanic for comfort. And his bride...

They wouldn't even look at Roddy, except from the corners of their eyes. Abruptly they all wanted to leave. Further discussion of leases and cattle and even tithes seemed to lose its appeal. When they came up one by one to tug their forelocks and make their awkward bows, there was an agitation that bordered on panic in the simplest of them, and a struggle to hold back superstitious uneasiness even in the more sophisticated. Roddy smiled in her friendliest manner and got nothing but grunts and monosyllables in return.

Rupert Mullane hung back until last, and dismounted in stiff dignity. He kissed Roddy's hand with a flourish. For the briefest moment he held her gaze, and her talent reacted, going down levels and levels of thought in an instant, past the pride and the despair of being too small to physically intimidate, past the anger at Faelan's highhandedness, past the wild schemes of retaliation down to the fear, real and deep, that Faelan could do what he promised—destroy Mullane's livelihood. And underneath that fear was animal instinct: the will to survive and prosper at any cost.

Faelan turned away and started back for the house as the gathering broke up into little knots of men who hurried off in pregnant silence. Roddy called softly to him. When he turned, she nodded toward the cottier and his two sons, who were lingering under the pretense of adjusting their leggings.

Faelan appeared to recognize the situation in an instant. "Send Martha," was all he said before walking on. "Meet me in the study."

Roddy nodded, glad that in this, at least, he had realized the delicacy of human psychology. The cottier and his sons were in a difficult position. They wanted to investigate Faelan's offer, but to be the first to do so openly would place them firmly in his camp, where they were not at all certain that they wanted to be.

With MacLassar at her heels, she hurried into the house where the maid Martha had begun a furious attack on the impossible job of sweeping out decades of accumulated rubble. "Those men—" Roddy almost shoved Martha out the terrace door. "Ask them in for tea, and then bring them to the study. Hurry!"

Martha gave her mistress a look which was as expressive as the astonishment in her mind before she gathered her skirts and rushed after the cottier family, who had begun to walk away.

Roddy pulled her shawl around her and headed for the "study," which was in fact only a room in the old servants' quarters which still had a dry roof. In the two days since Martha had arrived with their baggage, she and Roddy had been able to clear and arrange a makeshift desk out of two overturned cookpots and an old stall partition. It was so cold in the room that Roddy could see her breath frost when she pushed open the door. She found Faelan on his knees making up the fire.

"They'll be here in a moment, my lord," she said, crossing to the window. With the corner of her shawl, she wiped at the accumulated dust on the broken pane, trying to add more light to the dismal scene. She heard Faelan come up behind her and turned, brushing at her hands.

He caught one wrist and raised it, kissing a smudgy palm with a hard, brief pressure. His fingers were warm against her icy skin, but she felt the tension in them, saw the taut look about his eyes that had been there the night of the fairy ball. It was important to him, this meeting with three rough country peasants. It was life or death to the dreams he cherished.

Martha ushered the trio into the room with an air that would have been casual in London, but which seemed quite regal in this dingy place.

"Mister Donald O'Sullivan. Mister Evan and Mister Fe... Fac..." Martha bit her unruly tongue and took a breath.

"Fachtnan," said the tallest of the two sons, with a shy, sideways grin on his freckled face. "Ye make it pretty, miss, however ye speak it."

Martha curtsied quickly, blushing to the roots of her hair with pleasure at the small personal attention. She looked with shining eyes at Fachtnan. *Oh, la*, she thought, *he likes me*, and hurried to pump the ancient bellows and set the teapot on the hob. Roddy had planned to send the maid off and make the tea herself, but she hadn't the heart to cut Martha's little romance so short.

There were no chairs. Roddy hoped Faelan knew better than to lean against the unstable desk. He stood next to it, looking very much as he always did, which was enough to put the cottiers in a misery of tongue-tied unease. The rough surroundings only made him more elegant and mysterious and intimidating than ever, while at Roddy they dared not look at all.

The cottiers stood unhappily, not knowing what to do and expecting Faelan to speak. They had no notion of taking the initiative. The father had begun trying to remember an old tale he'd heard of a man who'd sold himself to the devil, uneasily comparing the details of the story to this scene. Roddy suddenly thought that the five-shilling offer was a mistake, that it was so low as to be suspicious. Here in this remote valley among ruins long dead, it was all too easy to believe in ancient tales. She kept her own eyes carefully away from the men and sought desperately for some way to undermine their fears. To make Faelan and herself human.

Martha began to set china cups out on the table for the tea, and the clatter seemed very loud in the silence. Redhaired Fachtnan cleared his throat nervously.

"Tea, gentlemen?" Faelan said finally.

In a fright that he would break the cup and humiliate them all, Fachtnan said, "No, thankee, m'lord. No, thankee. We don't take tea."

The others nodded agreement.

Roddy was still watching Faelan, afraid he would lean on the table and precipitate his own humiliation. She saw him shift his weight and reach out his hand, and stepped forward in quick reaction. Her foot encountered something soft. The next instant a loud squeal cut the tension in the air.

MacLassar shot out from beneath her skirts, snuffling and crying piteously. He ran between the elder O'Sullivan's legs, found no comfort there, and darted toward Martha's skirt.

The maid—no country-bred girl—shrieked, "A *rat*," and with a move that was completely unpremeditated threw herself headlong into Fachtnan's strong arms.

She nearly knocked him down. He staggered back, clutching her as much for balance as for giving support, but by the time he had recovered, a flash of very masculine appreciation coursed through him as his hands fitted around Martha's sturdy torso. He slid his palms upward in the guise of steadying her and his thumbs curved under her heaving breasts. "There now, miss. 'Tis no but a wee pig, do you see?"

"I believe it belongs to the countess," Faelan said calmly, reaching down to where MacLassar cowered with deep-throated, sorrowful grunting underneath one of the cookpots.

He handed the piglet across the table.

Roddy grabbed her charge hastily and slung him into his favorite position with his small forefeet dangling over her shoulder and his snout pressed lovingly behind her ear. She dared one glance up into Faelan's face. Fearing the worst, she took a moment to interpret the strange twist and hardening of his jaw.

Donald O'Sullivan coughed in a strained way. The air in the room had changed; Roddy felt the cottiers' eyes on the Devil Earl and his countess as they faced one another across the table. The vision formed in her head in all its absurdity—the dingy room, the china cups; herself staring apprehensively up at her husband with a piglet slung over her shoulder and Faelan with a belly laugh trapped behind the fierce set of his mouth.

Roddy bit her lip. MacLassar grunted and snuffled in her ear. Her body began to shake. "Oh, my," she gasped. "I'm so s-sorry!"

Martha giggled. Donald O'Sullivan began to chuckle. "Ah, well," he said. "An' we was after thinkin' m'lord and m'lady too fine and fearsome to traffic with the likes of pigs and poor dairymen."

Roddy met his eyes while the laughter still lit her own, and was pleased and astonished to find that at that moment he'd rather look at her than not. Everyone in the room was smiling at her—directly at her—and she felt as giddy and self-conscious as Martha had under Fachtnan's appreciative gaze.

A half hour later, the O'Sullivans had departed with the promise of twoscore cows in exchange for a pound sterling at the end of a year. They could sell their butter for cash to Faelan. Fachtnan and Evan were to begin work on the mansion house, and spread the word that the wage of fifteen pence a day was no dream, but real enough for any cottier who would come to work and lease Faelan's cattle.

Martha had seen them out with all the pomp that was possible under the circumstances. When they had gone, Roddy set MacLassar on the floor.

"You see," she said as the piglet snuffled and snorted in mild complaint. "He's good for something."

Faelan moved around the table. Success and humor lit his blue eyes with something that made her breath catch in her throat. "Little girl." He came close and drew her into his arms. "I know what won them."

"What?" She stood with a smile that changed to a giggle as he squeezed her.

"'Twas you, of course. Magical *sidhe*." He tilted her chin up to plant a deep kiss on her quivering lips. "'Twas you," he whispered at the edge of her mouth. "Because you're so beautiful when you laugh."

Seventeen

RODDY HUGGED MACLASSAR, SNIFFING THE SCENT OF THE lavender water she'd bathed him in and smiling to herself at the memory of Faelan's way of expressing gratitude. With Martha occupied by her new beau and Senach off wherever Senach spent his time, there had been a few hours of privacy that day in the empty stall where they'd made their bed.

It suited her better, she thought, to take a roll in the hay like a stablehand than play the gently bred Countess of Iveragh. It had been cold, but Faelan could always warm her; his words and his touch and the sky-fire of his eyes. A bed or barn, it made no difference when she was aware of nothing but his body hard and hot against hers.

That afternoon seemed long ago now, the last time in over a month that Faelan had been awake and hers alone. Winter was blowing in, and there was only work and more work in the sharp demand of the damp west wind.

Their cottiers had grown accustomed to the earl hammering beside them like a common laborer and the countess sweeping and hauling trash and bringing the workers tea and oatcakes with her pig and her maid in tow. That kind of acquaintance bred a measure of trust—at least they had stopped equating Faelan with the devil, by the simple logic that the devil would never have to work as hard as Faelan did to get a roof over his head.

Of Roddy they were less certain. Only the O'Sullivans spoke freely to her, and even with them the doubts would creep in if she happened to meet their eyes. It seemed that her difference was stronger here, and somehow more apparent. On those occasions, Roddy would smile at them and they would remember her laughing, and it set their minds at rest.

She wished it were so simple for herself. She knew now how it felt, that uneasy sense of facing a power beyond common humanity—knew it for reality, instead of through her gift. Every time her talent faded and slipped away and she looked up from whatever she was doing to find Senach's blind gaze upon her, her heart pounded and her legs trembled with the need to flee.

Public nakedness could not have been worse. She knew those empty eyes saw through her, pinned her and judged her: the petty fears and selfish needs, the times she'd used her gift to cheat—just a little, just a quick answer to spare her from a scolding, a remark made to sting and unsettle. And worse, far worse—the place in her heart that feared and adored and hungered for her husband, the place that cared not what he was, but only that he held her.

She could lose him. If he guessed her talent; if Senach told him and made him believe—

Roddy huddled in her cloak. The wind traced her exposed skin with cool, wet fingers, like Senach's lifeless, probing touch. She sat clutching MacLassar and his comforting small mind, where warmth and food were all that mattered and both were provided in plenty. But even as she drowsed there with him, she felt the connection slip away. She had climbed the hill to escape Senach. When she opened her eyes he was there.

"God bless," he said, and smiled at her. He was standing on the path below her, leaning on a staff. Farther down, the men still worked, and the sound of their voices blew away with the wind.

She took a breath, trying to slow the thump of her heart. "Good afternoon, Senach."

Her politeness was useless, all sham and humiliation; she knew that he saw through it to the loathing in her heart. *Go away*, her mind shouted. *Leave me be.*

"I've come," he said, "to show ye the way."

Roddy's arms tightened around MacLassar. The piglet shifted with a sighing grunt. "I'm just resting awhile. I wasn't going anywhere."

Senach's pale eyes found hers. She recoiled, refusing the challenge, jerking her face away to stare out to sea. *Don't. Don't look at me.*

"Your lad's father, he come here," Senach said. "He were a wee laddie thattime, and he come away up here to think."

Roddy looked down at her toes and fingered a tiny white flower that she had not noticed there before.

"Fionn's Kiss, he would call that wee blossom."

"It's pretty," she whispered.

"'Twill not last long. Away back then, in the olden times, the women would distill the wee petals and make a drink—no taste nor scent to it. 'Twould bring... sleep, of a kind. And other things, sometimes."

Roddy frowned at the gray and green spread before her, hoping that, if she showed no interest, Senach would go away.

He didn't. He went on, with a more certain rise and fall in his voice. A story he was telling, whether she would listen or not. "Aye, your laddie's father used to come here. He were a good lad, a stout strong lad, and smart as a whistle. But he were a dreamy fellow, do you know. Always looking for something, and it weren't there."

She found her eyes drawn to Senach's hands, resting like brown knots on the tall staff.

"The big men, the landowners, they sent their sons away," he said. "To the schools. For to be made into men. Most of 'em—ah, and many and many—they never come back. And if they do, they have forgotten. An' yer lad's father—Francis, that be his name—*his* father, he had to keep the land, do you know." Senach shook his head. "No blame in that, be God, no blame to him, though most say different. It's like a mountain, says I to yer laddie's father, an' the Catholics go up one side, an' the Protestants go up the other. But in them days, do you see, the big men, they had to be Protestant. They had to sign a paper, or say a few words renouncing

their creed—apostatizing, they call that—they had to become
Protestant, to hold the land."

Roddy stared at Senach's hands, caught up in the tale
despite herself.

"And yer lad's father's father—he did so," Senach said. "He
signed the paper, and he kept this land. He sent his son away
for to be educated with the English. And not for a long while,
a very long while, did he come back. We never thought to see
him come back atall."

But he would, Roddy thought. *If he were a dreamer, he'd come
back to this place.*

"Aye." Senach smiled. "He did come back. He brung with
him a wife—a quare lady, oh, she were that beautiful, with
fine clothes and fine airs, as fine as we'd ne'er seen."

Roddy sat there with her muddy cape and her windblown
hair, clutching a baby pig. *Not like me.*

The old man chuckled. "Och, but there's many a fine lady,
and don't he never think of none."

He lifted his opaque eyes to hers, and Roddy felt the chill
of blind sight like a shiver down her spine. She set her lower
lip and turned away.

"But this fine lady," Senach went on, "she were the
countess. She were the countess before you, do you see.
She had this boy—this one boy, and that be your laddie
away down there. And his father says to me, he says, 'I'll
not be sendin' that wee laddie away. I'll be educatin' him
meself. Ye and me, Senach,' he says. 'We'll be his masters.'
Because Francis, he had pined away for this place all them
years. He had pined away until he could not abide, and he
come home. And he took up the old religion, the Catholic
creed, in secret. At first it was secret. But then he began
to be seein' that there wouldn't be no other son; that this
son, this laddie of yours, he could hold the land all in one,
from here to there, and get out of the law that way—not
to divide it up amongst all his sons when he died because
he were of the old faith."

Senach turned, twisting his hands around the staff, and
looked down the hill. "I have to tell you that 'tis not so long

ago that if a man were of the Catholic creed, and his wife or son did what they call apostatize, as I be sayin', then they didn't any longer answer to him. They were set against him by the law, and free of him, and the land all went to the son, and the father were no more than his tenant."

Roddy frowned uneasily. "What are you saying?"

"Och, I'm saying that the rebellious wife, the unnatural son—they had only to convert to seize the land. A wee laddie, ten years old, had only to say that he were of the Established Church, and he would be taken from his father and put in a Protestant's care, and as much of the estate as the magistrate deemed fit and proper would be given over, and the father made a tenant, like the dairymen down there."

"That can't be true," she said. "A child—"

"A child of ten. He had only to say so, and the law gave him the land."

"Do you tell me Faelan did that?"

Senach made no answer. A light wash of rain spat a few drops onto his wrinkled hands.

"He couldn't have done that," Roddy said sharply. "He hadn't had the land until now."

"I hear crying," Senach said. "Do ye hear it?"

"No." Her fingers moved nervously.

"Aye. Oh, aye. I hear it. And Francis dead and murdered."

"What are you telling me?" she cried. "Say it in plain words!"

Senach shook his head. "Dead now and gone. Do the wee pretty pig be crying?"

"*No.*" The word was a sob. She felt unreasonable hot tears on her cheeks.

"Ye can help yer lad. 'Tis the truth ye be wanting."

Without meaning to, she looked down at the house. Through the sparkling blur, a single figure took shape, a fine, proud figure, black hair and white shirt against the browns and blues. He was working, rebuilding, and if she could not feel his drive and his weariness through her gift, she could guess it. She could remember every night for weeks, how he'd come in from working until midnight by torchlight, to eat and undress and take her in his arms and fall asleep as he buried his face in her hair.

Senach looked through her, and smiled. "He were a gallant lad, when he were childer. Aye. And then the dark come on him, and it has never left him from that day to this. 'Twere the day his father died, it was. The day the dark come on him."

She did not understand Senach. She was afraid to try.

"But you—" the old man said. "You be the flame. You be the light. Ye cannot go thinking of yourself only."

Roddy stared down at her knees. "I think of him," she whispered.

"Aye. Oh, aye. And when you think of him, ye fear."

No, she thought. And, *Yes*. She drew her legs up and hid her face in her hands.

"A gift ye have. Or so you call it. And you think 'tis a curse instead."

"It is," she cried into her hands. "I hate it!"

He chuckled softly. "Ah. 'Tis a sad sight. Cryin' and pityin', and who is that for, I ask ye?"

"Don't tell him what's wrong with me." She could not keep the quiver from her voice. "Don't tell him."

Senach did not answer that.

"Please," Roddy whispered. "You know I can't—with him. You must know. There's nothing. Nothing! It wouldn't be fair. He'd think I—" She stumbled on the enormity of what Faelan would feel if he knew of her talent, if he thought that she read him the way Senach read her. The horror of it almost choked her. "Oh, God, it wouldn't be fair. I could never make him believe I can't. He'd send me away. He wouldn't have me here."

"The truth, now."

She scrambled to her feet, pushing MacLassar aside. "That *is* the truth! You know it's the truth. He'd send me away."

Senach's blind eyes followed her with uncanny accuracy. She tried to make herself believe that it was coincidence, or acute hearing—anything but what she feared. Impossible, that he should share her gift. Crazy, to talk to him as if he knew. She was alone in the world. She'd always been alone. A freak. Somehow that was easier to accept than the notion that

Senach's words were anything more than the senile ramblings of an old, old man.

He leaned on the staff, his pale eyes turned toward her. *He's blind*, she assured herself. *Old and blind.*

And Senach began to laugh.

Her nerve broke at that. With a small cry she turned, abandoning even the nominal courtesy of a farewell. She began to run up the path, up the hill, with the rough furze dragging at her cloak and the rocks clattering beneath her shoes. She could hear nothing but that and the sound of her own harsh breath.

At the top of the hill she stopped and turned. MacLassar was struggling to follow, his small feet scrabbling for purchase on the wet, rocky slope. Senach was nowhere to be seen.

She stamped her foot, ridiculing the idea that no one of his age could have walked out of sight down the hill in that short time. There would be other ways, paths and hollows that she could not see—places an old man bent on terrorizing silly children would know.

MacLassar came panting up beside her. She picked him up and slung him over her shoulder, heading away from the mansion into the high hills and the mist.

She had no forethought about where she was going. She walked, because it seemed that she must put distance between herself and the insidious memory of Senach's words. The cold air stung her cheeks. Above her the black choughs followed and then wheeled away. The mists shifted, retreating and advancing, reaching out to envelop her.

Somewhere far back in her mind she was surprised that she did not stop. The path went on, though the world had gone to white and shadow. She followed it. Up and up, until her chest was heaving for air. MacLassar was strangely quiescent, bouncing along on her shoulder without complaint.

The path threading upward through furze and gorse had been easy to follow, but suddenly it leveled out and vanished in a stretch of rough grass and seemed to spread into infinity in the mist. Roddy paused. Around her, light shimmered through the atmosphere. She shifted MacLassar on her shoulder, and he gave a satisfied grunt.

There seemed to be some reason to go forward, and none to go back. She walked slowly into the open area. In front of her the paleness formed into shapes: flat stones set on end in a line that curved away like silent soldiers into the mist.

She walked forward. The only sound was the drag of her skirts on the dewy grass. As she moved past the line of rocks she could see that it curved back upon itself and made a circle, with a single group of odd-shaped boulders near the center. A few bushes grew among the spaces between, and a scattering of the tiny white flowers Senach had shown her, giving the group a softer, more welcoming look than the circle of brooding sentries.

She sat down on one of the rocks in the center. MacLassar wriggled until she set him on the ground, where he curled up at her feet and went to sleep.

Roddy went to sleep, too. At least, it seemed she must have, for when she looked back where she had come from the mist had thinned, and in a shaft of cool sunlight sat the woman who had danced with the militia captain on the night of the fairy ball.

Roddy recognized her instantly. She thought that she had even dreamed about her, so familiar did that face of winter beauty seem. The woman's hair was loose and long, a cascade of icy light. She sat with crossed legs amid a carpet of tiny, luminous white flowers, and looked at Roddy.

"How pretty you are," Roddy said.

The woman tilted her head and smiled.

"I'm Roderica," Roddy ventured again.

"I know," the woman said. She did not offer her own name.

"You helped us at the ball. I thank you for that."

The woman laughed, a sound that brought a pleased echo to Roddy's lips.

"Do you live nearby?" Roddy asked.

"Oh, yes. I do."

"We've only just come. My husband is rebuilding the old great house. Do you know it?"

The answer was a nod and another laugh. MacLassar lifted his head, and then came to his feet and ambled over to their visitor. He leaned against her, and Roddy felt his little shiver of pleasure as the woman touched his ears.

"Do you come here often?" Roddy asked.

"Often. To dance. Do you like to dance?"

"Yes." Roddy surprised herself a little with that answer. "I like it very much."

"Come back, then. Dance with me."

They both sat silent a moment, smiling at one another with the delight of discovery and new friendship.

The woman said, "I'll tell you stories."

"I'd like that."

"I'll sing for you. And you can sing for me."

Roddy nodded. "What's your name?"

"Fionn."

Bright and fair, that meant, though Roddy had no notion how she knew. "Like the flowers."

"Yes." The woman shook back her hair and rose fluidly. "You're called," she said. "I must go."

Roddy sat rooted to the boulder and watched as the slender figure was swallowed by the mists. MacLassar stumbled onto his short legs. With a happy, bucking leap, he shook himself out of sleep and ran to Roddy.

A moment later, she heard what Fionn must have: a voice shouting her name through the mist, hoarse with exhaustion and discouragement.

She stood up, and called out quickly in answer.

"*Roddy*." Faelan's outline appeared, a black shape, a rock that moved in the twilight atmosphere. He came through the circle with a determined stride, and only when he was very close could she see the strain in his face, the tight lines etched around his mouth and eyes. "Thank God!"

She thought for a moment he would pull her into his arms. But he stopped in front of her, his gaze sliding over her with a piercing urgency, as if to determine any hurt, and then he threw back his cloak and sat down hard on a rock. "I ought to beat you," he said fiercely. "God, I ought to beat you."

MacLassar trotted up and presented himself for an ear scratching.

"And you, too, you worthless beast," Faelan snapped. "I'll warrant you're the cause of this." He tore open the lacing at his neck and brought a leather pack and flask from beneath his cloak. "Here," he said, opening the pack and holding an oatcake out to Roddy. "Just eat a little at first. You must be half dead."

"I'm not hungry," Roddy said. "Give it to MacLassar."

"Christ. Don't get heroic on me with a goddamned pig. You eat it, before you fall down. Two days without food; I'm surprised you're on your feet at all."

"Two days!" She frowned at him. "Don't be silly. I broke fast and had tea, too, before I started up here."

"Sit down," Faelan said. "You're light-headed."

"No, I'm not. It hasn't been an hour since I—"

He grabbed her skirt and dragged her down beside him. "Sit down. *Eat.*"

Roddy sat. She broke off a corner of the oatcake and stuffed the dry morsel in her mouth. MacLassar came rushing up, and she gave the rest to him.

Faelan simply took out another and handed it to her.

"I'm not hungry," she said. "And you didn't have to come after me. I could have found my way back."

"For God's sake, are you feverish? You disappear for two days and then sit there and tell me I didn't have to come after you?"

"What are you talking about?" she demanded. "I took a walk, and I came up here and sat down for a few moments. I don't know what you mean—*disappearing* two days. I've worked just as hard as anyone! Yesterday I spent the whole afternoon on my knees clearing out the rubble you'd pushed down the drawing-room chimney, and the day before that I pulled down the last of the silk in the ballroom. With your help—or have you forgotten your grand fit of sneezing already?"

He looked toward her sharply. The concern on his face went to sudden wariness. Her question had been almost joking; his answer was soft, and deadly serious. He said slowly, "No. I remember that."

"Well," she said, as if that explained everything. But her heart began to thump in dismay.

He stared out at the circle of standing stones. The black mood came on him; she saw it in the way his eyes narrowed and his mouth curved. He stood up and walked to the tallest stone, put his palms flat against it as if he would shove it down. His teeth bared in that quick, savage straining at a hopeless cause. The rock never moved. With a jerk and a choked sound of frustration, he straightened, glaring at the gray-streaked surface as if some answer should be written there.

It was easy then to be afraid of him. Easy to suspect what Senach's story hinted. Unnatural son. Murderer. She could look at Faelan's rigid stance and believe there was a darkness in him, a demon that drove him and bowed to no morality or law.

She had married him because he was beyond her gift, and she clung to that fragile safety. She dared not probe too deeply. She could hope… as long as she did not *know*.

He swung away from the stone, and came to stand over her. "You're not hungry?" he asked softly.

Roddy shook her head.

"Nor tired? Nor cold?"

"No."

"I am," he said. He sank down onto his knees beside her. "All of them." His lashes sagged, a weary relaxation over blue-mist eyes. "Tell me. Tell me how that's possible if I dreamed it all."

"You've been working," she said.

He crushed some of the silvery flowers beneath his palm as he leaned on it, resting in the grass. "Roddy. I haven't slept since you left." He reached out, stroked the back of her hand. "I've been looking for you."

She could not argue with him. Exhaustion softened and blurred his features. "You've found me," she whispered.

His fingers interlocked with hers. "Yes." His eyes rolled shut. He drew her hand against his cheek and lowered his head to the ground. "…Found…" His words mumbled into indistinctness. Roddy saw a shadow move in the mist beyond him. She looked up, and Fionn stood on the other side of the circle.

The other woman laughed, a sound like bright bells on the wind. That joy washed over Roddy, banishing darker things.

She watched as Fionn came closer and knelt over Faelan's sleeping form.

Roddy was near enough to touch the sunbeam of hair that cascaded over Fionn's slim shoulders. Fionn looked up at her, with a hand over her mouth like a child holding back a giggle.

"Faelan." Roddy touched his face and rocked him gently. She wanted to introduce him to Fionn. But he only murmured and curled her hand more deeply beneath his cheek. She glanced at Fionn apologetically. "He's very tired."

"You can wake him," Fionn said. "When you wish."

Roddy looked down at her husband. His hard mouth was brushed with a faint smile; he looked younger, and infinitely precious. "I'll let him sleep."

Fionn reached out and drew her finger through his hair. "I know a story about him," she said. MacLassar came up, shoving his small snout jealously under Fionn's hand. She transferred her caress to the piglet. "I'll tell you someday."

"I'll listen now," Roddy said.

Fionn tilted her head with a sly smile. "Not yet," she said, and shook her head. "No. You won't listen yet."

It was the lightest of reproofs, but Roddy felt her pleasure shrivel into shame. She ducked her head, and touched Faelan's hair as the other woman had done. It curled through Roddy's fingers, smooth and cool and contrarily reminiscent of his hot sweetness.

I love you, she thought, with a faint despair.

When she lifted her eyes again, Fionn was gone.

Roddy had a moment's curiosity, a flutter of doubt about where Fionn lived and her comings and goings in mist and silence. But the importance of it faded and dissolved as Roddy's hand trailed through Faelan's hair and across his jaw. She felt his breath on her open palm. It seemed such a human thing, such a warm mortal weakness... it made her throat close and ache with wanting.

His lips brushed her hand. She looked down and saw his eyes still closed, but there was an awareness, a slight lift of the night-black lashes. He was awake. His free hand found her hip and slid upward, drawing her skirt in tow.

A spurt of hunger seized her. He shifted, pulled her down beneath him, and buried his face between her breasts.

She felt his hands cup and weigh her, felt his thumbs make rough circles around her nipples. The low, greedy moan of pleasure in his chest was sound and sensation both, a soft vibration against her breasts.

She spread her legs in wanton welcome, arching up to seek him. The breath that had caressed her so softly the moment before came harsher now, burning the tender skin at the corners of her mouth. "*Cailin sidhe*," he whispered. "*Cailin sidhe*. It's been too long."

Above him, far past him, the mists shifted and opened in patches, so that his black hair against the blue sky was like his eyes: bright and dark, the one drawing intensity from the other.

"Someone might come," she protested, thinking of Fionn.

"Aye." His thick lashes lowered as he fingered the ribbons on her cloak. "I've got searchers all over the mountain." At the slight stiffening of her body, he looked up. "Ah—you don't believe that, do you?" He grinned, his teeth flashing white in the moody atmosphere. He bent to her and spoke low in her ear. "You think I'm mad. I think you're mad. We're meant for each other, my love."

Her cape came free, falling back to form a bed in the damp grass. Her sash and dress followed under Faelan's knowledge-able hands. The cool air touched her skin like a kiss. She moaned, giving herself up to him, to the slide of his body on hers, to the arch and thrust of his possession.

She felt... like the earth itself. Like the earth beneath the wind, caressed and storm-tossed and then swept into the gale. He was rough suddenly, holding her face between his hands, driving deep with his tongue. Then he began to touch her, all over, to map each curve of her with his mouth and his hands.

"Roddy—" he groaned against her breasts. "Don't leave me again."

I didn't, she wanted to cry. *I never could*.

"I want you." His fingers went tight at her waist, pulling her beneath him, beneath his hot skin that had somehow gotten free of clothes. "I need you. Ah, God, if I wake up some night and find you've been a dream…"

"I'm not a dream," she mumbled, unable to think beyond that silly phrase under the weight of sensation his hands produced.

His throat rumbled with an aching laugh. "Little love, *cailin sidhe*—are you not? Sometimes I look at you, and the mist seems easier to touch…"

"No," she moaned. She traced the powerful curve of muscle down his back. "Touch me."

His body weighed on her, pressing her down as his teeth scored her shoulder. "Aye," he whispered fiercely. "I'm no saint. I'll hold you as I can." His hand slipped down to move across her inner thigh, guiding his hardness against her. "I know you this way. I know all about you."

"Faelan…"

"Love me, Roddy," he groaned as he found her depths and joined with her. "Stay with me. Don't listen to the rest of them." He lifted her, drove deep and hard, as if to brand her with his body. His words were a rasp in her ear: "My love. My life. Stay with me."

She did not answer. She could not, for the cry of pleasure and need in her throat. He took her up and held her, spun her like the whirlwind amid the rocks and the sky and the mist. His hands locked with hers. In a wide sweep against the silky-wet ground, he forced her arms over her head and pinned them, bending to suckle and tease her exposed breasts.

The move brought him into her with a throbbing power, an urgency that sent her exploding toward fulfillment. Each time she rose to meet him he made a sound, a sob of passion between his teeth. She felt the wet grass on her hands, and smelled the hot scent of exertion that shone in his skin.

It seemed she was expanding, that her senses and her talent swelled to encompass everything. As they swept together to the climax, it even seemed she was with him in shared ecstasy; that his hunger was hers; that the fire between them coalesced in one flame—dancing and joyous and wild, and bright beyond any imagining.

They lay together afterward. Awake. It was a strange inter-
lude, while the mists began at last to thin and lift, and the red
shafts of evening turned the ring of stone to a glowing rose. It
should have been cold, but it was warm. It should have seemed
wrong, to lie naked and entwined in the open, but it seemed
very right instead. Her cape lay in waves beneath them, and
Faelan's breath skimmed her neck and lifted a stray hair.

Eventually, in the same lazy, satisfied mood, they sat up
and began to dress. It was a slow process, teasing and touching
and helping one another. MacLassar accepted an oatcake with
dignity from Faelan's hand.

Dressed, they left the ring hand in hand like a pair of May
lovers. There seemed no need for words or questions; just
that contact of their hands, and the times when Faelan slid his
arm around her waist and pulled her to him for a kiss. Roddy
found the path as she had been sure she could. Below, the
whole coastline spread before them in a shimmering roll of
green hills and silver bays. It surprised her, how far she had
come in the fog.

It was dusk when they heard voices calling. The subdued
urgency in them caught her attention, and Roddy focused her
gift, stretching to overcome the distance.

It was Martha, and the older O'Sullivan, calling Roddy's
name with weary regularity. Faelan raised his arm and shouted,
waving. The movement caught O'Sullivan's eye, and Roddy
felt the strong and heady jolt of relief that swept him.

"Oh, mum!" Martha was sobbing when they finally reached
the lower path. She grabbed Roddy in a hearty and unservile
embrace. "Oh, mum, we thought you was gone for sure! They
been telling me *such* stories—about them soldiers and what
happened to 'em, and cliffs and wolves and all such, mum! Oh,
but I knew his Lor'ship 'ud find you; I just knew so! I said so
to Mr. O'Sullivan, over and over, and him thinking that one
night on the mountain be enough to murder a grown strong
man, and you lost for two, and then His Lordship come up
missin' the third! Oh, but I knew that if any could save you,
'twould be His Lordship—" In her fit of thankfulness, she let
go of Roddy and hugged Faelan, too. "Oh, sir, I'll do my best

for you all my days, for bringin' Her Ladyship home safe. I'll do anythin'!"

Roddy was barely listening to the maid's protests of eternal loyalty. She was looking at Faelan, and hearing Martha's "two nights" echo in her head.

"Martha," she demanded sharply. "Don't exaggerate. You can't possibly have been searching for me for two days."

"Oh, mum, we have indeed. Every minute of it, and I'm about dead on me feet, m'lady."

"But, Martha—I've not been gone but an afternoon."

"Oh—m'lady… She hasn't gone and knocked her head, Your Lordship—"

"Of course I haven't," Roddy snapped, driven to agitation. "I tell you all, I left the house just after tea. I spent all morning helping you churn, Martha—you can't think I've been gone so long."

Martha gave her a wide-eyed stare. In the face of Roddy's obvious emotion, the maid didn't dare contradict her mistress, but in her mind she decided that Roddy had indeed hit her head and needed immediate attention. Mr. O'Sullivan glanced worriedly at Faelan, and Roddy knew he thought the same.

"You're all being ridiculous," she exclaimed. "I know what I've done, and where I've been. I went up the hill, and while I was there I met a lady. Fionn is her name. I talked to her awhile, and then Faelan came. That's all. And if you're all trying to play some sort of silly joke, you needn't bother!" Her voice began to rise. "I won't fall for it, and I don't think it's at all funny!"

"'Tis no joke, m'lady," O'Sullivan protested anxiously. "We're after spending three nights out combing these hills—"

"*Stop it!*" she cried. "This is nonsense. You know I haven't been gone for three days. You *know* it!"

"Roddy—" Faelan's arm came around her shoulders. "Little girl, I—"

"Don't!" She shoved him away. "I don't know what you're all trying to do"—she took a deep, gasping breath as her words rose to a shrill—"but stop it! Just stop it!"

"Little one, little one—" Faelan pulled her to him again, this time binding her arms when she began to struggle. He held her back against him. "Don't panic." His voice was soft near her ear, but his arms were like iron. "Breathe slowly. Your heart's working like a cornered rabbit's."

"But it isn't true," she wailed. "It isn't—"

"Hush." He bent to her, held his cheek against hers as he rocked her like a child. "Shhh—hush. Listen to me. Listen to me. It won't help to fight it."

She took a sobbing breath and stared bleakly at Martha and O'Sullivan. "But they can't…" She trailed off, knowing that Martha and O'Sullivan weren't lying or joking. If she concentrated she could pick out memories, clear, recent visions of days and nights spent searching. It was that, more than their words, that sent the panic boiling through her.

But Faelan still held her, stroking her arms and her face. "Better now," he murmured. "Just relax a moment—"

"But you were there—" she cried, remembering suddenly. "Faelan, you just found me this afternoon, and they're saying you've been gone a whole night!"

"I know," he said. He held her hard for an instant, and there was an infinite weariness in his voice. "I know, Roddy."

"So they must be wrong." She bit her trembling lip. "Tell them they're wrong."

"I can't," he said.

Her voice was very small as she asked, "Why not?"

"Because—" He let out a harsh breath, and his hold on her loosened. He turned her around and drew her into his chest, splaying his fingers through her hair. "It's scary, I know. Losing time. It's terrifying. I know, Roddy. Believe me. I know how it feels."

She was silent for a long time. Then at last she put her arms around him and held on. "Oh, God. What do I do?"

Faelan laid his cheek against her hair and rocked her. "'Tis best not to think on it too much, little girl."

Eighteen

DOWN ON HER HANDS AND KNEES IN THE MUDDY SOIL, RODDY worked at a stubborn gorse root. She had hacked at it with a spade until it was crushed and splintered, but all of her twistings and whimperings were not enough to yank the slippery root from the center of her beginning garden.

She sat back on her knees finally, looking jealously across the sweep of land that spread below her to the sea. Under the lowering spring clouds, beyond the pasture where Faelan's bay racing stallion grazed in peaceful retirement, she could count no fewer than five pairs of men and ponies engaged in opening ground with the new castiron plows that Faelan had imported.

He had refused to give Roddy's project any priority. The precious plows were at work where he sent them: furrowing fields for potatoes and corn, for turnips or oats or wheat. It was the four-course plan, that Roddy could have recited in her sleep from all the nights he'd spent talking about it, how a field would grow wheat one year, and turnips the next, then oats, with clover undersown to be grazed by the cattle in the fourth year. The turnips would feed the cattle, and the rich manure went back to the soil to increase the cereal yields when the wheat came round again.

In all that, between the draining of the bogs and enclosing of the fields and plowing and planting and weeding, there was no time to spare for one small plot of flowers. So Roddy struggled on her own.

She grasped the root for one last mighty tug, standing up on her knees and putting the whole weight of her body into the battle. But despite grunting and huffing that would have done MacLassar proud, her fingers weakened and lost their purchase, and she fell back to the ground with a frustrated moan. The sound changed to a bitter cry as a splinter drove into her palm.

Her hands were too muddy and her fingernails too worn to extract the sharp sliver, but in her sullen mood she refused to be reasonable and made herself angrier yet by working at the tender place until it bled. Occupied with that annoyance, she paid no attention to the touch of familiarity in her mind until sudden recognition burst upon her. She twisted around, and stood up with a glad cry.

"Earnest!" She waved her arm and squealed in excitement at the pair of horses that cantered up the raw slash of reddish soil where the drive had been cleaned and reopened. MacLassar had been lazing on the steps of the great house, soaking up the weak April warmth. At the sound of her voice, he tripped down the stairs and trotted to the edge of the paved forecourt, too fastidious to join Roddy in the muck.

She was aware of Earnest's shock at her bedraggled figure, but she waited only long enough for him to swing off his horse before she threw herself into his arms. "Oh, Earnest," she cried into his muffling coat. "Why didn't you tell me you were coming? I've missed you—I've missed you all! You haven't answered my letters forever!"

He laughed and held her off. "Here, now, I can't have you muddying my best cape. I'm a veritable Tulip of Fashion in these parts." He shook his blond head at her. "Good God, Roddy, the last time I saw you looking like this, you'd just fallen off that crazy black filly of yours into a drainage ditch."

"I've been working in my garden." She looked toward Faelan, who stood back a few feet with the horses, and held out her hand. "And see what you've done, my lord. I've a splinter."

He tossed the reins to the small barefoot boy who came running up belatedly. "It's my fault, is it?" He took her hand

and spread her palm, ordering the stableboy over his shoulder to bring a bucket of water.

Roddy looked past her husband to Earnest, her gift full open with curiosity and eagerness, but instead of the pleasure she'd expected, her brother's thoughts mirrored his questioning frown. Finding her covered with mud in the weedy wilderness in front of the great anomaly of a house, with one barefoot servant and a pig running loose in the forecourt... to the overprotective brother of an heiress, it made a strange and suspicious picture.

But Roddy could see no way to counter Earnest's negative impressions without bringing them into the open in front of Faelan. That, at least, she was sure Earnest had not done. He met her eyes with a direct and silent question.

She smiled brightly, to reassure him. "Tell me everything," she ordered. "How is Papa? I haven't even heard what colt he's training for the Derby. And has Mark decided on his regiment yet? The last letter I had from him was so short that it was obviously written at gunpoint—Mama's, I imagine..." She went on in that gay vein until she had covered the entire family and reassured herself by Earnest's lack of agitation that they were all well and happy. The bucket of water arrived, and Faelan made her kneel in the grass to wash the soil from her injured hand.

"It's you I want to hear about," Earnest said when she ran out of questions. "Roddy—we had no notion of how isolated you are here. His Lordship told me you've posted letters once a week, but we've received nothing at home since the first of the year—and the news... that the whole country's up in arms, that the French are on the doorstep, that martial law's been declared—"

"Martial law." Roddy tensed, catching the frightening depth of importance of those words from Earnest's mind. "What's that?"

Faelan gently pried open the fist she'd made and continued to examine her hand. "Little girl. You are an uneducated heathen, aren't you? 'Tis when soldiers keep the peace."

"Aye. And make the law," Earnest exclaimed. "I ask you again, Iveragh—how soon will you bring her back to England?"

"Ouch!" Roddy pulled her hand away as Faelan found the tender spot. She frowned at Earnest, searching out the roots of the worry in his mind. "Go back—is there so much danger here?"

"Danger!" Earnest flung out his arm. "The damned country's in revolt! I landed at Cork to see five companies of light infantry and a detachment of dragoons march through. Their ultimatum expires tomorrow—after that, they free-quarter on the countryside until all rebel arms are surrendered."

"Rebel arms…" In her dismay, she allowed Faelan to take her hand again without protest. She looked at him, thinking of Geoffrey's guns, but he did not meet the panicked question in her eyes.

"Hold still," he said, probing at the splinter.

Roddy bit her tongue, glad of the pain. It gave her an excuse for the way she felt her face go pale. In revolt…

So Geoffrey's wild schemes had come to fruition. His United Irishmen were rising, and the guns were in rebel hands.

Faelan's careful fingers steadied hers, pressing the sliver free in one hard, skillful pinch. She drew in a sharp breath, and caught his eyes, finally. "Did you know this?"

"I saw a copy of the proclamation of martial law at O'Connell's. Several weeks ago."

"And you didn't tell me? You didn't do anything?"

He let go of her hand. "What would you have me do?"

"Come back with me," Earnest said. "If you won't come, Iveragh, at least send Roddy with me."

Faelan looked at Earnest, and Roddy felt the impact of that gaze as if it had been directed full at her.

"No," he said.

Her brother held his ground. Clear as speech, he promised, *I'll take you, Roddy. No matter what this bastard does.*

Faelan interpreted Earnest's stubborn jaw with precision. "She's my wife. She stays with me." He picked up Roddy's discarded spade and in one savage stroke sliced through the root she'd been struggling with all morning. "Think twice if you have any other notions."

"You don't care for her danger?"

Faelan went on digging. "Let me tell you about this rebellion," he said to the muddy ground as his shoulders relaxed and tightened in rhythmic exertion. "The peasantry don't fight for philosophy—they fight for their lives and their bellies. They hate the tithe. They're ground down to slave labor at the hands of tithe proctors and mean little gentlemen who live off the rack rents from a hundred miserable potato patches. They've got their Whiteboys and Defenders because violence is the only means they've found to keep themselves alive. And the damned gentry who've brought it on themselves are afraid to go to bed at night without a few of those miscreants they're pleased to call an army camped upon their doorstep." With one final dig and heave, he stood straight and tossed the spade aside. "The Irish army. '... formidable to everyone but the enemy.' That's how their own commander in chief describes 'em." His coat flared as he rested his hands on his hips. "And into this keg of black powder wades an open flame—a parcel of idealistic schoolboys with their talk of French democracy and free land." He snorted. "Aye. We'll have a revolution. And a thousand ignorant, starving cottiers will die for every musket-happy soldier."

"And you plan to sit here in the midst of it?" Earnest demanded. "I want my sister out of here."

"Are you going to take her by force?" Faelan asked softly. "She's safe enough here. I've paid the tithes and forgiven the arrears in exchange for the labor to open up new cropland. That alone makes me a hero."

Earnest's lip curled. "I suppose some do have to buy their heroism."

"I'm a practical man, Delamore. I'd rather buy it than die for it."

"With my sister's money."

"Earnest—" Roddy protested.

But Faelan only smiled his bitter wolf-smile. "As I said. I'm a practical man."

Earnest was prepared to say more. Roddy cut him short. "Come inside, Earnest. Come inside and see what we've done." Her eyes pleaded with him to drop the argument. He caught her look, and acquiesced reluctantly.

I don't like this. The phrase was silent and clear through her gift. *I want you safe.*

She took his hand as if to lead him up the steps, and squeezed it in answer. Deliberately she refused to acknowledge the second level behind his concern, the distrust that went beyond politics and revolution to fear of Faelan himself.

Up the wide steps, she pushed open the door—so new that the carved and painted wood had not yet lost its fresh odor. MacLassar shoved his way past her legs and trotted into the huge hall.

Roddy caught Earnest's jolt of dismay at the sight. "Oh, MacLassar is quite the most civilized pig," she assured him. "I consult him on all my household decisions. What shall we serve our guest, MacLassar? Will you part with some of your best French brandy?"

The piglet ignored her, heading through the hall toward the rear entry to the house and the servants' quarters. There, MacLassar knew, Martha would be struggling to understand the Parisian chef's pastry lessons and slipping her mistakes to any wandering pig that might happen by.

The interior of the great house was a peculiar sight. Just how peculiar Roddy had never really considered until she felt Earnest's confusion and shock as he followed her in. The chef, like the brandy and the elegant furniture and the fine white sugar for the pastries, was contraband.

Roddy could offer French spirits and an elegant meal if she wished, and serve it on a polished mahogany table—as long as she left the sheets draped across the shining wood to protect it from the dust of the plasterers at work in the dining room.

Eating in the midst of a construction site had never seemed to make much sense, so she and Faelan dined with Martha and the chef and the rest of the laborers in the large kitchen beside the servants' quarters.

Earnest stood in the front hall and stared around at the barren space, where the only things that had escaped the fire were the stone walls, the intricately carved mantelpiece of Italian marble, and the floor of black Kilkenny limestone.

He blinked up the huge opening in the rebuilt floor above, frowning at the narrow ladder which did service in place of the magnificent staircase only imagination could supply. "What in God's name happened here?"

"The place burned," Faelan said from behind. "Obviously."

"You should have seen it when we arrived." Roddy leaped in to reassure. "Faelan's done wonders. There wasn't even a roof. There isn't much to see down here yet, because we've been concentrating on the bedrooms upstairs." She grinned mischievously over her shoulder. "Faelan's tired of sleeping in the stable."

"The stable!" Earnest turned on his sister's husband. "You're sleeping in the goddamned stable? And just where is your wife sleeping?"

For an instant it was only a demand, a worry about comfort and responsibility. Then Faelan smiled, and even in the watery gray light from the second-floor windows, the slow sensuality was clearly evident. His hands slid onto Roddy's shoulders, drawing her back against him as they moved up her throat in a light caress. "Do you really have to ask, Delamore?"

Roddy opened her mouth, and shut it again, feeling her face go to scarlet at the picture that formed in Earnest's mind. She threw up barriers even as he hastily tried to concentrate on something else, casting about at the windows, the pavement, the doors. She had forgotten, living only with Faelan and Senach and kindhearted, dull-witted Martha, that her talent could precipitate such moments of agonizing awkwardness.

After that she stayed out of Earnest's thoughts.

It was difficult, though, to block his growing consternation as she led him through the house and out the opposing door where the wild hillside seemed to tumble down to the doorstep in a tangle of heather and gorse.

"What's this?" he asked dryly. "The formal garden?"

Faelan gave Earnest a bland look. "I believe Roddy was digging the lake and the Grecian grotto when we rode up."

She stomped ahead of them, reckoning they could nip at one another without her help. As they passed the stone enclosure where the barefooted boy had turned out their mounts, she heard Earnest make a caustic comment about the hospitality of the horses in vacating their stable. Faelan said he was certain Roddy would put Earnest up in the best available stall.

She reached the kitchen and found Martha and several cottiers, including the two O'Sullivan boys, taking tea with Monsieur Armand. In the babble of French, Gaelic, and English around the hearth, there was no thought of revolution. Faelan was indeed a hero to the men he had fed and employed. Roddy was no longer sorry to have put Mr. Willis out, though the Farrissys had been a much-loved family among the peasants.

But to Faelan, there were only those who worked the land and those who did not. When Mr. Farrissy's and Mr. Willis' leases had fallen in, so had the those of all their subtenants. Faelan had kept his promise. The homes of the middling gentry who had resisted his changes were empty.

Those evictions had won them no friends among the landed class. The only place where Faelan and Roddy were received by members of the gentry—Protestant or Catholic—was at the O'Connell house in Derrynane, where the improvements Faelan had initiated softened the impact of his blunt impatience concerning delicate political matters.

The men all rose when Roddy appeared, like a small respectful gathering of medieval vassals who stood with their hats in their hands as Faelan entered.

In six short months, his cottiers had grown to love him. He had thrown the squireens out, lowered the rents, brought seed and plows and hope. He worked the same backbreaking hours of the cottiers and more—*buildin' a grand house, a quare great house, fit for Himself and the Lady*—Many times she'd caught such a thought from a man standing back to stare up at the mansion. They had no notion of Geoffrey's democracy. Faelan ordered, and they obeyed, finding safety and a kind of childlike pleasure in the relationship. He was a lord in their old tradition: openhanded and patronizing, with an aristocratic manner that was as natural to him as breath, whether he dressed in velvet or homespun. *Aye, fit for His Lordship*, they said now, of anything fine or clever.

Monsieur Armand's hissed instructions sent Martha and the cottiers to abandon their tea and return to work. Faelan gave some orders as they left, and Roddy had the impression that he would have liked to accompany them. Instead he sat down with Roddy and Earnest at the hand-hewn table as befitted a decent—if not gracious—host. Roddy didn't think it was politeness for a minute. She knew his weakness. Tea would include some of Armand's hot buttered scones and fresh pastries.

"Really," Earnest said, with a mocking glance around after Armand and Martha withdrew. "This *is* the first stare. Are you sure the pig wouldn't like a seat closer to the fire?"

Faelan broke off a piece of his scone and tossed it to MacLassar—something which Roddy had never seen him do before. The piglet, grown now longer than his forearm, gulped the morsel and sat down next to Faelan's chair. He held out another bite, teasing with it until MacLassar rose up with his feet braced on Faelan's thigh and begged. Only the faint curl of her husband's lips indicated there was anything unusual about his actions at all.

Earnest took up the bait as readily as MacLassar went for the scone. "Christ, Iveragh—at least feed the filthy thing outside." He shoved his chair back from his untouched plate and strode to the tiny window. "My sister might as well be living in a barnyard."

"MacLassar," Roddy said with dignity, "gets a bath and a rub of lavender every other day."

"Which is better than you do." Faelan flipped another piece of scone, this time toward Earnest's boots. MacLassar trotted over and began a loud, grunting snuffle around her brother's polished toes. "When was it—a fortnight ago, that you visited Maire O'Connell?"

Earnest turned in horror. "Good God, you're not saying it's been a fortnight since she's had the opportunity to bathe?"

"We don't have a proper place here," Roddy said, trying to make herself sound as prim as possible. "Surely you can see that, Earnest."

"Then why in the Lord's name are you here? When Papa allowed you to marry this—" He stopped that phrase at a calculated spot, not quite ready for open warfare. "To marry, I'll tell you, he had no notion he was sending you to hold court in a pigsty!"

Roddy stood up. "It's not a pigsty, Earnest. It's a perfectly clean kitchen that happens to have a perfectly clean pig in it. MacLassar belongs to me, and I can assure you that in spite of Faelan's *display*"—she gave her husband a withering look—"he doesn't approve of my keeping him."

Faelan leaned back in his chair and crossed his feet among the delicate cups on the table. "Not at all, my dear. You may keep all the swine you like. I merely suggested that a pig who thrives on French brandy is an expensive pet, although I can imagine it might add an interesting flavor to the final product."

"Quite," Earnest said feelingly.

Roddy pressed her lips together, and pushed Faelan's boots from the table with one angry shove. "Leave off—both of you. MacLassar's just as clean as any of your silly hunting dogs that run tame in the house at home, Earnest. And twice as smart, I'll wager." She turned on Faelan. "And who got him started on brandy, I'd like to know, after we ran out of port?"

Faelan shrugged. "A man has to have some intelligent conversation along with his claret. After the ladies retire."

Earnest glanced at Roddy. She kept her barriers in place. What he thought of her husband was plain enough. That Faelan was doing all he could to reinforce the opinion was also clear. She gave an impatient sigh and sat back down. "Come and have some tea, Earnest. I assure you the cup's been boiled."

After a moment's hesitation, he did. He poured the fine, thick Kerry cream without comment and then looked at Faelan over the cup rim. "I had the pleasure of meeting your mother recently," he said. "In London."

Faelan had been sugaring his tea. He did not pause in his idle stirring.

"She was on her way here," Earnest said.

Faelan's spoon clattered. He steadied it and laid it beside his cup. "Was she? In spite of the rebels behind every bush?"

"Because of them. She was coming to fetch Roddy away."

"Indeed." Faelan's black lashes lowered as he sipped at his tea. "And you've been given the mission now."

"Yes. She feared she might not be welcome."

"Neither are you," Faelan said bluntly, "if you've come to kidnap my wife."

Earnest frowned. "I won't take Roddy against her wishes, of course—"

"Then you might ask what they are." Faelan's cup hit the saucer with a clash as he stood up. "I've noticed a singular lack of that little politeness in this discussion, Delamore."

With a restless move, he strode to the fuel bucket and threw fresh turf on the fire. Earnest watched, and there was something in his face which made Roddy loath to look behind it to the reason. She glanced away, controlling her gift with sharp discipline.

"I'll ask her, yes," Earnest said. "But I think she should know all the facts before she makes her decision."

Faelan squatted before the hearth. He tonged the turf into order and reached for the swab in the brass pot of oil.

"Your mother says that you're not… well."

The oil splashed against the turf. Flames leaped, throwing a furious red glare onto Faelan's face, creating light and satanic shadows. With a deliberation that was agonizing, he replaced the swab and tongs by the hearth, and turned slowly to the table.

Earnest glanced at Roddy, a look that asked her to open her gift, to listen to him. He knew she was barriered—for too many years he'd lived with her talent to miss the signs, the need for full conversation in place of the clipped and spare exchange of thought and words that marked a deeper link. Whatever was in his mind he did not wish to say aloud.

She refused him. She wanted to rush out of the room, to run away from what he would tell, in words or silence.

"Do you understand me, Roddy?" Earnest asked.

Her skin grew hot with the flush of panic. For six months, this had lain untouched. '*Tis best not to think of it*, Faelan had said, and she had not. She'd come back from the ring of stone missing three days of her life and gone on, building as if those days had not existed. It was easy, with Faelan to help her, to collude in the pretending. He knew how to do it.

He had experience.

The fire darkened. Faelan stood still, silent, with the waiting glitter of a cornered wolf in his eyes.

"Roddy," Earnest probed softly.

"No," she said. She stared stubbornly at her cup. "There's nothing wrong with Faelan."

"Look at me, Roddy."

"No!"

"Damn." Earnest came to his feet. "You tell her, then, Iveragh. You tell her she's not safe with you. God's mercy, man—think of what you risk with these… fits, or whatever you would call them. If you care for her at all, let her go with me."

"If you take her against her will," Faelan said, "I'll kill you."

Earnest exploded at that. Roddy's barriers tumbled before the blast of his frustrated temper. "Ah, you would, wouldn't you—you godforsaken bastard! In cold blood in my bed, I haven't a doubt. It's my belief that you're as sane as any other hound out of hell, but if it takes proving you're a madman to get my sister out of your hands, then I'll have your mother and your uncle and God Almighty on the stand to have you locked in the blackest pit in Bedlam." He crossed the room and grabbed Faelan's lapel. "Do you know what I saw before I left London, Iveragh? I saw your mother get the news that a Miss Webster had been pulled out of the Thames. Dead, brother-in-law. Drowned. Cast herself off Westminster Bridge. Care to tell my sister why? Or do you hide behind your mother's excuses—that you 'forget'; that you walk in your sleep or some such folderol." Earnest's mouth curved into a grimace. "Walk in your sleep," he sneered, and let go of Faelan with an excitement of disgust. "You must have villainous dreams, Iveragh."

Roddy was on her feet, pushing Earnest back. "Leave him alone! You don't know anything!"

Earnest gripped her elbow. *Come with me, Roddy*, he pleaded. *Get out of here.*

"No!" she said furiously. "I won't go. I'm not afraid of the people here—they'd never hurt us. Never. I *know* that, Earnest."

"The people be damned," Earnest shouted. "It's this—"

He broke off as a heavy pounding came at the door. In the heat of the moment Roddy had been aware of nothing but her brother's fury, but now the agitation seemed to spread as her gift expanded. Outside she heard the scuffle of many feet as Martha shoved open the heavy wood.

"Beggin' your pardon. Beggin' your pardon, Your Lordship, but Mr. O'Sullivan says to tell you there's redcoats coming up the hill!"

Nineteen

FOR AN INSTANT THE SCENE SEEMED FROZEN, WITH THE COTTIERS crowding behind Martha in silence and Roddy and Earnest standing in suspended confrontation. Then Faelan moved, swinging out the door and pushing through his workers, leaving Roddy and her brother in front of the glowing hearth.

Roddy picked up her skirts without a word and dashed after Faelan. She knew Earnest followed close behind, his tirade forgotten in sudden fear that he was too late now to rescue his sister from anything.

It was a picture of eerie familiarity in front of the great house, with Faelan standing on the steps with the wind in his face. This time, though, instead of the gathering of tenants and cottiers facing him, they were turned away, looking down the hill, watching uneasily as the company of redcoats approached.

Unlike the easygoing militia that had bivouacked and held halfhearted maneuvers for a few months on the road to Glenbeigh, this detachment marched with the discipline of experienced soldiers. Roddy tried to count, and lost the number after she reached a hundred rows of three abreast. Along with a mounted officer at the column's head were two riders who appeared to be civilian. As they neared, Roddy drew stiff in recognition.

Mr. Willis and Rupert Mullane. And with them, in full uniform and complete control of his horse, was the captain who had danced with Fionn on the night of the fairy ball.

Roddy felt for a moment that she could not breathe. It took no talent at all to read what was in their faces, these men who came with guns and soldiers at their backs.

Earnest stood behind Roddy, his hands tense and protective on her arms. As the scarlet company halted in front of the house and re-formed under hoarse shouted orders, she felt MacLassar come trotting up belatedly. He plopped down on the step beside her. The crowd of cottiers was growing as more laborers came straggling up from the fields below.

It was a complex shift of mood and emotion that came to Roddy through her gift: too many people and reactions to seem more than a babble rising in intensity. She caught the ugly turn of feeling as Willis was recognized, and a spurt of pure violence toward his deputy, Mullane.

Faelan had seemed a devil once, but now the memory of Mullane and his horsewhip burned stronger than any fading fears of their new lord. *Oh, aye—Mullane. He was the bully buck. He was the rogue. Didn't he raise the rack rent, and put a man out if it pleased him? Didn't he come beddin' an honest man's daughter, and hold the cattle and bid 'em out to strangers, and pull a man off his own wee harvest to do the big men's work?*

They looked at Mullane and hated, and Mullane looked back and feared.

Within the turmoil of the crowd, Roddy could glean no more from Rupert or Mr. Willis than that angry nervousness. Their reason for riding with the redcoats was lost in the swell of emotion.

The officer rode forward. The tumult of voices quieted, though the buzz of heated thought did not.

For a long minute of silence, he looked at Faelan. Roddy kept her eyes down, terrified, wishing her husband would fade back in the crowd, try to prevent the inevitable recognition. But he stood there, alone on the stairs, as striking and arrogant as Finvarra himself.

Finvarra. King of the Fairies of the West.

The captain had long suspected he'd been made a fool. Now, facing this mansion and Faelan's unmistakable blue gaze, he knew it as certainty.

Anger blazed in the officer, agonizing memory of the embarrassment he'd suffered, the ridicule from higher authority, the final indignity of transferal to another command when he'd persisted in broadcasting his folly. But now, as then, there was no way to call the fantastical bluff without exposing himself to scorn.

"Captain Norton Roberts," he snapped. "Under command of General Sir James Stewart. I've orders to effect the surrender of all arms, pikes, and ammunition in this district."

The crowd stirred, a mixture of fear and defiance. Faelan simply waited.

His calm, faintly mocking smile fueled Roberts' temper. The captain spurred forward to the foot of the steps as he had done once before. "You are Lord Iveragh?" he demanded.

"Yes."

"Then I place upon you the full responsibility of collection. We have reports that three hundred pikes and four thousand stand of smuggled arms have been concealed in this neighborhood. You have twenty-four hours from this moment to lay them before me."

The fear spread suffocating fingers from Roddy's stomach to her throat. Twenty-four hours. God, oh, God—where had Geoffrey taken the guns?

"I do not accept any such responsibility," Faelan said.

"I'd advise you to reconsider that, Your Lordship. My orders are to free-quarter my men. If the arms are withheld, I turn them loose to forage."

Almost imperceptibly, a muscle tightened in Faelan's jaw.

The captain caught that betrayal. His frown transformed to a wicked grin. "In fact, Your Lordship... I venture to predict we'll lay the country waste."

Mr. Willis started forward. "There's no need for that, Captain. I've lodged the information. An arrest, a simple arrest, is all that's necessary."

If not for Earnest's support, Roddy thought her knees would have collapsed beneath her.

Captain Roberts glanced at his informant with unconcealed annoyance. "We're here to recover the arms, Mr. Willis. There'll be no arrests without due process."

"But I've proof of his connection with Cashel—I've shown you the message I intercepted. That seditious rogue is hidden here now—" Willis flung out his hand. "Look at this place. It commands the whole bay. Iveragh's fortifying it, by God—he's gathered every ruffian in the district in to speed the process. The law's in your hands, man. Arrest him. Tear the house apart and you'll find Lord Cashel, I swear it. One judicious arrest, and you've cut off the dragon's head."

"I am not Saint George, Mr. Willis." Captain Roberts was sour and chagrined, but he was no hothead. He disliked Willis, and after the experience of the fairy ball, he was exceedingly tired of having people point out his supposed errors of perception, most particularly in public. "I shall carry out my orders as I see fit, without recourse to your schemes of petty revenge. Notes can be forged."

Amid the threatening murmur from the crowd, Willis flushed with shame and rage. "He's a damned traitor, with his damned cropped hair and French airs—"

"*Mr. Willis.*" Roberts' voice slashed across the other man's. "I'm well aware that Lord Iveragh has put you out of a comfortable living. That hardly renders him a traitor. I think you'd be advised to keep a civil tongue before you find His Lordship has you up on charge of libel."

"Thank you," Faelan said. "I hadn't thought of that."

Captain Roberts glared at Faelan, a look that warned. The officer had set himself a goal now, and that was to play Faelan as neatly as he himself had been played that night of the fairy ball. The officer knew the elaborate distraction had hidden something. Roberts was just as convinced of Faelan's treason as Willis, but the arrest of a peer on such flimsy evidence as vague notes and cropped hair could backfire all too easily.

The captain had seen the newly planted fields and the livestock and stores of food and grain that Lord Iveragh had imported. Roberts guessed with deadly accuracy that for Faelan the potent threat of free-quarters would be a more subtle and devastating victory than Willis' clumsy efforts.

As the officer sat there on his horse, well pleased with himself and his plans, Roddy felt her talent slip away. She turned, though she did not have to, knowing already that Senach was near.

He stood behind Faelan on the stairs, his blank gaze focused out beyond the red-coated company to the sea.

Roberts' horse moved restlessly. Then suddenly it shied, rushing into Willis' and aiming a kick that barely missed. In a thunder of hooves the other horses began to twist and rear, reeling out of control toward the scarlet row of soldiers. Discipline held the line until Willis lost his seat and his mount careered right through the column, knocking men aside and narrowly missing a murderous kick at the color-bearer's head. The soldiers broke and scattered. Roddy screamed, struggling in Earnest's grip as she saw a man take aim with a pistol at the officer's raging mount.

The animal quieted instantly.

The soldier paused, looking up from his sighting as if he weren't sure whether or not to fire. But Roberts was in control again, and the man apparently thought the better of shooting a horse out from under his senior officer.

Willis and Mullane were both on the ground. In a sweep of bannered tails and thunder, their mounts fled away down the hill.

Mullane struggled to sit up, but Willis lay twisted and utterly still. Another infantryman knelt over him, and looked up at his captain.

"Sir. He's gone and broke his neck, sir."

Roddy put her hands to her mouth and closed her eyes.

"Jesus," Earnest said under his breath.

She heard Roberts ride forward again. "Lieutenant!" There was a peculiar, controlled note in the captain's voice. "Have him taken inside."

"Forgive me," Faelan said coldly. "But I don't think I'm required to provide shelter for the body of a man who has just accused me of treason. I suggest you remove him from my property."

With the force of a blast furnace, Roddy's talent returned. She opened her eyes and saw Roberts' face; his fear and fury filled her as it had once before. He could not explain it, had no reason or logic to uphold it, but he knew in his soul that he'd been mocked again. *You did this*, his mind screamed. *How?*

This time, he knew better than to demand answers aloud. In a low, furious voice, he ordered a stretcher, and watched as Willis' body was loaded upon it. The men formed again in their blood-red columns. Roberts wheeled his horse and confronted Faelan.

"Don't think," he hissed, "that this means Willis' accusations are forgotten." He backed his horse and raised his voice so that all could hear. "We'll withdraw for one night, Your Lordship. One night."

With a snapped order, the troops fell in to march. Rupert Mullane struggled to his feet, glanced at the crowd of cottiers that began to flood into the forecourt in the army's wake, and began a limping run. He caught up with Roberts, and was trotting alongside, reaching out to lay an imploring hand on the officer's boot, when Roberts kicked him away and put his mount to a canter. The cottiers began to laugh and call out insults. Mullane was left to keep up with the soldiers as best he could.

Earnest gave Roddy a little tug. *Come.* She caught his thought, close and urgent, from among the emotion of the crowd. *Roddy, come away.*

But she could not. She stood watching the stretcher pass, the body on it covered casually by a military cape. One white hand dragged across the smooth terrace stones, bouncing to the soldiers' rhythmic step.

Earnest's persistent pressure finally pulled her bodily away from the scene. When she lifted her eyes, she saw Senach. His faint smile and empty eyes made the hair rise on the nape of her neck.

Without any sign from Faelan to stay, the crowd dispersed, some following the soldiers, most spreading out into low-voiced knots of men who stood about and asked one another what was to be done, in tones of mingled guilt and challenge. More than one of them suddenly had a pike burning a hole in his garden or thatched roof or hedge. But they took their cue from Faelan, who simply walked away into the house.

His Lordship. Roddy caught the thought from one. *Aye, His Lordship's standing buff. And wouldn't he do so, now, him the great man.*

Then, out of the thinning crowd, something familiar touched her gift. She stopped, ignoring Earnest's pleas. As she searched for the source her heart seemed to leap into her ears and deafen her with its pounding.

Geoffrey.

She recognized him finally, standing alone in the deep shade of an untrimmed bush. His hat was pulled down to hide his face, but cottier's clothes and soiled leggings made an ill disguise. The tall, unbowed elegance of his figure was a beacon to anyone who glanced twice.

He did not look at Roddy. He was watching Faelan disappear into the house and planning a way to gain his friend's attention.

Roddy pulled away from Earnest's grip. She could guess only too well what would happen if Geoffrey managed to contact Faelan.

Disaster.

Faelan would try to hide his friend. She knew he would. Amid this turmoil of redcoats and suspicions, with Captain Roberts out for the blood of the man who had made a fool of him, Faelan would offer shelter to a known rebel. And Geoffrey—romantic, stupid, idealistic Geoffrey—would somehow betray himself.

Willis' accusations would be fact. And Captain Roberts would be waiting.

There Geoffrey stood in the full light of day, a marked and hunted man, thinking that a hat and a laborer's coat disguised him, and knowing he had come to the one person who would not turn him away.

Roddy set her teeth. She could not, would not, let Faelan know his friend was near.

For once, she thanked God for her talent. No one else suspected Geoffrey's presence. Earnest was too occupied with his concern for Roddy's safety to pay any attention to the cottiers who lingered. He was rehearsing an impassioned tirade to deliver to Faelan. It was just as well. Roddy thought the best thing she could do at the moment would be to goad the two of them to a furious fight and then slip away and intercept Geoffrey before he revealed himself.

She gave in to Earnest's bullying and let him drag her into the hall after Faelan. "Iveragh!" Her brother's shout echoed off the walls as soon as they were inside.

Faelan walked out from the empty drawing room and leaned against the doorframe. He met Earnest's glare with a level look, but faint lines of tension touched his mouth. Though he crossed his arms in a casual stance, his fingers were white against his dark sleeve. "Yes," he said softly. "You may take her now."

Earnest had already drawn in his breath to begin before the meaning of Faelan's words hit him. "I can?" he responded stupidly.

"I think that would be best, though the overland route is out of the question." He glanced at Roddy. The gray walls surrounding him made his eyes seem vivid blue. "Pack your things, and you can be at Derrynane before dark. The O'Connells will ship you from there."

"No," Roddy said. "No."

Some of the tension went out of his face. He reached out and touched her chin. "Little girl. I've miscalculated the situation. I don't want you here."

"It took you till the damned Judgment Day to see it," Earnest muttered.

"I'm not going," Roddy exclaimed. "I won't."

Earnest took her arm. "This is no time to play the loyal wife, sister mine. You've got your husband's leave. Let's assume he knows best, and be on our way."

"No." She wrenched her arm away. "I'm staying here."

"There's no need," Faelan said.

She looked at him, demon-dark and sky-blue in the gloomy hall, and with a stab of desperation thought, *Oh, yes, there is. I won't lose you to Geoffrey's cause.*

"I don't care," she said aloud. "I'm not leaving now."

Earnest closed his eyes and ran a hand over his blond hair. "Lord spare me from idiots. The man just said he don't need you. Roddy—"

His voice trailed off in consternation as Faelan took a step forward. He pulled Roddy into his arms. It was an unexpected tactic, a smooth attack that for a moment sent reason and resolution tumbling away into unimportance. He held her, traced her jaw and her temple; lowered his thick lashes as his lips brushed her mouth. Roddy's chin tilted upward in unthinking response. The kiss deepened. She was melting, forgetting Earnest, and Geoffrey, and soldiers... forgetting everything, whirling away down the dark, vortex of his touch...

"You're going," he said.

Roddy stared up at him, weakened and bemused.

His arm tightened across her back. She could feel his chest rise and fall against her. "Is that clear?" he murmured.

"No." The word sounded too small, breathless with confusion. "No," she said louder. "I'm staying."

Earnest had turned away self-consciously. Faelan moved his palm up beneath her breast, his fingers barely brushing the eager tip. His other hand cupped the nape of her neck. "Little girl," he said, very low in her ear. "You'll do as I say."

His breath caressed her skin as he stood with his head bent so close and intimately. She knew what he was doing—distracting her, using his power over her body to twist her mind to his will. It had worked before, often enough. But there was more at stake now. Far more.

Geoffrey hid outside, awaiting his chance. She had to reach him, had to find a way to get him to safety without endangering Faelan. She could do it, with her talent. She could find a place that no one would know, and keep watch with a thoroughness no one else could. If someone became suspicious, she would feel it. If soldiers threatened, she could anticipate them. She could know whom to trust and whom to fear. For Roddy, Geoffrey was a manageable danger. For Faelan, he was poison.

She put her hands against Faelan's chest and thrust herself out of his arms. "Don't do that." She glared at him. "Leave me alone."

Her voice rang in the hall, strident with her inner conflict. It came out more shrewish than defiant, but she would not take the words back. For good measure, she added, "I'm not going. You can't force me."

A flicker of some emotion came and went in his eyes. He caught her wrist and bent it back with light but steady force, caressing her palm with his thumb. "I wouldn't put too much confidence in that, my dear."

"Just... don't touch me." Roddy pulled away from the sensual contact. She backed toward Earnest, who stood tensely, unsure of which side to take to accomplish his goal. He put his hands on her shoulders, more from distraction and habit than any real offer of protection.

Roddy saw Faelan's expression change at that. Like the mountain mists that could rise in a moment to swallow the sun, his face went to chilly blankness. His hand dropped. "Do as you please, then." He was already turning away. "I don't have time for this."

"Faelan." At the last moment, Roddy could not bear that coldness. He stopped and looked back, his eyes a bright, icy flame in the stone hall. "What about the free-quarters?"

For a moment his hand tightened on the doorframe. "Worried about your investment in the place?" he asked dryly. "Well, I shall do my best for you, my love."

A sudden panic took her, for the inflexible note in his voice. "What? What will you do?"

He laughed. The sound vibrated from the walls and the floors and had no trace of humor in it. "'Tis simple enough. I have only to prove that every living man in this barony is loyal to the Crown."

❧

That night, there was no sleep for anyone. Torches burned up and down the glen, and the ominous glow of red lit the drifting mist far below where the army was camped. The windows of the great house shone as they had on the night of the fairy ball, and dark figures passed in and out the wide door—figures bearing long, wicked wooden staffs with curved and sharpened metal points.

In the dining room, next to Roddy's shining mahogany table, the pikes lay piled against the wall in a bristling forest.

Earnest leaned over a rude map, his head supported by a weary hand on his brow, marking caches and making count, while Fachtnan O'Sullivan and his father and brother dispatched ragged couriers to every corner of the district.

Two local clergymen stood beneath a borrowed holy cross that had been hastily tacked to the wall: a Catholic priest and the elderly rector—the same who'd so narrowly missed murder by Geoffrey's men. As each cottier surrendered his arms, he repeated after Faelan a solemn oath of loyalty to the King, which O'Sullivan translated to Irish if necessary, and then a mark or a signature went down, duly witnessed and recorded.

It was the magistrate who should have accepted the oaths. But the magistrate lay dead, thrown from his horse onto the stones before the great house.

Martha bustled in and out, keeping the sweet tea flowing for the men who trudged in with their offerings of illicit arms—pikes and guns forged or stolen over years of misery under Willis and Mullane and the others like them, who'd drained the life from the land at a distance, safe in their comfortable houses in Cork or Dublin or even London, never questioning what was done in their names as long as the rents came due. Decades of oppression, of hate and rebellious dreams.

But now it was a kind of love that made them give up the weapons; it was the hope of better lives that Faelan had brought, and the certain knowledge that his ruin would be their own.

Some, lacking hidden arms, came with a chicken or a meager bag of oats, in a befuddled attempt to appease these higher powers that suddenly threatened. It was the only time that night Roddy saw Faelan's temper. He shouted at the confused cottiers that they'd do better to hide what they owned in the farthest hills than bring it to him. Then he sent them out to do it, and to gather all the cattle they could find and drive the beasts through the dark to the wild mountain fells where soldiers might not go.

After that, he sat down heavily, and made Martha cry by

snarling that she could take her damned pastries away and choke on them. Roddy smoothed over that by giving the maid a hug, and leaving the plate near his elbow. Ten minutes later, she tapped a snuffling Martha on the shoulder, pointing to the platter where only crumbs were left.

A contingent of small farmers had come and gone, and after their contribution was counted, Earnest swore. "Six hundred fifty-three pikes, twenty-two pistols, and five muskets. That's the last of the villages. There's only these two northern valleys left to go." He tapped the map and shook his head. "We've outdone the bastards by twice on the pikes, but where in God's sweet heaven did Roberts come by a figure of four thousand guns?"

Faelan did not answer. He only sat back in the carved French chair and stared at the half-finished ceiling with a bleakness that made Roddy want to cry.

Geoffrey. Oh, damn you, Geoffrey. You and your guns.

It was near three in the morning, and the flow of arms had become a trickle. Roddy had been aware of Geoffrey since dark, concealed outside the dining-room windows and waiting for a chance to catch his friend alone. Roddy had found no opportunity to contact him. He was growing dangerously impatient. He'd been thwarted all day and night by the crowd of strangers that surrounded Faelan. So now, when her husband stood up and walked to the door, Roddy rushed after.

She grabbed his arm before he reached the entry. "Where are you going?"

Faelan half turned, and the candlelight glistened off a trace of perspiration that had trailed down his left temple and his jaw. "Pardon me," he said, with exaggerated courtesy, "but you may have noticed that our accommodations lack a water closet."

"Oh." Roddy let go of his arm. She stared at him a moment, frozen with desperation, and then realized that Martha had gone back to the kitchen for more pastries. "You mustn't go that way," Roddy exclaimed, and then added meaningfully, "Martha just went out."

He accepted that without comment, turning back to sit down again.

Roddy said suddenly, "I'm going, too. While she's still there."

Faelan had already pulled the map toward him; he nodded absently and joined the conversation among Earnest and the clergymen about how best to take advantage of daylight when it came.

Roddy wet her lips, focusing on each man in turn to see that he was fully occupied, and then slipped out into the hall and through the front door.

Outside, she hurried down the stairs and skirted the house through the faint mist, keeping close to the windows. Geoffrey heard her approach, and she felt his sudden panic as he realized the unknown figure in the half-light was heading directly toward him. Just as he was preparing to scramble back into the undergrowth and run, she stopped.

Geoffrey waited. She dared not call his name, and so she began to hum, and then sing softly. It was a song he would know, the old, haunting love song that Geoffrey himself had taught her long ago:

> *Ah la, then he came to his true love's window,*
> *He knelt down low upon a stone,*
> *And through the glass he whispered softly,*
> *Are you asleep, love, are you alone?*
> *I am your lover, do not discover,*
> *But rise up, darling, and let me in,*
> *For I am tired of my long night's journey,*
> *And likewise, love, I'm wet to the skin.*

She did not have to sing the last lines, the sad stanzas of parting between a girl and her ghostly lover, come across years and miles for one night. Geoffrey relaxed, recognizing her voice and the message in the song. He did not retreat when she moved closer, but waited until they were both lost in the shadows to reach out and grab her arm and pull her against him.

"Poppet," he whispered, right into her ear. "I need Faelan."

Aye, Roddy thought, *and I won't let you have him.*

"The stable," she said, beneath her breath.

She felt his hard exhalation of relief, and did not correct his mistaken assumption that it was Faelan who would be waiting in the stable. She pulled away without speaking again and moved out into the luminous shaft from the nearest column of light. She looked up. Faelan stood there, outlined against the candlelight behind.

He gave no sign that he saw her. But she was sure that he must—the dewy air reflected and compounded the cool glow from the window, turning it into a shimmering prism that held her at its center. She bowed her head, pretending to straighten her skirt, and took up her song again. In a voice too soft to reveal the pounding of her heart, she sang:

> *When that night, it nearly was ended,*
> *And the early cocks, they began to crow,*
> *We kissed, we kissed, and alas we parted,*
> *Sayin' good-bye, darlin', now I must go.*

As she reached the end of it, she was saved from having to linger further by the arrival of a straggling party of dairymen. The shadow from the window moved and disappeared, and the group inside roused themselves from exhaustion to start the ritual of oaths and weapon-counting again.

Roddy slipped away.

The stable had many noises in the dark. There was the wind, ever present in the eaves, and a hundred small rustlings of mice and straw. An owl lived in the tree outside: Roddy had often drifted to sleep with his low mourning note in her ear, mingling with the deep, steady rhythm of Faelan's breath in her hair.

She heard Geoffrey scramble up in the straw as she entered.

"Faelan," he said in a low voice. "By the saints, I thought I'd never have a chance at you."

"It's not Faelan." Roddy moved into the thick, hay-scented darkness. "It's me."

There was a hiss of straw as he stumbled toward her. He came up against her and took a step back. "Ah—poppet. I can't see a damned thing in here. I nearly blacked my eye on a pitchfork. Where's Faelan?"

"He isn't coming."

She felt Geoffrey's quick surge of annoyance, but he kept his voice soft. "I need to talk to him—can't you get him away?"

"No. I came to tell you—he doesn't know you're here, and he isn't going to find out."

"What?" The annoyance changed to exasperation. He caught her arm and shook her. "Roddy, believe me, this is no game. I've got to have his help—"

"No!" She steadied herself against him in the dark. "I saw you this morning. You were there, when Willis accused Faelan. He can't take that risk, helping you. You have to stay away from him."

His hand tightened around her upper arm. "But you haven't told him I'm here? Roddy, you must. Aye, there's some risk, but I know Faelan. He won't think anything of that."

"Of course he won't," Roddy snapped. "That's why I want you away from here."

"But, Roddy—"

She shoved at him, angry and desperate. It was not so much that Geoffrey cared nothing for his friend's welfare; it was rather that he had an unshakable faith in Faelan's ability to handle any scrape. As if Faelan were somehow above human weakness, unable to make a mistake that might kill him.

"Geoffrey," she said between her teeth. "If you go near my husband, I will turn you in myself."

It was the only leverage she could think of. He took the threat in the light of a childish tantrum, but Roddy didn't allow him to open his mouth and say so.

"I swear to God, I *will*," she hissed. "If you think I won't see you hang for your stupid rebellion before I'll let you endanger Faelan, you mistake me at your peril."

It was bluff, pure bluff, for she could never have done it, but the words and her tone of voice finally sank in. For all her life, Geoffrey had thought of her as "poppet," as a child, a female: soft and submissive and not very bright. She suddenly dropped into a new category: a woman, who would grasp at any weapon to protect her man.

He might not respect her methods, but he developed a sudden and healthy respect for her resolution.

"All right," he said slowly. "I won't mistake you."

Twenty

Six hundred fifty-three pikes, twenty-two pistols, and five guns were not enough.

Nothing would have been enough, except the full shipment of Geoffrey's smuggled muskets.

Rain swept the great house in showers, throwing drops with a spattering sound against those windows that had panes, and puddling on the stone floor beneath those that didn't. The fireplace in the dining room leaked. There was a shiny dark spot on the marble hearth where a warm fire should have been.

But the smoke that drifted in with the drizzle was not the comforting, clinging smell of peat. The damp breeze carried a heavy, peculiar odor: the pungent scent of burning grain.

Faelan sat before the empty hearth. His face was a mask. He gave no sign of hearing the intermittent pop of pistol fire that heralded the systematic slaughter of his imported Frisian cattle.

Five days had passed since the army had come. At first the soldiers had only taken excess: poultry and potatoes and livestock enough to feed themselves royally. But as each day passed without the guns, Roberts had unleashed his men a little more, until by now they were angry, and impatient for results. They had taken all they could consume and more—far more—and the free-quarters had become free destruction.

Faelan's imported stores bore the brunt of their fury. Still gathered and awaiting distribution according to his careful plans, the cattle and seed wheat and commodities he'd brought for exchange in a moneyless economy were too easy to reach. It was more entertaining and far less trouble to burn sacks of grain piled high in a thatch-roofed barn than to search out the small huts in the mountains and seize a few year-old potatoes. And the soldiers did not stop with stores. The plows were broken up, the half-finished pier burned to the waterline. Even the lime and saltpeter Faelan had bought for the fields was carted away and dumped into the sea.

The oaths of loyalty had been futile. As long as the guns were withheld, Roberts said, he'd accept no false professions of good faith.

Roddy sat at the table with Earnest and smelled the smoke and listened to the guns and watched her husband stare at nothing until she could bear it no longer. "I'm going to take a walk," she announced.

Earnest roused instantly from his gloomy reflections. "I'll go with you."

The last thing she wanted was Earnest's company, with his eternal pressuring at her to leave Ireland with him. Beyond that, she had her other reason to be alone: Geoffrey, who had proved himself every bit as troublesome as she'd feared.

The hiding place she'd chosen for him, the remote cottage that had been MacLassar's first home, had stood vacant for months. Long ago Roddy had convinced Faelan to move the woman and her child to a better holding, where the widow had since become mildly famous as being favored by the *sidhe* because of the occasional small gifts that would appear in the night on the woman's new hearth. These Roddy attributed to Faelan, for she could find no other donor through her talent.

The *sidhe* luck must have rubbed off on Geoffrey, too. It was certainly no natural aptitude for concealment that had kept him undiscovered. He would not stay put; he took a ramble every morning and evening through the hills, and Roddy could not convince him that he couldn't build a smokeless fire. Someone had taught him the trick once, and he was certain that he had the way of it. As far as Roddy could tell, only the unfamiliar spread of smoke from the soldiers' fire kept Geoffrey's from instant detection.

"I'd rather go alone," she said to Earnest. "I shall be back before supper."

"Roddy—it's not safe." He automatically turned to Faelan for support. "You won't let her go wandering about alone."

Faelan looked sideways at her, a glance that puzzled Roddy, that seemed cynical and questioning at once. "I'll go with you, if you like."

Roddy wet her lips. His unexpected focus on her made her uncomfortable, burningly aware that she was hiding something from him. For days it seemed that he had looked through her without even seeing her. All night, every night, he sat in this cold, spare room waiting for more arms and watching the countryside burn. It had been easy to pretend, easy to go to bed in the stable and then sneak out after dark to carry what food she could conceal to Geoffrey. It was as if her husband did not know whether she was there or gone. But now...

She picked up her cape of bright green baize and threw it across her shoulders with a deliberately casual move. "That's isn't necessary at all. I'd really rather go alone."

Faelan rose. Roddy bowed her head, hiding the guilt she was certain shone clear in her eyes. She felt his light touch, and refused to look up as he traced her cheekbone and temple. Need struck her—a longing that made her throat close and her chest ache. She wanted to throw herself into his arms and cry for what the army was making of his dreams—of *their* dreams... for the future here had become hers, too. She wanted to confess her fears for Geoffrey, her hopeless inability to think of a way to get him safely out of the country. She wanted to lie again with her husband on a blanket in the clean, sweet straw, too tired from honest work to make love, but not too tired to be close, to feel his arms around her and his skin warm against her back.

But her secret stood between them, and she was afraid to meet his eyes.

"I'd like to go," he said softly.

"I don't want you." It was breathless, quickly spoken and ill considered. She stepped back away to avoid his touch.

From a safer distance, she dared to look up. If her words had hurt him, she could not tell it in his face. Only Earnest's irritated confusion reached her, his bafflement and concern at what he saw of their marriage.

"Very well." Faelan turned away to the window. His voice held a brittle precision. "Then go alone."

"No!" Earnest's chair made a scrape as he leaped to his feet. "I forbid it."

Faelan looked back. Roddy saw it then, like a mirror breaking. The mask of control cracked and shattered; Faelan's face went to violence and his body moved with savage grace—one moment Earnest was standing and the next he was sprawled back on the table. The blow took Roddy, too, made her stomach wrench and her knees stagger, and Faelan's snarled words came to her through Earnest's haze.

"*You* forbid it!" He jerked Earnest up by his coat. "You meddling bastard, you think I can't protect what's mine? You think there's a damned thing you could do better?" He let go, and Earnest stumbled, clutching the table behind. "You don't forbid anything here, my friend," Faelan sneered. "You don't open your mouth if I don't like what you have to say, because I own everything you can see, and that includes your precious little sister, and if I choose to sit on my backside while they burn the place down around our ears, then you can go or you can stay, but you'll damned well keep your mouth shut!"

Earnest found his feet. Roddy felt him gather himself, and thought for an instant that he would return the blow. He was almost of a size with Faelan, and no mean pugilist—it was surprise that had taken him down, not superior skill. But Earnest preferred finer weapons to his fists.

He fingered his swelling lip. "Of course." He looked down at his hand that came away marked with blood. "I can see that you have the situation completely under control."

Faelan made a sound, incoherent, and swung away.

"Admit it." Earnest followed up his parry with attack. "Admit it, man! You're hanging by a thin thread."

A gust of wind brought rain spatters and the acrid smell of

smoke in through an unglazed window. Faelan stood in front of the opening, ignoring the rain.

"What happens when it snaps?" Earnest asked with quiet menace. "I know about you, Iveragh. I've made it my business to find out. You may be a madman or you may just be an immoral beast, but either way you don't own my sister. You don't control anything. You'll be lucky if you don't hang for what I've heard of you—"

Roddy caught a vision of the dowager countess in Earnest's mind, a face crumpled in hysterical tears. *He can't help himself*, she'd cried to Earnest. *I know he never meant to do it! He was just a boy—How could a boy of ten mean to kill his own—*

"—Starting here, Iveragh," Earnest went on in that low, relentless voice. "Starting right here. You think I'll leave my sister with a man who pushed his father off a cliff?"

Faelan laughed. It was a terrible sound; inhuman. "I think you have the story wrong. My father died here. In this house." He half turned. "My mother didn't tell you that?" The smile on his face was a devil's insolence. "Ah, but she's always so anxious to protect me. To make sure no one knows the truth. The place burned. Senach found him after the fire, with his skull smashed on the floor of his own study."

Roddy stared at the dark puddle on the hearth. *I don't want to know this*, she thought, *I don't want to hear.*

But Earnest's wave of horror and disgust twisted her insides and kept her rooted to the floor. "His skull smashed. God, God…" Her brother's voice trailed off.

Faelan reached with one hand for the half-finished window frame. It was an unconscious move—Roddy thought it was—but she felt her brother's jolt of wariness as the motion dislodged a pike which had been leaning against the new wood. The weapon clattered to the floor.

Faelan stood, staring down at it.

"Little girl," he said in a tight voice. "I think you and your brother had best get out of here. Before we're all sorry."

"Aye. I'll get her out." Earnest gripped Roddy's arm and began to propel her toward the door. He stopped at the entry, his fingers digging into Roddy's arm as she fought to break his hold. "Any way I have to do it, Iveragh. I promise you. Any way on God's earth I have to do it."

⌇

Never before in her life had Roddy been physically restrained. And certainly not by one of her brothers—by her favorite brother, her best friend, who appeared now to have gone mad along with everyone else.

She sat in the dusty humidity of the abandoned harness room and fumed. The blow to Earnest's head had definitely injured more than his lip. He'd locked her in. Locked her in, for God's sake, as if she were a troublesome child, or an animal, while he went to Derrynane to arrange passage with the O'Connells.

He'd picked his spot well, though that was luck more than forethought. He'd pushed her inside in an unthinking rage, driven by the release of pent-up frustration, the need to *do* something after seven days of futile arguing. Then he'd shot the bolt home and left her banging at the heavy door and screaming at him to come to his senses.

But he hadn't. He was too wrapped up in this battle with Faelan, in which she had become a symbol, a pawn—a princess to be rescued from the dragon. He'd forgotten that Faelan had urged her to leave; glossed over any evidence that Faelan was not a heartless monster. Earnest saw, as well as Roddy, that while the soldiers were occupied with destroying everything Faelan had brought, they left untouched the cottiers' meager stores. But Earnest did not want to think of that—he was tired of gray; he was sick of fighting mist. He wanted black and white.

And there was no one blacker in his mind just now than the Devil Earl.

Roddy stayed all afternoon in her musty prison. No one responded to her pounding and cries. No one came near or heard her—no one but MacLassar, who sat himself down outside the door and waited patiently for her to emerge and feed him.

Through the high, barred window, she could see that the rain-swept sky had cleared as it usually did in the evening. Her throat was swollen and scratchy, her voice broken from futile shouting. Sweet, golden rays of late sun illuminated the room for a few minutes, and then the empty corners went to shadow and the night-gloom closed in. She strained her talent until her head ached, listening for Earnest, or Martha, or anyone.

As she sat there on a rotting tack-trunk she began to feel… something. Not a single mind, but the swell of consciousness that heralded a crowd. There was anger in it, and eager violence: a cheerful aggression—uniquely male, and beneath that a physical, almost sexual, pleasure in the lockstep rhythm of the march.

Roberts' infantry.

Roddy stood up. The soldiers' mood frightened her. They had not come near the mansion in force since that first day—it had only been Roberts and a small contingent who'd arrived each day to collect what arms had been brought in the night before. Yesterday it had been only five pikes. Today it would be two.

If she closed her eyes, she could imagine the scene. It had become a ritual—Faelan standing cold and silent with his cottiers as Roberts poured out a tirade against the evils of resistance to His Majesty's troops, carefully geared to humiliate and abuse as far as possible without crossing the fine line of direct accusation. Roberts was good at it; more than once, Roddy had seen Faelan go taut and heard the faint, faint tremor of rage in his voice as he repeated his own ritual speech: "The arms have been surrendered. The barony is loyal. There are no more weapons in this neighborhood to my knowledge."

Then Roberts would drip with scorn for liars, make veiled references to Faelan's reputation and more open ones to his connection with Geoffrey—and announce what his men would be turned loose upon the next day.

They were running out of targets. Faelan's imports had been decimated. There were only the scattered cottiers, and the great house itself.

She had the thought at the same moment that shouts erupted from the direction of the house. The words were lost with distance, the thoughts obscured by the multitude, but she recognized her husband's voice—hoarse with the same wild fury that had possessed him when he'd turned on Earnest.

In answer a sharp ragging pop cut the twilight.

That sound hit her the way Faelan's fist had smashed her brother's jaw: fear like a blow, an impact that sent her mind to black terror and her limbs to wax. For an instant it paralyzed her, and then she grabbed the first thing that came to hand—a long piece of metal, some underpinning of an ancient carriage that she'd barely been able to lift when she'd pushed it off the trunk to make room for herself—and swung it at the heavy door.

The crash of iron on wood sent pain to her teeth, but she hefted the metal club and struck again. The wood split at the hinges. She focused her attack at the point of weakness, sobbing with effort, swinging over and over until the lower bolts gave with a squealing groan, freeing the bottom half of the door from its hinge.

She forced her way through, clenching her teeth against the rough scrape of broken wood across one arm where her cape fell free and her sleeve ripped. MacLassar peeked out of the stall where he'd retreated, and rushed to tangle with her skirt as she scrambled to her feet.

She ran, throwing her cape aside when it hindered her. The shouting had become a roar, and through the lowering night she could see flames arching upward, blazing brands aimed at the upper windows of the house. One disappeared through an opening, faded to nothing for a moment, and then flared, filling the window with a rising red glow. Another found its mark, and by the time Roddy reached the crowd of weaving, shouting silhouettes in the forecourt, the upper story was ablaze.

She did not care. She searched the chaos frantically, screaming Faelan's name above the noise of the fire and the soldiers. Her talent was useless; without the strength of shielding she'd learned in London, she would have been writhing on the ground under the emotion generated by the mob.

Someone ran past her and shoved her roughly aside, heading for the stables. MacLassar squealed as she stumbled over him. She grabbed him up as she found her balance and threw him over her shoulder, plunging forward, crying desperate curses and shoving back viciously when anyone pushed her. Dark figures were running out of the house, carrying furniture and silver plate. Bayonets flashed scarlet sparks in the glow of the fire, still slung, but treacherous enough on the back of some gyrating soldier occupied with mayhem.

She heard Faelan before she saw him. His voice—strong and whole, bellowing her name over the tumult—made her stumble around toward the source in sick relief.

Two redcoats had him pinned by the arms in the dancing shadow of Roberts' horse. She ducked a shouldered musket, holding MacLassar close to her head and panting under his bouncing weight as she ran. Faelan wrenched free as she reached him. His captors moved to restrain him again, but Captain Roberts shouted, "Let him go! He can't stop it now."

Roddy saw Faelan flash a look up toward the captain, and even through her barriers she could read the triumph in the officer's eyes. Captain Roberts had had his revenge. He'd seen Faelan break; had found the chink in the mask.

Then she was in his arms, glad of the painful grip that made MacLassar squeal and wriggle. "I heard gunshots." She clutched at his coat. Her voice cracked under the strain of tears and relief. "I heard you and then I heard them shooting!"

"Roddy." He rocked her, his breath fierce in her ear, holding her with one arm and subduing MacLassar by main force with the other. "Little girl, little girl, I thought you'd gone."

"Earnest locked me in the harness room," she cried. "He's gone to Derrynane—he's arranging passage—"

A cracking sound drowned her words, and suddenly the soldiers began to surge backward. Faelan kept hold of her, pulling her along, cutting off circulation with the strength of his grip on her shoulder. The cracking grew to a steam-engine hiss, and with a slow, terrible majesty, Faelan's new roof bowed. Flames soared up through the spreading crevices. Slates began to crash down onto the rapidly clearing forecourt.

From a safe distance, the crowd watched as the roof structure collapsed into the stone walls with a thunderous groan, sending a thousand sparks sailing into night.

The soldiers cheered. Faelan's hand went tight and stiff on her shoulder. She felt him turn his face into her hair.

There was no comfort she could give him. Not even the pointless offer of her embrace, for MacLassar pummeled her with frantic feet, driven to panic by the noise and the smoke. It was all she could do hold the half-grown piglet with both arms. Someone stumbled against her back, jolting her free of Faelan's touch. In the same moment, MacLassar twisted and kicked, sliding relentlessly from her hold. She struggled, and lost him.

He was gone in an instant. The fire made a mockery of substance and shadow, confusing everything into a shifting blur of arms and legs and muskets. Then above the noise came a high-pitched squeal of terror, and she saw MacLassar lifted overhead in an infantryman's hands.

"No!" she screamed. "*No!*"

She lunged forward, and the struggling piglet leaped free. There was a wild shuffle and then with a yell of glee another soldier hefted MacLassar high above the crowd. The animal's shrieks only made the men more excited by their game: MacLassar jumped and escaped and was caught again, and one soldier made a motion of bringing the piglet down on another's bayonet. A jostle of the crowd made him stumble and miss, and MacLassar fell free and bolted.

Roddy fought through the mob in the direction the piglet had gone. She heard Faelan behind her, shouting her name. The sound of MacLassar's panicked squeals floated above the tumult as she shoved and slid through. It seemed to dawn upon several soldiers at once that there was a female in their midst, and amid renewed shouting hard hands grabbed at her dress.

She jerked away, and bounced back into another man's chest. His arm closed around her torso; she felt the knobs of buttons against her back and heard his hoot of pleasure as his mouth came down, revolting and wet on her neck. He swung her, and she kicked backward, connecting enough to make him stagger and overbalance. He hit his nearest comrade's shoulder and his clutch loosened. Gulping air, Roddy tore at his fingers and scrambled free.

She wasted no breath in screaming; it took all she had to duck and fight and narrow her talent to an arc of blazing clarity around her, channeling the energy she'd used for her barriers to catch the wild flow of intention around her, to separate minds and connect them to bodies, to avoid the reaching arm in front of her and slide away from the grasp that came from behind.

She was afraid; she was terrified, but there was no time for that. The fire lit her tormentors in lurid red motion. A soldier made a grab for her skirt and she spun away, knocking into another with enough force to push him facedown on the stone. She jumped, not quite across him, landing with her heel in his back and catching the sharp, nauseating lance of cracking bone before she thrust the sensation away.

Each time she turned, she reeled toward the side where her gift found the mob thinnest—away from the fire, toward the safety of darkness. She could hear shouts above the rest, demanding order, and from the corner of one eye she saw Roberts' horse silhouetted against the blaze as he waded into his men with his pistol pointed in the air.

The crack of gunfire caught the attention of the men around her for an instant; long enough for her to lunge free. One turned, yelling, but Roddy avoided his grasp and darted away, throwing herself to one side or the other in anticipation of the stragglers who stood between her and freedom.

She was in the open suddenly, but she kept running, heading for the cover of the overgrown shrubbery. Behind her the roar of the fire drowned out voices, but she felt the changing emotion of the troop as the officers began to restore some semblance of discipline. There wasn't much left for the men to set upon; the house and outbuildings been put to flame and the furniture bashed to pieces without resistance. Of rebels or even servants there were none to be found; no caches of hidden guns or gold. With no fuel for destruction, their excitement ebbed quickly.

In the receding emotion, Roddy picked out MacLassar's panicky flight. He was hurt and frantic, moving at speed away from the scene of terror. Roddy cast a look back at the mansion, burning steadily now, and plunged into the darkness after her wounded pet.

Twenty-One

THERE WAS ONLY UP AND DOWN IN THE DARK. UP AND DOWN, and rocks to stumble on and heather to tangle her feet, like living hands bent on dragging her to her knees. Each time it tripped her, she struggled upright, heaving for breath and plowing forward again, up the ridge, up and up until the earth tilted down again—and she stopped, staring bleakly into the dark.

She could see the line between the horizon and the sky, where a few hazy stars hung below the clouds, but the ground at her feet was a black and shapeless mass. In a few places the dim starlight caught the blurred outline of a bush or a stone, but the harder she strained the more the edges seemed to slip and waver, until she might have been standing before a smooth, safe plain or wavering at the edge of a precipice.

She thought of the militiaman who'd died the night of the fairy ball, and how a cliff must have looked like safe ground to him, until suddenly ground wasn't there at all. The more she thought, the harder it was to fight the metallic taste of panic in her mouth. She could imagine how it would feel. One step, and then nothing; the awful drop, the air rushing past… it would take a long time, a very long time, before one hit the bottom—

She stood frozen, breathing too fast, her stomach weak and her ears ringing with terror.

She'd long since given up finding MacLassar. Hours ago, she'd lost contact with his small, frightened presence among the dark hills. She'd stopped then, when she'd realized it, and turned back the way she had come, expecting to see the glow from the fire as a beacon.

But there was nothing. Only the dark, and the faint, silent wind.

Her gift was no aid; she found no rational mind nearby to help. There were creatures about, hares and mice and birds, with their little spurts of fear at her noisy approach, but for half the night she'd stumbled aimlessly without human contact.

She feared she had drifted into the mountains themselves, for in trying to find the fire she'd topped ridge after ridge, hoping at the crown of each one to see the blaze. It seemed impossible that the fire which had lit the whole sky could have faded so suddenly out of existence.

The logical part of her had an answer. There'd been little to burn on the half-repaired mansion. Once the roof and the new second floor had gone, there was nothing else to fuel the flames.

She blinked, trying to bring her mind into focus, if not her eyes. Beneath the fear was exhaustion, a deeper, heavier misery. Her legs trembled and her throat burned. Her skin was hot, but she was cold; her cloak long lost somewhere back at the stable and her French muslin dress never meant for the damp night air. She took a raw breath, fought back the paralyzing images of falling, and forced herself to put one foot in front of the other.

She crept along, feeling ahead with each step. She had an idea: to throw pebbles ahead of her every few feet and listen for the sound of them hitting the ground. It was slow, but it was progress, and she heartened a little as she edged down the hill without mishap.

A sound came to her. She thought it was wind at first, but it remained steady, a low rustle of water over stones, that grew as she neared the bottom of the valley. The vegetation thickened, rose up into bushes that brushed wet fingers in her face. To avoid the branches she kept her head down. The clinging vegetation opened. Her feet found a smooth rut among the plants: a cowpath, she guessed, and thought no more about it, only glad to have a guide and an easier place to walk.

A last spark of strength made her quicken her step. She could hear the stream ahead of her, and hoped that the path crossed at a shallow ford. As she was fuzzily contemplating the necessity of wetting her shoes, she put one foot into empty space.

She flung her arms backward. Her nightmares of falling took on shape and reality; for one infinite moment she hung in the air, her heart lurching wildly, and then water met her cry and choked it.

She came up coughing, tangled in her dress and slimy strings of vegetation. Splashing and stumbling in the knee-deep water, she cast about until she hit a bank, dragged herself up, and sat down on it, with her feet still in the stream and her arms clutched around her streaming shoulders.

She leaned forward, buried her face in her lap, and began to cry.

They were a child's furious tears, pointless and heartfelt, compounded of cold and fear and hopelessness. They swallowed everything, focusing all her mind on herself and her misery. For minutes she sat there—for hours... days... weeks. She was alone: the last person on earth, lost and doomed to wander the dark forever.

The touch on her shoulder made her jump and shriek. Her talent came into focus with a jolt, but she was already back in the water again before she recognized Geoffrey.

"Don't be afraid," he said in the dark. "I won't hurt you; I want to help—"

Relief poured through her like hot oil over ice. "Geoffrey—oh, Geoffrey, thank God—" She stopped suddenly, catching his shock of recognition as he heard her voice. "Of course it's me!" Exasperation followed on the heels of salvation as she realized he was disappointed—that he'd taken her for some unknown damsel in distress. Her cheeks warmed at his mental image of just what kind of rescue he'd hoped to offer.

But he was human and familiar, and Roddy waded toward him. "Give me your hand," she ordered. She could barely see him in the dark, just a vague light blob where his hair might be, and another one that moved. She took that for his hand,

and grabbed at it. After a moment's searching, their fingers locked. He pulled her up with a grunt.

"Lord, girl, you're sopping wet." He felt up her arm, and then lifted a dripping lock of hair and dropped it. "What the devil are you doing here? Did you run away from the fire?"

A quick memory of the flaming mansion accompanied the words, and Roddy suddenly realized that Geoffrey had been far closer than he should have. "You went down there, didn't you?" she hissed. "For God's sake, Geoffrey, they'll hang you yet, and Faelan, too."

He was instantly guilty, not for going to view the fire, but for why he was so late coming back. Roddy sucked in her breath and bit her lip to keep from shouting at him that consorting with stray cottiers' daughters did not count as offering comfort and consolation to the oppressed peasantry. Instead she clenched her teeth and began to shiver. A shaky sob escaped her.

"Come on." He took her arm and pushed her ahead of him into the gloom. "Don't cry. Poppet, poppet, don't cry. It was only a house, and half ruined at that."

"It's not the h-house. It's Faelan—"

He steered her around a bend in the path. "Faelan's all right. Didn't you know that? I saw him giving Roberts the devil of dressing-down—"

She stopped, and stumbled around as he bumped into her. "Just how close *were* you?"

"Up on the hill," he said, a blatant lie. Roddy caught a memory of the rioting soldiers from no farther away than the smokehouse.

There was no way she could castigate him for the exaggeration. "You shouldn't have been there at all," she snapped.

"Well, it's my hide, poppet."

"And Faelan's!"

"Faelan had best hold his tongue with a British officer, in that case—that's more liable to get him arrested than helping me out of my spot."

"No, it isn't." She turned and plowed ahead, only missing a tree because Geoffrey pulled her back just as the slightly blacker shape loomed up out of the darkness. "Roberts wants evidence before he makes any arrests. He's afraid of embarrassing himself."

The shivering began again, uncontrollable. Roddy tripped as she pulled her dripping gown up from where it was trailing off her shoulders.

"You'll catch your death from this," Geoffrey muttered. "Faelan'll have me out for pistols at dawn if you get sick."

"W-will he?" The sentiment behind that comment made her suddenly teary. "Do you think he really c-cares about me?"

"Lord, poppet—do you think he don't? He turns ten shades of purple if another man lays a hand on you. Including—*particularly*—me."

Roddy sniffed and shook. "That's just his way. He's j-jealous—"

"Jealous!" Geoffrey laughed with honest amusement. "Lord, we've shared more—"

He cut that sentence short, but Roddy could have guessed the end even without the flash of memory that accompanied it.

"Well," he finished lamely, "he's a changed man since he married, I can tell you that. Here we are. Take your shoes off and leave 'em outside. You can wear some of my stockings. Get that wet dress off. There's an extra blanket—that should do until morning."

"Morning!" Roddy set her feet outside the dim white bulk of the cottage. "I c-can't stay here till morning. I have to get home."

"If home is that stable you told me about, then it's nothing but a pile of cinders," Geoffrey said ruthlessly. He held back the musty cloth and pushed her inside. "Damn—wait a moment, while I find the tinderbox."

She hugged herself, trying to control the shivers. The shaking seemed to go to her head and muddle it. "Geoffrey… I h-have to get back. No-no-nobody knows wh-where I am."

Light sputtered and flared, then steadied as Geoffrey lit a candle. Roddy squinted at his face, underlit by the small flame.

"You can't walk another step," he said. "Here. Let me reach your buttons."

He turned her around, with no more thought of her feminine wiles than Earnest or MacLassar would have entertained.

Roddy clutched the blanket to her breasts as he pushed the sodden dress down off her shoulders. She tried to gather wit enough to protest, but nothing come out beyond a vague, sulky mumble. Her eyes would not focus, and Geoffrey's voice drifted in and out of her ears.

"There. Slide it off—oh, for Christ's sake, do you think I've a fancy for drowned rats? Get the blanket around you, then— here—here—stand up... are you fainting? Ah, hell... Roddy..."

❦

She didn't faint so much as fall asleep on her feet. Her dreams were vivid, and mixed with reality: lying down on a musty pallet on the floor, an incoherent argument with Geoffrey over starting a fire—it seemed fatally important to her that he not start one and vitally important to him that he did—and when Roddy could not remember her own reasoning she just burst into shivering sobs and accusations and buried her face in the blanket. Then she dreamed of a huge, hot blaze, that burned in her face and made sweat trickle down her throat, but when she woke sometime in the night there was no fire, though something warm held her pinned, and that warmth drifted into a dream of Faelan with his arms around her, and she snuggled down in safe content.

She woke again, with a start, to the taste of wet wool in her mouth and the cool half-light of dawn. She sat up. The blanket and her damp hair slid back off her shoulders, leaving her breasts bared to the humid atmosphere. In the moment of waking, there was something wrong, and something right. She focused her talent on the right, which was a touch of MacLassar's presence somewhere nearby—and then her blurred eyes found the wrong.

She blinked. The figure silhouetted against the light from the door took on hard outline, familiar features; arrested power in the broad shoulders and molded thighs. Faelan stood with the ragged curtain held back in one hand and her damp shoes in the other. A sheathed sword hung at his side and the dull pearl of a bone-handled pistol gleamed in the shadow beneath his coat.

She felt a movement against her back. Geoffrey groaned and tightened the bare arm that circled her waist, dreaming of a thousand soft, willing bodies that had lain in his loving embrace. She looked down in horror at his hand sprawled across her—male and possessive against her white nakedness— and then up into her husband's eyes.

For an instant she saw uncertainty, a look that took in the scene and would not accept: Faelan's mouth vulnerable with a greeting that had died upon his lips, and his eyes showing a kind of blankness, a shock; the first brush of recognition with some staggering loss.

"Faelan—"

Her voice was hoarse. It broke to a whisper, and Geoffrey stirred again. The name penetrated his half-sleep. He came awake with a physical jerk, gripping her and letting go, his hand clutching for his stiletto in instinctive defense. The bolt of surprise sent reason to his brain faster than understanding had come to Roddy. He saw Faelan and made the connection in an instant: no threat of redcoats pouring over him in frenzy, but one person—and a scene that suddenly balanced on a knife-edge of violence.

He rose up on his elbow, loosened his grip on the knife, and laid it slowly, deliberately aside. Roddy would have spoken, would have wrapped the blanket around her and run to her husband to explain, but Geoffrey's wariness stopped her. Explanations faded in her throat, impossible to prove, hopelessly weak—provocation and insult even to mention.

She pulled the cover up to her throat. Faelan's gaze flicked to the move. His mouth deepened into contempt. He leaned against the muddy doorframe and dropped her boots in front of him.

"Pardon me. I was under the impression that you were in need of aid, my dear. I see that I was mistaken."

Geoffrey said, very quietly, "Will you listen for a moment?"

"I think not." Faelan's lashes lowered. "I've listened for seven nights while my wife has made her excuses and left my house. I fear"—he looked up again, his eyes an inhuman blue—"I'm not in the mood for listening any longer."

Roddy could not help herself. She said in plaintive explanation, "I fell in the stream."

Faelan tilted his head. His smile was chilling. "A pity. I would have thought you'd know the way in the dark by now."

Which was true enough—she did know. *I was trying to protect you*, she wanted to cry, *I was trying to keep you safe*.

Geoffrey sat up behind her. She felt the sweaty slip of his bare torso against her skin. He was deeply uneasy—unarmed and uncertain of Faelan's temper, his eyes never leaving her husband's right hand.

"I've not dishonored your wife. Surely you know that."

Faelan said nothing.

Geoffrey took a breath and eased to his feet. Perspiration from where her body had been molded to his chest slipped down his rib cage and made dark markings at the waist of his breeches.

"Is it satisfaction you want?" he asked softly.

"My friend," Faelan's voice was equally soft, heavy with mockery. "Surely we're more civilized than that. You know I abhor violence in the name of honor."

Geoffrey half smiled, and shrugged. "I know you can kill me if we meet."

"I could kill you now, if I'd a mind to."

Geoffrey's glance rested on the sword and moved upward. "Do you?"

For a long moment Faelan stood, his dark figure still, his face carved in ice. Roddy felt Geoffrey's tension rise until the veins in his forearms stood out under the strain of holding his reaction in check.

With a vicious curse, Faelan turned abruptly away. He flipped the dirty curtain aside and strode out of the hut.

Roddy dragged the blanket around her and leaped to her feet, stumbling after him toward the door.

"Roddy—" Geoffrey's hand fell on her shoulder. "For God's sake, let him go."

"But—"

"You aren't going to catch him in that rig, anyway," Geoffrey hissed. He grabbed what was left of her limp gown off a hook in the dead hearth and thrust it into her hands. The sound of hooves thudded in the little clearing outside. Geoffrey looked toward the wall, as if he could see Faelan through it.

"He's gone." Geoffrey ran his hand across the back of his neck. "Lord God Almighty—I thought I was staring eternity in the face. I'll tell you, Roddy—"

He stopped short as MacLassar came hobbling on three legs into the cottage, batting the curtain aside with his snout. The piglet went straight to Roddy and sat up on his haunches to beg, waving one bandaged foot in the air.

Spare me this, Geoffrey thought as Roddy fell to her knees and hugged the animal.

"Go outside," she ordered Geoffrey. "I have to dress."

He bowed. "Oh, of course, Miss Modesty. I'm only the fellow who nearly got himself murdered for trying to keep your skinny butt warm without a fire."

"Don't try to blame *me*. This is all your fault. All of it. The stream, the fire, the guns—" Her voice rose as she recognized the connections. "The whole stupid *rebellion* is your fault!" She dropped the blanket and threw the damp dress over her head, wriggling into it with difficulty. Geoffrey paid no attention to her momentary nudity; he was busy buttoning his own shirt.

"I realize you're not very informed on politics," he snapped, "But I don't think you can pin the whole rebellion—*Ho!* I'm not sharing my breakfast with that pig!"

"Too late," Roddy said with vindictive satisfaction as MacLassar made short work of a loaf of hard bread. She lifted his foot and inspected the bandage, made of a ripped cravat and tied with careful skill.

Faelan did this, she thought, and suddenly her eyes went blurry and her throat closed. The memory of his face in that first moment of betrayal rose up in numbing clarity.

"I have to find him," she mumbled, scrambling to her feet. "I have to explain."

Geoffrey caught her by both arms before she reached the door. "Poppet. Maybe you'd best let him cool—"

She tore free. "He won't hurt me. He wouldn't."

"Wouldn't he?" Geoffrey gripped her again. "Roddy, you don't know him."

"I do!" She refused to acknowledge what was in Geoffrey's

mind. "You're as bad as Earnest. Those are all lies—those things everyone says."

Geoffrey's fingers dug into her flesh as he jerked her closer. "You saw him, just now. Do you think he wouldn't have spitted us both if it pleased him?"

"He was hurt," Roddy cried. "We hurt him."

"He was in a murdering rage, my girl. If you don't recognize the symptoms, I do. I've seen him shoot a poor bastard between the eyes with far less cause." *Chap barely out of leading strings—too witless to back down from issuing a challenge over his trollop of a fiancée.* Geoffrey's mind skipped back to the incident, and then to the girl. *Pretty little jade. Wouldn't mind tasting her wares again.*

Roddy shook out of his hold. "I won't listen to this," she shouted. She thrust her feet into her stiff shoes and swept MacLassar off the floor, ignoring his squeal of pain as she bumped his injured foot. With a snarl of disgust for men and their duels and their jealousy and their hypocritical morality, she stumped out the makeshift door.

⌘

"Your laddie." Senach's lined face seemed at one with the gray ruin, with the blackened, collapsed timbers and the slow smoke that curled toward the leaden sky. "Ye will not be findin' him here."

Roddy did not ask how he knew whom she sought. She shifted uneasily in her damp shoes, favoring a blistered heel, and said, "Have you seen him?"

"I be seein' him now." Senach looked into the heart of the dead fire. "Oh, och, aye, I see him."

She took a breath, willing herself not to turn and run. She hated speaking to Senach; hated being so close to him that her gift was useless and her heart thumped with fear of her own exposure. "Where is he?" she whispered, and then despised herself for asking.

As if she believed in his senile ravings.

"Never mind," she said, louder. There was no one at the burned-out mansion, not Martha nor Armand nor any of the little staff of servants who might know where Faelan had really gone. She started to turn away.

"Ye will not be findin' him," Senach said. "Not that way."

"Well—" Roddy stopped, covering her apprehension with churlishness. "What way, then, for heaven's sake?"

He chuckled. "Aye, 'tis nettled ye be. And 'tis a far piece to walk. There's better than that walkin'. There's bide a while, and listen, and ask what needs askin'."

"I have no patience for riddles," she snapped. "If you know where to find him, tell me."

"No patience. That I know." He shrugged, shook his head. "You're fearin' yet. Still fearin' your laddie."

A wash of guilt made her lips tremble. "What do you mean, fearing? I'm not afraid. I want to explain. I need to find him, and explain."

Senach tilted his head and smiled, in that blank, chilling way he had of laughing at her deepest terrors. "He won't credit it. Just words only. No, he won't credit that."

Roddy pressed her hands together. "You don't even know what I'm talking about!"

"Oh, aye—I do. You be speakin' of another man. Coming between friends. Wonderful friends, and ye come between 'em, and thinkin' there'll be blood on it."

She realized she was breathing unnaturally hard. She took a step backward. "That's not true."

"And how do ye know the truth?" Senach's whispery old voice took on a sharper note. "Ye with the gift, ye who be turnin' away and away from it, ye who could know if it pleased you."

"I told you," she cried. "I told you I can't! Not with Faelan."

"Cannot ye?" He looked her full in the face with his opaque eyes.

Roddy squeezed her lashes shut against him.

"Cannot ye?" Senach repeated.

The silence stretched. Roddy bit her lip. She was shaking as hard as she had the night before.

"Och, ye shame me, girl."

She heard him move, and when she opened her eyes, he was moving slowly across the empty forecourt. She watched him go with a relief that only made her shivering the greater, and a moment later turned away down the drive, running as fast as her aching feet would carry her.

She had no idea where to go. Her small store of energy ebbed, and she came to a stumbling halt at the place where the road branched. To the south was Derrynane and the O'Connells' home—miles away over Coomakista Pass. To the north was the army camp.

She sat down, defeated. MacLassar came hobbling up, dragging his dirty little bandage gamely. She had forgotten him. The sight made her feel guilty and sorry and angry at once—that he had to follow her in this aimless wandering about the empty countryside. The sun hung at zenith, a bright opalescence in the overcast sky. Wherever Faelan had gone, by now he had to be far beyond where she could reach on foot. The small fields and stony hedges lay before her in a patchwork; the mountains rose into the drowsing low clouds behind. She laid her head across her arms and closed her eyes, tired and hungry and unable to think.

She had no idea how much later it was when the touch of soldiers roused her gift. She lifted her head, stiff from sitting oddly, and searched the area suspiciously. After a moment, she saw them, a red splash against the green across the little valley.

She sprang up. For an instant she had no strength to take a step, and then she gave a despairing cry and began to run again—down the hill toward the path to Geoffrey's hiding place.

Twenty-Two

"Dearest Papa," Roddy wrote, and then stared at the paper.

Dearest Papa, I'm sorry, I'm sorry—

She made the pen move again. "I am writing with the utmost urgency. Two days ago, Earnest was arrested—"

Earnest, my brother… Oh, God, Papa, I'm so afraid.

"—along with Lord Geoffrey. They have been taken to Dublin to be charged with treason—"

*Papa, Papa, have you heard what they do to traitors? They're hanged, Papa, and then their heads are—*She closed her eyes and fought sickness. *Outside the prison—on the palings—Oh, Papa, I can't bear it—*

"You must come instantly. I have—"

She looked up. There were voices and footsteps outside Maurice O'Connell's study. Roddy felt her throat go dry as the lock turned and the door swung open.

Faelan paused on the threshold.

Seeing him was like a hard blow. She had expected to feel hate, disgust—but instead her heart reeled under the need to cling to him, to cry out her fear and desperation. As if he were deliverance, instead of treachery.

He shut the door. The others outside drifted away. They felt sorry for Roddy; they were horrified at this event. They thought she would be glad that Faelan had come at last.

But they did not guess what he had done.

She sat staring at him, unable to speak or move. She was glad that her gift was useless now, glad that she did not have to see into the mind that could conceive such vengeance. Better that he should have murdered her and Geoffrey at the cottage, in the heat of anger, than coolly plan this atrocity. It was no action of the moment. It could not be. At one sweep, the arrests removed all that threatened or vexed her husband. The soldiers had withdrawn from Iveragh, Geoffrey was in bonds, and Earnest—who had wanted only to keep her safe and who had made the mistake of trying to intimidate with reckless threats—Earnest, too, was brought down and obliterated.

Only Faelan was left, unpunished by law or decency.

He crossed the room, and reached as if to embrace her. He was so good at it, so perfect in deception, his face a mask of exhaustion and worry. His hand came within an inch of her shoulder.

"*Don't touch me.*"

A viper's hiss could not have frozen him so fast. He stiffened, and an instant later drew back.

"Forgive me," he said. "I'm not yet aware of the new rules of our relationship."

"Forgive you." Roddy turned away. Tears blurred the fragile lines and swirls of veneer on the writing desk. She put her fist to her mouth and whispered, "I will never forgive you."

The silence drank in her harsh words. She heard him move. A chair creaked, far away across the room.

"It seems I've been misguided about the way of things," he said lightly. Tautly. "I've been thinking that I was the injured party."

She turned on him. "Injured party!" Her mouth curved in vicious humor. "Oh, God, I wish you were injured. I wish you were dead! I'd kill you this moment if I knew a way."

He had been sitting and looking a little aside, out the window at the budding branch that whipped and scraped the glass behind her in the rising wind. At that he lifted his eyes. "Little girl," he said, "I think you know the way all too well."

She took a breath that became a sob. "Oh, no. I'm not like you, Faelan; I don't have that kind of strength. To turn on what I've loved and destroyed it—"

"But we aren't talking of what *you've* loved, are we? We're talking of me, of what's between us—" He stood up, strode to the desk, and took her chin in his hands. "You've destroyed that..." His fingers pressed painfully into her skin. "Or was there nothing to destroy? Was it all my hope—my fantasy—that we could make a life here? That there might be some affection in it. Some trust and loyalty." He let go of her suddenly. "At least a pretense of it." He shook his head and grimaced. "I've known better than to ask for love. The word comes too easily off your sweet lips, *cailin sidhe*. A fairy gift, all artifice and no substance. All shining surface, like a castle in the distance, and I've tried—God, when I think of how I've tried to reach it, like some besotted schoolboy—"

"Of course I don't love you," she shouted. She stumbled out of the chair and backed away. "I hate you. I hate you. You're a murderer—a beast—Why should I love you, when you'd as soon poison me as look at me, if I should get in the way of what you want? I'm *afraid*. Afraid of you. Afraid and sick at what you've done."

She found her words become chillingly real as she raved. When she spoke of hate and love, he was still human, still under control, but when she spoke of fear she saw the change, the cold rage that took him and drove the natural color from his face.

"Afraid of me," he repeated in a voice of sudden, icy calm. "It's late for that, my lady."

She stared at him, holding herself upright and trembling.

He glanced at the desk. "And what's this, then? A letter to Papa? A cry for rescue?" He swept up the paper and began to read in a loud sneer: "'Dearest Papa, I am writing with the utmost—'"

The words stopped as if garroted.

For longer, much longer than it took to read the few remaining words, he looked down at the letter. She could not see his face. The paper moved, crackled in his hand. He dropped the sheet as if it burned him.

"You trapped them," she cried. "As if they were nothing but animals!" She drew a choking breath. "If it had only been

Geoffrey I might not have guessed, but you *sent* Earnest into it! You told him where Geoffrey was and you told him to go there, and then you sent the soldiers after him with that trumped-up charge that when he'd tried to arrange passage, it was for himself and *Geoffrey*, instead of me."

Faelan grabbed her by both arms. "How do you know that?"

She would not tell him. She did not even want to remember those horrible moments when she'd watched them lead Earnest and Geoffrey past in irons—when Earnest had seen her and shouted in his mind for her to stay back, not to interfere—to stay free and get help.

Not from Faelan, Earnest had warned as he stared at her with his silent orders. Never trust Faelan, whose doing this was.

She glared up at her husband with furious hate. "It makes no difference how I know. It's the truth. I *know* it's the truth." She put both hands against his chest and shoved.

Faelan tightened his grip and shook her. "I told your damned brother to take you to hell with him," he snarled. "And I told him where to find you."

"Then you intended to include me too?" She twisted away, her arms throbbing where he'd held her. "Well—that part didn't work. I'm a coward—we have that much in common, you and I. I stood by the roadside and watched, and they thought I was a cottier woman." Her voice took on volume. "Do you understand that, Faelan?" She was almost screaming. "I stood there and watched them take away my brother and my friend—"

"Your *friend!*" he roared.

She took a step back, her heart thumping. Faelan narrowed his eyes. "You aren't a coward," he said softly. "Not while you stand there and say that to my face."

Roddy drew her shoulders back. "You're a fool, Faelan."

A wave of cynical disgust crossed his face. "Aye, I am that." He reached into his pocket and took out a small package. "O'Connell gave me this. It came with his last shipment."

He tossed the packet onto the desk. Roddy watched it bounce and slide on the polished wood with the force of his careless throw. When she looked up again, he was at the door. Without a word he slammed it behind him.

She stood with her hands locked before her, staring at the brown packet for a long time. It was marked with Faelan's name, and *Blake and Skipworth, Jewelers and Watchmakers.*

Her chest began to hurt. She put her locked hands to her mouth and pressed them against her lower lip. It seemed very hard to breathe suddenly; her throat was tight and aching and her eyes and nose stung. A little sound escaped her, a tiny moan of grief. She stood there until she felt the muffled thump of the O'Connells' front door, until she saw Faelan through the window, wheeling his horse out of the courtyard below... until moisture splashed onto the back of her hands and slipped down her wrists to make silent drops on the floor.

She swallowed, and drew a deep, ragged breath. Without looking again at the paper packet, she opened the door and ran out of the room.

❧

Roddy's hair whipped across her mouth, a sliding, pricking touch. She squinted, turning her head from the spray, watching Derrynane Bay roll past and break upon the strand in fountains of green and cream. The storm was rising. She knew she should return to the shelter of the house and trees on the hills above. Instead she walked farther out the spit of sand.

The ruined abbey drew her, set on its higher rocky ground above the tide. Through the arched, empty windows she could see the water and clouds beyond, driven by wind that moaned past the crumbling walls.

As she looked, a shadow took shape and life somewhere beyond. She blinked. At first it seemed a trick of sky and sea. She went forward, lost the thing behind one of the abbey walls, and then turned an ancient corner to find Fionn leaning against the stone transept.

She was dressed in the colors of the storm, white and green and gray that blended into the wild background and stood out starkly against the dark, wet abbey. Roddy opened her mouth to give a greeting, but Fionn laughed and called, "Come away! Come away, I can't stay here."

Roddy gathered her cape and followed, down the hill toward the sea. Some confluence of land and wind created a space of calm in the tempest, a little cove where a seal lay resting above the reach of the waves. Fionn ran ahead, faster than Roddy dared, and stopped to stroke the seal's silken head. It relaxed under her hand and rolled over luxuriously. When Roddy neared, the animal gazed at her placidly from a liquid brown eye.

"Go," Fionn ordered, and gave the seal a little flick about the nose. "Soon it will be too rough to chance."

The seal opened its mouth in yawning protest, then rolled upright and made its undulating way toward the water. It paused, breast-deep in the waves, and looked back once. Then it was gone.

Fionn sat down in the sand. "I can't stay long." She looked over her shoulder toward the abbey. "That place is none of mine."

Roddy smiled, not understanding, and not caring if she did. "I'm glad you came. It's been a long time."

"Has it?" Fionn smirked and giggled. "Has it?"

"I tried to find the ring of stones. I never could. I'm sorry. I would have come again if I could have."

Fionn tilted her head, gazing out at the sea. Her hair blew in golden waves across her shoulders. "Perhaps you'll learn the way someday."

"I don't think so." Roddy bit her lip. "I'm leaving here. I doubt I'll come back again."

Fionn lifted a strand of her hair and played with it idly, batting the tip to and fro. "I said I would tell you a story."

"Yes." Roddy huddled on the sand, lost in a sudden, piercing melancholy for what it would mean to leave this wild land. "Please."

"There was a king," Fionn said. "A great king with three daughters, and the oldest wished to be married. So she went up in the castle, and put on the cloak of darkness which her father owned, and wished for the most beautiful man in the world as a husband."

A wave crashed high upon the sand and rolled almost to their feet. Fionn did not flinch or waver.

She said, "The king's eldest daughter had her wish. As soon as she put off the cloak, there came a golden coach with four horses, two black and two white, and in it the finest man she had ever laid eyes upon, and took her away."

Fionn looked sideways at Roddy with her laughing sly smile. "When the second daughter saw what had happened to her sister," Fionn said, "she put on the cloak of darkness and wished for the next-best man in the world."

Roddy pulled her cape closer around her as the sky darkened to greenish black and the waves rose to pound the sand. They seemed very near, and yet their sound was muffled and distant. She rested her chin on her arms and listened to Fionn's musical voice above the wind.

"The second daughter put off the cloak, and instantly there came, in a golden coach with four black horses, a man nearly as fine as the first, and took her away." Fionn still looked at Roddy. "Then the third sister put on the cloak, and wished for the best black dog in the world."

Roddy turned in puzzlement, and Fionn laughed. "Straightaway he came," she declared, "in a golden coach and four pitch-black horses, and took the youngest sister away."

"A black dog?"

"Aye. And when the first man brought his new wife home he asked her: 'In what form will you have me in the daytime—as I am now in the daytime, or as I am now at night?' And his wife answered, 'As you are now in the daytime.' So the first sister had her husband as a man in the daytime, but at night he was—" She paused dramatically, as if to see if she had Roddy's full attention. "—a seal!" Fionn covered her face, her merriment pealing out over the sand.

"Oh," Roddy said, and felt quite stupid.

"And the second man asked the same question of the second sister, and had the same answer, so the second sister had her husband as a man in the daytime and a seal at night." Fionn was smiling, apparently certain that Roddy was enjoying this story immensely. "Now, when the black dog brought the youngest sister home, he asked her, 'How will you have me be in the daytime—as I am now in the day, or as I am now at night?'"

Something stirred in Roddy: a suspicion, a flicker of premonition. She gazed warily at Fionn. "What did she say?"

"She answered, 'As you are now in the day.'" The other girl drew a pattern with her finger in the sand. In a strange, gentle voice, she added slowly, "So the black dog was a beast in the daytime, and the most beautiful of men at night."

Roddy put her palm to her face, feeling it grow hot with confusion. "Is that the story?"

Fionn looked back out to sea. She nodded.

"But that's not the end," Roddy cried.

"Is it not?"

"No. That can't be the end! It was only at night he could be a man."

Fionn rose. "I must go now."

"You can't go. Tell me the rest—"

The sky lightened, and Fionn's clothes seemed to fade into the background of clouds and sea. Her hair drifted in a golden mist around her head. "I don't know the rest," she said.

"Oh, no," Roddy moaned, burying her face in her hands. "I need to know the end. Please."

Her only answer was the sound of the wind. She looked up, and the strand was empty. The day had turned bright and blue around her. In the light ripple of waves, a seal dove and splashed, looking back at Roddy for a moment before it gave an echoing bark and disappeared.

She stood up, and began to run. By the time she reached the O'Connells' house, she was gasping for breath. Maurice was just emerging from the stable to join his huntsman and the pack of beagles milling in the court. He looked up at her stumbling figure in shock.

"Mr. O'Connell—" Roddy took a gulp of air. "Mr. O'Connell—do you know where my husband has gone?"

"Lady Iveragh, are you all right?" He strode toward her. "Where in God's name have you been? Saints above, child, we've been searching shore and hills over for you!"

"His Lordship," Roddy repeated. "Is he here?"

"No indeed. He left four days ago, just before you disappeared." Maurice reached out. His thin, strong hands closed over her shoulders, his sharp eyes searching her for signs of injury. "I don't know where he went, but I've been in a dread that he'd return to find you gone. We were just going out with dogs again. My dear child, my dear, dear child, we'd given up hope. *Where* have you been?"

"I've been on the island." She waved vaguely back toward the bay and the abbey. "Not long."

"Not long? My lady—four nights we've been searching." He let go of her, and spread his arms to take in the ravaged trees and littered lawn. "Four nights and five days, and the worst spring storm in fifty years."

Roddy found herself on a red-coated arm as she descended the gangplank onto Pigeon House quay. "'Tis all come to naught," the Dublin yeoman said positively, in answer to a question she had not even asked. "All the jails are full, and we've had quantities of pikes surrendered. I've seen none of the flogging, but 'tis awful to hear—" He stopped himself, remembering that he was trying to reassure his companion, not regale her with the stories of how it had taken three hundred lashes before some of the conspirators would reveal where the pikes were hidden.

Behind her Martha was paying no attention to the yeoman's talk, occupied fully with extracting her skirt from a splintered barrel where the hem had caught. Young Davan, the O'Connell cousin who'd leaped at the chance to escort Roddy to the capital, managed to hide his dismay. He'd had high hopes of plunging into the heart of the rebellion that his more conservative relations in Kerry had looked upon askance. The easy surrender of arms in the remote southwest had been uninspiring, but Davan had been certain that in Dublin the rising would succeed. He'd only prayed that they'd not be too late for the pitched battle, in which he was certain he would find a chance to perform some deed worthy of glorification in a song or an epic poem.

It appeared that his prayers had gone unheard. The yeoman led Roddy down the quay, between two hasty fortifications of sandbags manned by armed and confident soldiers, but there was no sign of disturbance. In the long, golden shadows of late afternoon, the Liffey flowed peacefully between its stone embankments. Along the curving riverside avenues crowds moved and shifted beneath the fine new facades and across the arching bridges: ladies borne in open litters and ragged beggars with their outstretched hats, gentlemen on horseback among the brilliant abundance of scarlet uniforms.

Davan and Roddy joined the throng, unable to hail a litter for the short ride to the inn where she planned to wait for her father. She had not mailed the letter she'd written in Derrynane, but hoped she could summon him faster by sending it directly from Dublin. The mood of the crowd flowing past was strange and artificially gay: a tightly tuned instrument robbed of its performance, a rising exhilaration as smoke from neighborhoods suspected of rebel contamination curled silently into the clear air.

The innkeeper asked Roddy and Davan to share the public parlor while her room was prepared. "The crush, Your Ladyship," he explained hastily. "The past week—you can't know. Everything's in upset."

Roddy barely listened to him. She sat down in the chair offered and stared dully at her teacup, listening to the street noise from the open window and breathing the familiar smell of burning timber.

Three other ladies sat around a table in the corner, exchanging rumors. "Did you hear what they planned for the Kingston trial?" one asked as she buttered a thin slice of cake.

"Oh, that came to nothing," another said. "All that excitement over the trial of a peer—imagine, outfitting the Commons to hold all seventy-one lords just for a silly murder where the prosecution didn't even make an appearance!"

"No—no, that's not the half of it. The viceroy was there, do you see, and the lord chancellor, and—well, the entire *government* of the *country*, do you see. And they planned to take it! Right then and there, without a shot fired!"

"The Unitedmen?" The first woman gasped. "Lawks, you don't mean it!"

"Oh, aye, that's what I heard. My housekeeper is as loyal as the day is long, but she has a sister-in-law whose cousin's son is high up in their councils." The first woman nodded, and took a bite of cake. "Without a shot fired, do you see."

"Well, they didn't do it, did they?" the third said complacently. "'Tis crushed now, my husband says. There was a motion in the House this morning to execute *all* the rebel prisoners. Right away. If they wait upon trials, they fear it might be too late."

Roddy's teacup slid from her fingers and broke in a tinkling crash upon the floor. The ladies all looked toward her, and the one who'd spoken of the executions jumped up. "Oh, dear, what a shame—your pretty dress, love, here, quickly now—" She began patting at the stain on Roddy's skirt with a handkerchief. "Do pull the bell, sir! What a shame. But soda and chamomile will take it right out, my dear, I promise you."

Before Davan could reach for the bell, a change came in the crowd outside. The high-strung, confused gaiety faltered and the noise hushed. For an instant a weird silence settled over the streets; the pedestrians stopped and the horses were reined in, and the sound that had alerted them came clearly through the evening air.

Drums. The urgent, rolling snap echoed above the poised crowd, calling to arms, sending the redcoats suddenly scrambling and the ladies in their litters crying to the bearers to hurry on, for God's sake. The women in the parlor looked at one another in horror, and then, like Roddy and Davan and everyone else, ran for the door and stumbled over each other down the stairs, where shopkeepers and businessmen and residents were pouring into the streets.

Davan was first to reach the entry, in a pitch of renewed excitement. He grabbed at a running soldier, and got a shove and a curse for his pains. "The news!" Davan shouted after, his bellow nearly lost amid the noise and the drums. "What's the news?"

"They're massing at Santry!" A youth in civilian clothes lunged for the door. "Out of the way, man—I've got to get at my uniform!" The youth squeezed and pushed his way in,

losing his hat and panting apologies to the ladies. "Mama—
Mama—my coat—"

"Santry—where's—"

"To the north," one of the ladies said wildly. "So close!"
The press of other guests and servants behind them began
to push Roddy and Davan out the door. She clung to the
frame, unable to pick individual thought out of chaos.
Davan was looking about wildly; he took a step out into
the street and stumbled under the force of collision with an
aproned shopkeeper.

He grabbed the man by both arms. "The United army," he
yelled. "*Where is it?*"

"Rathfarnham," the shopman cried in triumph. "Six thousand already, and more coming."

"How do I get there?"

The shopkeeper tore himself from Davan's arms. "Are
you a friend? Go to Newgate—they'll need you there! Lord
Edward's to be freed to lead the attack!"

Roddy reached out, trying to catch Davan's arm. She knew
that name—Lord Edward Fitzgerald, the Duke of Leinster's
brother, the center of Geoffrey's circle of aristocratic radicals.
But one of the women from the parlor caught her back.
"Attack! Are they going to attack?"

Roddy turned for an instant, just long enough to shake
herself free. When she looked back again, Davan was gone.

Roddy stared into the surging crowd, unable to open her
gift to this intensity. It pressed at her through her barriers,
frighteningly like the night of the fire, a crowd-mind that
knew no reason, no sense, but only swept and swayed with
wild emotion as the drums crackled their dread message
through the streets.

She squeezed her eyes shut, trying to escape it, trying to
think. Someone ran into her, and she had to move to avoid
falling. She opened her eyes and saw a cavalryman urging his
frantic mount forward, almost on top of her. She pressed back,
trying to avoid the animal's hooves as it half reared and came
down, knocking a porter aside. The press of people caught her
up; she had to move to keep from going to her knees.

She was pushed one way and then the next by the surge and shuffle. The color of the crowd seemed to be gaining red as the barristers and attorneys and merchants and bankers and students and apothecaries of the city threw on uniforms and became yeomen desperate to reach their mustering points. She stumbled along the riverside in their midst, already far down from the inn where she'd lost Davan. The sun was setting, throwing the buildings and milling crowd into high relief. Still the drums went on, calling and calling for the men who were helplessly jammed in the press.

Reason seemed impossible in the noise and confusion. At first, she tried to battle her way back toward the inn, but the general movement was opposite, and she exhausted herself without making headway. Shorter than the rest, she could not see which way to move, could only follow her perception of where the crowd thinned.

The river flowed like a silver dagger down the center of the mob. She found herself at a bridge, and grabbed a yeoman's hand and shouted in his ear for the way to Newgate, receiving a vague wave and an uninterpretable shout in return. Like a stream branching around a rock, the people around her pushed her along onto the bridge, across it, and into the mass on the other side.

She shouted again for the way to Newgate, and this time a barefoot beggar boy answered, not with words, but with a tug on her arm and a motion to follow.

She hung on to him until sweat popped out on her palm and made the contact slippery and hard to keep. But his small, dirty fingers dug into her skin, pulling at her, squeezing her through among shoulders and arms and legs while dusk settled into shadows.

They left the river far behind, but the crowds did not lessen. It was almost all uniformed men by now, and a strange hilarity had begun to grow among them, made of fear and helplessness and determination. She heard laughter, and saw bottles of porter making rounds. Many of them tried to move and make way for Roddy as they saw a gentlewoman in their midst. "Get along home, ma'am," someone cried toward her. "We're standing buff for your defense!" A spate of encouraging calls followed, but Roddy had not time to answer, clinging to her small guide, afraid she would lose him as darkness closed in.

Past a church, down a wide street, twisting and wriggling among the throng. Roddy began to think the child was leading her a dance; it seemed that they must have doubled back twice, and she could smell again the evening odor rising off the river. Rumors flew—reports that shadowy figures had been seen assembling in the churchyard they'd just passed, where pikes were buried by the hundreds; that rebel couriers had been heard to cry, "Liberty, and no King!"; that mounted sentries posted outside the city had been driven in by the rebels advance guard; that a secret column of rebel sympathizers was already among them, preparing to set fire to the House of Parliament. At one point they scraped by a crowd of well-dressed women, and Roddy heard one arguing strenuously that she and her companions should seek the protection of a Mr. Beresford at his "interrogation center."

The thought of being caught between Unitedmen and loyalists in the narrow, packed streets was terrifying. "Here 'tis, mum!" the urchin cried, before Roddy could decide whether or not she should try to join the group of ladies. She looked up at the dark windowless walls of the prison in despair, not knowing what she was doing there, not wanting to believe that Earnest and Geoffrey were really barred behind those stones, liable to be executed at any moment in the rising tide of fear.

The child hugged her hips, holding out one thin hand. The crowd was thinner here, and Roddy had room to bend and take off her shoe, slipping out the emergency shilling her mother had taught her to carry always. The boy grabbed it and vanished into the growing darkness.

Roddy stood, indecisive and miserable. The prison itself drew her, though she was sure that she would never find Davan here. She doubted he had made it this far.

There seemed nowhere else to go. An alley beckoned, walled on one side by the prison, on the other by the backs of closed and boarded shops, mercifully empty of yeomen or confused citizens. She slipped between two arguing university students and sought the relief of a space of solitude. She could not plunge back into the surge of people, not yet. Drawing a breath of river-laden air, she moved down the narrow lane.

With relief, she relaxed her taut barriers, keeping alert for any threat. Never had she been alone in a city. It scared her more than being lost in the black night at Iveragh. Her fears then had been mostly in her mind, but here the danger was painfully real.

She heard the intruders enter the alley before she could separate them from the crowd-mind that she'd set at a distance. Quickly, she drew back into a doorway, batting aside a rug that had been left out to air. It took no effort to focus on the strangers approaching. They were already at a fever pitch of excitement, and their intentions reached her with blazing clarity.

Her fingers closed and twisted at her skirt as she recognized Davan's wild enthusiasm among the approaching group. They spoke in whispers that kept breaking to agitated louder speech.

"'Tis the only chance," someone hissed. "Without the rest of 'em. It's been done before, mark me—if no one falters, we can make it."

"Och, are we here to falter?" That was Davan. "I'm a Kerryman—I've run cargo past the King's best men and thumbed my nose."

There was a scuffle. "Go on, I've thumbed me nose a' a few Orangemen in me own day. You'll be bringin' up me rear on that ladder, Kerryman."

"Shut it," another voice warned. "'Tis no schoolboy prank. We should have been thirty, and with a horse waitin' to take him. We'll likely die of this, takin' it on with half a dozen."

"Are you afraid of it?" Davan's voice dripped scorn. "'Tis a fine enough way to die."

They were directly opposite Roddy now. She heard something metal clatter, and a pike fell at her feet, its blade glittering underneath the rug in the last of light.

"I'm not afraid." That was a lie, fierce and quick. The rush of feet carried them all past her. "Lay down your weapon, and I'll be glad enough to show you with my bare hands!"

"Give over. We've no time for that. Where's the rope?"

"Who's going up?" someone asked. The voice's owner had to work hard to keep it from shaking with excitement and fright.

"We'll draw lots. Hand in your cockades. Green go up; white take the gate."

"I haven't one," Davan said impatiently. He was torn, not sure if the assault by ladder or front entrance would be more heroic.

Roddy drew in a breath, preparing to step out and put a stop to this nonsense, when the one who seemed in command said, "Those that go over the top—don't waste time looking for Lord Edward. Just finish off the first guard you see, take their keys, and start opening doors while we have them distracted in front."

She had a sudden, wild change of heart, a thought that perhaps they could do it. If Earnest happened to be in the right cell…

"My friends," a new voice said, low and smooth and star-tlingly familiar. "I don't believe you'll be distracting anyone just now."

Roddy's stomach went liquid with shock. She made a move for the rug, pulling back the folds, peering through the dimness at the little knot of men in the alley and the broad back of the red-coated and bewigged British officer who held them at pistol point.

She knew that back. She knew that voice, and the unmistakable taut grace. She knew every muscle and limb of the man who held a gun pointed at Davan's head.

Twenty-Three

"IVERAGH," DAVAN SAID. AT FIRST IT WAS ONLY STUNNED surprise, but an instant later the youth put the uniform and the man together. "Great God, you're a King's man!"

"Your acuteness astounds me," Faelan said flatly. "You and your companions may lay down your pikes."

Davan took a breath, and tightened his grip on his pike handle. His companions stood straighter behind him.

"*Lay it down*," Faelan said.

Roddy bit down on her tongue, holding back sick fear. She could not allow Faelan to murder a silly boy for his silly dreams of glory. Her husband could do it; *had* done it— Geoffrey had been witness. And the wild chance—maybe the only chance—to save Earnest and Geoffrey was evaporating before her eyes.

The pistol didn't waver, still aimed at Davan's forehead. Roddy's eyes stung with fright. Any moment—any moment and the gun would explode and Davan would crumple, shot down like the cattle at Iveragh. Roddy swallowed bile. She held the curtain back and bent over, easing the pike at her feet upward into her hands. Her heart was pounding so that her fingers would hardly move for their shaking. She felt Davan's second shock as he recognized her behind Faelan in the shadows.

Davan blinked and then stared at the pistol, unable to accept the possibility that it might be his death. It seemed to him only a piece of metal, but as he looked at it he had a vision, clear and graphic, of what it might feel like to take a ball between the eyes.

He dropped the pike.

"The rest," Faelan said. When no one else obeyed, he cocked the gun. "Do you dislike your Kerryman so much?"

One by one, the other four pikes fell with a clatter onto the pavement.

The young rebels all had the sense to keep their faces under control as Roddy lifted her weapon and slid one foot silently out into the alley. She had to remind herself to breathe. The pike handle was smooth and heavy in her hands, with a damp spot where it had fallen in a tiny puddle. She took another stealthy step, coming into the open.

"You won't turn us in," Davan said. "You wouldn't." It was half to gain time, that question, and half a real fear. His eyes were locked on Faelan, trying to gauge Roddy's slinking approach from the shadows. *Sweet Mary, will she hit him? Her own husband...*

Roddy took another step, and another, and suddenly she was within range of Faelan's head with the pike handle.

"I ought to," Faelan said, "God knows, you're an inconvenience to me."

Roddy's grip tightened. It seemed impossible that he did not know she was there.

Davan's eyes narrowed. "Bastard," he said softly. He had to strain to keep his eyes from Roddy. "Damned slimy informer."

"Don't try my patience, O'Connell. You have half a minute to disappear."

Roddy stood, within range, with the pike handle lifted to deliver the blow. She held it there, staring at her husband's unprotected back.

I'm here, she cried silently. *Don't you know I'm here?*

Davan's lip curled. "You peached on the others, didn't you? 'Twas you who put Lord Geoffrey's head in a noose."

And my brother's. Oh, God—Faelan...

"I'll not listen to that," he snapped. "Get out of here, you damned bumbling puppy."

He motioned with the gun. Davan's eyes widened, but he stood his ground, expecting Roddy to strike. Her arms were trembling under the weight of the weapon, and still she did not swing.

Davan took a breath. Sweat was breaking out on his forehead in his impatience for Roddy to move. *Hit him*, Davan screamed in his mind. *Hit him now.*

A huge lump built in her throat. She swallowed, and swallowed again. Her eyes began to blur.

Do it, Davan urged. *For God's sake, do it!*

The pike burned her palms. She could not breathe. A hot tear slid down her cheek.

Hit him! Davan was verging on hysteria. *Hit him, hit him, hit him!*

"I can't!" she sobbed.

Faelan jerked around.

She saw Davan move, diving for the pike and sweeping it up into a murderous thrust. Roddy screamed. Her arms moved without her mind's command, swinging her weapon in one long, violent arc. The passage seemed to take place like a strange, slow dance: she heard the whistle of the handle through the air, saw Faelan duck and evade, saw Davan's pike rise up toward Faelan's chest... and then felt impact shudder through her body as the wood in her hands met the steel point of the other pike and smashed them both into splinters against the pavement. An instant later, Faelan completed his own lithe turn with a blow that took Davan down in an explosion of pain and blackness.

The youth hit the pavement, already unconscious. His companions fled, all but one, who only hesitated long enough to see Faelan take aim again with the pistol.

Her husband caught her with his free hand as the others disappeared, curling his fingers around the nape of her neck. "Little bitch—you stupid little ass—did you talk them into that insanity?" He let her go with a hard shove that sent her stumbling to her knees. "You won't get your precious lover free with those buffoons, but you came damned close to murdering me, didn't you? Get up."

He dragged her up by her shoulder, trapping her wrists behind her back. She whimpered, not fighting, finding her legs somehow outside her command. She leaned into his familiar strength in complete surrender. With an oath, he slid his arm around her shoulders, half pushing and half carrying her back toward the main thoroughfare.

At the corner of the alley, he fought through the crowd along the stone wall of Newgate. Soldiers still milled outside the prison gates. Faelan stopped a few yards from the entrance, glaring down at her. "You want Geoffrey and your brother out?" he hissed. "Stand here and watch."

He left her with her knees wilting in delayed reaction. His figure melted into the throng, lost quickly among the others in the last vestiges of twilight. At the gates, lamps were lit, shedding pools of yellow illumination down onto the guarded entrance.

Roddy stared numbly at the prison entrance, still shaking too much to question or think. A few moments later, a scarlet-coated officer parted from the crowd. He strode directly to the guardhouse and returned the salute of the soldier on duty.

Roddy stood bolt upright.

With an effort of will, she focused her talent, too late to catch the guard's thoughts before he took some papers from Faelan's hand and disappeared. Faelan stood back, just inside the gate, his hands behind his back and his feet spread in an attitude of careless patience.

A long time went by. Roddy stared at him, her lips parted, while her sluggish mind finally began to awaken to the moment. The last of the day faded, and the night was full of hysterical laughter and uneasy people. The rest of the lamps were dark; up and down the street the crowd was lost in shadow. Only the prison gate was a pool of mellow light.

It came upon her slowly. No thunderous revelation, but something like the soft mists of Iveragh, that crept through her and filled her, twining around her heart and squeezing. She looked at Faelan and wanted to cry for the mistake she'd made in judging him. He stood motionless in the center of the light, his face obscured by the shako's brim. A King's man, in a uniform that when she looked closely did not quite fit: too tight across the shoulders, too generous around his lean waist.

She had not been able to hit him. Not because she was too weak or too noble to take a man down from behind. She would have struck Davan senseless in an instant if the threat had been reversed.

No, her hesitation had not been weakness. It had been a choice.

I love you, she thought, gazing at his still figure. *I love you. No matter what.*

Faelan straightened. The returning guard passed back papers, and Roddy felt familiar minds. A spike of wild hope shot through her. Between four yeoman guards and the jailer, Earnest and Geoffrey appeared in the gate.

The papers came out again. Roddy watched in a misery of tension as the jailer looked at each one carefully. She narrowed her gift, straining to find his thoughts among the crowd. It was impossible. She caught his doubt, a sense that this release of prisoners was peculiar, but the pitch of strain from Earnest and Geoffrey mixed with the jailer's concern and the crowd's babble, until she could make nothing clear.

She saw Faelan shrug in answer to a query that was lost to her ears in the noise. He waved a hand toward the crush outside the gate.

Shorthanded, that seemed to mean.

The jailer looked again at Faelan, and even through the confusion, she could feel his meteoric rise in suspicion. He asked Faelan something else, but before her husband answered, a disturbance rippled through the crowd outside. A heavy, shambling man began shouting and waving toward the prison, and as everyone stopped to look, his drunken oaths rose above the throng—wild, incoherent curses directed at the jailer.

The jailer looked that way, stretching up to see through the crowd. His hand with Faelan's papers fell to his side. A whisper and then a roll of recognition went through the street. "Neilson," she heard someone say. "By God, isn't that Sam Neilson?"

The huge drunk stumbled about in the little open space the crowd made for him. "Gregg," he shouted, and the jailer turned sharply around. "I'm back! I'm *back!* You been—" He swung around, nearly falling. "Uni—united! We're come! A damned, damned—Gregg! You hear me?" He laughed. "You, boy, you damned—boy—"

Roddy held her breath. The crowd was tightening, closing in on the drunken man. "'Tis that printer—the *Northern Star*—" she heard. "—was he out?" "—sedition—four years ago—" "—paroled him, but he's in it again—" The jailer had turned to the yeoman guards. They formed into a quick knot, and slipped out into the street. An instant later they surrounded the big man. Danger suddenly seemed to penetrate his besotted brain; he bellowed something and charged the guard, swinging wildly. The scene erupted into a brawl. Roddy backed against the wall, and found herself jerked roughly away from it. Faelan's hands shoved at her, and she had a moment's image of his face, locked in concentration. "The alley!" he shouted, and then Earnest was there, his hands bound behind his back, looking at Roddy for the way to go.

She grabbed his elbow and turned, pushing toward safety. Once someone flew against her, knocking her breathless against the wall. She staggered, still clinging to Earnest's arm while he braced. "Hold on," he yelled, setting his feet against the crush from behind. She dragged herself upright, catching a glimpse of Geoffrey and Faelan behind. Her husband's intent face steadied the rising fear in her—Faelan was thinking, he was not panicking, and she could do the same.

Think. Hold Earnest's arm and don't let go. One step, dodge. Think. The sudden fight was dying, people were looking at her strangely. Suspiciously. Someone caught her shoulder. She let her knees go to water, sliding down out of the grip and yelling a fishwife's imprecation in a drunken blur. She held on to Earnest and rubbed herself against him. Another hand came down on her shoulder, hard, and Faelan dragged her up like a drowned kitten. "He's not much good in irons, my pretty." He swept her into his arms and pushed on. "Spend your wares on a man with his hands free."

Suspicion dissolved into knowing laughter. The crowd of loyalists suddenly seemed to think Faelan might need help with his prisoners. A few opened way, hissing at Earnest and Geoffrey as they passed. The mood began to darken, but the alley loomed ahead, barely visible as a deeper shadow in the unlit facade. Roddy slipped out of Faelan's arms, and stumbled into the open space. She turned in the pitch black and found her brother and Geoffrey shoved in behind her.

❧

Roddy sat her saddle on a stolen horse by willpower alone. Dawn brought a tinge of color to the surroundings, giving line and definition to the rich fields and hedgerows and the mountains to the east. It was her fourth dawn in which the sun seemed an enemy, a blazing beacon rising to shine down and expose their small party to the forces which now burned over the land.

No rebels had materialized that night in Dublin, but the imagined United army that had thrown the capital into a frenzy had become a reality in the counties outside. On the midnight ride out of the city Roddy had experienced her first taste of murder—vicious murder, when the mail coach ahead of them on the Cork road had been halted and burned by the rebels, and the passengers hacked to death.

They'd been too far away to see it, she and Earnest and Geoffrey, but her gift had frozen her in the pain and bloody terror as they stood in the dark and waited for Faelan to return with a report of the bonfire that lit the horizon. Earnest held her in front of him on his horse while she shook too much to control her own. When Faelan returned, he said little, but it was enough. They turned away from the main road.

Since then, she had seen enough of death. What the rebels accomplished with their pikes and firelocks, the loyalists answered with equal ferocity. Faelan had led his little group around the towns, but Roddy had seen the corpses hanging from trees, and the bodies left to be scavenged in the fields. She heard the stories, and caught the memories in old women's minds—of sons tortured for information, of the caps of burning pitch and the half-hangings and the flogging. In one place a whole garrison had been murdered in their beds by rebels,

and the commander—notorious for his torturing methods—
burned in a barrel of pitch. In another the panicked loyalists,
deserted by the retreating army, had taken all prisoners out of
the jails and shot them without trial.

Now, in the quiet dawn, such things seemed impossible and
far away. But she saw a pair of ravens circling a dark spot across
the field, and she turned her face and would not look closer.

All right? Earnest asked, a silent question between them. She
looked up at him riding beside her, and nodded.

"Where are we?" he said aloud.

It was directed toward Faelan, and tingled with faint
belligerence. Roddy felt a surge of annoyance at her brother's
lingering distrust of her husband.

Faelan squinted at the low mountains on their left. "That
should be Sculloge Gap."

"Is that the road to the coast?"

Faelan nodded.

"Aren't we going to turn that way, then?" Earnest was
anxious to reach a port, not for his own sake, but in his determination to get Roddy to safety.

To her surprise, her husband did not answer immediately.
Up until now, it had seemed as if he'd had everything
planned, and his crisp orders had swept them all along in his
wake—even though Geoffrey was burning to rejoin his rebels
and Earnest was stewing over the disgrace of having broken
out of prison when he'd been falsely arrested in the first place.

Roddy pursed her lips. She wouldn't have believed six
months ago that Earnest could have been so stupid as to care
about something like that.

Faelan halted his horse and turned back to face the rest
of them in the narrow lane they'd been following. He'd
exchanged the red uniform coat for something dark and
nondescript. Where the early light touched the shape of his
cheek and jaw, the grim outlines were blurred by stubble.
"You may go east, if you please."

"I thought we were trying to make for a port."

"That's certainly what I'd do if I were you." Faelan
unstrapped his water flask and upended it. A trickle of

moisture slipped down and made a random trail through two days' growth of beard.

"Well—" Earnest said impatiently. "How am *I* supposed to know which direction to take?"

With a leisure that was maddening to Earnest, Faelan recapped his flask and twisted to flip open his leather saddle pack. He held out a folded paper. "Forgive me. Have I been monopolizing the map?"

Earnest snatched it. "Damned right you have. I'd been hoping all this doubling back and forth was to some purpose."

"It was. Staying alive."

Geoffrey had been staring at the mountains. "I keep telling you, we've only to find the United headquarters to get protection. Bagenal Harvey's our man in Wexford."

"It's inconceivable to you, I suppose," Faelan said dryly, "that the country may still be in the hands of the regular government?"

"You heard the news at Kilcullen!" Geoffrey's horse danced. "Dublin's fallen, man!"

"I heard what a scruffy schoolmaster with a broken musket wanted to hope."

"The militia's retreated. That's a fact."

"Aye." Faelan frowned toward the north, where at Narraghmore they had watched at a distance as the Suffolk Fencibles and Tyrone militia had marched out of town, leaving it completely undefended. "Aye, and I was impressed with the expertise of your United soldiers. The army itself could hardly have plundered better."

Geoffrey, unable to think of a suitable excuse for the half-wild mob that had taken over Narraghmore in the wake of the militia, said, "They must be short of officers. I'm heading for Wexford."

Earnest looked up from his map. "Yes. That's closer than Waterford, from what I can make out." He squinted at the rising sun. "Things look quiet enough. I think we should risk pushing on. We could make the foothills at least, before the horses need to stop."

"Let's go." Geoffrey urged his horse past Faelan's, with Earnest close behind.

Roddy looked after them, and then at Faelan. He met her eyes, and for a moment there was something in his face—a depth in his look, a kind of intensity, as if he were memorizing her features as he must have memorized the folded map.

He looked away before she did, and swung his leg over the saddle.

Roddy blinked down at him. "Are you stopping here?"

He was already loosening his horse's girth. "Yes," he said. That was all.

She lifted her knee off the sidesaddle and twisted, sliding to the ground beside him.

"Roddy." Earnest had paused. "Are you too tired to go on?"

"Faelan is stopping," she said simply.

Earnest rode back. "Oh—come, Iveragh, do you really see the need? Every hour we dally, this damned thing is exploding around our ears. I want Roddy off this cursed island."

Faelan's mouth tightened a little, but he went on stripping his horse in silence. Roddy reached for her girth.

"Dammit," Earnest snapped. "I think you've given orders long enough. You've no more notion of the situation than the rest of us. All this dodging has done nothing but keep us in the midst of the worst of it. Leave off that, Roddy, and come along."

"I'm staying with Faelan," she said.

Earnest took a breath. She could feel his temper slipping. "Roddy." He spoke aloud—for everyone's benefit—very clearly and slowly. "Come now, or by God, I'll leave you here."

Roddy grabbed her saddle and flung it to the ground. "Well, Earnest," she said, equally slowly and deliberately, "*by God*, why don't you just do that?"

Earnest opened his mouth. She didn't give him time to marshal his response.

"Go on!" she cried. "You won't be missed here—you *or* Lord Geoffrey. I'm sick of your carping, I'll tell you that, and I surely don't blame Faelan if he's had his fill of it! He saved your necks; he walked into that place and he got you out, and have either of you said one grateful word?" She yanked the saddle pad off and pulled a rubdown towel from between its folds, going after her mount's coat with vigorous strokes. "No. Oh, no. You just go on griping, as if you were both a couple of royal princes who deserved to have a decent man risk his life for you every other day."

Earnest dismounted behind her. "Roddy, you're exhausted—"

She whirled on him. "The devil I am," she swore. "I'm just tired of your company. I'd ride another hundred miles if Faelan told me to."

"Lord, girl, are we back to this? You shouldn't be here. You owe no loyalty to a man who don't even try to keep you from harm."

"No loyalty—" Roddy dropped the towel. "Are you blind, Earnest? Are you deaf and dumb? *I love him.* I love him, and when I think of why we're here—" She broke, off, unable to control her voice, and dropped to her knees to retrieve the towel.

A leopard don't change his spots without reason, Earnest thought. *Remember that, Roddy.*

She threw up barriers, refusing to let him make arguments she could not acknowledge aloud. It was unfair, and he knew it. "Spots," she sneered recklessly, just to show him she was aware of his tactics. "You don't know the first thing about spots. Or loyalty either. To rescue you and Geoffrey—that's loyalty. That's friendship. What have you done for Faelan? Nothing, except badger him and threaten him and plague him to death. And as for Geoffrey... do you know what my husband thinks Geoffrey and I did?" She saw Earnest's brows rise, and cried, "Yes—you might as well be shocked, I don't care. He thinks Geoffrey and I cuckolded him. Stupid Geoffrey and his stupid rebellion; my husband thinks I'd rather love his best friend—" Her voice began to shake and rise. "His idiotic friend who isn't worth the ground Faelan walks on; who's never lifted a finger to plant something to eat for people who are starving; who thinks fine speeches are reason enough for this bloodbath; who can ride through what we've seen and call it victory—"

She was shouting by then. A rough hand caught her shoulder and came across her mouth, stopping the sound. Faelan pulled her back against his chest. "Little girl," he said in her ear. "Must you broadcast our quarrels to the whole county?"

She froze for a moment, realizing the danger she'd courted. Her muscles went limp and she turned into her husband's body. "Faelan——" The word was a sob. "I'd never go to Geoffrey. You can't believe I'd be such a fool. I was so afraid for you, I didn't want him near you—and he kept making fires, and then I fell in the stream, and I was lost! I was lost and I fell in and I was wet and he was going to make a *fire*, and he doesn't know how to do it, even if he thinks he does—you can see the s-smoke from everywhere! Please——" She clutched at the sleeves of his coat. "Faelan, please say you believe me!"

He was stiff for a moment, unyielding. Roddy pressed her forehead against his chest, her mouth trembling on a dammed sob. Then he made an odd sound, a peculiar, strained chuckle, and stroked the back of her neck lightly. "That Geoff can't build a decent fire? That's easy enough to believe."

It was not an answer, exactly, but there was a note in his voice that made her throw her arms around him and bury her face against his dusty shirt.

"It's the truth," Geoffrey said softly, meaning more than the fire. "God's truth, Faelan. I feared she'd be down with pneumonia."

Roddy felt her husband's slow, harsh exhalation. "Yes. And so you rendered the only aid you could think of. I might have known it would involve taking a female's clothes off."

"She's all yours, my friend." Geoffrey's voice held a tentative grin. "Not in my style at all."

Roddy turned. "Of course not. Any female with a brain in her head isn't in your style," she said waspishly.

"You see what I mean."

"This is all very affecting," Earnest said, "but we aren't making much progress toward a port."

Roddy straightened. "I'm staying with Faelan," she declared. "It's you and Geoffrey who'd best leave the country."

"I'm not leaving without *you*. That's the only goddamned reason I'm here in the first place! God knows, I'd rather be on my way back to Dublin to clear myself. I don't fancy carrying the title of escaped felon all my life."

"'Escaped felon'! When Faelan risked his life—" Roddy almost choked on her ire. "Earnest, do you know what the House of Commons did that morning before Faelan got you out? They almost carried a measure to execute suspected rebels *before* the rebellion! *Before it!* So unless you're looking for posthumous vindication, you'd better take yourself off smartly!"

"Lord, poppet," Geoffrey said. "Where'd you learn words like that? 'Posthumous vindication.' It sounds like something your husband would say."

"It sounds to me more like something you'd say," Faelan drawled, "but consider the sentiment seconded."

"Then how does it look, for God's sake?" Earnest's voice quivered on a note Roddy had never heard from him before. "Escaping with the same damned rebel I'm supposed to have been helping in the first place?"

"It appears to me you're in prime shape." Faelan let go of Roddy and hefted her saddle from its sprawled position on the ground. "Covered on both sides. If the rebels have Dublin and the French are on the sea, you're a red-blooded patriot for aiding our hero here." He nodded toward Geoffrey. "If the thing's crushed—then... what do you know of it? Butter couldn't melt in your mouth. You've never seen a radical, never heard of democracy, never imagined an upstanding gentleman like Lord Geoffrey was a sleazy closet republican. You're just a poor English sod who came over to help his sister and got caught in the cross fire."

"Ever-practical Faelan," Geoffrey said indulgently.

Earnest looked exasperated. Roddy suspected it was because he had a notion that Faelan was right. For now, with the rebels apparently in control of most of the countryside, Geoffrey's company was more safeguard than menace. And later, once Earnest was out of Ireland, Delamore money and prestige would be standing against the flimsy evidence. And if the evidence weren't Faelan's, it would be flimsy—of that Roddy was certain. Earnest would very likely never even come to trial, unless it was for the escape itself. And surely that could be excused under the circumstances.

Earnest stood, glaring at Faelan and Roddy. She would not open to the question in his eyes, but instead answered by moving closer to Faelan. "Tell Papa that you did your best," she said in a softer voice. "But I can't come with you, Earnest. I can't."

His glance drifted over Faelan with lingering distrust. "Can't?"

"I won't." Roddy pressed back into her husband's arms.

For a long moment, Earnest hesitated. Then with an angry sound of defeat he turned to Geoffrey. "So. It's Wexford, is it?"

Geoffrey grinned. "You and I, comrade."

"*Comrade*." Earnest spun away in disgust.

Faelan worked open the leather bag attached to Roddy's saddle. "Take this." He pulled out a second pistol, a money purse, and a packet of powder and ball. "It throws left a hair. Remember that."

Earnest took the offering. He met Faelan's eyes with a level look. "Thanks," he said dryly, and then with a reluctant twist to his mouth: "For everything."

Faelan nodded, curt, and turned away. He repacked the saddlebag and held it toward Roddy. "We'll stop here for an hour to eat. I want to push on west while it's quiet."

Twenty-Four

THEY REACHED KILKENNY BY NOON. THE TOWN SEEMED drowsy with Sunday quiet, but Roddy had learned that horror could hide beneath the calm. They crossed the river Nore in view of the old castle walls, and she looked with eyes of weary apprehension at the scarlet coats of the occupying garrison stationed at points across the broad lawn. There was evidence that the area had been "disarmed" with the government's brutal effectiveness. She and Faelan had passed burned-out cottages and stripped farms, and no single soul had appeared on the road, though Roddy knew that the inhabitants were there—in hiding, watching from hedgerows and empty barns.

Faelan stopped just over the bridge and gave her a smile that looked strange and fierce in the dark stubble that shadowed his jaw. "Will you go another hundred miles if I ask you?"

Her whole body ached and her eyes burned. She'd been riding since midnight: she was hungry and thirsty and bruised and scared.

She looked up into his eyes and said, "Yes," without flinching.

He reached out and touched her cheek as their horses stood with heads lowered together. "Little girl. You're turning into a heroine on me."

"Am I?" She managed a smile in return. "It must be rubbing off of you."

He looked down at that, with a faint frown, as if it had been an accusation instead of praise. He swung off his horse and handed her the reins. "I'll see what I can find out."

A quarter of an hour later, Roddy was walking stiffly into an inn with the promise of at least a few hours' rest. "Not longer," Faelan said. "Nothing's reported to the south and west, but communication's cut off from Dublin. We're not far ahead of it."

"Thank you." She sat down and threw herself onto her back on the deep feather bed. "I'll certainly rest better for knowing that."

He pulled his boots off with the jack and sat beside her, smelling of horse and sweat and black powder. Roddy knew she could be no better, except for the powder smell. There was a smudge on his face where he'd used his arm as support once—aiming over his shoulder at a deserter who'd tried to take Roddy's horse.

She saw his lashes relax and lower as he looked down at her. His glance traveled the length of her body.

Roddy smiled and shifted her fingers, rubbing the back of his hand where it rested on the bed. "Too tired," she murmured. "Too tired." She closed her eyes and concentrated on the feeling of him, on the fine muscle and the bone beneath; his hard, steady warmth.

The mattress moved. He leaned over her. She felt his breath on her skin, and then the scratchy touch of his cheek as he buried his face in her hair. "I'm sorry, love. God, I'm so sorry to put you through this."

She patted his back, the only part within easy reach. "It isn't your fault. 'Tis all the Geoffreys and the Mullanes and Willises in the world, who look at people and only see chess pawns. Who play with fire and think it's clay."

He rolled away and rested on his elbow, looking down at her with dark amusement. "Ah. She's become a philosopher now." He tangled his fingers in a strand of her hair and said slowly, "I'm sorry you're here, I meant, and not safe in England as Earnest would have you."

"Earnest," she said with disgust, and then bit her lip.

She turned suddenly, pressing her face to Faelan's shoulder. "Oh, God, I hope they make it."

He stroked her hair. "They will. Your brother has some sense, if Geoffrey doesn't."

"At least they had a chance." Her words were muffled in his coat. "Because of you."

His hand paused, wavered over her hair. He drew back and sat up. "Don't harp on that," he said harshly. The floor creaked under his feet as he stood and paced to the open window, where green light filtered through leaves and made a moving pattern on the wall.

She sat up. "No." Her words were soft. "I won't harp on it, if you don't like it. But I wanted to say—" She stopped, searching for words, and then shook her head in despair. "…'Sorry.' That's not enough. That's not nearly enough. The things I said to you—the accusations—"

He turned on her. "Aye, you had every reason to doubt me."

"All I knew for certain was that you'd sent Earnest to the cottage." She could not tell him of her brother's suspicions, of how his interpretation had shaped hers. She shrugged, and looked at the plank floor. Color mounted in her cheeks. "You had far more reason to doubt me than I did you."

He shook off his coat and threw it over a chair. "Did I? You don't think I might have arranged Geoff's arrest in a jealous frenzy? And thrown in Earnest too, when I saw the chance?"

"No."

"'No, not anymore,' you mean." He stripped off his waistcoat and cravat. "You saw me break them out, so you think it's only logical that I didn't put them in."

She stared at him, suddenly uneasy with his words. "What are you saying?"

"I'm saying," he snarled, "that I don't remember what I did after I sent Earnest to that damned cottage to find you. I left there, and when I arrived at Derrynane—" He bent his head, leaning into the windowpane, staring out as if there were demons in the yard below. "When I arrived at Derrynane—" He stopped again, and then like an explosion the words burst out of him. "—you were *there*, with that letter that said '*two days ago*.'"

❧

He refused to talk about it. The confession seemed to have been a rush of water from a weakened dam, quickly repaired and plastered over. That afternoon in Kilkenny, he had not allowed her even to respond, but only told her to go to sleep while she could, and pulled on his boots and left the room. Two hours later he'd woken her from exhausted unconsciousness and they'd ridden out of Kilkenny, driven by a rumor of rebel columns retreating south out of Carlow.

Now, close to home, she had finally begun to feel safe. In Kenmare, in the shadow of Iveragh's mountains, they had left the reports of uprising far behind. The country was in upset, but the rumors had become wilder and more unbelievable, and through her talent, Roddy picked out no one who had actually experienced any violence. The government repression in the area had been the same as in Iveragh—directed against property, not people. Roddy had come to understand how lucky the southwest had been in the restraint and humanity of the army's commanders there.

Over a quiet supper in one of Lord Kenmare's excellent inns, Roddy screwed up her courage and attacked the subject she'd been brooding upon since Kilkenny. "I think we should investigate," she said, between bites of stewed apple in their private parlor.

Faelan didn't look up from his lobster. "Investigate what?"

"Who betrayed Geoffrey and Earnest."

Instantly, she regretted her choice of words. He glanced at her, a flash of icy blue, and went back to his meal.

"The O'Sullivans and O'Connells can help us," she added doggedly. "Between them, they know everyone in the barony."

He poured himself another glass of wine.

"I've thought about it," she said. "It must have been someone who followed Earnest from Derrynane. No one but you and I knew Geoffrey was at the cottage, and only someone at the O'Connells could have known Earnest was trying to arrange passage for two people."

"Leave it, Roddy." He stood up, his plate only half touched. "Just leave it alone."

"I won't leave it alone."

"Dammit, you *will*." He took a large swallow of wine and turned to stare into the fire.

She sat back in her chair. "I need to know—did you meet anyone on the road after you spoke to Earnest?"

"I said leave it, curse you!"

She was focusing her gift, testing the blank wall. "Did you meet someone?"

The wineglass hit the table with force enough to crack it. He twisted Roddy's chin up. "Did you hear me? Don't press your luck, little girl."

She refused to flinch before his black glare, though his fingers bit painfully into her skin. When he let go of her, she forced herself not to reach up and soothe the lingering ache. "Now," she said, "you see that intimidation hasn't worked." She gave him a small smile. "I believe that seduction is usually the next stage."

He looked down at her, frowning savagely.

"Go on," she said after a moment. "I'm quite prepared to enjoy your efforts."

He took a deep breath. One corner of his mouth curved—more a grimace than a smile. He reached out and touched her face again, this time a caress. The backs of his fingers skimmed her temple and cheek. "Are you?" he said softly. He bent and drew her mouth up for a long kiss, light at first lingering and sweet, and then his palms spread to cup her face and his tongue drove deep into her mouth.

Her loins melted, hot liquid fire that leaped with unexpected strength. She had meant to let him kiss her and then ask again. Senach had told her—he had said she could read Faelan if she tried. She clung to her focus, letting the feel of his hands on her flow into it and add power and connection. For an instant, it seemed... "Did you meet anyone?" she gasped.

The image flashed and was gone, incomprehensible. She made a small sound of frustration and reached up to put her arms around his shoulders, arching toward him, searching for that touch that had escaped her.

He groaned, his hand sliding downward, molding her breasts, slipping beneath her back and knees. The room tilted and spun as he lifted her, and then she was on the bed in the connecting chamber, and Faelan was slamming the door behind him and working at his neckcloth.

Roddy moistened her lips, watching him undress in the evening light that filtered through the lace curtains. Shadows slid and flowed over his skin, dark against pale gold. Naked, he leaned over her, his arms braced on either side of her head.

"Did you meet anyone, Faelan?" Her voice sounded thin and unreal. Breathless.

He buried his face in her throat, his hands pulling at the shoulders of her dress. "No," he growled, and drew his tongue down her skin, following the neckline of her gown. "That satisfy you?"

He was lying. She was certain of it. Before she could answer, his fingers dragged the gown down off her breast and his lips found her exposed nipple. Her body jerked and writhed as he teased at the swelling bud. She slid her hands across his back and underneath, spread her palms across his belly, circling the hot, smooth thrust of his manhood. The sound he made in response sent passion arcing down her spine.

He moved, pushing her skirt up as he knelt over her, shaping her thighs and hips with his palms. Roddy panted and tried to think, tried to keep her gift focused, but he never met her eyes. She only saw black hair and smooth skin; his jaw and his neck and his shoulders, the curve of his back as he mounted her. "Faelan—" One last attempt. "Faelan, did you—see anyone—"

The memory came: a face, strange eyes, old; old, and familiar and frightening. He gripped her shoulders with a moan like a child's whimper. "Not now." His body shuddered and pressed into hers. "Ah, God. Not now..." The image vanished; reason dissolved into sensation as he penetrated. She tilted her head back, feeling her body and her gift expand, drinking in passion that seemed more than she had ever felt before. She knew what he wanted, what he felt; she moved beneath him in perfect answer. His need was to drown himself, to lose all thought and logic in the joining. He drove toward that, to be part of her: domination and submission, life and death, a mystery and an answer in the dark, hot oblivion that her body offered. His explosion took her with him, tore her into a thousand glittering sparks and put her back together, her own self, her own skin—alone again.

She realized it only from the loss. She *had* reached him, in that moment of fulfillment. But now the touch was gone. He lay on top of her, his sweat trickling down her shoulder, his palms damp in her hair. Outside the open window, a carriage rattled into the court below.

He slid to the side. His hand sought hers—an odd, obsessive move. He locked their fingers together and rested heavily against her. As his breathing slowed, his body softened. His fingers loosened; his arm and leg went slack across her, holding her down with warm, solid weight.

There was still late-evening light pouring in the window over the bed. She turned on the pillow and looked at him, at his thick lashes that lay like devil's wings against the taut skin beneath his eyes. His mouth was relaxed; his chest rose and fell in deep rhythm.

It was his peace that defeated her, rather than his threats or his sensual distractions. The question that had risen again on her lips died there. She touched his cheek and traced the line of his brow, and then turned over in his arms and let him sleep.

～

They rode into the O'Connells' yard at midafternoon two days later. Almost before Roddy hit the ground, MacLassar trotted out from the stable behind the house. He seemed much bigger than she remembered—finally grown too large to lift in the month that she'd been gone. She dropped to her knees, calling him, giving him a hug and a scratch in his favorite spot while he grunted and snuffled in excited welcome.

Faelan walked up behind them. "I'd forgotten that beast," he said, and then belied his disgusted tone by tossing MacLassar a leftover pasty from their dinner on the road. Roddy turned and smiled up at him, but as he met her eyes his blue ones faltered. His thick lashes swept downward and he found somewhere else to look.

Roddy bit her lip. It had been so since Kenmare, since she'd touched him with her gift: the old and miserable experience of seeing someone's glance slide away from hers as if it burned.

She hugged MacLassar again, a hard squeeze to hide the way her mouth crumpled up and her throat went heavy and too thick to speak. He squealed a complaint and show out of her hands, bounding after Faelan in hopes of more food. Roddy came to her feet slowly, watching her husband walk away without waiting for her.

He didn't realize it yet, but Roddy knew already who he would find inside. The babble of thought reached her, an incoherent stream, instantly recognizable amid the quiet surroundings of Derrynane. Before Faelan came to the front steps, the door burst open and the dowager countess swept out.

"Thank God!" she cried, running down the stairs with a quick, nervous tripping. Her blue eyes seemed huge in her thin face. "Roderica, my love—thank the Lord. They've been telling me—I can't credit it—we must leave immediately. Faelan, you will arrange for it on the instant. My God, the reports we've had, and Lord Geoffrey and your brother part of the plot! I can't imagine—Did you have any idea? Your own brother, my dear—You must be crushed. To think that *I* suggested that he come in my stead. And for you to go chasing off after him in that way—But Faelan's brought you back now, and we'll be out of this horrid place tomorrow. I should have insisted long ago; I knew I should have…"

Roddy drew back, uncomfortable and dizzied by the dowager countess' wild dance of thought and speech. The monologue went on at length, and then suddenly broke off, as the countess looked up at Faelan with that way she had—the expression of having just seen him standing there.

A shock of fear blazed through the countess, even as her mind whirled with expressions of affection. She went forward toward her son with hands outstretched. The sickening force of that strange, vivid juxtaposition of thought and emotion made Roddy's eyes blur. She pushed it away with frantic effort.

"Faelan, it is dreadful, isn't it?" The dowager countess' words seemed to come from a distance to Roddy, so powerful were the barricades she'd been forced to raise. "Lord Geoffrey. I can't credit it. He'll hang now. He'll hang for certain. And betrayed... hunted down like a dog! Who would do such a thing? Who could destroy that man—that good, kind man— He's been your friend for years, through everything you've—"

"Your Ladyship," Roddy said, holding tight to her barriers and trying to stop the unfortunate flow of words. "I'm so sorry that you came out of worry for me. You should have stayed safe in England."

"Aye." Faelan walked past her without offering his hand. "You know how much you dislike the place."

"But for Roderica's sake." The dowager countess seemed insensible to her son's antagonism. "I couldn't leave her here. Oh, no. I never wanted you to bring her here. It was a crime, Faelan. A crime."

He left her talking on the step. She turned to Roddy, her fine lips set in a pout. "Infuriating boy," she said. "I don't see how you abide him. Come in. Come in, Maire O'Connell is waiting to greet you. I've been here two weeks, and we've all been on tenterhooks. Tenterhooks, my dear. The things we've heard, you simply would not believe..."

Roddy took a breath, knowing she would have to endure the countess at least long enough to express proper greetings to their host and hostess. And worse, she dreaded to tell them that she had no news of Davan, who she'd last seen lying unconscious in a Dublin alley.

Her fears of prostrating the intrepid O'Connells with worry on that score proved groundless. "Abandoned you to join the rebels?" Maurice roared when he heard. "Curse that brainless pup. Dublin stands—we've had that news a week since. By damn, he bids fair to make his exit on the scaffold if he don't get clear and hie himself back on the double."

"He's an O'Connell," Maire said, in her voice of ancient and fine-tempered steel. "He'll be making his own choices and living with them."

"Aye. Or die by 'em." Maurice looked gloomy. "Stupid young hothead. Wasting himself on this outrage, when I might have made a man of him in our own operations."

"I'm sorry," Roddy said, with heartfelt regret. "But I couldn't stop him."

"'Tisn't your fault, lass. 'Tis this craziness that's got the country by the throat. Great God, it's madness! Sheer madness. What could be worse for us than French purges and French republicanism?"

"No tax on French brandy," Faelan suggested dryly.

The elegant old smuggler inclined his head with a brittle smile. "True enough, my friend. God knows where this business will end."

Roddy escaped finally, pleading headache and backache and anything else that would get her at a distance from the dowager countess' incessant mental babble. She had forgotten how it plagued her—or perhaps it was worse here, where everything about her talent seemed worse. In her room, she changed from the ill-fitting riding habit she'd managed to obtain from a seamstress in Clonmel into a familiar skirt and shawl, and slipped out the rear garden onto the path that led to the bay.

She knew what drew her. The hope of meeting Fionn again was like a sweet, distant melody that called Roddy to come, to listen closer and learn the song. She pulled off her shoes and stockings and walked along the sand, allowing her barriers to ease as the cool water slid up the beach and ran between her toes, sucking the sand from beneath her heels as it retreated back to sea.

She squinted against the late sun on the horizon. The abbey and its little island were cut off by the tide. No gay, golden figure beckoned to her this day; no seal played in the gentle surf. Roddy sat down on a rock, disappointed.

She thought of Faelan. It was easier at a distance, just as it was easier to think of Fionn if Roddy did not try to visualize her features too clearly or concentrate too hard on the memory of her voice. Roddy's mind skittered away from those things, from contradiction and illogic, from a reality that shifted and slid as easily as the beach sand drained from beneath her feet.

Time lost. Days. *I don't remember*, Faelan had said, and it was either lies or madness. She was caught between what she did not want to believe and what she did not dare to.

He would not look at her anymore. That frightened her most of all.

The empty strand seemed to mock her with its memory of a storm-swept day. *You've lost time, too.* Yet the thought seemed so impossible that she dismissed it. To give in to such doubts was dangerous—a commitment to irrationality that, once made, could never be recalled. There would be some explanation, some logic, if only she could find it.

She stood up and lifted her damp hem, climbing above the wave swash, carrying her shoes and stockings, picking her way among the wrack, across the small dunes and up the path. Sand clung to her ankles and fingers. Strange leaves padded the path beneath her bare feet, odd tropical shapes that Roddy had seen nowhere but in the peculiar mild climate of Derrynane that was different even from Iveragh's just over the nearby pass. Here where the mountains made a palisade to the north and the wind blew off the warm sea currents, it never grew cold enough to frost and the plants grew in green profusion.

At the top of the path, she stopped to drag on her damp stockings before walking through the stableyard. A fallen log made a spongy seat as she worked at the gritty wool. Half consciously she began renewing barriers, sensing the countess even at a distance. But the sound of a voice made her look up and open her gift.

Rupert Mullane walked out into the yard with one of the many O'Connell cousins—one of the younger ones, who claimed no seniority or authority. It angered Mullane; his mind was full of offense that he had been pawned off with this junior member of the clan. *Too busy*, he fumed over Maurice's blunt excuse. *Too damned high and mighty.* Rupert took his horse's reins from the stableboy and mounted, giving a curt answer to the young man's offer of a later appointment. *Thinks I've not the means to buy. He'll be finding out, aye, he'll be seeing that my gold's as good as the next man's.*

He wheeled the horse. Roddy stood up just his gaze passed over her.

Their eyes met. A shock went through him: guilt and fear, and Earnest's face. For an instant Mullane held her look, and then he put his heels to his mount and galloped out of the yard.

Roddy dropped her shoes. She began to run, into the house and up the stairs, calling Faelan's name. He stepped out of Maurice O'Connell's study, frowning question at her windblown figure in stocking feet.

"Faelan," she panted, grabbing his arm. "I have to speak to you. I know——" She stopped, looking toward Maurice, choking back the words that wanted to tumble off her tongue.

Their host smiled indulgently as he walked into the hall and waved back toward the study. "Please. We can finish our discussion after dinner."

Roddy preceded Faelan inside without ceremony. The door shut behind Maurice. She managed to control herself until she was sure he was out of earshot, and then turned to Faelan. "I know who did it!" she blurted. "I know who informed on Geoffrey and Earnest!"

He'd been looking toward her, frowning at her feet. At that, he raised his head. His face went suddenly and utterly neutral.

"It wasn't you, Faelan. It wasn't. It was Rupert Mullane." His shoulders stiffened. "How do you know that?"

She opened her mouth, and found herself without excuse. In her anxiety to tell him, she had not stopped to think. Hastily she said, "He told me."

Faelan's glance was too penetrating. She looked away, fingering her skirt.

"Told you what?"

The question was like a lance. Roddy sought madly for a plausible answer.

"He said he did it. For the reward. It was a thousand pounds sterling. I'd been thinking——you know I had. I figured it out, and when I saw him in the yard just now I asked him, and he said I was right."

The last came out fast and breathlessly, and ended on a swallow as Faelan gripped her shoulders. "He admitted it?"

This time it was she who could not meet his eyes. "Yes."

"You're lying." He pushed her away. "God, don't do this to me."

"I'm not lying!" she cried to his back. "Mullane did it. I swear."

He put both fists behind his head. "I don't remember." His harsh sound rang in the room. "*I can't remember.*"

"I'm telling you—you didn't do it!"

"You're lying, damn you." He turned on her savagely. "Mullane never told you that."

"You saw him! Faelan, think of it. Try to think of it. You must have seen him on the road that day."

He looked at her, met her eyes. The wall cracked—one instant of desperation, of fury and raw fear. The face that broke from his memory was not Mullane's. It was older, and younger—female and male, impossible and inhuman. It faded into her own: her eyes and chin and cheekbones. Faelan recoiled. "No," he shouted. "No, damn you, God damn you—*Leave me alone.*"

Roddy raised her hands uselessly, too late and too little to hold him. The wall had slammed down. The study door slammed behind him with the same furious rejection, leaving her alone.

Unwanted. Fearsome.

Sidhe.

Twenty-Five

THE BLACK RUIN OF THE GREAT HOUSE SPRANG OUT OF A HILLSIDE of purple and gold—of heather and gorse that blazed in the late-spring sun. Where Roddy had worked to tame a garden, the wild Kerry flowers waved glorious ridicule, mocking any civilized plant to match their form and color.

She walked along the forecourt where weeds already pierced through the cracks, and watched as MacLassar rooted beneath the crowded, untrimmed shrubs.

Faelan moved beside her in silence. He was not even looking at the house; he was staring at the weeds, his hands in his pockets and his mouth set.

"It's not too late to begin planting again, is it?" She gave her voice a deliberately optimistic air. "Perhaps you'll plow me a garden this time."

He looked out at the sea. "You don't have to stay here, Roddy. You don't have to spend all your money on this."

Roddy pursed her lips. For her the lowest moment had come when she'd seen the stable, roofless, with a few weak new stalks of grass among the scorched walls where their bed of sweet straw had been.

She reached to take his hand, but he moved away. He picked up a loose stone and sent it skipping across the pavement with a quick, savage move.

"Go home with my mother," he said. "She seems eager enough to have you."

And you're not.

Roddy said nothing aloud. Her chest hurt. It was a worse hurting—a duller, deeper pain than the piercing doubt of those days after the arrests. She had cried then, but this pain was beyond tears.

He did not want her anymore.

She recognized the signs. It took no talent to read the way he avoided her, the way he cut his answers short and found excuses to leave a room when she entered. She had touched him with her gift, and now she was exiled, as she had been all her life.

He drifted away from her, up the hill behind the house. She had a moment's thought of following, and then of the welcome she was likely to receive, and stayed where she was in the forecourt.

The wind blew in the gorse and through the empty windows. She sat down on the steps and held out her hand to MacLassar, who came and plopped down beside her—a small comfort, an animal, who had no hopes or vices or needs beyond the moment; nothing to hide, and nothing to fear from her.

"Nothing to hide," a soft voice echoed her thought, and Roddy looked up to find Senach leaning on a staff on the step below her.

Once she would have fled, as Faelan was escaping her, but now in her misery even Senach's uncanny company seemed better than the loneliness. She sat still on the steps and looked at him.

"You're changin', Lassar. You're learnin', I do believe."

"Am I?" She lowered her eyes, staring listlessly at the dark, heavy wool of her skirt where it stretched across her knees. *Learning what? That everything I wanted is impossible?*

Senach smiled. "Dreams," he said. "What is it you want?" His voice had changed. The old man's quaver, the thick brogue faded. "What is it you want, and what is it you fear?"

"I want Faelan," she whispered to her knees.

"And your fear?"

She bent her head and hugged her legs.

"What do you fear?" Senach repeated softly.

"I fear…" *Faelan.*

What he might be.

What I might be.

"All your life," Senach said, "you've been turning from this."

She looked up. For less than an instant, Senach shimmered in the wash of midday light, something far and different from a stooped old man. Then she blinked the glare away, and he was only Senach.

Only Senach.

"What do you want?" he asked again.

Faelan.

"He's lost. 'Tis dark."

I have to help him.

"He fears you, Lassar. He fears you as he fears himself."

I'd never hurt him. Never. How could I hurt him?

"The truth is yours. You've touched him, and he sees you for what you are."

She stared at Senach in despair.

"He doesn't want me now," she whispered.

"No," Senach said with gentle cruelty. "He doesn't."

She closed her eyes against his words. "I love him."

"You do not know him."

"I *know* him." She scrambled up and cried, "He isn't what they say."

Senach shook his head. "You think so. You hope so. You do not know."

"He didn't betray my brother and Geoffrey."

Senach moved his hand, a wave of dismissal. "'Tis darker than that. Far darker."

Roddy's breath quickened. "He's not mad. He never killed his father." She backed a step. "He never did that."

The blind eyes looked through her, mocking her certainty.

You think so. You hope so. You do not know.

"He didn't! I love him!"

Senach stood before her, a weathered tree, brown and ancient and all-wise. "Not enough."

She cried, "What, then? What's enough?"

"The truth."

"But—" She stopped, the words lost in fright and sudden understanding. "No," she said. "He's forgotten it. He's buried it. I won't use my gift to plague him over what's past and done."

"Your gift. Your curse. You're afraid, Lassar. You make excuses."

She closed her eyes. "I won't," she moaned. "I won't do it."

She felt Senach's sightless gaze like cold burning on her skin. He said, in a voice of taunting lightness, "Why will you not, Lassar—if you think him innocent?"

She looked down at her hands, twisted white before her. "Oh, God, let us stay as we are." Faelan suffered her now, at least. He did not force her away. By her folly of trying to help, of finding a crack in the wall, she was reduced to this: that he tolerated her and held her at a distance. How much worse if she should do as Senach asked—

"*Let* you," he echoed. "You beg that of me? But the power is none of mine. 'Tis in your hands, this choice. On your head."

"I don't want it. *I don't want it!*"

"Aye. As you don't want the gift you have. But I will tell you, Lassar. 'Tis more than a gift. 'Tis what you are."

"But if he finds out… oh, please—if he should guess…" She remembered her mother, and the mark of a blow on a little girl's cheek. Panic began to rise in her breast. "It can't be the only way to help him." Roddy drew a sobbing breath. "He'd hate me for it. Do you understand? He'll hate me!"

Senach only waited, with something old and implacable in his face. There was no pity there. No sorrow for what might come of what he asked. He understood, well enough. And still he asked.

She licked her lips, tasting tears. Below her the green land and the sea shimmered. A dark blot took shape on the road to the mansion, a rider—two riders: the dowager countess on a dainty gray, and another, bareback, on a seal-brown mount. It was Fionn who cantered ahead into the court and slid to the ground with her pale hair blowing and a laugh like distant bells.

Though Senach's presence drained Roddy's talent, she saw the countess' look of unease in the company she kept. At first, the older woman refused to dismount. "I only came to see the house—" she began, but Fionn tossed her hair back and laughed again.

"Do stay," she said, the mildest of invitations, and the dowager countess stiffened as if she'd been slapped. Senach moved forward and offered his wrinkled hands. The countess stared at them, and then slowly placed her palms on his shoulders.

Her feet touched the ground. Fionn giggled and flicked her mount on the nose, playful, but both horses seemed to take exception. The gray barb skidded back, and the earth-brown steed with the liquid eyes pawed the courtyard slate, sending sparks. The day that was bright grew gloomy as clouds rolled off the mountains. In the greenish storm light, Fionn's solid presence seemed to fade. The odd sunbeam broke through, lighting Fionn and skittering away across the pavement, making her seem cobwebby and transparent with her hair of gold and her mantle of moss and misty white.

The air was still, brittle, with the waiting quality of thunder about to break.

Roddy looked at the dowager countess. The older woman was staring up at the house. There was such a strange horror in her face that Roddy turned, too. But it was only the mansion…

…the mansion, whole and unscarred, with a roof and sash bars and glazing at the windows, with a grand door and heavy draperies…

…and then, on a blink, a ruin again, with only imagination and the blackened walls to hint at what it once had been.

"Madame." Faelan's voice was chilly. He stood in the gaping doorway, a dark, insolent devil-figure leaning against the gray stone frame. "I never thought to see you here."

"Faelan," the dowager countess said, and no more—breathless and uncommonly tongue-tied.

He stood a moment. His glance rested on Roddy, on Senach, and then moved to Fionn. The scorn in his expression wavered, shadowed to something painful, and he looked away as a man might turn from a light too bright.

"What do you want?" he asked hoarsely, in a tone no friend would use.

Fionn smiled. It was a look without softness. Without humanity. She seemed to grow older before Roddy's eyes. "Justice," Fionn said. "Only that."

Fine, pale lines of tension gathered around Faelan's mouth. He stared at the steps before him.

"I must be going." The dowager countess gathered her skirts and stepped quickly toward her horse. "Senach," she said imperatively. "Help me mount."

Senach made no move to do so. The countess reached for the gray's reins, but the horse eluded her with a snort. She grabbed again, and missed. The barb danced just out of her reach, with arched neck and nostrils flaring.

"Senach!" She stamped her foot. A note of hysteria quivered in her voice. "I want to go."

"Let her," Faelan ordered, with a touch of his old imperative. "'Tis myself you want, if there's justice to be done."

But Senach only stood, silent in a strange reversal that made it seem the master pleaded with the servant.

Faelan said, louder, in a less steady voice, "The crimes are mine. You've no quarrel with the others."

The wind rose and howled through the blank windows, a sound like an eerie laugh.

He glanced at Roddy. "Go with my mother. Now."

"No." Fionn spoke before Roddy could gather her wits. "Never think we are so kind."

Faelan stood straight in the doorway, his hands gripping the frame. He had a cornered look, a wolf-look, his eyes bright blue and dangerous and wary. "I know what you are. Why you come. 'Tis late—years late for vengeance for my father's murder."

"Is it? Call it years, then, if you please. The guilt grows greater with each passing."

"'Twas I who killed him. Seek your justice with me, and let these others go."

Fionn shrugged and stroked the nose of the seal-brown steed. "Easily said. Easy to call down our curse on your self. Have you considered? He was our friend, your father. Do you know what we ask in return for his life?"

"I can guess," Faelan said roughly. "Let my wife go."

Fionn smiled, her sly smile, bright and somehow terrible to look upon. "Ah. You think to bargain. Your wife. Do you care for her so much?"

He wet his lips. He seemed about to speak, and then did not.

Fionn laughed, merry and cruel, and the wind blew hard and the clouds grew low and dark and roiling green. Faelan stood like a man in chains, as if his hands were bound to the stone that framed the door. Fionn's voice came again, soft now, and chill as falling snow. "How much does she mean to you?"

Faelan looked at Roddy, and suddenly in the force of that look she knew his mind—felt his love that was almost desperation, a tangled, driving, aching need. *Everything.* The thought came clear... his thought. He closed his eyes on it and turned his face away, leaving her weak with the knowledge.

"That is what we ask, then," Fionn said, "in payment for this guilt. *Everything.*"

"No." The word broke from him. He opened his eyes and looked at Roddy again with new fear.

"She always belonged to us." Fionn's words were gentler than before. "You knew that."

Roddy blinked, not understanding. Faelan took a step toward her. She saw him stumble, and felt the weakness in his limbs that drove him to his knees. He cursed and looked wildly in her direction.

She frowned at him, finding mist in her eyes, a slow fading of the hill and the house and her husband into white light, as if the mist claimed them. "Damn you!" Faelan's despairing roar came from a distance. Fionn and Senach and the brown horse grew more real and solid as the others dimmed. "Don't take her!"

She looked wide-eyed at Senach, saw him changing: ancient eyes in a young man's face, the twisted hawthorn staff leafing and exploding into green. It was like a dream—like a nightmare—as the brown horse took on wolf-shape, and seal-shape, and horse-shape again, and Fionn grew in brightness until Roddy could not bear to look.

"Faelan," she said, confused and frightened. "*Faelan.*"

She saw herself through his eyes, the day turning night around her, the wind strengthening, a ground mist flowing in the fading light. She lost way to the wind, staggered back, and the paleness began to rise around her.

Mad, he thought, watching her go to wavering light. *This is a dream.*

And she felt the heart-deep fear that grew in him, that he would awaken from this with nothing, not even the memory of her face, but only the echo of light and laughter that had plagued him all his life. He had been afraid of that since the day he'd first seen her—strange and lovely under a lad's cap, with that fall of sun-gold hair. To find luck and love so suddenly, so easily—

But he had known it for what it was. In his heart, he'd known. She was a dream, and he was waking now…

She raised her eyes. "No," she cried. "Don't let them make you believe that."

"Roddy—"

"I love you." She moved toward him, but the wind rose and moaned, and her skirt billowed, plastered against her. She fought a step, and another. "I love you. Help me. Faelan… Faelan… help me. Believe *me.*"

She strained, trying to reach. But there was no anchor, nothing but a hazy outline that appeared and then faded. She felt herself slipping, losing even that contact in spite of all her strength. She cried out in dismay, but there was nothing to hold, nothing to cling to but his thoughts—

"I love you." He heard her voice, thin and distant. Desperate. "Faelan!"

She loves me.

He did not believe it. He had never believed it. How could she love him? Murderer, blackmailer, cheat. Lunatic. He'd held her with his passion, pleasured her and burned for her, worked the land until he ached to his bones to build something that would hold her. And it all turned to mist before his eyes. To nothing.

She loves me.

Is this a dream? Was it all a dream? Little girl…

Will I forget you?

He fought to stand against the weight and weakness in his knees. That one thing he refused to yield... mad or sane, dream or lost reality—he would not forget her.

He tried to see her image in his mind—her face and eyes—but they seemed to shimmer and flow, at one with the strange light and the blowing wind. It was the memory of her smile that came clearer.

Stay with me. He'd said those words before—somewhere else—where?

But he could not remember; he only thought of how she'd lain warm and trusting in his arms, an heiress in a bed of straw. His wife... a *sidhe* gift, but there was more to her than moonbeams. There was what he'd come to love—plain stubborn guts and a lavender-scented pig, and faith enough to keep her with him through a countryside in flames.

Roddy, Roddy. Little girl. Stay with me.

"Leave him," Senach said. "Stay here in the light, and leave him in the dark."

"No." Roddy sobbed. "Faelan!"

"'Twas your choice. He would hate you, you said."

"He loves me!"

"He always loved you." On Senach's head a crown of budding green leaves shone bright in the mist. "Too late, Lassar. Too late to cling to that."

"It's not too late!" She stared at Senach and Fionn, felt the world receding, slipping away and away in the mist, and Faelan... she could not even hear him now; it was all silence and white shimmer; it was sliding from her, everything she'd loved...

"*No*," she screamed, and squeezed her eyes shut to gather her talent, to draw into herself the gift she had despised. She did what she never done—called on all her power, the part of herself she'd been afraid to touch, deep and silent, that suddenly seemed to have been waiting for this day, this moment, when the discipline she'd learned from suffering cities and crowds made a focus and a forge, turning mist to weapon and bending it to her will.

She sent it out, across the distance, and for a moment it was enough. For a moment she saw the house through the light, saw MacLassar on the steps and the dowager countess with her hand on her mouth and her eyes blank with horror. But the door—at the door the mist was too bright and thick, obscuring Faelan from Roddy's sight.

Fionn smiled at Roddy—friend and enemy—shining beautiful and terrible in the vapor. *She always belonged to us*, Fionn had said, and Roddy knew now what it meant. Her talent and her strangeness had been echoes from another world, a world that touched reality only in the green and empty places of the earth—the faint remnant of a dying song on the brooding moors of Yorkshire and a burst of living magic here at the edge of humanity's reach, where the wild land swept down and fingered with the sea.

She was a bridge between, belonging to neither, and to both. *Faelan.*

She was losing him. A crowd of memories engulfed her—MacLassar with his bandaged foot, a mare with her newborn foal... Faelan's hands, sweat-grimed on a pitchfork; his face in the firelight, and in an open field with the play of sun and shadow on his glistening chest... the funny half-wry twist to his mouth when he threw a morsel to MacLassar... "Damned pig," he would say. "Worthless beast." And throw another bite.

Faelan, she thought in anguish. She would not lose him, not like this, as some fey punishment for an ancient crime. Whatever he had done—it did not matter. She put her whole self, her whole soul, into reaching him. All the love that had lit those winter days of work and laughter, all the dreams she had learned to share...

The light grew blinding, but she felt him in it, touched him with her gift, drove deep, gathering all of him—everything, what he was now, what he had been—love and dreams and memories, and a dark place...

Suddenly he fought her, resisting that, struggling away from the shadows she would bring to light. *I don't remember*, his mind howled. *I don't want to remember*. She felt his panic and

overrode it, gathered him close as if something threatened and
she could protect him… *I'm here. I love you. No matter what…*
While the white dimmed to shadow and shape…

Twenty-Six

IT WAS DARK IN THE HALL. MAMÁ HAD TOLD HIM TO WAIT, and he waited, far too old at ten years to admit that the black shadows still scared him a little. But not as much as the voices—not nearly as much. He swallowed and shifted uneasily, hearing through the closed door his mother's tone grow shrill.

"I'll not suffer it," she cried. "I tell you, Francis, I won't live like this—branded with your Popish ways. We might as well be animals, shut up in this godforsaken place while you mouth your mumbo jumbo and traffic with foreign priests. I live in fear, Francis. I lie awake at night and think of it, that any moment we'll be informed upon and everything taken—the house, the land—the very rug wrenched from under our feet. Do you hate me? Do you hate me so, that you wish me cut off from every friend—"

"I don't hate you," his father shouted, with that frightening tremor in his voice. "Don't say that."

"*Yes!* I say it! You don't care what I feel; you don't care what I suffer for this. Married to a *Papist*. I daren't touch my own fortune, daren't show my face in a decent drawing room. I can't go to the capital, or to London, or to any civilized place, for fear you'll expose yourself—crawling off to some mass-house like a drunkard crawls off to a tavern. And *why*, Francis—"

"Because it's what I am," his father roared. "Because this family has kept faith for six centuries, and I'll not be forgetting that we're Irish, or let my son forget. There's change coming—we'll live to see these damnable penal laws repealed. I'll see it, and I'll be certain that Faelan knows his father didn't bend to every wind that blew. Not as my own did." Disgust tinged the bitter words. "I'll keep my family's land, and my family's honor before God."

"Honor," his mother spat. "You call it honor, I suppose, that you no longer come to my bed for fear that I'll conceive another child!"

"Great God, Christina—"

"Oh, yes—look shocked, if you will! I know your mind, Francis. One son, and you think to keep this miserable stretch of rock and mountain undivided under the law. Lord knows, you're right enough—no more than one paltry country squire could make a living off of it. But the Dublin leaseholds—you've income enough to be adding to them, to be building something substantial for your precious son, so he won't be scratching like a plowboy in the dirt. But you can't do so, can you? A Papist," she sneered. "You can't purchase *anything*."

The sound of her footsteps made angry thumping toward the door. She flung it open and candlelight rushed into the shadowed hall.

"Faelan," she snapped, imperative, and waved him into the room.

He went slowly, hating the violence in their voices, the way his mother breathed fast and uneven beneath the heavy braiding and shiny blue silk of her gown. His father looked tall and furious, barricaded behind the great polished width of his desk. He only glanced at Faelan and then back at her, his dark brows drawn down and his mouth fierce.

"For God's sake, woman, do you think I'll have him subjected to our quarrels?" He came out from behind the desk and reached for the bellpull by the fire. In a kinder tone, he said, "To bed with you, son. 'Tis late—"

"He has something to say." His mother stepped between her husband and the dangling velvet, holding herself erect, trembling. "Listen to him, Francis."

His father's hand dropped, a fall of white lace against his blue velvet coat. There was a look on his face that made Faelan's fingers curl into nervous fists.

"Faelan," she said. "Tell your father what you told me this afternoon."

Faelan looked from her to his father, his throat too tense to manage words.

"Go on," his mother said. "The lines you bespoke me." Her face was very white, her eyes bright and feverish as they had been that afternoon when she had consented to sing while he had practiced on his harp. She had even hugged him hard at the end of his performance—a thing she never did, a thing that made him feel hot and giddy with pleasure—though he knew she hated the instrument and his lessons, as she hated all of his father's ideas. Faelan thought he must have played with particular excellence to deserve that attention, and in a burst of pride and confidence he had been eager to please her again by learning the catechism she'd brought him.

In the Name of the Father, the Son, and the Holy Ghost, he had memorized, *I recant the Roman Catholic religion, for that is the way of damnation.*

It had been easy enough to learn. It sounded much like the things Father O'Coileain taught him—damnation being familiar enough, and "Father, Son, and Holy Ghost" having the same awesome ring as "Holy Mary, Mother of God," although "recant" was not a word he knew yet.

He looked at his mother, and she smiled at him with that same quivering, nervous eagerness—that look that his fine new pony had when he restrained it before a challenging fence.

He took a shaky breath, and began to recite.

He faltered halfway into it, letting the huge silence swallow his thin voice as his father's face grew flushed and terrible.

"Do you know what you're saying?" His father's whisper was hoarse. Outraged. "Do you understand this?"

Faelan blinked. He bit his lip, not knowing the right answer to that. To be ignorant—that was the first sin before his father, but it seemed now that knowledge was worse.

His mother stepped behind Faelan, put her hands on his shoulders. He felt the brush of her stiff skirt against his back and legs. "He's quite old enough to make his own decisions. Let him speak."

His father ignored her. In a low and frightening voice, he said, "You had best be sure you understand it, boy. Understand it well, for if you finish those lines, be certain that you're no son of mine."

Faelan blinked, hearing the dire tone more than comprehending the words. He stood, caught between his parents, while his mother's fingers hurt him, digging into his shoulders.

"That's not fair, Francis—"

"Not fair!" His father made a furious move toward them. Faelan took a step back against his mother's skirts, frightened of the wild look on his father's face. He felt her accept that move, slide her hands across his body and forehead and pull him into her protectively.

"Don't touch us," she hissed.

"Not fair," his father repeated with a sneer. "You speak of that, when 'tis you who taught him this abomination."

"I want what's best for him!"

"You want what's best for yourself. 'Tis easy enough to see. You want your assemblies and your ball gowns and your theaters—"

"Yes—I miss all that," his mother cried. "Of course—when every happiness is denied me, when I'm locked in this great haunted prison, I wish for some small relief! I married you for love, Francis, in an Anglican church—against my parents, against my brother—against all those who knew best. I never thought you'd return to this Popish mummery and force me to waste away in a place that gives me nightmares—" She was weeping now, stroking and plucking at Faelan's hair, her fingers shaking with her voice. "These strange servants and weird airs—'tis unchristian! 'Tis no work of God that makes music play in the dead of night—and the lights—that damned harp of yours—"

His father glared. "Imagination," he said sharply. "You let your nerves run away with you."

"I don't! Oh, Francis—Come to me again, don't make me stay alone." She held out her hand. "I need you. I need you with me when it's dark. It's been so long, and I'm so afraid—"

His father stared at her, the hard line of his mouth changing, weakening. He turned abruptly away. "I can't. I know you, Christina. You'll use it against me. You twist everything. Another child—How should I risk that, when already you bribe my son to damn what I teach him? How much worse if you had another pawn, to whisper in their ears that they might steal it all if they forswear their religion and their heritage?"

"Francis—"

"*No.*" His father gripped the curtain with white fingers.

"All right," his mother cried. "Live here like a monk, then! I'm taking him. My son won't grow up in this place, surrounded by priestcraft and night hags."

"*Your* son!"

"Mine. You said he was none of yours. The law will take him from you anyway, when he professes the Established Church." She was pushing Faelan toward the door in a rush of stiff skirts. "My brother will be guardian—"

His father cut off the words, grabbing her arm and dragging her around to face him. "By God, you forget yourself. You're my wife—you won't be stealing my own son from me."

"Freeing him! Look at him. Do you think he wants to stay with you? I've only given him the words to get away."

Backed into his mother's skirts, Faelan looked up into his father's eyes in a misery of confusion and fear. He hated it when they shouted, and this time was worse than ever before.

"Is that true?" his father demanded. "Do you want to go away from here?"

"No, sir," he said quickly.

"And that damned blasphemous oath she's taught you— you won't be mouthing that to any man?"

Faelan swallowed and shook his head.

"Faelan," his mother wailed. "We can leave here. We can go away and be happy. He won't be able to stop us. Just speak your lines to the vicar, and we're free of this."

"Swear to me." His father pulled him forward, both hands on his arms. "Swear to me you'll never do so."

Faelan bobbed his head. "I swear, Papá."

"Oh, God!" His mother gave him a jerking shake. "You don't know what you're saying!"

His father grabbed her wrists, shoving her hands away. For a moment they fought, his mother's panting whimpers loud in the room's quiet. But without effort, his father pulled her off and held her. Faelan saw her then, her face a mask of rage and frustration, like some cornered animal hissing in a trap.

"Mamá," he said, in muffled dismay.

His father let her go, with an oath and a push, and swung away. And like an animal again she moved, reaching for the nearest thing, the heavy iron stand where the fire tongs hung. The tongs fell onto the hearth with a ringing clatter. Faelan watched in dumb fascination as she lifted the stand by its dragon-shaped head, looking dainty and small and impossibly weak against his father's broad shoulder as he looked back. But her face—her face had nightmares in it, and the metal swung and his father fell, still turning, with a noise that went to Faelan's bowels and wrenched them, and the black iron rose and came down again…

He stood there, with his mouth slack and his mind blank. When it was finished she came to him and knelt, holding his face between her hands. "This is your fault. Do you hear me?" Her teeth showed as she spoke, like a vicious small dog's, and there was nothing human, nothing of his mother in her voice. "You did this, Faelan. You should have listened to me."

Her fingers came away from his cheeks, sticky, darkening red. She looked down at her hands, and up at him. As if he were still a child, she tugged out his shirttail and wiped her fingers on it, and he stood there and let her, unable to move then, or later when she tipped the oil pot and spilled it across the floor and threw the candle down. Only when she grabbed his hand and dragged him from the rising flame did he move, tugged out the door and into the black hall.

"Papá," he whispered as the door slammed shut on the reddening glow. "Papá."

His mother yanked him behind her.

Someone wept.

He thought it should have been himself, but it was his mother, sitting on the ruin's steps, curled and rocking like a child.

Faelan looked at her, huddled and small and terrified, unwilling to look beyond to the bright figure that burned there.

"I came," the other said to him. "That night, when she left you—right there, at the edge of the drive. The fire she set was yet small. She went to Derrynane, to pretend she had not been here. Do you remember? I took you... elsewhere. I let you sleep in my arms."

Faelan raised his eyes. As if it were only a moment's time, the memory came clear in his mind—a shining in the darkness, a voice like the wind. "Yes." His man's voice was hoarse, recalling a child's anguish and a strange comfort. "I asked you to undo it all."

She answered softly, "I did what I could. I made you forget."

"Kindness." He leaned on the doorframe, seeking solidity, feeling the stone cold and hard against his spine. *Still crazy*, he thought. *This is not real.*

But the memory of his father's murder was a true one. That he knew.

All those years, and finally he knew.

He said, "Your kindness is a curse, *sidhe*."

She was sunlight and moonlight, and she shrugged like the blithest youth. "That is the way of it, sometimes."

He blinked at her, his eyes defeated by the taunting shimmer. *Still crazy.*

"And the rest—" he said bitterly, to the threshold at his feet, because it was easier to look there. "All the other times. Have you been so kind as to make me forget every wickedness I've done in my life?"

"That is another matter. Another trespass. Ask this one who weeps for it."

He looked up again, though his mother would not. She only curled tighter, moaning softly.

Above her it seemed that the bright figure opened a palm, and a white blossom fell from it. Like a small wave breaking foam upon the shore, the luminous flowers sprang up from every crack in the pavement and spread across the hill. "Ask her what can be done with stolen perfume. She's taken my flowers and made you sleep, my friend. Done murder in your name. The gentle things, the small creatures, grieve us most—tortured and sacrificed at her bidding. You were but a child then, and she would have you believe in your own madness."

He remembered those midnights, dragged up from sleep to stand in line before a hard-eyed master. Even now the sweat broke out on his palms, a child's sick fear to see the blood on his nightclothes, to be sure that something hideous and alien lived inside his skin.

Mamá, did you do that to me? Did you hate me so much?

The bright one leaned on her horse's shoulder, sliding her fingers through its shaggy mane. Where she combed, he thought strands of silver and gold grew in shining profusion, trailing out in the wind. "As for the rest... I cannot speak for human machinations. A draft of this to make you sleep, a note in your handwriting, a word of falsehood whispered to a foolish young girl... and when you wake, you wake miles from where you last remember. I think much evil can be done in such a way. But she can tell you."

He thought he must be truly mad, to listen to light and shadow speak and think it proved his sanity. But he clung to the words, to the hope that it was truth. "Drugged," he said harshly. "Have I been such a fool as that?"

"A fool, aye. A man convinced of his own guilt. A man who feared to look into his own mind. The answer was easy, if you had but questioned." She smiled, a sharp, slim figure of mischief and dreams. "But I gave you another gift, my friend. Have you not guessed it yet?"

He had guessed. He looked at last where he'd not had the strength to look before—at his wife, who was storm light made into sweet reality, who had haunted his waking and his sleep, as bright and golden and elusive as the one who stood beside her.

But real. Flesh and blood.

He smiled then, because Roddy would not return his look—a slow, sensuous smile as he thought of her body beneath his, warm as sunlight on the earth. "Little girl," he said huskily. "Come here." He wanted to hold her and make love to her and lose them both in it forever… the way she felt, the shape of her, the warmth and scent and softness…

Roddy obeyed him, finding her cheek pressed hard against a solid chest. His arms were around her, his breath blew harsh against her ear and throat and temple, his lips seeking, defining, as if by brute contact he could hold her and make her real.

She turned her face into his body. She could not look at him. It was still too new, this clear touch of her husband's mind. Still too raw. To know the way he wanted her—spur to his memory, the force that had battered down the wall…

There had been no skill in that, none of Fionn's elegance or Senach's wisdom. If Roddy was one of them, she was sadly lacking in their mystic grace.

But she had done it.

He was open to her now.

Tentatively she lifted her eyes. His hands sought her cheeks and helped her—forced her—until she looked directly up at him.

The intensity hurt. It made her throat ache. The fortress of pride and defiance lay in ruins. He was not the Devil Earl—he was only a man, and he needed her. Wanted her. Let her look at him and see his soul laid bare and still loved her, with a fierceness that made her want to laugh and cry at once. The way he saw her… she never would have guessed: her strangeness he thought beautiful; her obstinance he called courage; her childish whims were joy and laughter to him, who had never known innocent laughter before.

Wind and mist gathered, made a voice that murmured, "Is this your choice, then, little sister?"

Roddy turned her face, still leaning in Faelan's arms. Fionn sat the brown steed with her long hair mingling in its silver mane. There was a sadness about her bright figure, a gentle dimming of her light.

"Fionn," Roddy whispered.

"Shall we let you stay?"

Roddy felt her husband's body, firm and real against her. She bowed her head and said, "Yes."

"It is not a gift. There is a price."

"What price?" Faelan's voice was gruff, his hands tightening around Roddy in suspicion.

Fionn looked at him. "My friend, it matters not to you what price. For you there is a debt, not a payment." She gestured toward the dowager countess, still huddled in blank misery on the steps between them. "Tell me that first, then—how is justice to be done?"

"I care nothing for your justice," he said harshly. "Leave my mother be."

Fionn smiled, heartless and sly and shining. "A fit punishment. As she is, so she will be. A frightened child for her lifetime."

"Curse you—"

"Do not curse me, Faelan Savigar. We stand fair and even now."

Roddy felt him take a deep breath, but he held back the oath that blossomed in his throat.

Fionn said softly, "Lassar, little sister—have you guessed the price of staying?"

Roddy nodded and blinked, seeing only a shimmer of light through sudden tears. "You'll not come back," she whispered. "I'll not see you again."

"Does that trouble you most?" One of last summer's leaves skirled across the ancient steps. "You give up other things as well."

Roddy shook her head. She could not speak. No farewell would come through the ache in her throat.

Wistful laughter blew on the failing breeze. "You will not see me, little sister. But perhaps I will be there."

"Fionn," she said brokenly.

"Is it what you wish for…" Fionn's voice was fading. "Do you give back all our gifts?"

Faelan's grip shifted and found Roddy's hands, closing hard, a silent plea. But she knew the answer. She had always known it. She twined her fingers gladly with his, choosing Faelan, choosing love, over any other magic. "Yes," she whispered.

"'Tis done. The gifts returned." Sunlight broke through the vanishing clouds, making transparency of Fionn's lithe figure. Then suddenly she smiled, still mischievous even in her passing. "I leave you—with one more."

Roddy opened her mouth to speak. But farewell was too late. Fionn was already gone. A gust of wind took the flowers, lifting bright petals in a whirling cloud that made MacLassar sneeze and Senach shake his weathered head, and streamed like snow across the dowager countess in her huddled place on the stairs.

The white mist drifted out across the wild hills and the empty fields and the fire-blackened pastures. It spread down to the sea and up to the mountains and over all that Roddy could see of Iveragh.

And wherever the mist settled, its radiance sparked and then faded, and the land turned to living green.

About the Author

Laura Kinsale, a former geologist, is the *New York Times* bestselling author of *Lessons in French*, *Flowers from the Storm*, *The Prince of Midnight*, and *Seize the Fire*. She and her husband divide their time between Santa Fe and Dallas.

Lessons in French

by Laura Kinsale
New York Times bestselling author

HE'S EXACTLY THE KIND OF TROUBLE SHE CAN'T RESIST...

Trevelyan and Callie were childhood sweethearts with a taste for adventure. Until the fateful day her father drove Trevelyan away in disgrace. Nine long, lonely years later, Trevelyan returns, determined to sweep Callie into one last, fateful adventure, just for the two of them...

978-1-4022-3701-0 • $7.99 U.S./$8.99 CAN

MIDSUMMER MOON

BY LAURA KINSALE
New York Times bestselling author

"The acknowledged master."
—*Albany Times-Union*

IF HE REALLY LOVED HER,
WOULDN'T HE HELP HER REALIZE HER DREAM?

When inventor Merlin Lambourne is endangered by Napoleon's advancing forces, Lord Ransom Falconer, in service of his government, comes to her rescue and falls under the spell of her beauty and absent-minded brilliance. But he is horrified by her dream of building a flying machine—and not only because he is determined to keep her safe.

"Laura Kinsale writes the kind of works that live in your heart." —Elizabeth Grayson

"A true storyteller, Laura Kinsale has managed to break all the rules of standard romance writing and come away shining."
—*San Diego Union-Tribune*

978-1-4022-1398-4 • $7.99 U.S./$8.99 CAN

THE
PRINCE
OF
MIDNIGHT

BY LAURA KINSALE
New York Times bestselling author

"Readers should be enchanted."
—*Publishers Weekly*

INTENT ON REVENGE, ALL SHE WANTS FROM
HIM IS TO LEARN HOW TO KILL

Lady Leigh Strachan has crossed all of France in search
of S.T. Maitland, nobleman, highwayman, and legendary
swordsman, once known as the Prince of Midnight. Now
he's hiding out in a crumbling castle with a tame wolf as his
only companion, trying to conceal his deafness and desperation. Leigh is terribly disappointed to find the man behind
the legend doesn't meet her expectations. But when they're
forced on a quest together, she discovers the dangerous and
vital man behind the mask, and he finds a way to touch her
ice cold heart.

"No one—repeat, no one—writes historical
romance better." —Mary Jo Putney

978-1-4022-1397-7 • $7.99 U.S./$8.99 CAN

SEIZE THE FIRE

BY LAURA KINSALE
New York Times bestselling author

"Magic and beauty flow from
Laura Kinsale's pen." —*Romantic Times*

AN UNLIKELY PRINCESS SHIPWRECKED
WITH A WAR HERO WHO'S GOT HELL TO PAY

Her Serene Highness Olympia of Oriens—plump, demure,
and idealistic—longs to return to her tiny, embattled land
and lead her people to justice and freedom. Famous hero
Captain Sheridan Drake, destitute and tormented by nightmares of the carnage he's seen, means only to rob and abandon her. What is Olympia to do with the tortured man
behind the hero's façade? And how will they cope when
their very survival depends on each other?

"One of the best writers in the history of the
romance genre." —*All About Romance*

978-1-4022-1396-0 • $7.99 U.S./$8.99 CAN